ip '73 6.95

Intensive Care

Also by Janet Frame:

Janet Frame

INTENSIVE
CARE

a novel

George Braziller, New York

Acknowledgments

Grateful acknowledgment to The Yaddo Corporation, The Macdowell Colony, The Henry Foundation.

To

Sue Marquand and Bill Brown
for the possible and impossible
greeting and parting.

1.
Kindness Itself,
Happiness Itself,
and Delphiniums

1

In the dream in the dream
the child played a poem
protected by mild adjectives
gentle verbs and the two
pronouns teaching the
division of earth and sky
night and day
object and show; and the separating
personal eye.

In the dream in the dream
the child danced, sang, smiled
to the faces unmasked
and the boy with the luminous eyes
and the watch face telling
the time by the permanent sun
in the permanent way of heaven.

All others were born dead or sent away
to institutions where they played
with pebbles in a graveyard
licked clean the poisonous red paint
from the toy sewing machine
and the red pram with wheels
and a handle, but no sleeping doll.
All others were murdered or hanged
left out in the rain overnight,
tripped, trodden on, pulled apart
limb by limb, bonfired
in feast explosion and orgasm.
In the dream in the dream
child alone, child alone.

The mother plunged from a high tower
broke her neck falling
on a complicated steel structure
went down to the cellar and met

the brick wall and said, Brick wall, eat me, and was eaten,
her fate secret.
She will not come here again,
he said to the child.
Both smiled.

2

Tom had great big waterproof boots on.
Tom had a great big waterproof hat.
Tom had a great big waterproof mackintosh.
And that said Tom is that.

Why did Tom have great big waterproof boots on?
So he wouldn't be splashed with blood blood blood
when he trampled the body of the dead dead dead
enemy enemy into the mud!

3

He woke in the sun. He was lying outside on a rug on the
grass where they had carried him, and the English nurse,
Ciss Everest, sat beside him holding a blue and gold flower-
printed sunshade over him. He looked up at her dark hair
knotted like a black-shining button at the nape of her neck,
and her deep violet-colored eyes, and all afternoon he lay
watching her move among the wounded. She was not con-
ventionally pretty. Her face was pale with freckles around her
mouth and across her nose. Her mouth was big. When she
opened it he had a pleasantly dreamy sensation of being
swallowed into softness. He wanted to kiss her.

He watched her every movement, and then as soon as the sun withdrew he was carried again into the crowded ward to his bed on the floor where he had arranged, as signposts of his territorial rights, his army boots, one on each side, his trench coat, canvas bag, his first-aid kit with the yellow oozing ointment, the bandages stuck to the oiled silk, the tin rusting with the writing on it blurred with brown spots; and his gas mask, his precious gas mask that no one could take from him. When anyone came near his bed he seized the mask and hid it under his bedrug. And Nurse Everest understood. She was the only person who understood. His wife of two days and one night, Eleanor Madigan, thirteen-thousand miles away, an image dissolved many months ago by the chemical action of spilled blood, would never have understood.

He was only eighteen and he had been shaving for only eleven months and after he was wounded his voice kept returning to its boyish pitch.

"Nurse Everest!" he would call; then stop, surprised.

And Nurse Everest would laugh. Her laughter was quick and graceful like the movement of her body. And of course he was in love with her. Is that how it was? Was that Tom Livingstone mad in love as all the Livingstones were, their passions as generation succeeded generation resembling an assortment of old Scottish ballads where to be a human relative was to be, inevitably, one of the murderers or the murdered?

After the War, any war, haunted by Ciss Everest, Tom returned dutifully to his wife. He was not brave. He killed because there had been company in the killing and he liked company. After all, the world was full of people, wasn't it, ordinary people going their ordinary way and killing when they were asked to kill? And when he returned from the War he was a frightened man—afraid of poverty, of becoming a drunk like his father, known all over the pubs of Waipori City,

3

of losing his job as furnaceman in the cement factory, of being overwhelmed by his wife's family with their oblong faces and large chins, her sisters like female cardinals and her brothers like bishops, all making blackmailing use of their exclusive personal God to form a protective body for Eleanor, trying to preserve Tom's inflexible love as if it had been a gold bar that no amount of heat or pressure could soften or twist, when in fact it too had dissolved with the endearing image of Eleanor.

Returned from the War, Tom became a member of the Union and the Lodge, a respected citizen. He who had fought and been wounded in the trenches attended lessons in the art of applying tourniquets, removing bee and wasp stings, removing foreign bodies from eyes and ears, restoring to consciousness the drowned and the suffocated, administering antidotes for phosphorus, belladonna, aconite, strychnine; after which he gained his first-aid certificate and became a member of the St. John's Ambulance Association.

A returned soldier, entitled to wear the R.S.A. badge on his lapel, to march in memorial parades, to be buried, at a discount, in a soldier's grave, to receive a discount for purchases in local stores—ten percent on saddlery and leather goods, thirty percent on jewelery, including diamond rings, thirty percent on furs including mink and Russian sable, ten percent on electric toothbrushes and cake mixers—after living with death, set up for life. A returned soldier with remnants of gas in his lungs, shrapnel in his back, and a passion in his heart for Ciss Everest alias the War, the first person he had seen on waking from his drugged sleep, as if his ordinary life had been marked from that moment to be lived in obedience to the dictates of myth and legend where the first person seen on waking is the natural, only person to love, to be haunted by, and where the haunting may last from five seconds to five-hundred years and beyond.

When Tom Livingstone's wife died he made his return

4

journey to find Miss War, Miss Everest. Gods unrelated to
Eleanor's jealous God attended him and through their guidance he had been in London only three days when he stepped
on the black November ice of a London pavement, slipped,
broke his leg, and after a time in hospital was transferred to
Culin Hall, the Recovery Unit.

All dreams lead back to the nightmare garden.

4

Culin Hall, a former stately home, was set on the edge
of the heath among English trees—oak, ash, plane, dark-
braided sycamore, larch—and many acres of lawns and gardens with two revolving summer houses on the back lawn
near the rose garden and a goldfish pond with a rock garden
in the middle of the front lawn. Glimpsed from the entrance
to the wide curving driveway the two-storied brick house
appeared formidable with its black-painted window frames
and tall silhouetted Elizabethan chimneys rivaled only in
modern architecture by the chimneys of factories and crema-
toria. Now that it was autumn, the leaves were in their last
shades of gold, strewn across the lawns and gardens, and the
late-blooming marigolds and early chrysanthemums bordering the path near the house set the brick aglow with reflected
gold; and in the evening when the London sky sprawled like
a burnished one-eyed tiger, the brick trapped the bloody
glare of the sun-eye and the yellow and gold and black of the
smoke-and-cloud body. One could imagine Culin Hall as a
home furnished with works of art, fine silver, antique furniture, canopied beds from which idle aristocrats set out each
day to hunt and kill their golden fox. It was difficult to imagine the house as a Recovery Unit peopled with the sick—the
limbless, the one-lunged, the wombless; for poverty, as one
attribute of sickness, if only the poverty of health, was not in

keeping with the majesty of the house and the extravagance of its architecture. Even the front door opened into an admissions hall where the ceiling was as high as a barn and the vastness of the room invited its use as a store for a year's harvest with the stacked wheat and barley enticing golden echoes of their light from the brown polished walls and floors. The only harvest it received, however, was the winnowings of sickness that at this time in history were still preserved and cared for.

Tom Livingstone with his personal file and the morning mail was delivered to Culin Hall Recovery Unit at ten o'clock one morning. He sat in the deserted hall, his white plastered leg stretched in front of him. No one came to admit or deny him admission. Presently another patient, delivered by ambulance, arrived and sat near him. Both sat for half an hour unattended. Suddenly the woman looked desperately around her and began to cry, her cry changing to a wail.

"It's my first day up. Isn't anybody here?"

Tom's voice was tired. After the intensive care of the hospital he was feeling neglected and unwanted.

"Someone will come along soon. This is Culin Hall where you recover."

The woman burst into tears.

"It's my first day up. They can't treat you like this on your first day up. We're sick. We have to be looked after. They can't leave us like this to ... to ... we might even die!"

A nurse appeared carrying their records. She was kind but brisk. She guided them upstairs in the lift to their wards, each of which was named after famous fox-hunting men and women, masters and mistresses of the hunt. A polished brass plate on each door described each benefactor's services to blood sport.

Tom's ward held two beds. A pale young man was sitting in an easy chair by the window bed, overlooking the front garden.

"Another leg?" the young man asked, smiling. "Are you keeping it?"

"It's only broken. Of course I'm keeping it. I'm Tom Livingstone of Waipori City in the Antipodes.

"The what? Oh, I see. Your summer's our winter. Of course. I'm Peter Bridge. I didn't mean to be personal about your leg, but we do get very possessive about parts of our body here. You'll meet Miriam. She's just finished with her pylon."

Tom frowned, startled by the esoteric language that sounded strangely agricultural, like a quotation from an article on animal husbandry in a farming magazine.

"I slipped on the ice," he explained.

"Here on holiday?"

"Not really. I was last here in the First World War. I fought for my country. I was wounded and nursed back to health."

(I'm sixty-five now, old enough to be getting the pension, and my wife, thank God and unthank God, has been dead a year and I've come to London to find my first only love, a young woman of twenty-three, Miss War of Nineteen-Seventeen, dark-haired, violet-eyed, with breasts like wine bottles and a kissing mouth.)

No, he did not say it. Nor even think it. He was feeling lonely and homesick and afraid that now he was an old man they wouldn't bother to care for him, he'd heard what people were saying about the old men and women cluttering up the hospitals.

"We've no other broken legs. The rest are more serious. A few lung cases. I had my left removed, you know. One or two waiting to go to nursing homes. One hopeless cancer. A stroke here and there. It makes you wonder why they bother to look after us but it's human nature, isn't it, to care for the sick. Thank god!"

"And what do you do all day?" Tom asked, stowing his

toilet things in the top drawer of the locker by his bed.

"Oh this and that. Eat. Read the paper, walk in the garden, sit in the summerhouses—they revolve you know to face the sun—when it's shining; watch TV. Rest. Some have physio in the physio room. There's occupational therapy if you want it—baskets, weaving, painting, a few books downstairs, all very civilized; mostly we do nothing, we're all so tired; just wander around the garden and look at the goldfish and the dead waterlilies; and sleep. For people who are well like me," Peter added, clearly closing the door tight to the dark cave of his lost lung, "it's a bore. I get up early and help with the morning teas."

"You're cheerful," Tom said.

"I know. I'm awfully cheerful."

He lay down on his bed, closed his eyes and fell asleep. His face was pale, sweat-glistening, with a flush on each cheek. He was mapped more by bones than by flesh. His breathing was shallow. The temperature chart at the head of his bed described a perilous alpine region of towering peaks and deep ravines.

Tom lay on his bed with his eyes closed, not sleeping, until he was roused by the sound of creaking wheels in the corridor.

Peter woke. "Lunch," he said. "You either go in the lift or down the stairs."

Using his crutches Tom eased himself from his bed and limped from the room to the landing where three patients in wheelchairs waited for someone to operate the lift. They turned toward him, smiling, smiling, smiling, an unfamiliar kind of smile that did not speak merriment or greeting or signal any promises; a demanding smile that persuaded him to limp forward, press the lift button, wait for the doors to open, and wheel each chair into the lift. When the ground floor was reached, rather than face again the smiling concert, Tom at once wheeled the chairs out on the landing where other patients took over the responsibility of attending the smiling ones.

"I'll not be caught again," he thought resentfully. He was unused to seeing so many disabled people who, clearly, were not wounded in battle and had no glory attached to their disablement, only the overwhelming demands of complete dependence on others.

"Wheelchairs first, wheelchairs first."

It was tyrannical. Flashing silver, the seats and backs grained plastic, like frowning human foreheads, the wheels new hard rubber, the spokes whirling, the privileged wheelchairs moved towards the dining room. Tom found himself at the end of the queue advancing slowly, slowly, staring curiously into the side rooms along the corridor. A ward. A men's ward of four beds and flowered screens. An old man white-haired, white-bearded sitting at a desk with books open in front of him.

"A famous scholar," Peter whispered. "Comes here every year to give his family a rest. Never see him at meals. Blind. And deaf. What's the holdup?"

Two patients in their wheelchairs were stranded on the upper floor because no one had come to wheel them, and other patients had hobbled by with gaze averted from the responsibility of accepting the smile, smile, smile of their helplessness.

The queue waited. The old man at the desk stroked the open books with the palm of his hand, his head on one side as if listening to his hand that made a sound like slow washing on the smooth surface.

"Wheelchairs first, wheelchairs first!"

Smile, smile, smile. It was their only web to trap their necessary servants. Its weaving had been learned slowly as a political trick of the helpless, replacing the petulance and complaining that brought no response.

The procession entered the dining room, a large airy

room overlooking the side lawn and the summerhouses and the misty heath. The wheelchairs settled at their tables. Other patients limped, hobbled, crutched to theirs, with insightful redirectioning and rearrangements as those who knew the territory found themselves about to be condemned to sit with someone who "talked about it all the time." Although at first all the patients in the Recovery Unit talked of their illness, some used more words, for a longer period, than others, and these were avoided. The hysterectomies, for instance, lamented restlessly like birds who'd had their nests stolen— and the fledglings too—"all my pretty ones at one fell swoop."

Each newcomer was initiated into the hierarchy of illness, receiving subtle often unspoken guidance in his own status and what was expected of him. Tom found himself at a table with Miriam (in her wheelchair, unable to bear the first use of her new leg), Peter, wombless Mrs. Bertha Noble from the Argentine who talked in a Scots accent about windmills, the new patient, Cherry Millow, pale, gaunt, pituitaryless, who wore a cap over her baldness and had spent several years, she said, in the diplomatic corps. Conversation turned to the woman upstairs who never came to meals and who was waiting to be transferred to a nursing home in the same street.

"She shouldn't be among us here," Mrs. Noble said. "This is a recovery unit. Patients don't come here unless there is hope for them."

"Is she young?" Cherry Millow asked.

The others, who knew, looked at Cherry, at the cap over her head, and turned away, to look out of the window, or take another spoonful of curried stew, or make finger patterns on the tablecloth, or merely close their eyes facing the darkness with its ripples of light.

"She's old," Mrs. Noble said. "About seventy, surely.

She's had it for years, they say. I don't know what she's doing here in the *Recovery* Unit."

She turned to Tom, explaining.

"We're talking about Miss Everest. Have you met her?"

"No," Tom said.

He folded, creased, unfolded, refolded his paper napkin. His hands and arms began to tremble and a feeling of sickness struck at the base of his throat where words begin or are buried.

"I used to be able to make an airplane shape, and a boat shape," Peter said.

"I can make a rosette," Miriam said. "What are you making, Mr. Livingstone?"

"Nothing," Tom said.

"You're not feeling sick are you?"

"Not at all."

"The first day is always terrible. They leave you alone. Nobody does anything for you. It's all for your own good, to get you well quickly. People still care about getting sick people well, you know."

"And why shouldn't they? It's human isn't it?"

Peter looked across at Miriam, blushed, and said mercilessly, "Even if we stamp our feet (if we have feet to stamp) in rage no one is going to give us back our lost lungs and legs and wombs."

The others appeared embarrassed. Their eyes glanced at that part of their body that was precious to them because it was diseased, or a dream. Tom felt guiltily whole. He longed to share with his new companions, to rip off his leg and cast it into the heap like an old wooden chairleg on a Guy Fawkes bonfire.

"What did you say that old woman's name was?" he asked. "The old woman upstairs?"

"Miss Everest. Cecily Everest."

11

5

Dear First Dad, up Central the summer heat is nightmarish beside the valleys bleeding with raspberries and the river bleeding green with melting ice. The sky is brilliant blue, the hills are brown and yellow, like burned flesh, like khaki, like polished brass buttons and buckles, and the light furs the faraway hills with purple and golden leather. In the War that followed your War, I was young—remember? I was Naomi Livingstone, student, typist, writer-of-verse. I picked raspberries, hemorrhaging them into a tin bucket. Then as typist in the ration pool I went to Wellington where I met and married the stranger Alfred Whyborn, in peacetime a history lecturer, while Pearl, your other daughter, went to live in Auckland with her husband Henry Torrance, the bank clerk, and their son Colin. The names are well worked out, aren't they, dear First Dad? And the people placed as neatly as the flags on the battlemaps of the War.

I shall never escape from the first white and gray winter. Newspaper scraps in the street, bare trees, sticks, twigs, wires overhead. The absence of color terrified me. I walked through Woolworth's. I bought blue and white and gold soap powder and arranged it on the windowsill. I feared the smooth white walls, the smooth white freezer in the kitchen, the smooth white pulp of the tinned vegetables and corn. The apartment lights were pale. I drank them like lemonade.

And it was an unbelievably pale shade of loving, in winter light. "Are you sick?" I said.

He replied, "Oh no, it's the central heating, I'm not fighting a war now."

"Are you sure?" I said.

He grew paler and smoother and fatter and we had nothing to say to each other. I thought, in the beginning, that each of us was carrying load upon load of personal treasure to the common pool, a kind of emotional acclimatization venture, but when I looked in the pool I saw nothing but my own face, and he saw his own face. Now that was strange, for in the beginning, in the sun, his voice flowed like yellow waves, but our love went away or was misplaced because suddenly, faster than the speed of light, it was not where we had left it and neither of us could find it.

"Have you seen our love?" I asked calmly.

"Have you seen our love anywhere?" he echoed.

Then we panicked.

"It must be somewhere. You've hidden it."

"No, I swear I haven't. You had it last, anyway."

"Oh did I? You mean *you* had it last and now you've lost it and won't admit it."

It never appeared again, though at night and in the daytime each of us in our separate ways put out tender bait for it, but when one of us, one night, discovered that its distinctive odor filled the house, we knew that it had died and was decaying somewhere in a secret place and we would never find it again.

The seas, then, were distant on our coasts. Dry wood, dry sands. The creatures were shriveled and dead in their shells.

Dear First Dad, remember you were the War? I remember that first winter away, how the woods were full of war and the snow made its own light, magnesium, mercury, splendor and flash in a sunless world. I saw the soldiers standing blind with the blood falling disguised as snow in the persuasion of purity. I looked again. They were pine trees. I inspected the withered limbs, the storm-blasted faces and bodies, all the seasoned carnage where sunlight, now and again on blue days, opened the wound of the scene showing—say—only a giant tree uprooted on its side, a half-headless hero drained of blood, his muscular convolutions of thought—chiefly his killing-pattern—exposed, his hope cramped in fetus shape. He wore a cap of icicles pointed and tasseled like a jester's, and his huge foot in its dead-leaf boot stuck in the sky. And no one came to bury the dead. Only the snow buried and uncovered, buried and uncovered, and the streams washed the bones, and the brown-and green-mottled army coats that others might have mistaken for dead leaves; and season after season the hummingbirds shuttled their patches of light across the eyeless faces.

Dear First Dad, the swords of the dead still hang like icicles to weep above the living.

And it stays, everything stays. The winter stays, while from my window here in the Recovery Unit I see the autumn woods and the squirrels picking up nuts to hoard. I see the burning leaves blown in small whirlwinds along the path as if the goldfish have been uplifted from their pool. I hear the stumbling limping, halting tread of the patients, the scrape and squeak of the wheelchairs; a thrush sometimes, singing; or I see a blackbird with its head poked forward like a shopper in search of a bargain at the opening of twilight, hurrying across the lawn; black-bonneted with long black skirt of black feathers; all in the Victorian world of Culin Hall.

Blessed is he whose sin is recovered.
I do hope to recover the city by nightfall.
The woods hope to recover their primeval silence, intervals and
    rests and music, the heart its belief and hope.
The day will recover its night.
The night its morning.
The death its birth.
The valley its lost mountain.
The mountain its departed valley.
"Stop! Stop!"

What are you doing old man, staring like a madman at my blonde transformation or wig?

6

The meal finished, those who could walk stood aside respectfully while the patients in the wheelchairs were taken to the lift. Following at the end of the procession, Tom avoided the small group of waiting wheelchairs and crutched up the stairway, and as he went along the corridor he heard weeping. Miriam was sitting crying in a chair in her ward. On the spare bed beside her, her new leg lay encased in its black lace-up shoe.

"They promised me a knee, they promised me a knee," she said, looking up and seeing Tom.

Tom hobbled a little way into the room. He didn't know what to say. His mind was chiefly on "the woman upstairs," Ciss Everest, and the appalling possibility that it was *his* Ciss Everest.

"I had two daughters," Tom said. "They're older than you. They're grown up and away long ago. I'm sorry they didn't keep their promise about the knee."

"They promised! Look at that shoe. It's like a Salvation Army foot. They said as soon as I was finished with the pylon I could have a real bending leg."

She stopped crying. She pushed back her long brown hair, sniffed, wiped her nose, and looked curiously at Tom.

"What was wrong with you at lunch time?" she asked. "You're not losing your leg are you?"

Tom tapped his white leg in its white pod.

"No. I'm keeping it."

"You probably don't understand then."

"Oh I do, I do!"

Peter had said that Miriam was a violinist. "You've still got your music."

Miriam made an exclamation of anger and impatience. "Oh, it isn't *like* that! Why do you old people always play the game of adding and subtracting with remainders and so on, as if everything's equal to everything else, and if you lose something, well you've something else left, as if it were all coins. Yes, I agree, I've still got my music. And this!"

She gestured towards the leg lying on the bed.

"There are others," Tom said, "worse off."

"Oh I know, I know, but how does that help? It only makes it worse, it doesn't balance it, just because there are others. I'm an intelligent person, Mr. Livingstone. I know that nothing balances like that. This is living, not keeping accounts. How does it help to know others are worse off? Look at poor Miss Everest."

(The dead lying on violets and daisies like food on a decorated plate; a spring and summer dead more terrible than the winter dead in snow that is their shroud.)

"Is she very very sick?" Tom asked.

"Hopeless," Miriam said abruptly. "Are you feeling bad, Mr. Livingstone? Is your leg hurting?"

"I'm tired. I believe they're making arrangements for me to fly home."

"You're a long way from home. Where exactly do you live?"

"Waipori City. Quite a small place for a city. Our country leads the world in social legislation and experiment," Tom said, suddenly aggressively proud of his distant country.

"Do you have anyone to visit you here?"

"No. I think I'll go to lie down."

"Some can't rest. Peter is very brave."

"He's in my ward. A nice kid."

"His whole life is broken by this. Everyone here is seeing and experiencing revolution. Attack, assassination of the

16

body followed by revolution and the new government."

"Sounds too political for me."

"It is," Miriam said thoughtfully. "It's the politics of helplessness."

Tom said goodbye to Miriam and limped along the corridor. He passed two nurses.

"She can't be given it so soon."

"The effect wears off. You know that."

"But we must keep to the regular hours to give out medicine."

"Miss Everest's in pain. You know what pain she's in."

"We must think first of the smooth running of the whole ward. We're short of staff. We have to check every visit to the medicine cabinet and we simply can't unlock it every half-hour for one person only."

Tom limped on past his ward to the women's four-bedded ward at the end of the corridor. He hesitated at the door and went in. Three of the beds were occupied by women resting clothed under the bedcovers while the fourth was screened from view by the usual rose-patterned screen that must have been a standard worldwide hospital design. Tom could hear the patient behind the screen whispering to the nurse.

An elderly woman, her neck, wrists, body set in a plaster splint, lay smiling, smiling, smiling. She saw Tom and directed her smile at him.

"You're the new patient? Having a look around? I'm Mrs. Dockett."

Smile, Smile. She wore glasses with black rims like the rims of the wheels of the wheelchairs. Her eyes gave the impression of spinning, spinning, spinning, their spokes whirling.

The nurse looked out from behind the screen.

"Mr. Livingstone, let the ladies rest. Go back to your ward."

Tom listened. He felt sick and faint. The woman behind the screen was Ciss Everest, *his* Ciss Everest. He had thought of her for so many years with love and longing. He'd made her his shrine where his praise and his blame could be set, and time had so sanctioned for him the certainty of her perpetually remaining a shadow that her reappearance had the effect of toppling the pillars of love surrounding her and exposing their foundations of fear and hate and youthful uncertainty. He listened for her to cry out from behind the screen in her strong young voice: "Livingstone, not Tom Livingstone?"

He heard no one calling his name. Rage came over him that a woman who had spread so wide in his world, for so many years that she had sucked up his life as the sun sucks up the sea and all the streams and rivers, should be lying so near him and yet make no sign to him. Unable to help himself he moved towards the screen and peered behind it as a surgeon, after making his incision, might peer in at the diseased place. He saw a frail golden-haired woman lying with her fist in her mouth and her mouth biting on it to suppress the cry of pain. She turned her eyes towards him. They were violet-colored eyes, startling in her pale face, against her golden hair. She was Ciss Everest yet with a doll's hair in golden curls. She stared at him. She did not recognize him. She did not say: "Tom, Tom Livingstone!"

Well he could throw away the photograph he'd kept for forty-five years, the one of him lying in the grass and her with the sunshade; and that other photograph taken at Stoke Poges. He'd protested at the idea of going there, saying that visiting graveyards was a morbid English custom. It was a bitter January day; he was a gloomy young man in his soldier's uniform, she a love-haunted young woman; the photograph, taken by the sexton in dim light, showed the snow-flattened battered grass, the gray putty-colored tombstones, a color of sickness, the locked budless trees with their branches like rods of iron. The scene was an aristocratic mockery of the vast European fields of putrid abominable death.

And when the sexton had gone, they sat together on the stone bench inside the porch, facing the weather-stained notices. They held hands. Tom remembered the sensation of the surrounding stone and the warm flesh hand. They kissed, scarcely a kiss, a light brushing of the lips and thistledown breaths, surrounded by the dead who, should they waken from beneath their stone, would breathe heavily and greedily.

Well he could throw away all those cherished memories, with the photograph, for he now possessed the image of an old tart with dyed hair, a life-sized doll mechanized to cry out in pain every few minutes, to groan in the night, to whisper her pleas for morphine. The Ciss Everest Cancer Doll. This way to see the Ciss Everest Cancer Doll. Real hair that can be washed, dried, combed, permed. Real face that can be made up to hide the age and the tears. This way, this way to the Ciss Everest Cancer Doll, Doll of the Years, Doll of Forty-Five Years, This way to Miss World War I!

Tom huddled, suddenly in pain. A fever speckled his forehead, like something crawling over his skin. He cried out and a nurse came to help him.

"You've no right to be wandering in the women's ward like this." She fetched a wheelchair, helped him into it, and wheeled him to his room.

"On to your bed at once to rest, Mr. Livingstone."

He drifted into a feverish sleep where he dreamed not of Ciss Everest or the War but of his work. He dreamed of his work as furnaceman in the factory. He dreamed of the flame he had cared for, almost for as many years as he had dreamed of Ciss Everest, and all the years he had lived as tormented inadequate husband to Eleanor, and bullying dutifully loved father to Pearl and Naomi. He dreamed of the Flame. He saw

19

himself, his eyes shaded, opening the furnace door, inspecting, judging, reading the Flame, translating its shape and color and temperature and sound as a scholar translates a foreign language. No one ever knew the Flame as he had. He could see the respect in the eyes of his workmates as they watched him judging, measuring, changing what they would never understand.

He woke when the late afternoon was darkening outside with heath mist and city fog.

A nurse came to read his temperature.

"Not feeling too well, Mr. Livingstone?"

"I'm fine, fine."

"I think you should have dinner upstairs this evening. You can sit in the other ward with Miss Everest. She sits up for dinner. We like to have her up for an hour or two."

"Oh no, I'm having visitors," Tom invented desperately.

"Visitors? We'll send them up to you, don't worry."

Tom dozed again, waking at suppertime when he eased himself from his bed, peglegged to the washstand and splashed his face with cold water. A low fever still burned on his skin. Peter was already downstairs watching television while he waited for the supper gong. It sounded, as from deep in a well, like a summons. There was the grinding movement of wheelchairs being hurried to the landing, then the swift footsteps like those of someone who naturally flew but who, out of discretion and sympathy, now chose to walk. Those steps were always those of the staff, as no patient walked easily, for although all were not crippled, each learned to deflect possible envy and to make himself acceptable and in harmony with his surroundings by acquiring a token limp or an awkwardness and slowness of movement. Firm healthy walking was not recommended.

A nurse passing Tom's ward looked in.

"Suppertime, Mr. Livingstone. You're having supper in Miss Everest's ward?"

No, no, no.

"Yes," Tom said.

He moved slowly to the ward and opened the door. Dressed and blanketed, Miss Everest sat in a deep armchair near the window overlooking the front garden. Tom hobbled over and sat in a chair opposite her, with the supper table, already set, between them. He stared at her, coldly, curiously, trying to read the past in her face, to extract it like some kind of invisible writing beneath his glance. He thought of Eleanor, eaten, early in their marriage, by the two children who swung from her breasts like little monkeys dangling from the buds of a tree; and then eaten by his own impatience and coldness and his longing for another woman.

He watched Ciss Everest's face. She did not recognize him. He saw that the clear violet eyes had grown an opaque film, like pondweed. She must be seventy now, he thought. She was an old woman and he was an old man. And as he stared at her she became an old woman he had never known, and he almost believed that her name and the repeating of it by the patients and the nurses and his own mind was a trick he was playing upon himself, for when he glanced away from her and turned quickly back, almost before he himself realized it, she resembled his own daughter Naomi, she *was* Naomi. Now how could that have been? And then once again she became the Ciss Everest with whom out of politeness and sympathy he had agreed to share a meal, eating, munching, knifing, forking, scraping, saying ah ah, oh oh, yes yes yes, and smiling, smiling, smiling, for he too was learning the politics of helplessness.

"Good evening Mr. Livingstone."

He started.

So she did recognize him. He stared harder at her face. He remembered his passion and haunting, the pain and delight her memory had caused him. But where had his memory gone? Where had the time gone? There was so little room in

21

his mind in which to keep what remained. He had tried to preserve it all so painstakingly—indeed, in "taking pains" he had been forced to endure them and distribute them among his bewildered family.

But she had gone from him now. Nothing stayed. Only his childhood stayed. And the War? The older he became the more his childhood years became clear to him, seen in a new light manufactured by the accumulation of years and switched on, full voltage, day and night by the luxurious necessity of approaching death. A room with no corners shadowed. A room where, because one had not yet learned to read, one imagined the many warning notices were entertaining pictures. Tom had had ten brothers and two sisters, like a family in a fairy tale, the tale where someone was always missed out when treasures such as wings were being distributed. All the brothers and sisters were dead now except Leonard, the black sheep, the drunkard.

"Good evening, Miss Everest. Have you had a good day?"

(He had learned the ritual. In the morning: Have you had a good night? In the evening: Have you had a good day?)

Miss Everest smiled a floating smile.

"Not bad at all. A bit niggly. Yes, definitely niggly at times."

The nurse brought two plates of scrambled eggs and toast and tea, bread and butter and raspberry jam, and two pieces of chocolate cake with chocolate icing half an inch thick.

Tom rebeled against being classified as a "scrambled egg" patient. If he had been dining downstairs he would have been eating beans or sausages or curried stew, indelicate dishes that gave one the illusion of being in stout health.

"And have you had a good day Mr. Livingstone?"

He answered abruptly.

"My leg's mending. Plaster comes off tomorrow."

22

He wondered what she would say if he asked: "Do you remember, Ciss, that time in London when I first met you? I was a wounded soldier and you gave me special care and you let me keep my gas mask and sleep with it under my pillow, because I could not bear to part with it. I never did part with it, Ciss. I took it home with me to Waipori City and I've had it with me all my life. I showed it to my wife and two daughters, by God I showed it to them, and it scared them all but it didn't scare you, Ciss Everest."

But Miss Cecily Everest, floating on the ebbing tide of her morphine, wanted only to chatter.

"I've been ill a long time you know. It started years ago. I used to be a nurse, so I know something about it. And now at last they've broken the news to me. They've broken it to me gently."

She waited, perhaps for him to ask what they had broken to her, but he said nothing.

"The news of course," she said impatiently as if he had questioned her. "The news that I shan't recover; they're sending me to a nursing home not far away—that's why I'm here in the first place, waiting for a bed."

She leaned forward. Her face was flushed.

"It's not far from here. This is a Recovery Unit, you know. I can't stay here. Promise to visit me when I go to the nursing home to die. Promise!"

The demand startled Tom. Perhaps she had recognized him after all?

"I'm sure you'll have many visitors," he said soothingly.

"Promise."

"Of course."

"I like having supper with you here. It's like being at home. I never had a home of my own. I've just lived in hospitals as a nurse and then as a patient. I never married. This is like our home, isn't it, just us two sitting here eating our supper."

Tom played the game.

"It is indeed."

"I used to go down to the noisy dining room, but now I just sit here. They dress me for supper on most evenings. It's quiet up here, just us two, like around the fire at home. I can pretend I've invited you to supper."

"Yes, yes."

They finished their meal. Tom had a horrifying glimpse of Ciss Everest in the reality of her hideous long blonde hair. Meet Ciss Everest, Miss War of Nineteen-Seventeen, the World's only cancer doll, Doll of the Year, Doll of Forty-five Years, Doll of the Future.

The next moment he had the privacy of his nightmare ripped open with a brutality that he had often practiced himself but could not forgive in others. Leaning forward suddenly, Ciss Everest raised her hands to her head and removed her long golden wig, exposing her bald head.

"See," she said. "I wear a transformation."

Hearing her say it in her slow dreamily deliberate way, callously as if she were trying to convey some fearful message to him, he felt himself growing dizzy, his heart beating heavily with a turn-over gurgling of blood around it. She had recognized him, surely!

"Since the radiation made me bald I've worn this transformation."

He'd never heard a wig called by that name before. The word horrified him in its exactness of meaning and description. He felt that if she repeated it with such mocking deliberation he would jerk his hand forward and slap her face.

Then he began to cry. He sobbed. His shoulders sagged as if they were made of straw, suddenly buffeted, the prop removed.

"Nurse," Miss Everest called. "Nurse."

She pressed the bell by her bed.

A nurse came at once into the room.

"Nurse, this old man's crying."

"Now now Mr. Livingstone, we can't have that, and you with only a broken leg while here's our Miss Everest so ill, and you're upsetting her."

The nurse turned, speaking gently to Miss Everest. "Would you like to go to bed now?"

Miss Everest raised shining, craving eyes to the nurse. "I'll have the injection now," she whispered. "I'll have the injection."

The nurse led Tom from the room. "An old man like you!" she exclaimed.

He felt too tired and sick to protest that he was not an old man, he was only eighteen, a young soldier wounded in the War. He'd seen more blood and sickness and death than this Recovery Unit would know in a hundred years; and he was only eighteen, too young to kill and be killed. He had a right to cry, a right to scream if he wanted to, with rage and unhappiness.

7

Did you think you were a king? Where is my box of jests? Am I not my own fool to amuse the courtiers and frighten them into the bargain? With my hand I puff out the squashed gray face of the gas mask with the ridged rubber tube leading from the mouth and nose and the oval window-glass eyes, working my hand inside it like a hideous puppet, putting it over my face and looking through its eyes into the world's eyes, moving my puppet face, my breath hissing, my gray cheeks inflating, deflating, closer and closer.

Dear First Dad, you were such fun. Oh such fun, and you knew how to dance and sing the war songs but the War lasted too long after you came home from it, and just when we thought you had finished with it the films came to tell us of it. All was so quiet on the Western Front, and do you know why? Because the War had gone away from the Western Front, it was home, at home in our house on Eagle Street, and when we looked out of the window at the pine trees in the valley we saw the War and the soldiers, and when the trees died in a storm and the branches fell we saw the dead soldiers, and when we walked in the pine plantation in the valley we walked up to our ankles in blood, all among the dead, and no one but us knew.

Uncle Leonard was in the War, too. He came to see us once, I remember, when we were children, and he said to me, "When I was a boy of ten. . . ." A boy of ten. The time of life when people pass by without looking, because the scaffolding and the boards are up on the outside while the building is being constructed in secret. Uncle Leonard told how he used to read at night, to burn a candle at night, a candle a book, getting the tales of history, of the bad and the weak, the good, the dates, the wars, blood more than flowers; and reaching into tomorrow where all the marvels lay.

"Get away old man with your waving crutch. I am whoever you want me to be."

The stereotype—war, woods, snow—stays.

And Victor Hugo was a boy of ten at the time of the retreat from Moscow.

The stereotype—war, woods, snow—stays.

But what of men dressed in light-green uniforms the color of rotten milkweed? The hot copper sky; the soft earth; the obscene uncontrolled growth of trees with huge leaves that shine as if they sweated; the monstrously beautiful flowers in primary colors; the air an accumulation of tiny suns whirling in the steaming light; the rain a succession of avenues of burning fluid mirrors; no antiseptic scrub of an ice-gloved wind on the exposed wound, not even the freezing, once out of the mouth, of the words of love and hate; a feminine war engulfing in softness and warmth; the shining forests crowned with brilliantly patterned snakes; decay the staple food, decay sown thickly as fields of rice; the natural scene invaded by men's hate; not kinder or unkinder than snow and plain and dark woods yet upsetting the simple death-cold stereotype, infecting other life, the propagation of bacteria; we and they; they the rats, the insect scavengers, the crooked line, the broken circle that lets the difference flood in; the triangle that is not equilateral or isosceles or scalene; the new triangle wedging its unwanted difference into the geometrical harmony.

The flame-colored summer War.

The busy War, the dead not isolated in snowy shrouds, but attended by the scavengers that they in their death encourage to multiply, the dead used as houses for the hungry mindless life, the corrupting guests, the mouthing maggots that have no potentiality to write or speak a sonnet.

Dear First Dad, all wars have fused, even the ancient ones where the battles had foreign unpronounceable names, even the wars that were dropped out of history books because by some extraordinarily callous melodramatic standard "nothing happened in them."

Get away old man with your limp and your crutch, your walking stick, thought stick, life stick that would recover from the room of memory the lost translation of your love.

8

He planned to surprise her, to creep into the ward one day when no one else was there and confront her with, "You remember me, Ciss Everest?"

Do you remember a young wounded soldier, Tom Livingstone?

All her answers must be yes, yes. He needed the strength and support of her memory to recreate his own. If she did not remember he imagined that he would "deal with" her as he had dealt with his children when they were young and would not "tell," grasping their shoulders with impatient rage, shaking, shaking, "Tell the truth, tell, tell, you did, you did!" He'd seen his daughters inflict the same treatment on their dolls—the Christmas dolls they had one year, golden-haired with violet eyes and pink knitted clothing.

"Tell the truth, you did, you did!"

So the next afternoon, on a pretense of going for an exploratory walk now that his leg was out of plaster, Tom again went to the women's ward. It was near the end of the rest period when two of the women were up washing and Miss Everest and Mrs. Dockett lay in bed. Ciss Everest had emerged from sleep and from the morphine dullness, and once again she was in pain, needing another injection. Her eyes shone with pain. She was pressing her fist into her mouth to stop herself from crying out. If she remembers, Tom thought, she will remember now.

He felt he had to know. Cancer Doll, Doll of the War, tell the truth, tell, tell.

The nurse was out of the room. The other two women, slowly completing their after-rest toilet, flapped slowly with slippered feet around the tiled bathroom. The nurse would return soon. Tom could see the thermometers and charts set out ready for the afternoon readings. He drew up a chair by Miss Everest's bed.

"Hello, Miss Everest."

She turned to him and smiled. "Hello."

"How are you feeling?"

She sighed and bit her fist. "A bit niggly, a bit niggly."

He leaned close to her. "Miss Everest, Ciss!"

"Yes?"

Then she drew his attention to her new mohair bed jacket.

"Look. I had this knitted for me. I've two bed jackets now, for when I go to the nursing home. It's not far from here, it's just along the street. They say it's lovely. I've been sick a long time. They've broken it to me, you know. They broke it to me gently."

"You're Ciss Everest, aren't you?"

"Ciss? Of course, Cecily."

"And you nursed in the First World War."

"They used to call it the Great War didn't they? They're always changing the names. Yes, I was a nurse. In the War. I'm so tired. Will you come to supper at my place again tonight?"

"So you remember me from last night? Do you remember young Tom Livingstone from Down Under, a great friend of yours, a boyfriend?"

"Oh yes."

Miss Everest sighed and closed her eyes. A frown creased her forehead and a small smile played about her lips.

"Oh yes, I remember Tom. The love of my life. Did you know him? He would be about your age now, but of course he was a different type altogether. I would know him the moment I saw him. A very quick eager young man. Poor dear Tom."

"You were young too."

Miss Everest looked surprised.

"Oh yes. It is a long time ago now, and I've been sick so many years. In the early days they used to send me to the recovery unit by the sea; so cold and lonely and gray and all the places boarded up along the pier and the sea eating all the color out of the paint. I like here best. I like the traffic in my ears."

Her gaze was beginning to wander to the bedcover. She

caught sight of her fist, clenched it, and drew it up to her mouth, biting hard on it. Her face contorted with pain.

"It's niggly again," she said. "It's so niggly."

Tom was seized with absurd fierce anger. She had failed him. Maybe he hadn't asked the correct questions, yet she had failed him, she had denied his existence, for since he had known her, his whole life had been built upon the memory of her.

Reaching forward he grabbed her fist from her mouth—it was so small and light and sharp that for a moment he thought it might break in pieces like a twig. He held it tight while she struggled weakly. "I'm Tom Livingstone," he said. "I'm Tom Livingstone! I came to find you."

Calmer, he released her fist and looked furtively around him. There was no one in sight now. Mrs. Dockett was fast asleep, snoring in her plaster case like an old wrinkled pea in a white pod. There was no sign of the nurse. Taking hold of the bedspread Tom lifted it to Miss Everest's face and pressed it upon her mouth, firmly, while her eyes grew wide with alarm and disbelief. He pressed the cloth harder on her mouth and nose and now upon her whole face. She scarcely struggled, merely twisted once or twice with the pain of her illness. He turned his face away as he felt her sigh and then grow still. Then quickly, unable to look, he arranged the bedspread as it might have been had she become trapped in its folds while she struggled against the pain.

Taking his crutches he limped from the room. There was still no one in sight. He heard the clattering of cups as the nurse in the duty room washed the afternoon tea dishes. Presently the nurse would appear and take the temperatures. She would discover Miss Everest.

Tom moved slowly along to his ward. There was no sign of Peter. He swung himself onto his bed and lay with his heart thudding, thudding. He could not believe what he had done. She knew me all right, he said to himself as he lay with his eyes closed and his palms and forehead damp with sweat. I tell you she knew me. She had to, she had to know me. Where have I been living for the past forty-five years if not directly in her shadow?

He dozed, restlessly, and when he woke he found that everyone was talking about it, though no word had been given officially. Miss Everest, in a spasm of pain, had pulled the bedclothes to her face and suffocated. No one knew exactly what happened, but all agreed, with the arrogance of ignorance which the living show towards the dying and the dead, that her death had been "a merciful release."

That evening Tom went to the dining room for supper, and afterwards he watched television, an old film where the heroine's face was so pale it appeared blue, and the hero had black eyes like a cat. They made love in a brass-knobbed bed and then he went away to the Great War. The last scene showed his grave among the poppy fields, a beautiful sight with the sun and the dappled shadows and the sky, the lightly trembling spring leaves on the trees, the hard dry earth, firm to walk upon, the rippling cornfields. And no trace of mud. No battle tracks, duckboards, shell holes, dead men and horses, trenches, no decayed fruit at all, shell fall from the blossoming orchards of War.

9

So he returned to his home in Eagle Street, Waipori City, South Island, New Zealand, the World. In the Recovery Unit and its nightmare the time had traced him, in dream and reality, with the carbon, so to speak, crumpled and twisted. Home in Waipori City some agent—he himself or the place or the summer thunder and lightning or the brilliant black-and-white night sky and the daytime polish and sparkle of the summer leaves, or the fact that Leonard his brother now lived in the lower house on the sloping hill section and could be used to quarrel with or complain about and ask advice from—whatever it was, agent or fact, it succeeded in smoothing the tracing paper, putting dream and reality edge to edge, the two in harmony. What was left to do, then, for an old man, but sleep?

The concentration of time necessary for the traveler who stores a multitude of impressions may cramp the time also, like a foot in a pinching shoe, and the hurt persists when the traveling is done, and when the constriction is about the heart instead of the foot the pain is intense. It is better then for an old man to sleep.

He slept. His nightmares—of the annihilation of Ciss Everest, of himself and his love, were many. He looked for his dead wife too. And for his two daughters who had left home early in their lives and never returned. He watched his pet bird die—a yellow budgerigar in a cage—and could not bury it. It used to say "Hello" and "Oh my, I don't want to die." And he liked to fondle Samuel the cat and feel the thread of its purring.

His leg neither improved nor deteriorated. He talked of it to the grocer and the baker and to Leonard. My broken leg. When he had been a young man he was playing football and broke his ankle and all the members of the football team had visited him in hospital and signed their names on his plaster. It was a custom, autographing plaster of paris legs and arms, and cricket bats and footballs. Young Colin his grandson, who was said to be a promising cricketer, might one day be autographing the cricket bats of admiring youngsters. Colin was taking up accountancy. Such a clean occupation. No mess to wipe away after working with figures; no leaping and threatening and changing mood and color and temperature like a flame in a furnace; no need to confine figures in a cage and wear an eyeshield to examine them; oh no, they stayed where they were put. No mess at all. No sickness in numbers

—broken legs, lungs legs, wombs removed. Oh no, now there was something to clean up. And ah! The world was getting cleaner and cleaner, and everyone wanted it that way. Who wanted blood and hair on the weapon after the murder?

But his leg still hurt and he made an appointment with Dr. Friar downtown, Dr. Friar who lived in style like all the doctors in Waipori City, in a large two-storied house with the Spanish flat roof that was in fashion at the time, set in a landscaped garden surrounded by a high brick ivy-covered wall. The doctors' houses were the town palaces, and the doctors' children were educated at private schools, and the sons were handsome and the daughters were beautiful. And young Chris Friar who was studying to take over his father's practice was slim, sandy-haired, gentle, a favorite with expectant mothers, a man with the gynecological touch.

So six weeks after Tom returned to Waipori City he sat in Dr. Friar's waiting room. The surroundings subdued him. A poster hand was pointing at him asking: *Do you have a sore that does not heal?* He shuddered and picked up the *Weekly News* from the magazine table and turned the pages of photographs—sheepmustering in the high country; autumn days in the mountains; deep sea fishing; American tourists and deer hunting by helicopter in the back country; inside a butter factory. He put down the *Weekly News* and stared at the painting on the wall—a dark blue-and-green oil of paradise ducks in flight. *Consult your doctor without delay.*

A woman came into the reception room. Tom glanced at her and suddenly leaned his head in his hands and closed his eyes, for there was no mistaking the way her face and body, like an index, made reference to the past. She was middle-aged, in her late forties or early fifties, but big violet-colored eyes emphasized by heavy makeup stared out of her face, and her hair was golden blonde, piled high on her head and fastened with a brown wooden comb. She spoke.

"Excuse me, what time is your appointment."

33

Tom looked across at her. He felt sick with the sudden shifting of the balance of his life. Why, she was nothing but an old tart.

"Ten thirty," he said.

"Mine is too."

He tried to still the trembling of his hands when he heard her speak. It was impossible, impossible. He was dreaming.

"I'm Peggy Warren," she said.

There. It was impossible.

"My leg," he said confusedly. "Broke my leg."

"Oh," she said, and began to talk. She told him she was alone in the world, she had a live-in job as a nurse's aid at the Bideawhile Old People's home at Maheno, the next town north of Waipori City. This was her day off, though usually she had only an afternoon, but as her blood pressure was playing up she had come to consult her old family doctor.

While she talked he stared at her. Oh, there was no mistaking her though she wore disguise. Her eyebrows were thick and heavily marked, her eyelids shadowed a mauve color with little spots at the corners like the spots on foxglove petals, her eyes were that dark delphinium blue-to-violet, her face was cemented pink. She wore a tight-fitting dark blue costume and while her body was trim and her legs, with their pointed feet in high-heeled open-work shoes, were thin, her breasts swelled like full porridge bowls.

She was staring at him, studying him. Tom picked up the *Weekly News* again and flipped over the pages, gazing at the sun-and-snow-filled photograph of Fox Glacier and the caption, "A field or body of ice formed in a region of perpetual snow and moving slowly down a mountain slope or valley; glaciers also carry rock debris in their basal parts and this grinds, scores, and polishes the surface over which the ice moves."

Well he knew all that. That was glaciers. "I wear a transformation," he heard Ciss Everest say. And there was her

34

bald head like a world globe without continents or islands or oceans, a blank world.

Fifteen minutes later with Peggy Warren boldly taking his arm he walked with her into the street towards the Dainty Doris Tearooms, as if he and she had always been together, and anyone seeing them might have thought so too. There goes Tom Livingstone, too old to have his heart broken, maybe, but not too old to have his pocket picked, if he hasn't emptied it already on that wild-goose chase of an overseas trip. There's Peggy Warren, Furcoat Peg, Miss Second World War. Ha, ha. Off into the Dainty Doris Tearooms. Hold onto your pocket, Tom.

They found a table for two inside the door.

"I like to look at people," Peggy said.

Tom said nothing. A feeling of extraordinary lightness came over him as if his whole life had been wiped clear, his dead wife flying away like a flame to the heaven she wanted to be in and had waited patiently for; the dark burden and nightmare of Ciss Everest buried under its own weight yet remindingly, excitingly present in Peggy Warren; Naomi out of the picture, not heard of for years; Pearl sitting pretty up north with her husband the bank clerk and her son the accountant, never visiting, sending the regular birthday and Christmas handkerchiefs and ties; and now Peggy as close as Eleanor had never been. The resurrection of an old love, even in spite of murder, and wasn't that the way the world was supposed to turn, and a hundred years from now, sooner, the lions and the lambs and so on, that Eleanor used to rave about?

Tom's view of Eleanor had been like the view one has when one's eyes are being tested and the optometrist keeps blocking the view by twisting mirrors this way and that, by shading one eye, thrusting in lenses that one can't see through at all, or which magnify or diminish, never getting the correct focus, and then when the correct focus is obtained at last, the optometrist suddenly removes the lens, saying, "I'll send this away to be processed." And for some reason the only lens that gives correctly focused sight is mislaid and never returned. It had been this way with Tom's view of Eleanor, a continued guilty muddled peering this way and that through hazes of mustard gas and shell smoke and fire and strands of Ciss Everest's dark hair. The golden curls were new—a transformation.

They had their pots of tea, sardine sandwiches, and a meringue. Peggy talked of her life in hospital, of the day spent turning and lifting and washing the old men and women.

"We'll be like that some day," she said. "Being washed and turned. And what do you do all day?"

She asked the question in such a way that Tom's day and its many many hours seemed suddenly like a treasure-house of pleasant surprises. He told her how he worked most of his life as a furnaceman at the cement factory but now he was on the pension, and with his leg he didn't think he would be getting another job. "I could have had a career," he said, in a satisfied way, "but I stayed a furnaceman."

"Sounds good."

Peggy laughed, distributing her body, her legs shooting under the table with the impact of her own laughter. No woman he ever knew had laughed that way, so certainly and immediately, whether or not there was something to laugh at, except their next-door neighbor who used to laugh regularly every Friday night, pay night, when her husband came home drunk. She used to come out to the top of the steps on their back porch and throw back her head and laugh and laugh, like a horse whinnying. You half-expected some animal to answer her back. And then she'd go inside to her old man and he'd take out his block and tackle and have a go at her in full view of the kitchen window.

"Oh. Excuse me," Peggy said, rearranging herself.

Tom felt suddenly nervous. He cleared his throat.

"Don't mention it," he said primly.

They finished their snack. The waitress, smart in black and white frilled apron and cap and stick-on cuffs, brought the bill. Peggy pushed it towards Tom. He picked it up and looked at it.

"My God," he said. "They sting you."

He said he was not used to paying so much for a measly cup of tea and sardine sandwiches.

"Come on, cough up," Peggy said, smiling so gaily that Tom could not help smiling.

"Why not?" he said.

Once outside the Dainty Doris they stood, deciding. People passed on the footpath and Tom bumped against Peggy's arm. She took his arm in hers.

He wanted to whisper urgently, "Who are you?" But he kept smiling instead. Who are you? Why are you?

Her arm, nicely plump, felt soft as a feather pillow.

"I'd better catch the bus back," Peggy said. "It's been nice meeting you, Mr. Livingstone, and thanks for the cup of tea."

She sighed. "I suppose I'd better catch the slow old bus."

"Wait," Tom said, "I can drive you in my little Hillman. It's a good day for a drive. I've got all day to myself."

"That's kind of you." She giggled. "I was hoping you'd ask."

He drove her along the State Highway and over the river to Maheno. She promised to meet him the following week. And maybe, he said, she might like to come to see where he lived.

He felt instantly guilty. Home was still Eleanor's territory. Even Ciss Everest had never been allowed in it, not by Eleanor. And it belonged to Naomi and Pearl, though they were long ago vanished. He was not brave enough to begin apportioning love and property, as King Lear had not been brave enough also—to conceal his own cowardice, putting upon his daughters the responsibility of measuring and weighing out love. "On second thought," Peggy said, "after all we're both by ourselves aren't we?"

He patted her on the shoulder, but she swooped him into her arms as if he were a puppet. "I could have waited forty-five years for this for all you care," she said. "It's no use trying to keep your dignity, it's like keeping a bank book with no money in it."

"It's all over Waipori," Leonard said, grinning, when Tom passed the cottage and the valley pine trees on his way up to the house. "Peggy Warren picked you up."

Tom frowned. "Peggy Warren? I'd be careful what I say. She's a clean-living decent woman."

"I won't argue," Leonard said. He didn't think Tom knew that she used to be called Fur Coat Peg, Miss World War Number Two.

Leonard looked lonely as he said in a complaining tone, "The paper's there by the gate. No news."

Leonard's regular comment on the newspaper was that it never had any news, though he read it right through down to the advertisements, lost and found, personal, radio, cars for sale, electrical repairs. Neither the morning nor the evening paper carried the news he searched for.

"Nothing," he said again. "Not a drop of news."

As if it were a well gone dry, and he might soon die of thirst in a desert world.

"Never is," Tom said, picking up the newspaper from between the bars of the gate and limping up the hill towards the house.

"Sammy, Sammy, puss puss," he called as he came round under the pear tree to the back door. "Puss puss, Samuel."

Leonard must have him at the cottage, he thought. "All right, cat, have it your own way," he said aloud as he opened the door and walked in, and sat in the chair by the window where he could look down the hill at the pine plantation in the valley. He felt as if he had missed something, a bus or train or plane going somewhere important. He felt uneasy and lonely. Looking out into the holly and lilac bushes he fancied he saw the cat's eyes staring back at him, changing color, blue-violet, green, glittering with mockery.

Inside, the house seemed to grow darker while outside the day still glared and gazed like a searchlight. He looked out, longingly, at the day. But what's the use of going outside, he thought. He felt resentful against Peggy Warren. He felt afraid. By some trick of the daylight—that was it, by daylight robbery—she had taken home to her hospital room not only her own abundant supply of enjoyment and gaiety but his meager supply also. She'd picked him up all right. Eleanor would have disapproved of her. Everyone he ever knew could invade the privacy of his mind to offer opinions and advice, and all disapproved of her. Even Ciss Everest the Culin Hall Cancer Doll? Ah. He began to sing softly, leaning in his chair, knowing and not wanting to know the many hours of daylight that remained hard and knocking against the sky and the house, while inside grew darker every minute, the light slipping away fast because there was no one strong enough to want to keep it—what was the use? Tom sang:

I want to go home,
I want to go home.
I don't want to go to the trenches no more
Where the bullets and shrapnel are flying galore
Take me over the sea
Where the enemy won't get at me
Oh my I don't want to die
I want to go home.

But he was home now wasn't he? He got up from his chair and switched on the radio. Mantovani and his orchestra. "Greensleeves." If the world were coming to an end they'd play "Greensleeves." He switched to shortwave. Underwater gurglings, high-pitched squeals. No hope.

Then he went to the cage where the dead bird lay in its yellow shroud of withering feathers. "I'm damn sure I'm not going to bury you," he said.

Then he stretched out on the sofa by the back window and closed his eyes and fell asleep.

It was a spring morning. The year seemed vague, the time kept changing. The cement factory stood in the background like a huge process of digestion with the sand and clay being swallowed at one end, submitting to change and movement, action and reaction, and finally excreted as cement into the concrete silos that stood like tall chamber pots outside the delivery end of the factory, where the railway trucks connected by branch lines to the railway station. For miles around you could see the factory chimney with its smoke and the ever-burning Flame that swayed and danced as it consumed the foul gases. The furnace room where Tom worked was at the lower intestine, so to speak, and to reach it Tom had to climb a steep iron staircase. It was cozy and warm inside the furnace room and if Tom and his assistant felt the need of fresh air they could always go out to the narrow stair landing and look out over the factory and feel the cool breezes blowing from the Taeri Plains across the river.

This day, all over the grassy slope down from the house, the morning sun was undoing the crumpled yellow knots of the daffodils, and blossoms clouded the trees with pink, and the pear tree with white, and the wattle brushed its yellow dust upon the sleeve of the passing wind; at last, winter had been trodden underfoot into the earth like an old cracked acorn.

Tom set out early for the factory. There was a war in the world. Another war. The news troubled him. He'd bought a map of the world at the local stationers and he'd pinned the flags of the nations in appropriate places, moving them backwards and forwards with each battle and defeat and victory, playing a child's game, the game the generals were playing. That morning the newspaper had listed as dead the son of the laughing woman down the road; blown to bits thousands of miles away. The War. The Flame. A new machine had been installed in the furnace room. Anyone could turn a switch, read a pressure gauge. How many like Tom could judge the Flame correctly with their own eyes?

The War. The Flame. Ciss Everest. And Eleanor clinging to him, abasing herself in a way that made him despise her so much that he finally closed the valve of feeling for her and accepted her only as a presence providing food and clean clothes. He had grown used to escaping from home each day to care for the Flame. But what escape was there now, when his skill had been replaced by the new machine?

From the bus stop to the cement works was a short walk past the slaughterhouse. He found himself dawdling as he used to do in childhood on the way to school, staring and standing. If school had promised something fearful he used to plan to run away for the day or forever, to run away from home, to take a ship to the Californian gold fields or maybe only as far as Australia, to the gold fields and Calgoorlie and Coolgardie. Calgoorlie, Coolgardie. The names echoed in his head. He stopped by the sheepyard with its rust-colored wooden railings touched with late frost, and the mob of sheep enclosed by them, waiting patiently huddled together with twinkles of frost glistening on their wool, their heads showing above the surface of the sea of wool "like swimmers whose strength is going." As one sheep moved the others rippled in a wave. They were mostly silent sheep—sheep were usually complaining, communicating animals, bleating and pushing and struggling—that turned Tom's guilty thoughts of escape to an overpowering gloomy calm, as if he were one of the waiting sheep. He stood watching them. They stared back at him with a nothingness of expression that was worse than plain hostility or pity or curiosity or disdain in that it provided a blank pool for the watcher to sink his own feelings.

Tom walked abruptly away from the silly sheep, and arriving at the factory he clocked in, fetched his overalls and eyeshield from his locker, and climbed the stairs to the furnace room, where to his surprise the manager, Scott Howard, was waiting for him.

"Ah Tom," he said.

Howard was dressed in evening clothes—black suit, white shirt front, black tie, black-polished shoes. He wore gold cuff links, too. Perceiving Tom's surprise he smiled an embarrassed smile.

"I suppose you're wondering why I'm dressed like this but I always dress for such occasions."

Tom waited for an explanation.

"You see, Tom, you've been with us a long time. You and I have worked side by side and seen almost all the Portland in this country being born and put to use. You and others like you have helped to build the great prisons that are our country's pride; cellblock upon cellblock; and factories; and hospitals; dams; wharves; homes; walls, walls, walls. In these you and others like you are leaving behind great monuments. Oh, I'm not such a fool as to think that everyone will remember the furnaceman, but your presence will be there, it'll be there, durable in the works of man. I've been proud of your work with the furnace, Tom. I know your attitude to our new electronic gauge. I know how you feel at the thought that instruments have taken over to do the work you learned to do with your eyes and ears and brain. And believe me, Tom, I've been worried since that new machine was installed. I don't like to see your skills made redundant in this way. I want to see you practicing the skills you are proud of."

Tom stared in surprise. He'd never heard Scott Howard talk in this way before. If it hadn't been happening before his trusted eyes and ears, he would never have believed it. Scott Howard was not that kind of man. He was tough, quick tempered; what I say goes and no monkey business.

"I know you're unhappy with the new machine, Tom."

Tom blinked his eyes, closed them, and opened them again. It was no dream. Scott Howard, in evening clothes, stood before him in the furnace room of the cement factory. What is more, he held between his two hands a huge hammer.

"It's all yours, Tom," Howard said, smiling as he gave Tom the hammer. Tom could hear the sound of the works— knocking, pumping, hissing, grinding, the metallic snap as the clinker dropped from the furnace. He fancied he heard far away the contented bleating of sheep on the hills in the heat and cool breezes of a summer day. A train whistled, birds called. The door to the furnace room was opened. He could see the iron stairway and the squat ugly buildings of the laboratory where Jim Talbot, the assistant chemist, spent his time baking and testing trays of cement biscuits and dreaming, in the midst of his cookery, of the career he might have had with the D.S.I.R. And beyond the laboratory Tom could see the green of the Taeri Plains.

To the right of the laboratory the sun shone on the slurry pool, pressing a gold metallic light like a lid over the gruel-gray surface. Tom felt and saw these details as if in a dream, as taking the hammer, and disconnecting the machine, while Howard stood watching approvingly, he proceeded to smash the machine to pieces, blow after blow, with the sweat oozing on his forehead, his sleeves rolled up and the veins on his arms standing out like inner tubes. There was a sighing sound from the Flame lying in its long steel cocoon, as if it turned in its sleep before it resumed its steady roaring. Tom stopped in his frenzied destruction to listen. So many years of his waking life had been spent close to the Flame, observing it as a doctor observes his patient, or a man close to the woman he loves counts her heartbeats because his own life depends on them. He had listened to the speech of the Flame because it was to him and only him that it was speaking, and for him only it changed color, moved, gained or lost degrees in temperature.

Tom put down his hammer and, not even stopping to put on his eyeshield, he opened the small round furnace door and looked in at the Flame, as a father might look in at a sleeping child or a lover upon the woman he loved. Immediately, with the new machine lying destroyed under the high-speed impact of his hate, he faultlessly gauged the pressure, temperature, color, shape, and reaching to the old switch on the old fashioned gauge he adjusted the Flame as his skill dictated it ought to be. That was that.

He closed the furnace door. The manager, the remains of the new electronic gauge, even the hammer had disappeared. Contentedly Tom returned to his work as if nothing had happened, sitting down first to see what kind of sandwiches Eleanor had packed for him in his black high-domed lunchbox. To his dismay he found the box was empty. Eleanor had forgotten his lunch! How dare she. He realized he was hungry, too, after his destruction of the machine. Not a sandwich, not sardine or salmon and shrimp or onion. Disgusted, he was about to go back to his work when he heard footsteps on the iron staircase and Scott Howard, dressed now in overalls that gave off a blue sheen like some kind of bird's feathers, lightly sprayed with cement dust, appeared on the landing.

"Ah, Tom," he said. "Let Herb look after the Flame for

a moment. Your wife's here with your lunch. She's waiting outside by the slurry pool."

"Coming," Tom called, though there was no need to call out. He was surprised by the youthfulness and hope in his voice. He called Herb from downstairs to watch the Flame and hurried down to the slurry pool where Eleanor was sitting on the concrete edge with a small shopping bag at her feet. She was dressed as he had not seen her dressed for years. She looked young. Her long brown hair was wound with a velvet ribbon. She wore a gold-patterned spring dress and light cardigan. She appeared as she was when they first met, on the launch trip in the Marlborough Sounds before the great great Great War.

She'd better be careful, sitting there, he thought suddenly. He felt young and gay. He fancied he heard the sheep bleating again, the young lambs with their trembling calls to the ewes, the ewes with their anxiously identifying, reassuring calls to their young, all on a hillside on a summer day under a blue childhood sky with crickets knitting the light and sound into the grassheads of cocksfoot and soldier grass. Tom's eager steps gave way to a slow tread. Eleanor, suddenly older, nearer, smiled beseechingly at him.

"I forgot your lunch, Tom."

He did not answer. He frowned.

"Here, I've brought you onion sandwiches and two salmon and shrimp."

He sat down beside her on the edge of the slurry pool.

"Forgot it again!" he exclaimed.

"I've never forgotten it before."

"Haven't you?"

Both turned to look into the pool. Eleanor shuddered.

"This gives me the creeps. It looks bottomless, it's like ... it's like a sore filled with pus—oh Tom!"

She clung to his arm. Her fingers felt small and strong. He grasped her fingers, then her hands, then moving to

45

grasp her upper arm he swung her around, holding her arm with one hand, gripping her thigh with the other, and quickly, though she now began to struggle, he leaned her further back towards the slurry, pushing, pushing while she still struggled, and with his hand now over her mouth, stopping her cries, he leaned with her, feeling his face close to the gray plasticine-smooth surface that splashed up suddenly hitting him with gritty wetness as she fell and sank, and the smooth lightly sand-starred surface closed over her.

He wiped his face and brow with his handkerchief—his birthday handkerchief. He wiped the splashes of slurry from his overalls. Then he picked up the shopping bag and looked inside and took out a small parcel, unfolded the waxed paper and saw the sandwiches, onion and two salmon and shrimp, just as Eleanor had said. Hungrily he began to eat, sitting there on the edge of the slurry pool. He saw Scott Howard, on a tour of the works, passing in his car. Howard smiled with his new false teeth with the acrylic-resin gums. Tom smiled back showing his ordinary human teeth.

"That's got rid of her, hasn't it?" Howard called, opening his mouth again in a flashing laugh. "Knew you'd do it, Tom."

The manager's car turned the corner by the laboratory. Tom sat munching his sandwiches, keeping the salmon and shrimp until the last because he liked them best. No, he thought, it was not even murder, it was nothing, nothing.

He looked once more at the surface of the slurry pool. No sign, not a ripple, not even an arm raised for help. Nothing.

He crumpled the waxed paper and threw it into the pool and taking the shopping bag he returned to the furnace room.

The manager made no further visits that day to the furnace room. A notice was pinned in the locker room requesting that lunch wrappers be disposed of in the receptacle provided, not in the slurry pool. Tom worked for the rest of the day conscientiously, heart to heart, eye to eye with the Flame and when the whistle sounded at five o'clock he knew he had done a good day's work. Walking past the slaughterhouse to the bus stop he did not look at the sheep waiting in their pen, yet again the silence of the new flock impressed itself upon him—the morning's flock would already be strung up in freezer rooms. He remembered the nothingness in their smooth-surfaced eyes. Why didn't they bleat or bawl or go mad when they so obviously knew what was going to happen to them? A great silencer, knowledge of doom. Tom heard, enclosed within a shaft of memory, the dread, dreary silence that came after battle when the cries and the still-booming guns and crackling gunfire still sounded, yet in a separate listening world from the dull used silence; a kind of nothingness of the spirit; a numbness to get fast into sex, with himself or others; or merely sit tapping his foot or twirling his hat like an angry schoolmaster or anxious suitor.

The bus was on time. Eleanor was dead. Ciss, and the children they'd had together, would be waiting for him, Tom remembered. And when the bus stopped he saw them, Ciss as usual lovely, dark, smooth, and the two little girls Ciss and May with their violet-blue eyes, their Everest-Livingstone eyes, waiting to kiss him hello. In the morning before he left from work they would cling to him to try to stop him from leaving. Ah, he remembered. That was how it was and how it had always been. He put his hand across his eyes and wiped away a terrible dream.

Ciss was older, with smile lines and love lines around her eyes and mouth. Her shoulders were plumper, her used breasts enticing like familiar warm breakfast bowls.

"I've picked wattle," she said.

The home was warm and yellow with light.

He kissed her on the ears, on the neck, and on her mouth and a quick fear came and vanished as he remembered his map of the world and the small brightly colored flags that pierced the different territories, charting the progress of the War.

His meal was ready. He ate. The children talked happily of their day at school. Ciss smiled and dished out food, mountain on mountain of food. His appetite seemed without end.

After dinner he worked a crossword puzzle from the evening paper, solving all the clues without a dictionary and without asking for help. And when Ciss (Cecily) and May came to him with their homework he made a map of the gold fields of Australia, saying, "There's Calgoorlie, there's Coolgardie." He repeated the names: Calgoorlie, Coolgardie.

Enchanted the children took up the refrain, "Calgoorlie, Coolgardie. Calgoorlie, Coolgardie."

So that was it. There was no War, he had only dreamed it, there were gold fields and gold mines and he was head of a happy family in a world forever made safe for—happy families.

"It's the Australian gold fields," he said, smiling at Ciss who had not studied Australian geography, Calgoorlie, Coolgardie.

Suddenly tired, the little girls stopped their fun and shut down their faces as a prelude to sleep. They looked wisely and seriously at Tom.

"Bedtime," their mother said, enfolding them.

The evening passed in quiet domestic harmony. Ciss and Tom had not much to say to each other, they merely glanced, murmured, smiled, while the stove gleamed warm; and later when they lay in bed together, again at peace, they slept as the happy are reputed to sleep, dreamlessly, though once, waking, Tom fancied that he heard the faint bleating of sheep from the faraway hills of summer.

And the time became a dream. Eleanor's body was never found in the slurry pool, it was as if she had never existed.

Her shopping bag vanished from the furnace room. She left no trace. And Tom never again saw the manager in evening clothes in the furnace room nor heard him mention Eleanor. It was always Ciss he asked after, and Cecily and May, never Pearl and Naomi. Tom's days at work were satisfying, his evenings at home full of happiness. The years passed peacefully and the two little girls grew up wise and beautiful and clever and good and though they never married, as naturally they wanted most of all to be near their father, they lived full lives with the opportunities they had. May becoming a teacher of elocution and Cecily a teacher of the piano, both with their studios in a building next door to the family home. And it was only when Tom retired from the cement works that the new electronic gauge was once again installed in the furnace room.

When Tom retired he felt a period of loss, as a cliff might when years of persistent weather suddenly demolish part of it into the sea. I might have pursued a different career, he thought then. I might have been someone in life. Still, I learned my trade and was happy in it, and the world is at peace and it's a great little country I live in, with its compassionate social reform. I live a simple life with my wife and two daughters, with my fishing in the weekend, the radio to listen to in the evenings, the garden to dig and plant; and never a moment of boredom, my fishing flies to inspect and identify, my salmon spoons to cut and polish and count, my lead sinkers to fashion with the soldering bolt, the crucible and the spirits of salts; friends to talk to; and Ciss Everest whom I loved and married, to be with me, a part of me; and memory and dreams through which to recover what is lost and dead.

And one night about this time Tom dreamt a strange dream, and May dreamed also, and in the morning at breakfast they told each other their dreams.

Tom, articulate as always, said, "I dreamed there was dancing down in the pine plantation in the valley with a band

49

and a host of dancers all in white swaying to the music. It was a dance arranged to celebrate a victory which all knew of but none talked about. You could see everyone exchanging glances and smiles, sharing the good news. It had been raining, I remember, and the pine needles were damp and as they were being used as a dance floor, they enmeshed some of the women's high-heeled shoes, tripping them, and even breaking ankles. I knew none of the dancers. I suppose they were from out of town, miles away. I could not make up my mind where in the world I was, although the pine trees were our Waipori City, northeast valley pine trees and the night sky was ours with the Southern Cross showing. Then suddenly I saw myself as one of the dancers leading a charming young woman in a circle around the pine-needle floor while at the same time I sat under the trees next to an old hag who had twisted her ankle. I kept appearing and disappearing. I heard in the distance what I first thought to be the sea around the bay, roaring as it does at night, and then I realized that it was the sound of guns, a natural sound, as much a part of my life as the sea and the wind and the sheep bleating and the sounds at the cement works; a large world-heart beating unsteadily to ensure a circulation of death. It was War. We were dancing in celebration inside the War and it kept changing from being something magnificent, watched over by the Southern Cross, to something small and quickly crushed and devoured, like withered peanuts rattling inside their shells.

"I thought of food and I decided to go to a large wooden table where the food had been spread, and help myself to something, but as I approached the table I saw that the only food was heaps of long rusty nails which a few dancers were eating hungrily, while the drink was nothing but glasses of drainwater and urine which the dancers drank thirstily. The women's white clothing had been as white as the pear blossom at the beginning of the dance; now their dresses were stained like rotten lettuces. I remember feeling confused and

50

cheated because when the dancers ate and drank they made no sign they were not getting the usual party food. I wanted to go to them, to seize them and shake them, try to make them see the food as I saw it but I was afraid to because they were all so powerfully real and full of belief; and then I devised a plan to startle them by driving one of the rusty nails through the heart of the most beautiful young woman. I seized a ten-inch nail from one of the plates. I realized that the most beautiful young woman was the one dancing with my other observed self. I sat on the wooden seat under the trees and waited until the dance brought myself and her near to me and then suddenly I stood up—I remember the old hag tried to stop me—and thrust with all my strength at the woman's heart. She wavered, like water, not as in a dream but in a film convention of a dream. I saw my other self spring to confront me. And then I woke up," Tom said. "That was the end of the dream."

"My dream was strange too," May said. "I dreamed that I was living happily underground and had never been above the ground. There were other people—vague presences—and they too seemed to be living happy lives underground in almost complete darkness. The dim light was not light as we know it, not daylight or twilight but the kind of light you see against your eyelids when you close your eyes, full of streaks and spots and mysterious shadows, like the light shed by your own blood. I'd heard about the sun and the daylight and the moon and the night. I think I must have heard about it from deep in my bones because much communication was between bones and mind, and bone speech was the accustomed language. I knew there was one entrance to the daylight world and the longing grew in me to go above ground and I began to spend my time—if there were such a thing as time—I should say I had begun to spend my heartbeats at the small gate trying to make up my mind to open it and go up to the daylight. I had the feeling that the journey was forbidden, that if I made it, something dreadful might happen to me, but this again was another communication from my bones which, however, I trusted. We all knew, underground, that bones and skin and blood were the most trustworthy friends. Then one day—*day?*—I mean one heartbeat, I pushed open the small gate and crept up and up and crouched on the earth like a little rabbit, I'm sure, with my eyes closed because I knew that daylight and the sun were perceived chiefly through the eyes and I wanted to experience them in a sudden dazzling moment.

"I opened my eyes.

"I felt keenly disappointed. I felt that I might just as well have stayed beneath the earth, for I found that all was dark here as down below and there was no immediate sensation or knowledge of daylight or sun, and a feeling of frustration came over me as I realized that in expecting to see the sun I had not known how to recognize it when I saw it, I did not know what it might be, or when, or where. Therefore I began to grope about on the earth. How sweet-smelling it was, covered with coarse fur, like that of the underground animals I had known, but soft and wet. My hand sprang up and down upon it. Then I touched something hard and round. I tapped it and bruised my fingers. I closed my fingers upon it and found I could grasp it. I pulled, and suddenly I held it in my hand. It was round. My bones told me the sun appeared round. As my hand warmed against it it grew warmer and smoother. My bones told me the sun was warm.

"And then I felt lonely. As far as I could make out there were no walls to the earth. It seemed to go on and on without curtains as we know them or clay mountains, and there was no sign of a roof, though when I looked up I could see that the aboveness was not as dark as the beneathness; but my loneliness became too much for me and persuading myself that I was satisfied, that I indeed held the sun in my hands though it was not all my bones told it should be, I retreated again through the small gate to the underground place, taking the sun with me, and when I arrived I had much prestige from my display of the sun, for no one not even I, knew that the round smooth stone I had picked up and warmed with my hand was not the sun.

" 'So you've been above the earth,' " they said to me. " 'If you've seen the sun you should also have seen the daylight. What is the daylight?' Knowing they—the shadowy presences—would believe everything I told them, I explained that the daylight was a series of small suns placed edge to edge upon the earth, and some were sharp enough to pierce your flesh but others were smooth and round and warm, like the one I had brought back with me. And the daylight, I said, believing it myself and feeling a heavy sadness inside me— the daylight is a heaviness that will crush you to death, and nothingness. And that was the end of my dream. I woke up. I thought when I was waking that I should have the stone in my hand but my hand was empty. That was a strange dream wasn't it?"

And after breakfast that morning May returned to her studio to give her usual ten o'clock lesson. Her pupil recited:

The moan of doves in immemorial elms,
And murmuring of innumerable bees.

And,

White founts falling in the courts of the sun,
And the soldan of Byzantium are smiling as they run.

And the next pupil, a boy of ten, recited:

John had great big waterproof boots on;
John had a great big waterproof hat;
John had a great big waterproof mackintosh—
And that said John is that.

53

Tom drowsed on the sofa and waking in darkness he reached to switch on the bedlight near his locker. There was no locker and no bedlight. He touched something wet and soft lying on the floor ... the wetness might be blood ... Peter's lost lung.

"Stupid," he said, his mind awake and foursquare, the corners and shadows of sleep darkly inaccessible. "How can he breathe without his lungs? I, I got friends all over the town."

10

Dear First Dad, it has rained all day and each hour the green of the grass and the trees becomes softer and deeper —I see them from where I lie in bed—and the sky grows layer on layer of pearl, blue upon blue—gray and silver with the fusion of thunder light, sunlight, and darkness driven down to cling black against the boles of the trees; and I lie here as life is lived half in a dream, identifying pain and relief from pain, embroidering both in a tapestry of hope and despair on a frame of memory. I had a dream that the doctor came to restore all those parts of my body that have been taken from me, that instead of the usual search and destroy operation of War he performed a healing restorative operation, recovery, but before he returned my body to me he arranged the parts for my inspection: raw, dead, ugly objects to be flushed away, I thought, with the lid shut.

"Here's your me," he said.

That made me smile. My me!

"It's easier," he said, "if I treat you as a flower and name the returned parts of you as petal, stalk, and so on."

Then he gathered the dreadful things, dripping with blood, into his hands, and said harshly,

"Take your guts and lights and so on."

It was a silly dream because snow kept falling and the great trees in the valley lay as I remembered them, capped with icicles, uprooted, dead; and the evidence of War lay everywhere. I think I refused to accept my "me" because it was a stranger in its separate becoming; it was raw, dead, ugly—cat's meat.

Then in the dream Ciss Everest, whose photo you always kept at home among the birth and death certificates, appeared and claimed what I had thrown away, seeing in it a becoming that was valuable to her.

She said, "I don't see rawness, death, ugliness here."

I think I disappeared, or perhaps I watched from a height while she took my place in bed and became instantly the dying me, and you entered the room and your leg was in plaster and you were eighteen-years old like the photo of you in your soldier's uniform and because Ciss Everest did not recognize you and thus denied your existence you killed her to escape annihilation, and then when she died she disappeared as your only witness to yourself at eighteen, the only witness to you in love, and you became an old man with a broken leg in a fever from the pain in your leg.

I dreamed it.

The snow fell around the knuckled feet and roots of the trees.

And when the nurse brought the thermometer and thrust it in my mouth and said, "Don't move your head or this fragile thermometer will burst in your mouth." I stayed still and when she read the thermometer she plunged it into a bath of crimson liquid the same color as the cochineal we used to stain the coconut ice; cochineal gathered from the crushed bodies of insects, you said, for you gave us knowledge, the quiz crossword sharpness that stored the diamond fields of South Africa; the gold fields of Australia; a love for; a depository for the bones of the dead; a European lychnis with white woolly leaves and large solitary flowers, thriving under alternate periods of dryness and moisture or of heat and cold; the highest mountain in the world; the geological ages; a Spanish dish made of rice; falsehood; pertaining to; a black jewel; and a bird rising from its own ashes.

It has rained all day. I dreamed the leftover snow lay heaped against the trees; not your battlefield snow, not this snow but that snow, Alfred's snow. It melted. All the ice melted that starred the roadways and the eaves and puddles and pools; it was the season of waking.

The pain returns. I identify each pain. Each is different and does not exist; and does; and is; narrow, broad, deep, and shallow pain; absorbent transparent hard resisting pain; traveling lightning-swift pain; immoveable dull heavy ache with no edges; pain with edges sharp as icicles; still center, traveling circumference; triangular, three-pronged; circular; dark-red pain, dark-blue pain; a dull-yellow spotted pain like a poisonous plant; round smooth beads of pain; sharp crystalline beads caught by a thin thread of white pain that snaps and rejoins to itself with needle thrust; long thin aluminum limb pains; darting finger-and-toe pains; crisscross webbed womb pains; clenched shoulder and neck pains; circular and columnar head pains; stabbing chest pains. And the pain of grief brought to birth by thinking, a thinking into its sweetness and anguish. My catalogue. My summer and winter catalogue. My journey. My book of knowledge. Amphibious creatures inhabit both land and water, the sun is ninety-three million miles from the earth, demos means the people, philos means loving, logos means the word. Delphinic is pertaining to or derived from larkspur, or delphinium, those blue flowers that grow tall enough to look in the windows of tomorrow and therefore, senseless, make with the help of shadows, a mirror image of their lives.

11

A hot dry nor'wester blew from the north plains down the valley street to the bus shelter. Already the day was stifling with a taste of heat and dust in the mouth and the sting of heat in the eyes. The day was burning up like some old dry-grassed ruin with sick white convolvulus flowers clinging to its broken windows and crumbling brick walls.

Layered with heat and clay dust from the unmade road between Maheno and Waipori the bus nosed into the North East Valley shelter. It was farmers' shopping day in Waipori City. The passengers, mostly women and children, spilling out of the bus, had their mouths open as if they were eager to swallow the hot dust, and all carried large shopping bags carelessly unzipped showing dark shapeless pockets of emptiness, and as they came from the bus they drew their bags protectively towards them and looked earnestly around them, getting their bearings, sorting their plans for the day, settling the problem of food, shopping, place, and time.

Tom watched Peggy alight. He felt as if he had been meeting her at the bus stop for a hundred years and his feeling was deepened by the permanence of the farmers' day without which Waipori City would never survive. Peggy carried a trim shining handbag with an outer large compartment. She wore white hat and gloves—the conventional summer attire—and a blue suit with a tight skirt. Tom shook his head to get rid of his sudden disbelief that here he was at Waipori bus station meeting an almost total stranger; his disbelief was replaced again by his certainty that he had met Peggy week after week for a hundred years. Nothing changed in Waipori City! And yet the time was swift, so swift that it seemed to flow beyond his range of being and set him simultaneously in the past and present and perhaps in the future; it was crazy crazy to be here—what of the Recovery Unit, wheelchairs first. All these women with their infants crowding from the bus, with never a thought for those in wheelchairs—ah, there was someone, a folding chair that the driver unpacked from the luggage boot and there was a young man —Peter?—being helped into it by his companion, a woman —his mother? his wife?—and now he was being wheeled away into the walking dancing skipping peopled world, as if the bus had delivered him, like a new product, all the way from the Recovery Unit.

Tom limped forward to speak to him but he was gone.

"Know him?" Peggy Warren asked. "I thought you were going to leave me stranded to follow him."

"Never seen him in my life before," Tom said, reminding himself that Peggy Warren was fun, that he needn't be a lonely widower and what had he to lose, alone in the world with his own home and car and pension, and nobody, as in past generations to "take" him when the time came for old age to "give" him like a bad bargain, suspiciously free, to relatives who would keep him in storage until the time of winter virus, the fall on the ice, the discovery of the long-embedded disease, the sudden death knot in the narrowed artery; for grandad could no longer be given the back room and induced to stay there until he died, while the children, the children alone, remembering for the rest of their lives, enlarged their sense of wonder in the unconscious contemplation of age upon age upon age, and were educated in death and came to know it as a sleep that shut grandad's eyes when he was tired, and stopped his body from hurting when it was worn out with being used. And drew down a blind of calm upon his last confusion. What had he to lose when day after day the authorities, the specialists, were adding up the numbers of old bodies and forgetting to add the human experience that young people were hungry for, and were getting ready to swill their answers down the economic drain? Ha!

Peggy burst over Tom with a laugh. "I bet if you knew how to say things you'd say them," she said. "By the look in your eye then, I wondered if you'd remember me. I'm not in the habit of picking up men in doctors' waiting rooms."

Tom was indignant. He reached forward to take her bag or coat or something but she kept her handbag jealously guarded.

"If anyone did the picking up," he said, "it was me."

They walked towards the Hillman. Peggy sat beside him in the front seat. "Home James, and don't spare the horses."

Tom sang the line to the tune he knew.

"As I was saying," Peggy said, "there's not much fun in doing nothing on your afternoon off. As it is I have to be back for evening duty, serve tea to the old folk. They're a laugh you know. One day you and I will be there tottering around."

"There you are," Tom said, waving his arm. "The homestead. How do you like it?"

Peggy frowned, seeing only Leonard's cottage in the pine trees.

"Primitive isn't it?"

"Oh that's brother Leonard's cottage. It's his day for lunch at the R.S.A. Lunch and booze. The black sheep of the family."

"Married?"

"No. Bachelor."

"One of the boys?"

Tom frowned. "I'll have you know," he began.

"Poor black sheep."

They walked up the path to the house, Peggy prodding the earth with her high heels.

"Watch your ankles."

Tom limped with his hand on the side of his thigh to help his leg forward. Peggy's breasts swung like shopping bags being carried by an energetically anticipating shopper. Her legs had little leg-shape; they were straight up and down like wickets.

"What a crazy world," Tom said.

Peggy turned. They were just over the slope near the house.

"What's crazy?"

"Nothing," Tom said. "See the view. Swampy and Flagstaff. Well this is it."

He looped the big key from the nail inside the lean-to, said, "Mind the pear branches and don't trip on the lumps of coal," and opened the back door.

"Why don't you prune this tree?" Peggy asked as a branch pinged at her face. "It must be the oldest pear tree I've ever seen. Look at its trunk, all gnarled like an elephant. And if you're not careful it'll grow right inside your kitchen door. Not to mention blocking your view and your light and the insects that will come in."

"Make yourself at home."

Tom rubbed his sleeve over the cleanest yellow cushion on the sofa by the window and said, "Here, sit down, forget about the pear tree, take the load off your feet. Do you know that one?"

He began to sing from the old song he used to hear over the radio,

Make yourself at home, make yourself at home,
Put your feet on the mantelshelf
Open the cupboard and help yourself,
Make yourself at home, make yourself at home.

Peggy listened. She smiled, with a trick of her eyelids widening her eyes as she smiled.

"You look tired," she said. "Show me where things are and I'll make a bite to eat."

Eleanor would turn in her grave, Tom thought, as Peggy, dismissing the coal range as "a load of trouble and work" turned to the old rusted electric range to try to make it go.

"The element's all right," Tom said.

"It's a wonder," Peggy said sharply. "With all those burnt crumbs and bits of bacon stuck to the hotplate. Where's the electric jug?"

"Oh we use the kettle on the coal stove," Tom said meekly.

Peggy spoke shrilly. "We? Who's we? There's only you and me now."

She spoke the truth. She had arrived at it by an unmannerly shortcut, yet she spoke it and both recognized it.

"I'll soon put a stop to black kettles on old coal stoves," she said, dissolving all her sharpness with a sudden laugh, like sun on icicles.

"Pork and beans it is."

"Ha, ha," Tom said.

Peggy got the electric element glowing under her touch, dished up pork and beans and tea on a large child-marked table over which she had thrown a blue and white checked tablecloth.

"You need curtains for your back," she said.

"Curtains for my back!" Tom threw back his head and laughed. They both laughed.

"New curtains for the house," Peggy said seriously. "I'm only suggesting. You must come up to see where I live. Run up one day in the car. We can go to the lookout over the beach or to the gardens and eat in the kiosk and feed the pigeons and the ducks. We can go to the races if you like, have a bet on the double. Or the pub."

"I'm not a drinking man," Tom said.

Immediately he corrected himself. "I drink only now and again," he said.

"I've brought some with me, anyway," Peggy said, reaching in the compartment of her handbag and drawing out a small bottle of gin.

"Gin," Tom said in alarm that sank under a wave of cliché and memory. "It used to be called the lady's drink in my time."

"What do you mean, in your time? You're still alive aren't you? If you are you'd better prove it to me. I hate to say it but gin's a leg-opener."

Tom asserted his authority over fear and the past and his mother and Eleanor and Naomi and Pearl and Ciss Everest the suffocated Cancer Doll and Peggy Warren the ghost and everyone and everyone.

"You don't hate to say it. You like saying it."

Peggy grinned. Something, at least, was understood.

"And I do," she said. "People can't go through life, even through old age, pretending they're made like kewpie dolls out of Woolworth's with undented celluloid bodies and legs stuck together and nothing, not a thing, down below."

She grinned, scooping up the last of the beans with a shovel of bread.

"Celluloid's inflammable, what do you know. And burglars use it to pick locks and open doors where they're not supposed to go."

So that was that.

After lunch they had a glass of gin and a small cuddle-up on the sofa and Peggy inspected and judged the house and its furniture and furnishings and she told Tom about her family, how her father died when she was a girl and her mother found work as companion help on the big sheep stations, taking Peggy, the youngest child, with her; how Peggy had correspondence lessons instead of going to school; how her mother died in a stupid silly way.

"You'll never believe it," she said. "It was like a joke death. Mum was drowned in the sheep dip. Go on, laugh your head off. She never learned to swim. She panicked."

"It's no joke," Tom said. "It's a pretty horrible death. We used to joke about it too, you know, 'Go and drown yourself in the sheep dip.' A chap at work, a wife and three kids, was drowned in the cement slurry; just fell in, no hope of getting out; fancy drowning in cement!"

"Jake Lewis, wasn't it?"

"Yes, from Five Forks."

"His eldest was up before the Court the other week. Borstal. Now sing us something, Tom. I heard you were something of an entertainer at Smoke Concerts."

"I was," Tom said, remembering.

"Give us a song then."

"I can't just off. Another time."

"Will there be another time?" she asked. Her face was serious. She looked as if she were about to cry and her tears would wash away all her gaiety and her makeup; they would start, like streams, in her violet eyes the color of distance in the mountains, and maybe erode the whole landscape and the life in it.

"We're good company, don't you think, Tom? We'll have some good times. I've waited so long for this."

"You haven't been lonely," Tom said, disbelieving, "You've had plenty of company over the years, from what I hear."

Peggy frowned dreamily. "But it was to mark time," she said. "To mark years and years. Let's talk."

Tom talked about Eleanor, Pearl, Naomi, family affairs, worries, history. Peggy told of her childhood and girlhood. Two lonely people covering almost as much ground as God when he created the world in such a hurry you might have thought he was afraid of losing either his blueprint or his inspiration. The honeymoon period of telling! As the afternoon passed Tom and Peggy found themselves being blessed with the mutual warmth that is the starting place of love; yet it was the telling known also in childhood when

63

"best friends" compare and contrast their lives, loves, fears, hopes, accomplishments, blemishes, beauties—Can you crack your fingers? Can you flap your ears? Stand on your head? Walk on your hands?

Tom drove Peggy to the bus stop and when he returned Leonard was at the gate as before with the newspaper.

He spoke, as before, of Peggy Warren.

"It's all around town," he said. "Don't you know she's supposed to go out with just about every man this side of Wellington, and beyond?"

"That's not my business," Tom said. "And less yours. Any news?"

"No news. There's never any news."

Leonard walked back to his cottage. He staggered a little with his knees bent and his elbows poking out. His brown suit was crumpled at the seat and from the back he looked like some kind of trick ape dressed in a man's clothes. He was muttering, "No news, no news, never any news."

Tom limped up the hill. He felt dispirited again with Peggy gone, as if she had robbed him. It mustn't be this way next time, he thought, I'll have to do something, make plans.

He called the cat, "Puss puss, Samuel, Samuel."

No answer.

"He's down with Leonard, I'll be bound," he said angrily, going into the already-dark house.

12

Where's Tom, the character
with the ordinary name
who did something in the War
put his boot in place
on a dead man's face
and thought that pulp was made of apples and pears

and decay a dropped core
in a mellowing orchard; that hearts were never red
and only sheep bled.
Where's Tom?
Home home to the kitchen
Culin, kiln, the furnace,
Tom, expert translator of the Flame
poor Tom acold, Livingstone.

And Eleanor is dead who bore
Naomi and Pearl
in a marriage where love lasted
less than a week followed by
forty-four years of heartbreak.
Tom went journeying
to find and kill Cecily
Miss War the Cancer Doll with the blonde transformation.
And who cut the grass
and grew the cabbages back home
if not Leonard
and envied Samuel the cat his breathing
and Harry the bird his yellow shroud?

Colin will account for the days of everyone's grief
with four lives, a conservative tally
but this isn't war any more, only domesticity
the kitchen, Culin, kiln, the furnace.

In the dream, when Leonard was discharged from the
army in the First World War he received every incentive to
live the life he chose. While he was still in France the army
gave him a rehabilitation grant which did not have to be
repaid and which was generous enough for him to take his
French bride, Claire and their son Leo and their daughter
Rosa to live on a sunny Mediterranean island where he became proprietor of a small harborside inn. He and Claire and
the children had no difficulty in learning the language—they
knew it the moment they settled on the island. They read

newspapers and books, talked to people, dreamed, and after a few years unless you had known Leonard Livingstone in his former years you would not have been able to tell him apart from a typical Spanish innkeeper. He was handsome too, for not having returned home after the war he had not had the motorbike accident that broke his nose. His teeth were straight and white. He was happy. A bottle of wine, siesta asleep in the sun against the stone wall while the fishermen mended their nets. The evening gaiety, dancing, eating in the dining room that looked out over the harbor to the other side of the island where the reflection of the buildings and the olive trees shimmered in the clear water; and on Sundays and holidays a walk in the Square with the children dressed in their best clothes and the brass band playing; the meal again at night, with Leonard as host, the local violinist playing romantic music for the tourists; the excitement of the lottery, winning of course; and the children going to school and learning and being clever and loved, and Rosa wanting to be a bride when she grew up, and Leo wanting to be a lawyer with a practice on the mainland; church on Sunday; the festivals; the processions; the summer evenings with the whole family cycling along the white dusty roads past the olive groves into the red-earthed countryside with the riverbeds dry and stony and the oxen ploughing in the fields; noon, the shadows on the buildings sharp and small as deadly penknives; the light-green pines; for Leonard and his wife it was like paradise. There was not even the weather to complain of, for though the days of the mistral were ice cold the sky stayed blue and the sun shone fiercely. It was a happy life for the Livingstone family, for dreams are the smallest circle and like blood platelets on a square centimeter of blood cell, only the correct number of dreams are allowed and should others invade or overpopulate the result in dreams and blood may vary from ordinary discomfort to extraordinary disruption and death.

And it happens with dreams dreamed and controlled by the dreamer who is separated from the dream; and one day, therefore, the church bell in the steeple tolled all day for the many dead who having had too many ideas and dreams were shot by the firing squad; and one was Leo, seventeen, who had escaped, as the young will do, from the shelter of his father's dream.

And the poor women, their rope-soled shoes tied about their feet, walked miles into the country to pick up the shriveled windfall olives for food. And the landowners dined on beans fat as a woman's fat arm in its green sleeve; and on cabbages tight and round as a globe.

And Claire was an old woman, old before her time, with greedy black eyes and skin like leather.

And Rosa grew thin and sick, mourning her lover among the dead.

And Leonard was so tired he drank pitcher after pitcher of raisin wine and lay down in the street under the eucalyptus trees and the fleet-footed pink-nosed island dogs licked his face as they passed.

And deep in the tunnel of the esteemed monument the shit of the children formed a new mountain and memorial.

And Leonard was home again, in the dream dying on his iron bed with the sagging mattress and the heaps of old newspapers and the sugar sack of photographs, and someone knocked at the door of his bach and he called, "Come in," and recognized his old schoolteacher, now an old man, who sat down on the apple box by the bed with his hands clasped over his skinny knees and spoke in a feeble voice.

"Livingstone, we'll give you a reward for good work today. We'll send you out to work in the garden.

"Livingstone, Leonard Livingstone, I've come to apologize. I know it's too late. We're both old men and dying. I should never have sent you from your books into the garden to work. You were a child for books and I denied you them.

I don't ask forgiveness as I don't believe that would be possible. I merely apologize and acknowledge the terrible injustice done to a boy of ten. A boy of ten!"

Leonard felt neither pleased nor sad. His schoolmaster, droning on and on, could have been telling him anything for all he cared, naming the planets, the list of rivers of South America, the chief cities of Europe.

"I do apologize, Livingstone," he said again.

Still Leonard made no reply.

Then the schoolmaster bowed his head and Leonard saw with some indifference that he had changed to a withered chrysanthemum on a thin brown stalk propped on the chair beside Leonard. A miracle. He had become his own apology. Leonard made arrangements for him to be buried with the eggshells, the tea leaves, the pear and apple peelings, and the sour contents of the chamberpot sitting like a bowl of cider under the bed.

And now it was the first time since his childhood that Leonard had a house instead of lodgings or a rented room to live in. There were two houses on the Livingstone property—the family house and Leonard's cottage with one room, a lean-to kitchen and scullery, and an outside lavatory or dumpy. While Tom was in London, Leonard who had been for many years beyond the family orbit in an outer darkness of drunkenness and disgrace, agreed to look after the house and live in the cottage. He brought his few possessions—his old leather kitbag of tools, his few clothes, his radio, the sugar sack of old family photographs that had been sent to him when one of his brothers died. On his first day at the cottage he made up his bed with the four dark gray army blankets from the army surplus stores and the two light gray Hong Kong fleecy sheets, set up an apple box shelf by his bed on which to put his radio, stowed his battered suitcase and his sack of photographs under the black-painted iron bed, dangled his two suits from a hanger behind the door, and was at home. In the small kitchen with the rusted two-ring electric stove he arranged his army-style pots and pans and his knife, fork, and spoon; set out his shaving gear, toothpaste, and soap on the wooden shelf above the chipped enamel sink, swept the rough wooden floor with a soft broom and the concrete square of back yard by the tank (his only water supply) with a hard broom, arranged the two brooms side by side against the wall in the sun, made himself a cup of tea, and was more at home.

Since his return from the First World War he had spent his life wandering through the country working as a garage mechanic, engineer in electric power projects, rabbiter, rouseabout on farms, often being fired for his drunkenness. The only creatures who did not fire him were the rabbits he spent many years trapping and shooting and eating, selling their skins, carrying his ferret from place to place in a little bag, and when he found a place to sleep constructing a cage for it and feeding it bread and milk. He never named his ferrets. He despised them. He disliked the color of their fur and their stink and their mean habit of biting. Up Central he lived on raspberries and apricots and stewed rabbit and billy tea and pancakes tossed over a manuka stick fire. He slept in huts abandoned from the gold prospecting days and as a rest from rabbiting he sometimes panned for gold in the shallow places of the river, storing his few clay-colored grains with their occasional bright telltale gleam, in an old screw-top jamjar.

He claimed to have "a son in France" as a relic from a love affair with a French girl during the First World War. "I should have stayed in France," he used to say. "It's love rules the world; love is the only hope." He never married and the one woman who tried to persuade him destroyed all her chances when she asked Leonard to sign a temperance pledge written on a gold card, bordered with angels blowing trumpets and stamping with their strong angels' feet upon the devil's bottles of wine.

So he stayed alone and unwanted, for a motorbike accident had broken his nose and battered his teeth and he was ugly, and by those who perpetually reckon such things his life was accounted a failure because of his drunkenness and because he was known to be a clever man who never made actual the potentiality admired in clever men of being able to "buy up half the country if he wanted to." Leonard Livingstone never "bought up" anywhere, he had not even a home until Tom offered him one, after Eleanor's death, nor had he many friends and acquaintances, though each year some member of the family found his address, a box number or rural delivery, to send a Christmas or birthday card with handkerchief, tie or socks, few of which parcels he opened, thus collecting a supply of bordered initialed handkerchiefs, patterned ties, and arrow-patterned socks that lay untouched in his battered suitcase.

He was now sixty. He looked tough and repulsive. His teeth slanted like broken fence posts. He enjoyed his own company though he spent many hours at the Returned Soldier's Association, where he read the newspapers, the weekly scandal sheet and the provincial morning paper, the local evening paper, the weekly racing news, and the weekly pictorial. He had accumulated a pile of old newspapers which some paralysis of the will prevented him from burning in the oil drum he used as an incinerator and which gradually became as much a part of his gear as his battered suitcase and the sugar sack of photographs which visiting mice had gnawed so fiercely that a pile of photographs spilled onto the floor under his bed. And he would kick them impatiently further out of sight and they would spread fanshape, renewing their avalanche like the movement of a yesterday's glacier. At times he picked up one of the photographs to examine it—a wedding or farewell, the train steaming ready, the troops going, family and friends with hands joined singing "Auld Lang Syne," his father there, shrunken in his advancing age, with his curly faded handlebar moustache, his mother in her long black dress with her big smooth face and dark eyes and her jar-shaped belly, his sisters with veiled hats and smiles, farewells, the family home, a small square house on a small square plot of land with the lattice fence and he and his mother and father and sisters and brothers standing hands behind their back in front of the veranda, toes turned out as if at a dancing lesson. What a tiny fellow he was! He'd look at his photograph and tears would smart in his eyes when he saw the tiny boy with his head on one side and his eyes screwed up against the perpetually shining childhood sun. In that photograph his sister already had her first boyfriend and worked in one of the big houses on Maori Hill and he, a little fellow, used to carry messages between her and her boyfriend at the garage. He kept his mouth shut. They could trust him. She married that same boyfriend, too. And now they were both dead.

In those days the street was earth, clay colored like the faded photograph, and the rest of the world was sun and sky, sky, sky.

Leonard's formal education finished at primary school as soon as he found a job in a local garage. At school his most wonderful discovery had been books and reading. Then in his final year, because he was brighter then the other boys, he and the second boy in the class were given a reward by the headmaster—the task of weeding and planting the school garden, while the other pupils toiled at their lessons in the classroom. "There's nothing a boy likes better than to get out of the classroom, I know," the headmaster said. Remembering this exchange of pen, pencil, ink, and paper, for hoe, spade, and gardening fork, Leonard thought with bitterness of the long blue days outside in the garden planting, weeding, staking, and trying to understand why a supposed reward should have inflicted such punishment. That year he used to cry in bed at night, his tears dropping with the candlewax into the candlestick as he pored over a book that he'd had to steal from the classroom as he now spent so little time there. When he left school he gave up the habit of reading although at the sight of a hard-covered book he still experienced the kind of agonizing nostalgia that a man might feel upon an unexpected unhoped-for glimpse of a long-lost love. His boyhood dream had been transformed to a reminding nightmare by the properties of Paradise—spade, fork, hoe, a garden with flowers, trees, grass. And now the further irony in his life was that the other nightmare, the World War he fought in, should provide him, in the R.S.A. Memorial Hall, with the only place where he could pass the time of day in human company.

The R.S.A. Memorial Hall had been built as a memorial to those who fought in the Second World War. In Waipori City each war had its memorial—the Boer War had produced a soldier on horseback, the First World War, a Digger presenting arms. The Memorial for the Second World War had been planned conservatively as a group of three figures—navy, air force, army, with their arms around one another, looking down from a stone pedestal upon the post office, the stationer's shop, and the town mortuary. When an anonymous citizen increased the budget by a large cash gift the concept of the memorial changed. People were tired of statues, someone said. They wanted their money to be used. Statues were seldom looked at or cleaned, and used only as deposits for wreaths on Anzac and Armistice Day and for pigeon shit every day. What about a home for handicapped children? Scholarships for sons and daughters of veterans? An addition to the Peter Pan statue at the Gardens? Or a memorial that could be used as well as looked at, a garden with rose arches and flower beds and graveled walks, like a cemetery without the dead, set in front of a social hall and club rooms where the old soldiers could meet and eat and drink and read and talk. And the club rooms would not only serve their purpose as a memorial, they would help to beautify the surroundings and draw attention from the neighboring timber yard with its piles of seasoning timber, the nettles and docks growing around the timber, the scrap iron nearby, the rusted railway engine and old-fashioned railway carriage that in a country of determined swift progress were not yet enshrined in a museum where they might surrender their secrets of past journeys, of family picnic excursions to lonely gold and green and silver beaches now overcrowded with holiday homes, the wild yellow broom cut down, the black swans shot or dead in polluted waters, the lagoons monstrous with abandoned car bodies.

While the Memorial Hall was being planned, someone suggested it would be a happy occasion if the building were opened by the Queen on her next visit to the country. What a triumph that would be! That one time, at least, she would be bribed into staying in Waipori City instead of bypassing it to visit the lakes and catch the fish that had been deposited there especially for her. Oh no, this one time the Queen would stop overnight in a suite in the best hotel known for its royalty of plumbing, and what a triumph indeed that would be for Waipori City—both the Queen's acceptance of the plumbing about which she was known to be fastidious and her opening of the Memorial Hall before an invited audience who would sit on the hard seats and listen carefully to digest the details they would regurgitate for many days afterwards. Unfortunately the Queen and her consort did not visit Waipori City. They traveled to the lakes where they caught three huge trout each. The Memorial Hall was declared open by the Governor General who happened to be in the neighborhood attending a boy-scout meeting and who declared himself not ashamed or embarrassed to be wearing boy-scout uniform because, as he said, it was the boy scouts of the nation who grew up to become the young shining-eyed men who had sacrificed their lives so gloriously to defend the cause of freedom and democracy.

He quoted to the hushed crowd:

If I should die think only this of me.
Take up our quarrel with the foe:
To you from failing hands we throw
The torch; be yours to hold it high.

and so forth.

We shall not sleep, though poppies grow
    In Flanders fields.

A beautiful poem! The crowd stood hushed. Veterans of the First World War, wearing their poppies, bowed their heads. A hymn was sung, the voices sounding strong and resonant above the timber yard, the scrap iron yard, and the real roses.

O Valiant hearts who to your glory came
Through dust of conflict and through battle flame,
Tranquil you lie your knightly virtue proved
Your memory hallowed in the land you loved.

How true it was, how true! A bugler played the "Last Post" while the audience stood with bowed heads.

At the last moment the Governor General had asked his aides to find him a poem about the Second World War so that he could let the new veterans share the honors, and perhaps break away from the tradition of skylarks and poppies if only because so few people these days saw a skylark, and poppies were suspect as a source of opium. The aides had not been able to find a poem that expressed such simple faith in the work and destiny of a soldier; indeed, the verses spoke of the dead as neither heroic nor at peace, but simply dead.

74

Burnt black by strange decay
Their sinister faces lie
The lid over each eye.
The grass and colored clay
More motion have than they
Joined to the great sunk silences.

But you my brother and my ghost if you can go
knowing there is no reward, no certain use
in all your sacrifice . . .

Not poems, the aides decided, for a mass memorial-in, and therefore the Governor General distributed his skylarks and poppies, the larks bravely singing above the new R.S.A. Memorial Hall, the poppies brilliantly flowering, and the fact of the bomb forgotten, that it had been dropped not only on cities of the world but on large areas of human imagination and what was growing from the devastation was beginning to reveal its hiedeous deformities or, if nothing grew, the barrenness made a grim shelterless world without, and within, in that part of the mind where once man had been able to retreat and recuperate.

The crowd disappeared, their hearts thudding with the orgiastic

They went with songs to the battle, they were young,
Straight of limb true of eye steady and aglow.

while the small remnant of "afters," some limbless, some blind, cheered one another in the new hall over their glass of beer.

13

You see, I have brought you home.
I have taken you in.
You are an old man.
With some, rage stays,
with you it has gone.
You will whimper soon
here in this room
beside my bed where I die
today or tomorrow.
I have brought you home, father.
I have recovered you.
And you have recovered yourself.
As a child of ten you flew
from the roof
on brown paper wings
and broke your arm
your green willowstick arm
that fished in the creekwater
for eels and trout
and speckled cockabullies
back and forth
back and forth
sky to water to earth.

As a boy you cracked
the coconut shells
together to make
the horses gallop
into the dream
and mounting them
you rode away
nearly three-score years
to Love and War. Say,

     who cares about Innocence?

It's only a taste
found and lost
like my mustard waste
and your poisonous past.
Soon death
like a gray mask
will cover my face
between springing flag lily
and river stone.

*Breathe in the gas mask, father,
or poisonous life like a scorpion
stings your lung.*

14

Each week now Tom met Peggy at the bus station and always she arrived with her shopping bag laden with goods. One week there were new curtains for the kitchen. "Homely and in fashion," she said to Tom as she showed him the pattern of teapots and teacups and saucers with steam rising out of the cups of poured tea, but as this was her first attempt to change the furnishings of Tom's home she did not unpack the curtains until they had shared their usual bottle of gin.

"I've brought you something to brighten your days," she said, and fetching her shopping bag she unzipped it, drew out the brown paper parcel and like a conjurer performing his act she shook out the new curtains, unfurling patterned teapots and cups and saucers.

"There. Kitchen curtains."

Tom frowned, suspiciously.

"Not bad."

"Shall I hang them this afternoon? Tear down these ugly old faded pink rags?"

"What's wrong with the curtains already there?"

"I just told you. They're ugly old faded old rags."

Peggy pulled a face.

"Oh you can see what's wrong with them. If I try to wash them I bet they come to shreds in my hands."

"If you try to wash them?"

A woman in the house again, washing. Curtains, sheets, pillowcases, towels. Boiling up the copper on a fine windy day of scuddy clouds. Planning the night before: "Do you think it will be fine enough to put on the copper tomorrow? Red sky at night a shepherd's delight, or was it a red sky at morning a shepherd's warning. What does the weather report say? But yesterday the hills were close, and dark purple; yet all day the smoke's been going straight up out of the chimneys and no seagulls are flying inland. . . ."

Tom smiled at Peggy. "Why not try to wash the ugly old faded old pink rags? They're quite new. When you come next week I'll have a supply of wood, there are some old borer-riddled four by twos that I can chop up—Leonard will help me—and I'll collect a few pine cones from the plantation and that tree where the magpies nest and make such a row on an autumn morning? . . ."

He frowned as he noted a change of expression in Peggy's face.

"What's up?"

Peggy's voice was sharp with indignation and a hint of anger.

"Boil up the copper indeed! I wondered just how far you'd go. That sort of thing might be all right for some people, but I'm not a pioneering fool and it's not my kind of life, thank you."

"But, Eleanor . . ."

"Yes, Eleanor but not me."

Tom frowned. Even two weeks before her death Eleanor had "boiled up" the copper. It was the Scottish way wasn't it,

for the womenfolk to work for the menfolk, the womenfolk
to be the slaves and the servants? He remembered his own
mother and father, how when his father came home drunk
from the pub down by the wharf where he'd been drinking
with the sailors, his mother would receive him at the door as
if he were royalty, as if she were a nurse and he a patient
being admitted to hospital, or she were an angel welcoming
a guest to heaven. She'd calmly undress him, fold his clothes,
put him to bed, make him warm, and when he woke the next
morning there would be fresh clothes ready for him, ironed
with the old flatiron; his shoes would be polished, a clean
white handkerchief would be set, folded in four, on the dressing table for him to blow and cough and spit into as soon as
he woke. And Eleanor had administered to Tom in the same
way, though Tom was not in the habit of being drunk. Eleanor had even tied his shoelaces if he did not feel like bending
to tie them himself, or fastened with her nimble fingers the
trouser buttons to his braces, put the studs in his collar if he
were going somewhere important enough to need the wearing of studs—a Lodge or Union meeting, or Smoke Concert.
Not to mention the ordinary household tasks like cleaning
and washing and cooking. Eleanor had never rebelled. She
had known her place in the house.

"You mean to say your wife boiled up the copper every
week?"

"The pioneer women did," Tom said coldly. "So did my
mother."

"Times have changed, old sport. Speaking for myself, I
like a washing machine and hot water out of the tap or it's no
go."

"Well are you going to wash the pink curtains or aren't
you?" Tom was at home with alternatives. Did you or didn't
you? Tell, tell the truth. Yes or no."

"Tell you what. I'll take them home and wash them and
in the meantime we'll hang the new ones."

Dutifully Tom looped the pink curtains from their rods while Peggy put them in her shopping bag. Then she shook the new curtains once more.

"Nice aren't they?"

They fitted exactly.

"How did you know?" Tom asked.

Peggy smiled. "Magic."

The following week she brought new matching covers for the sofa and the two armchairs.

"What about the pink curtains?" Tom asked.

Peggy smiled. "Who likes to do a good turn? There's this woman at the hospital, nurse's aide, a husband off work, four or five kids, and she was talking about curtains for her kitchen and that brought yours to mind, so I washed them, and they didn't fall to pieces—told you so!—and I thought you wouldn't mind as I know you like to do a good turn, so I gave her the curtains."

"You can't give away other people's property like that!"

"Other people's property? We share and share alike don't we?"

They agreed then that they were both alone, that two could live more cheaply than one, and if they were married he would be there to make arrangements if she should "go" first, and she would do the same.

"I'd hate them just to find me," she said. "And have no one to supervise it."

"You're young yet, Peg."

"What about you? You're not senile!"

"I'm too old. I'm tired."

Peggy gaped. "You mean . . . no bed . . . no love-a-dove? What have we been leading up to these afternoons on the sofa I'd like to know."

"I've a father's responsibility," Tom said confusedly.

"Father's responsibility my foot. Your girls are out of it, married or fled the country. Do they ever write to you?"

80

"Cards and presents from Pearl. And Naomi's got this disease."

"Cancer?"

"I don't want to talk about it. Haven't heard from her for years."

"Didn't you see her in England? What did you go traipsing halfway across the world for, if not to see her? Anyway what have they got to do with bed? Surely you didn't love-a-dove them?"

Tom reddened. "I'll have none of that talk in my home."

He was sitting on the sofa. Peggy was just about to bring out the bottle of gin. She crossed to the sofa and sat down beside Tom. She took his hand in hers.

"I should think," she said slowly, "that with me's the first time in your life you've acted your natural self. I bet Eleanor wouldn't let you fart the way you do when I'm around. You sound like a regular motorbike starting up. And a man at your time of life gets nice and wicked—so what? Can't we live in the present for a change and leave tomorrow to the others? You've earned it. All this fighting for democracy. Democracy! That's me—us."

"Knock knock who's there," Tom burst out suddenly, in tune with the "fun," the radio comic dialogue that had sustained him for so many years, rescuing him in moments of embarrassment. "Knock knock who's there?" Ivor. Ivor who? Ivor Bun. Iona. Iona who? Iona teashop."

"Knock, knock."

"Your hair's gray but it's all springy. Look."

Peggy fingered his chest curls.

"Knock knock."

Peggy knew the game. She frowned, trying to think. "Have some gin first."

"No, knock knock who's there."

"I give up."

"Oh, come on, think of one."

"Well . . . Phyllis then . . ."

"Phyllis who?"

"Phyllis up again, ha, ha."

They drank a glass of gin each. Peggy unbuttoned her blouse.

"Let's sit on your knee," she said. "Whoops! Don't say you don't like it you guilty old soldier."

Tom took in a sudden sharp breather, seized Peggy by the shoulders and shook her and shook her.

"Oh you wicked old . . . wicked old . . . not there silly, stop it . . . you wicked old."

Tom stopped abruptly.

"A good old fashioned cuddle is what we both need," Peggy said, nestling close. "Oh let's cuddle up some more, Tom!"

Her voice had an infantile plea.

They cuddled.

"You're welcome," she said, shaking her breasts out of their pocketfolds of blouse. "My headlights." She giggled.

"Shall I put a little tickle down there?"

Then "Oh, oh!" she said fiercely and breathlessly. And gasped. And began to sing:

To market to market
to buy a fat pig
home again home again
jiggety jig—

"Oh Tom!"

The following week Peggy brought new pillowcases embroidered with pink roses and a pair of floral-patterned sheets. Without waiting for an invitation she went towards the front bedroom.

"I'll make the bed for you."

She opened the door and walked in. She stopped abruptly. She was looking into an old man's room. She worked in a home for the aged, she knew the signs, she could smell the smells, see the twisted yellowing bedclothes on a bed that had not been made for donkey's ages, the long pink Roslyn woolen underpants with their stained crotch hanging, still with their shank shape, over the bed rail; heaps of dust fluff gathered in ridges against the wall, the skirt of the dressing table, the foot of the bed like decayed foam left by a long-departed tide. The place was more of a nest than a bedroom. The entire upper part of the built-in wardrobe had collapsed and the green-painted boards stuck out like dislocated limbs while the ceiling was riddled with borer holes surrounded by stains of sawdust; and one of the blind springs on the double window had broken and the blind hung askew like a half-shut eyelid on the face of a paralytic old man, while across the other window a piece of faded lace curtain had been dragged and hooked on a rusty nail

Tom's voice behind Peggy was entreating but sharp.

"Don't go in there, Peg! It's like nothing on earth."

"Don't I know it," Peggy said grimly. "Don't I know it."

At least the room offered nothing but Tom Livingstone —any trace of a woman had been wiped out years ago.

"Oh don't Peg. I tell you it's a mess."

Peggy smiled confidently.

"It won't be for long, Tom. This is what I've been waiting for. Now you go and busy yourself about anything you like but this is my job for the day. Turn on the hot water will you, love? And if you've got such a thing as a scrubbing brush, a mop or broom or something, find them. And remember this is once and for all, Tom. The place'll take care of itself in future, just you see. Only you'll have to have rules, know where to put things, you can't go slopping around like an old bachelor."

"It's what I am now, Peg," Tom said, teasing.

"All the same," she said uncertainly as she watched man and house about to disappear through a crack in the earth.

"Hey, wait a bit, you're no bachelor!"

Fifteen minutes later dressed in an old smock with a torn pillowcase safety pinned around her head—"to protect my coiffeur," she explained—she began cleaning the bedroom in every nook and cranny, vigorously scrubbing out memories, lost hopes, arranging a new view through the curtain, and two hours later she finally smoothed the eiderdown over the bed and plumped the pillows in their new embroidered pillowcases.

"We—you—need new blankets, an eiderdown, a new duchesse runner with crocheted edges, a couple of rugs on the floor, sheepskin, pink or apricot I should say, so your feet won't be cold on a frosty morning, and you're set. As for these old sheets"—she held the dirty sheets up to the light to show their threadbare patches—"you can shoot peas through them. They're out."

When the bedroom was cleaned they had a cup of tea—no gin—and a cuddle-up on the sofa.

Peggy ran her fingers through Tom's hair.

"All these springy gray curls. Come on, Tom, what's eating you?"

"Well Peggy, I only get the pension, you know. I don't know if I can afford your kind of style. And I've nothing saved. And I've come home with this leg into the bargain. If we . . . get together—you won't have your job—or do you want to keep on with it?"

"Oh, I'll have the house to keep in order! Maybe you could get that part-time job at the works."

Tom sighed.

"I haven't the heart to. Not after being there all those years."

"That reminds me. Did you bury that bird yet? Where's it gone? Did you bury it?"

Tom hesitated. He sighed again.

"It's out in the cage in the wash house, under the sewing-machine cover."

"That's another thing I want to talk to you about. A new sewing machine. Electric. Not treadle. But first, that bird. How do you think I'd feel if I went out to the wash house and came across that yellow corpse by surprise?"

"But you know it's there. I've told you."

Peggy stared thoughtfully at Tom.

"You know, Tom Livingstone, there's something about you I don't quite get. You're softhearted. You won't bury a filthy bird that's been dead over a year. And yet I bet you're cruel, oh I bet you've a cruel streak. You were in the War weren't you? They teach them in the army, they soon teach them how to be cruel. I used to know a chap, he'd been wounded in the First World War, he died crazy, he just didn't seem to care what he did. I went to visit him once up the line. His face had got big somehow, like a balloon, and burned by the weather, and his beard and hair went white, and he was in this park where the grass was worn off with them walking round and round on it; and it was all the War."

"The War's a long time ago now," Tom said, speaking very slowly as if each syllable were a year passing.

"But you were there, you saw it, you killed people."

"You're the one with the cruel streak, Peg. Women are like that. They . . . I knew someone—the gentlest person . . . a nurse . . ."

"Well?"

Tom glanced at Peggy. He fancied that her violet eyes were mocking, that he or she had become disembodied, formless, timeless.

"Did Eleanor ask you about the War?"

"The War's over I tell you."

"Did she care about it, Tom, what it did to you?"

Tom's voice was sharp. "What do you mean, what it did to me?"

"Did she care?"

"Of course she cared."

"What happened between you and Eleanor to make it how it was all those years?"

"I never told you how it was with us."

Peggy shrugged. "You wiped her out as long ago as the First World War."

"Ha," Tom said.

He had no intention of telling Peggy about Ciss Everest. He reached down and touched his hurt leg.

"It's paining me," he said. "It's supposed to have healed."

"He told you it takes longer at your age. You need more calcium."

"I know, I know, everything takes more time when you haven't much time left."

"Go on, you'll live to be a hundred yet."

Tom grinned. Peggy with her violet eyes and her bleached hair was good for him, for the level things of life, the earthy things, the facts. Sitting here on the sofa in the kitchen-sitting room with the painted cups of tea steaming on the new curtains that moved slightly as the breeze came in the opened window, here with another Christmas and New Year gone and the chill of autumn coming in the air, and the Recovery Unit far far away—a kind of homeless dream because the people and the places that folded their reality around it had gone.

Peggy waited for him to speak.

"How was it then?"

"Eleanor and I weren't right for each other."

"From the first?"

"From the first."

"Then why didn't you do something about it?"

Tom shrugged. "It's a long time ago now," he said with some bitterness.

Peggy looked at him shrewdly.

"Like the War, eh? A long time ago. I suppose it was because of the children?"

"Maybe."

"How do they feel about you and me? Have you told them?"

"They're not exactly children," Tom said, addressing his denial to himself as well as to Peggy. "I told you they're out of my life. I think Pearl's heard about it, though, from some gossipy tart."

A delicate subject was being approached. It was time, Peggy thought. She looked demure and grave. She took Tom's hand in her two hands and smoothed it into a warm capture.

"They know of course," she said distinctly, "that when a man marries again his new wife inherits."

She pulled a face of pretended surprise at her daring, and giggled.

Tom grinned. He was escaping to home ground, to the old radio comedies and music-hall jokes where nothing need be looked at clearly, where he could hide beneath the comic character and sing, sing, sing his heart *in* and not *out.* Jokes about wills. That one about the chap being left an armchair, how did it go?

How they tittered, how they chaffed,
How my brothers and my sisters laughed
When they heard the lawyer declare,
Granny has left you her old armchair.

And how the payoff came when the chap sat on the chair and the chair collapsed.

And there to my surprise
I found before my eyes
A lot of notes ten thousand pounds or more.
Oh how they tittered, how they chaffed,
How my brothers and my sisters laughed
When they heard the lawyer declare,
Granny has left you her old armchair.

"The will, the will," Tom said, recalling another comedy. "I've nothing to leave. Except the house. And the bit of land. And the pear tree with its annual crop."

"How much land is it?"

"About an acre. Could be subdivided I suppose, a right-of-way put in. After I'm gone. The girls won't want it certainly."

"You might be surprised—hasn't Pearl any children?"

"Colin. He's married, couple of children himself."

Peggy looked at Tom curiously. "Don't they really keep in touch with you?"

"Oh, I told you, birthday cards. Colin does the same. They write any news at birthdays and Christmas. Pearl wanted me to go to live near them—she's a real fattie now. Pearl, I believe, but . . . I don't know . . . it wouldn't work."

"It's often a man's children that turn against him," Peggy said, trying to sound wise but sounding merely vague. "And when you die everything's flushed out into the open."

"What do you mean when I die? Who's talking of dying?"

"I mean generally speaking," Peggy soothed. "You're right though. When we get older we can't expect to hang around the younger fry. I've got nieces and nephews who give me that sly look when I visit them, as if to say, It's the old people's home for you, Aunt Peg, when you can't manage for yourself. And there's so much in the newspapers about growing old, it gets on your mind that you're apart from everyone else."

"The papers make you get a lot on your mind," Tom said sternly. "I don't read them right through the way Leonard does. A great reader, Leonard. He reads every word in the paper, even the financial pages and the woman's page and the recipes for foreign food. But you can't help knowing you're old and unwanted if they keep telling you about it. So much percent of the population over sixty, what's the definition of death, what's the right age to die, as if old age were a national disaster. Who saved the country in two wars, I'd like to know. If we'd guessed, I tell you if we'd guessed what the end of it would all be!"

"At least we're not a barbaric society. People care for people. It's not what condition you're in, it's just that you *are*, it matters that you *are*. In our society, anyway. And never mind, Tom, we've each other, we don't have to rely on relatives to bury us and pokenose around, and we've both a good few years left. When your leg stops playing up. . . ."

"I'll have to go to the quack with it again this week. There's this pain." Tom bent down and rolled up his trouser leg showing the white leg with its new soft blue-lined skin, like a column of pale cheese.

"It's here," he said, pressing a point just below the knee. "It hasn't set or it's ricked or something."

Although Peggy's work was in an old people's home she did not approve of disease or distress of the body. The only discomfort she had known in her life was that of sex, and that could be relieved. She accepted age with its gradual decay of faculties and energies as an autumnal dignity that did not exclude the messier aspects and processes of autumn, but she did not accept pain or discomfort and when her attention was drawn to it she became impatient or resentful. She tried to be sympathetic about Tom's leg but she was beginning to wish he would forget it.

"It will improve, just you see. In a few weeks' time you'll have forgotten about it."

She sounded unconvincing and unconvinced and Tom, sensing she wanted to possess him with goods and chattels but without complaints, resolved with a feeling of disappointment that in future he might do better to keep his mouth shut. Other men had told him Eleanor had "spoilt" him and he had always denied this but since her death when his daily dose of attention ceased, Tom had suffered badly from withdrawal symptoms. When he was visiting London he liked to talk about his troubles and pains to people waiting in bus queues and serving in shops, but here at home this freedom of commerce in complaints was denied him. He was known in Waipori City, he had lived most of his life there, he had dignity to retain, appearances to keep up. He longed sometime for the langorous anonymity of the big overseas cities where he might have talked his heart out to strangers whom he would never see again.

Also, he had no one to talk to about Peggy and his plan to marry her. Leonard dismissed her as a tart. Pearl had written on her Christmas card that she'd heard rumors about him and Peggy Warren and were the rumors true? He felt the need for someone to whom he could say, simply, definitely, "I'm going to marry Peggy Warren."

Just that. No explanation. No discussion of her morals or her past. Just the fact, spoken quickly.

"I've decided to marry Peggy Warren," he said once or twice, to himself, testing.

Or he said conversationally to no one, Peggy and I are getting married.

Except that the innerspring mattress almost made him change his mind. The day it arrived Tom was standing at the front door and before he knew what was happening the mattress was there leaning against the passage wall, and he was holding the delivery note which read, as far as he could make out, that he, Tom Livingstone, had bought a luxury padded quilted innersprung mattress on time payment from Prop and Fancy.

"Good God!" he called to Peggy in the kitchen. "My God!"

"Come here, Tom," Peggy said cheerfully.

They sat on the newly covered armchair and she put her arm around him.

"Don't worry about my finances," she said. "All these things are off your account with Prop and Fancy."

"That's what I mean ... good God! ... my account!"

"Your credit's good with them, Tom. And when I explained we were getting the house refurnished ..."

Tom was bewildered.

"But you didn't have my authority. I didn't sign anything."

He drew a deep breath, and when he spoke his voice was angry.

"I don't want any innersprung mattress. I can use the old flock one."

Peggy shrugged and smiled.

"You mean—*we?*"

"But how did you get these things without my signature?"

Peggy spoke patiently and clearly as if to a deaf person.

"But you remember," she said, her eyes under their purple-shadowed lids widening to show violet depths (she had practiced and perfected this look when she was thirteen). "You remember when I wrote the note asking you about the blankets, would you like new blankets, and you sent that postcard the week I couldn't come to town as I was otherwise engaged, and you said, you said distinctly on the postcard: Get what you like. Prop and Fancy have them. Blankets, any bedding necessary. And you signed your name, Tom. And they know you, and they know you'll pay."

"Do they now?" Tom said grimly. "I can't afford an innersprung mattress."

"But it's only a fraction a month, so little you won't even notice it. You can put it right out of your mind. Just give me the housekeeping money each week and forget all about it."

"Well!"

Peggy cuddled up to him.

"And you know we're anxious to get everything settled, you said so yourself, and I've never been married before, Tom, it's natural for me to make some mistakes, and I've waited all these years for you. I suppose I'm just an innocent fool."

She began, surprisingly, to cry. Real tears. Now when Eleanor, Pearl, or Naomi had ever shown distress, Tom had felt his heart harden against them; their tears made him contemptuous. His feeling for Peggy, uncomplicated by as many overtones of love, hate, dependence, resentment, habit, stopped halfway along the scale of contempt at pity, striking the note that prompted him to take her in his arms and say her name softly, without anger, "Never mind, Ciss."

Absorbed in her moment of helplessness she did not hear the name at first. Then she frowned.

"Sis? I'm to be your wife, not your sister! None of that sister-brother racket for me, thank you very much."

Tom had been startled to hear himself say Ciss. He'd not been thinking of her. Her name had been delivered to him as it were, in response to a long-standing order. Too late. And yet with Peggy he was aware of a kind of background of Ciss Everest. Also he knew that if he had brought Ciss home after the War, people would have disapproved of her as they seemed to be disapproving of Peggy. Adulteress, tart. He knew the whispers.

"I'm sorry to upset you, Peg," Tom said gently. "Of course we'll take the mattress. But nothing else unless I say so, mind!"

"O.K. then."

92

Peggy dried her tears. She had really gone crazy with excitement at the thought of furnishing a house after living most of her life in a bed-sitting room in an old people's home; a member of the staff, certainly, but there were times when she realized that if her bedroom were only a few yards from where it was she could be termed, technically, an inmate of the home. Sometimes she slept out, and she had a good friend, a live-in barman at the local pub, and one or two others who were always willing to offer a night's hospitality for services rendered. Lately, however, since she met Tom, she had spent the night away only once, with Ted the barman, who told her he'd heard she was "going around with Tom Livingstone and planned to marry him to get a nestegg for her old age."

"What is it to you?" she asked Ted.

"It's not that," Ted replied. "He's a tough old bloke. You mightn't know what you're letting yourself in for. His wife hadn't much of a birthday party with him, let me tell you. They say he drove her to the grave.

"And those two kids of his—I saw them once or twice—as scared as ever I've seen. It's a wonder they didn't turn mental. Tom Livingstone was a war case, I heard."

Peggy's retort was sharp.

"Tom's a good sort. He's kindness itself to me."

Tom had formed the habit of sending Peggy chocolates or flowers or nylons to her room at the Bideawhile, the foundation for the habit being made when Peggy herself wrote unashamedly on a postcard, "Dear Tom, how about a present now and again to cheer my lonely heart?" After a few weeks she decided it should be nylons only, for, as she said, flowers fade, chocolates get eaten and make you fat, nylons run but at least they're used.

The afternoon of the innersprung mattress ended for Peggy and Tom in snoring sleep upon the innersprung mattress.

15

In the dream in the dream
want was get
wished-for absence was death
a thorn was a sword or nothing
men cabled
summer by first return of sun; also
hands and feet mattered as never again
the twice-ten servants bringing
food and comfort when there was none.

The unsurprising
ease of perfection
the overturning of
the bitterest enemy
the tally of the dead
lying head to foot
reaches a life-time
where moments are inches
reaches the moon without cost, funnels down
the Sea of Tranquillity for human use and pollution.

In the dream in the dream
simplicity is a necessity
but luxuries, inevitably, come
and are not sent home.
Others are born alive and beautiful
mother is a secret trapeze artist
child alone
in the dark dream
mother warm
with poison, and father, the other
pronoun, a terrible child-eater
masked to perform the celebration of death.

In the dream in the dream
pearls have the shine of clouds in the early morning
the sun's first flush has turned from them
saying, I take my blood elsewhere, leaving you
the faint shadows.

She had not been, then, Pearl,
tremendous in childhood
as a live oak of flesh.

Now add up her gray accounts
in the red in the black
out of the dream out of the dream
Henry has eyes like bicycle wheels that never turn back.

the act as final unrepeatable
his and her shroud a model
used once only
abandoned to Charity.
She thought
he said
he thought
she said.
Their history hung
like clothing added over the years
in the wardrobe
and never worn again or looked at
except for an occasional dry clean
the garment returned
without a stain
on a black wire hanger free
from the company.

For the company got in
deep enough to stay
and gate-crashers
hung in their privacy,
the castoffs from their castaway lives,
and all the world's loving had a say.

Accept. The child accepted, wanted
except the global story,
some mismanagement of sunlight;
dream it is a train to catch
heard of, waited for,
caught in half an hour,
the landscape loved, familiar,
enough sky, trees, water,
fairest share.

                                        Rivalries begin.

She plans a journey.
He plans a journey,
a worldwide cruise stopping at every port,
a hundred in the shade; condemned
for owning much and looking through
glass-bottomed boats at the golden fish swimming
in paradise. First speech a hook
the angler caught in a gasp. All right,
get it over with, pull it out,
the world will be a small marble or pearl again
and was not, is not,
is not ever again.

They said there was dancing in the streets of the city,
the dancers were pelted with pearl-precious stones
quarried from the immobility, awkward to desire,
of the distant planetary
woman called by the children Crazy
Vulc-Anny, Vulc-Anny.
Turned out of house and home
battering the children with hailstones, the bodies of the un-
      born,
in search of a syndrome.

16

After the birth of her son, Colin, Pearl grew fat and fatter and fatter. She surged like a moving mountain whenever she walked. This act of treason by her body was so unforseen and incredible that it put her in a continual state of shock and helplessness. She who as a child dreamed of becoming a dancer had been exiled from her body. From time to time she tried to fight the sentence of flesh imposed on her by following diets and courses of exercise, by wearing garments bought by mail order from the back pages of magazines like *Confess!* and by consulting doctors whom she begged to supply her with "something for her glandular trouble." As the years passed she had drawn an increasing supply of bitterness and resentment into herself, and from herself, from where she erupted it, like a fountain or volcano, upon her husband and child and neatly proportioned foursquare home. Henry early in his marriage, and Colin, early in his life, learned to retreat from Pearl's bitterness which changed on its way from her to her family to a suffocating love and concern for them.

A rainy morning.

"Where's your coat, Henry? Have you got your coat? Are you wearing those socks I washed yesterday? You need a closer shave."

"Colin, come here and put on a singlet. You know how damp it is outside. Take your raincoat to school. I saw you bring it back yesterday and hide it."

A sunny day.

"Drink plenty of fluids, Henry. You'll be dehydrated."

"Where's your sun hat, Colin? You'll get sunstroke."

Henry and Colin grew more silent, absorbing themselves in activities that Pearl was unable to see and criticize.

She could supervise neither Henry's work at the bank nor Colin's accountancy studies. She could control the house, though: decorating, redecorating were her passion. Every few months she moved the furniture, recovered the chairs and sofas every two years, hung wallpaper, varnished, painted, rearranged the lighting—one year diffused indirect lighting, the next, according to fashion, direct lighting with pastel-colored bulbs and black shades. She made lampshades from parchment, covering them with postage stamps and luggage labels, made frilled skirts for the dressing tables, put up shelves, put down shelves, lay carpets, linoleum, tiles. When the lavatory cistern overflowed she startled the assistant in the local hardware store by asking for a Croydon Ball Valve and a plumber's wrench. She had read or heard that activity burned up calories. Not in her; her bulk stayed. Her body adopted the unwanted size and shape as its permanent container while Henry and Colin moved like snake-thin deadly shadows in and out of doors, up and down streets, up and down neat columns of figures, balancing budgets, canceling feelings and accounts; shadows thin, they almost became transparent with the world showing through them as if they were moving pictures of ghosts; but putting on, putting off substance as hard cash.

One morning Pearl received a Save the Children card from an old school friend in Waipori City, and scrawled beneath the greetings was the sentence, "The rumor is that your father and Peggy Warren (Furcoat Peg) are going out together and plan to marry."

Pearl's sense of betrayal and shock forced her to sit down. She was trembling. She'd not been to her old home for years. Both she and Naomi left home as soon as they could. They had pitied and hated their mother and hated the textual God who looked down on them from mantelpiece and wall and cabinet, never from sky, with Peace Be With You, Honor Thy Father and Mother, Remember Thy Creator in the Days of Thy Youth, Blessed are They—the Mourners, the Peace-makers, the Pure in Heart, the Poor in Spirit. They had pitied their mother and feared their father. Pearl had not even returned home for her mother's funeral. Each year her conscious act of memory was performed through the birthday and Christmas cards, with photos of the family, of Henry, of Colin as he grew—the first step and tooth and so on, while her news of Waipori City was gained chiefly through the Old Girls' Association of her high school, though her visits to the meetings were few. She would look out through the arrow-slit windows of her castle of flesh, feeling herself trapped, besieged, as any creature might do that has undergone a transformation and cannot make its explaining voice heard, while she listened with horror to the faithfully quoted Old Girls' Refrain passed from mouth to mouth: "You haven't changed a bit, you're still the same!" with a sick feeling as if she were having a conversation with her own vomit.

Rereading the message on the Save the Children card, Pearl calculated how long her mother had been dead, to try to give herself some reason for her emotional outrage at the news. Her mother had not believed in remarriage, though as she had many times righteously asserted: God allowed it after the death of one of the partners. In the heaven or hell their mother dreamed of and vanished into she would be waiting at the gate for Tom Livingstone, alone, and his arrival as husband also to Furcoat Peg Warren was alarming to contemplate. Yet it was not this which angered Pearl, it was her own sense of betrayal, as if her father were committing a crime against her.

"It's not fair, not fair," she quavered.

Then a practical thought was thrust forward as food for her hungry unhappiness.

"If he marries her everything will go to her when he dies. The house, the land, any money he has. It's not fair. The tart," she said vehemently, "the dirty little cheap little tart.

And Dad will lap it up. Just lap it up. Men of that age do."

She thought of Naomi. She'd had birthday and Christmas cards from her for a number of years since she left the country with that Yank. Colored photographs of foreign places that filled Pearl with envy and longing for a past she had never known and places she had never seen: the Turkish mosques, the beautiful breast curves that transfigured, not disfigured, the landscape they rose from; the vast ruins and golden memories of Mexico City and Stonehenge; the huge dignified speechless gods of Easter Island. She felt she wanted to recover, restore, redecorate the world, not merely her foursquare home on Stuart Street, Birkenhead, Auckland, New Zealand. To grow oranges in the sky, not a miniature tree in the back garden with the twigs tied like sore thumbs with small scraps of cloth.

Naomi in her postcards had once or twice mentioned her illness, how surgeons were removing parts of her body. Pearl had a feeling of envy, of being a subject in anarchic unreality at the thought that Naomi was diminishing in size and content while she increased, almost as if she were recovering for herself what her sister was losing. During the past year there had been no news from Naomi. She could be dying, or dead, Pearl thought, finding this as easy to accept as the mail or the morning paper or the cases she met in her part-time job as social worker for the Society for the Prevention of Battered Children, commonly known as the Battered Children's Society, where she visited homes, inspected the battered children, and made recommendations about their welfare. She seldom thought about her own childhood. Her past, Naomi's past, was done with, dead, dead, dead, dead. And now why should she worry that her father planned to remarry?

The unfairness of it overcame her and she cried. She sat down and cried. It had been years since she cried—not since she saw a film about a dog sentenced to be destroyed, "put to sleep," while the owner, a small boy, pleaded for its life.

"Don't kill Ole Bony," he cried. "Don't kill Ole Bony!"

And Pearl, at the matinee, in town on one of her shopping visits, when Colin was ten or eleven and at Intermediate School, found herself repeating the child's plea under her breath while tears stung her eyes and she swallowed and could not look at the closeups of the mournful-eyed mongrel.

She hadn't cried since. Even that surrender had been unexpected and humiliating, and she had never been able to account for it. She and Naomi had been rather tearful as little girls but she had grown out of that, she had grown so strong, so strong, and the only advantage of her bulk was its power to increase her appearance of strength—why, she could be champion heavyweight of the world—oh God! She'd never cried over a dog in her life, until then. And now there was her work among the battered children, among bruises, broken limbs, burns where the flame had been applied deliberately, scars that could not be explained away by protecting, loving parents, children shocked dumb with such an air of inward defeat like members of a beaten army that they had made the move of such an army, retreating across no-man's land to a place inaccessible to the enemy—battered child after battered child and no tears came to Pearl. She was brisk, businesslike with the children. And she did not cry or mourn.

And now she sat and cried with rage against her father.

When Henry came home from the bank that evening he saw that Pearl was unhappy. He'd had a pleasant day at the bank where he was in sole charge and overlooked from his desk a small park bordered with pohutukawa trees and the sea beyond. In summer he could watch the pohutukawa bud and blossom, and the blossoms drift down in showers of blood-colored dust, and he could see the red and yellow and white sails of the yachts in the harbor. That would set him dreaming about his brief days in the navy, of places he might have visited but which now, as far as he was concerned, had

101

vanished from the face of the seas, while in his mind he constructed in detail his dream yacht, a beautiful blue and white high-stepping trimaran with three decks and many flags, bulkheads of the finest varnished wood, shining railings, luxury cabin, galley, bathroom. He had seen one moored at Nassau, a millionaire's yacht, and it had set him dreaming of the Bahamas, and his dream then and now was that one day he'd leave home, he'd leave Pearl with her sad bulk and her domineering ways and her obsessive visits, first to the local doctor, then to Symonds Street where the doctors' rooms were known as "chambers"—tall, white-painted buildings fronted with Grecian pillars, where the doctors wore suits all the year round and not, like the local shore doctors, shorts in summer, and charged fancy prices; and her resentful maneuvering of her body. Her voice sounding from room to room like a foghorn might have caused amusement had it not been that the special sound of the foghorn breaks the dim habitual acceptance of it to warn of the reality of possible disaster, to remind that ships are still wrecked or lost in fog and many are never recovered. And he'd leave his son Colin with his pale haunted poring over his accountancy, his restless searching away from his wife and their two children for an "ideal woman," a new unpatterned woman upon whom he could impress, with the starvation of a personal never-used printing machine, his own self or his image of it —an ideal love that would begin perhaps in adultery with sordid details and end God knows where. Yes, Henry dreamed, he'd leave them all and cruise in his yacht forever and ever, up and down the Spanish Main; he as captain, crew, and the yacht responding to his every desire.

He'd leave them all: this year, next year, sometime, never.

"Something happened?" he asked Pearl.

"Dad's getting married again. He's turned into a dirty old man."

Henry said nothing. Lately he'd had some pleasure in telling risque stories to one of his clients, a young woman, a captive audience who could never leave until he had cashed her check. He enjoyed her company and had told her most of his stories remembered from the War, including the one where he found himself renting a room in a brothel. He liked to see her innocent eyes "take the veil" as it were, until any thoughts she might have about him passed out of sight.

"Your father's lonely, Pearl. And he'll never accept our offer to come up here. There's no one to keep him company."

"But what about Mother?"

Pearl's voice was deep and fierce. Henry reached for his armor, helmet, shield, and all.

"These things happen," he said. "A man doesn't want to die alone."

"But if you knew who he's chosen! Some tart known the length and breadth of the country."

"Who?"

"Peggy Warren. Furcoat Peg."

"Never heard of her."

"There, you see, you're as innocent as Dad, you don't even know what goes on in the world, you've never known, you didn't even learn in the navy. There you are in the bank all day with your money, and you haven't a clue to what's going on. Milly Parson's child died in hospital last night after the beating they gave her. What do you care? The Petersons' child has had to be put into welfare. You don't know half of what goes on. And Colin's the same with his wife and kids, goodness knows what's happening there, I tried my best to train him, they don't even phone us now, not even at night on the cheap rates, and look how we bloody well struggled for him. At least he didn't have the childhood Naomi and I had, an insane father acting the War all the time, you'd think he was the country or the world."

Pearl's face had flushed a dark red. Once again, her body told. It would never keep out of an argument, always it must have its say, to humiliate and control her.

She sat down, abruptly.

"I suppose it's Dad's business who he marries," she said more calmly. "I would have thought that for once, though, he'd think of his children."

Henry frowned. She saw the frown.

"Naomi and me."

Henry looked at her as he might have looked at a child. She saw the look and hated it. Yet she marveled at the continuing surgery of habitual love which could cut through so much unwanted flesh and so many years to create her as a little girl again, with Naomi, at home, while Mum and Dad showered unhappiness like climate, not passing weather, on them both; and the War came, in their home and on the films, and there was that time when she and Naomi were trapped in the torpedoed submarine. She could not remember how many hours it lasted and it had not seemed strange that two little girls should be locked in with grown bearded members of the crew; they suffered together, and in the last hours when there was no more fresh air to breathe she remembered how they had crawled around the mess room and the engine room and the narrow corridors, grasping at each other, making animal noises, clawing at each other's face, only to get at, to unlock the fresh air from the world; and in the end Pearl and Naomi, their pretty blue- and white-print dresses with the gathered yolks and the puffed sleeves, torn and stained with oil, died side by side with the submarine crew. In the War. Torpedoed in the War. Then how was it, that the next week they died also, in the cockpit of an airplane, one of the early models with the open cockpit and simple controls like the joystick? Everyone knew that if you thrust the joystick forward the plane descended, if you pulled it towards you the plane soared skyward; their plane was on fire with bombs,

104

and Naomi and Pearl in their pleated skirts with the calico bodices and knitted jumpers, brown and green, died with the pilot and co-pilot when the plane crashed. Died.

Died and died and died in the War. Because the War never ended, they forgot to find the trick of ending it, because they didn't know it was still going on and on and on, and if they saw it was there they kept looking away and pretending it wasn't there, like with the mental people.

And Naomi and Pearl lived the next week to see dancing on the stage where the films were shown—dancing and singing and elocution by the other children of the neighborhood. *Come follow, follow, follow the merry merry Pipes of Pan*, they sang. And they recited, *John had great big waterproof boots on, John had a great big waterproof hat.* And *White founts falling in the courts of the sun.* But Naomi and Pearl did not dance or sing or recite, they did not learn to, they had to go to the trenches and in the submarine and the airplane when the dancing and singing were finished.

"No," Pearl said, "I suppose it's best for Dad not to die alone. Though who's talking of death? The question's remarriage."

"Has he written to tell you?" Henry asked.

Pearl showed her anger once more.

"Not a word. It's underhand. Him with his broken leg and wasting his savings on an overseas trip."

Henry's voice was gentle.

"He's not accountable to you. Not any more, Pearl."

Pearl buried herself in her flesh. If Henry tried to retrieve her he would be hurt now, as one is hurt withdrawing a thorn. Her voice was harsh.

"Accountable!" she exclaimed. "You work in a bank all day but what do you know about accounts?"

17

My schooner and I
have a pattern of life
that definitely
excludes a wife.

I anchor her
in ports unknown
and her deck lies bare
as a sunburned bone.

Her sails lying
under my hand
are shining
blonde.

Our talk is murmur
hush-hush
softest murmur
of seabird in the seabush.

My schooner and I
can fiercely fight
a storm at sea
ten hours of the night.

Long can she sleep
with my long fish
deep
in her mouths' salt wash.

My dream is old,
we rise and fall
like the gold
standard or the green swell

till late or soon
the tumbling tide

will invite us down
to the seabed.

and like a furnace
roaring love
the tide will possess
all we have.

18

Dear First Dad, Alfred and I and the children, Thomas, Ellen, Milton, have been thinking and talking so much about you lately. The family never tires of asking me about my childhood in Waipori City and Alfred who teaches history at a local college is always pestering me to "write down" something of my early life and again and again I confront him with —my life has been so happy, where is the history of a happy life? Why wasn't I raped as a child? Why didn't you and mother beat me? Why were not Pearl and I brought up in poverty, forced to walk barefoot through the snow, to witness distressing scenes between parents who never loved each other and took no pains to conceal it, why were we not subjected to subtle cruelties that I could describe in detail? Where are the family skeletons, the uncle who drank and came to our bedroom and got into bed with us, the mad uncle who cut his throat when we were alone in the house, the blood spurting like a fountain over the gold-embroidered cushion on the sofa? Where is the sweet taste of sex that was served to us at the wool store and shearing parties, in the pine plantations, down by the wharves in the dark streets by the grain store and the flour mill? What about the scene in the butter factory or that summer holiday down on the farm when the big hairy rouseabout took me among the milking machines in the cow shed?

Dear First Dad, our life was one of happiness and calm,

107

as you wanted it to be; and always your wishes came first. What happy times! Pearl's dancing and music lessons and the prizes I used to win for elocution in the competitions every May holidays. I remember how we came home from school when we were very young and we asked in turn if we could take dancing and elocution lessons.

"Father, may I learn dancing, tap, and National?"

I remember your kind understanding smile. Your reply came instantly. There was no furious raging about money money money and who did we think we were that we should be privileged to learn dancing and elocution while so many children were crippled and dumb and had to spend the rest of their lives in an iron lung and silence, who did we think we were that we should want so desperately to dance and sing and speak?

"Children dear," you said. "Of course you may learn to dance, you may learn anything you wish. You shall have the best teachers in Waipori City. A dressmaker will sew your costumes. Money is no problem."

"God always provides," Mother said.

And it was true. Mother was a religious woman and her religion was inspiring and it never caused us to make fun of her, demanding what kind of a God she believed in that never acted as he promised to act, that never answered prayers, that "stood by" while millions suffered and would no doubt "stand by" while the human race brought about its own destruction in body and spirit; and since when had God, by the way, who provided, footed our grocer's bill?

Oh no, it was not like that. .

God provides, Mother said. And God did. Always.

What happy days they were! We learned to dance and we wore kilts and an Irish dress and a Dutch costume with clogs and we danced in the competitions and won silver cups for dancing and singing and reciting and music. You remember how the competitions were held in the old opera house that was used also as a cinema to show the war films; one evening death by shellfire and gas, the next:

Have you seen the fairies in their neat white silk
Their gossamer wings and their teeth like milk?

The gossamer War, a merging of the two?

Dear First Dad, you were so proud of us. All our silver cups were arranged in the hall at home so that everyone who came to the house noticed them and praised our talents, and on New Year's Eve when we had our midnight feast and a dark handsome man came to firstfoot us we always drank champagne from one of our silver cups, and he kissed me first, then Pearl, to welcome the New Year. And I think it must have been about this time that you sent Pearl away to boarding school where she stayed until she grew up, without ever coming home again, even for a holiday, and you and mother gave me her toys and anything of hers that I wished for, not forgetting the big sleeping doll with the pink knitted dress and bootees and mittens and bonnet that had been sent to her by mistake. The man from the post office came to tell us it was really addressed to me—remember?

Also when Pearl went away you and Mother came to me and said kindly, "Now Naomi we want you to think of yourself as our only child. We have a secret to share with you. Pearl is not really our daughter. We adopted her. We did not want her as we wanted you and now we have sent her away forever."

Any dreams I had had about the romantic possibilities of being an adopted child immediately vanished. Poor Pearl, I thought. It's her own fault though. It's her own nasty piggish pink-sleeping-doll fault!

So I took my big sleeping doll with its pink knitted clothes and put her in her doll's pram and wheeled her up and down, up and down, and people passing in the street looked over the gate and said, "There's Naomi Livingstone, a talented beautiful only child who has so many medals and cups for dancing and reciting that her father has begun to melt them down to make a silver mountain in the Livingstone's back garden, under the pear tree." How well I remember that silver mountain, with each day more silver being added, and soon it grew so big we could add no more and we had your photographs taken standing in front of it, you and I, dear First Dad.

"Naomi Livingstone, famous dancer and reciter of poems standing with her father by the Livingstones' silver mountain under the Livingstones' pear tree." The paragraph went on to say that I was an only child, my sister having died at birth and a great future lay ahead of me, in Hollywood, and in spite of my fame I was not at all spoiled, I was still the same popular, charming Naomi Livingstone.

It was not long after that, I remember, that Mother died. I was ten years old. Ten years. I remember Mother had been sick in bed and though I was only ten I had the responsibility of looking after her and of preparing her medicine every afternoon when I came home from school, before I went to my elocution class. It was only the flu she had but it was a bad flu and she was too ill to get out of bed. Now, at that time I had a small garden plot where I grew cucumbers, mustard, and cress, and I was trying to grow a sunflower so I could make believe I lived in Russia, but the weeds kept growing in my garden plot, and wanting to get rid of them I measured some weedkiller into a small bottle but (by some tragic confusion) the weedkiller found its way into my mother's medicine, and mother died in horrible agony and when it was discovered why she died everyone was very sad and sorry for me, saying what a tragic mistake for a child of ten to make —a child of ten; and the psychologists said that a child of ten had no moral judgment or responsibility and lived a life that was, strange to say, largely unconscious; and everyone patted

me on my blonde curls and kissed me and cried over me.
Poor child! And poor Mother. We buried her in the cemetery,
and you said she would not have wanted a headstone to mark
her place, therefore we did not buy one, though we could
have used part of the silver mountain, and she lay in a plain
plot with the weeds growing over it, and if you visited the
cemetery today you would not know where to look for her
grave.

After her death a housekeeper was hired to do all the
work, taking her instructions from me. I had no work to do
at home. The housekeeper even used to run my water into
the silver bath each morning, for I had said, "No thank you,
dear First Dad," when you asked me if I would like a personal
maid. A chauffeur now took me to school and elocution and
dancing lessons and wasn't it that year, dear First Dad, that
you and I went on that long sea voyage in the luxury liner?

Sometimes in the evening you would sing to me because
you liked to sing. The songs were always happy songs. You
never sang of the War, you never sang:

I want to go home I want to go home
I don't want to go to the trenches no more
Where the bullets and shrapnel are flying galore.
Take me over the sea
Where the enemy won't get at me.
Oh my I don't want to die
I want to go home.

Oh no, you never sang that song though you had been
in the War and when I asked what you had brought back from
the war (I being led to believe that the War had been a kind
of holiday), you did not show the gas mask and the first-aid
kit with the bandages still dark with blood and the paybook
with your will written at the end, and the puttees you wound
around your legs to keep them dry in the mud of the trenches

111

and the identity disc you wore around your neck; no you brought back none of these from the War. All you had as your souvenir was a clay tablet from Egypt pictured with storks and ibises and beautiful hieroglyphics—some of the first writing, you said, a piece of civilization, to be rescued at all costs from the War; you had brought back a piece of hope, you said, for the future of man. How kind and wise you were! And even when I broke your best, your treasured watch, silver with jewels and a silver compartment you said, "Naomi dear, what a shame my watch is broken, do not worry, my love for you is worth more than a broken watch." You never showed anger, desire for revenge. And I remember so well the way you fostered my dramatic talent.

Each year Guy Fawkes was a celebration for you and me and the neighborhood, culminating in the fireworks and a bonfire—sparklers, sticks of wire that we held and waved around like a baton while the sparks showered, Catherine wheels pinned to a tree trunk or a plank of wood, spinning in the midst of their flame; ordinary sheets of dark-red crackers strung together by their fuse that could be lit one by one or in a burst of shots from some while others, fizzers we called them, lay hissing, never exploding, while yet others danced as if alive, crackling, leaping until they were exhausted; and then there were the throw-downs, silver three-penny-sized crackers that burst when you threw them on the ground; and skyrockets set in an empty bottle and lit while we watched the slow crawling of the flame along the fuse to the rocket and heard the first hiss as it made ready to fire itself into the air, then whoosh-whoosh there it was away, see where? Where? There. Where? Making a trail of sparks and fire, and we never knew where it really landed, though sometimes the next day or weeks afterwards as we walked the hills or in the streets or even in the garden we might pick up the charred damp remains of a dead skyrocket. And then there was the bonfire, fueled with old broken-down chairs, tables, manuka scrub, tires—any rubbish that would start the fire that would end by burning Guy that the neighbors' children had trundled through the streets all afternoon crying:

Guy Fawkes Guy
String him on high
A penny for the Guy.

The particular Guy Fawkes Day I write of was when I was fourteen and at high school and in love with a boy who lived on the next street. Though handsomeness at that time was much in demand in boyfriends, with the first question being asked by girlfriends, "Is he handsome?" meaning does he look like a film star? Donald Parker was not handsome, his cheeks being too ruddy and his eyes too small and his hair too much like straw, but he was clever and I admired his cleverness and his eyes were shy and gentle when he said hello to me. I was hoping he would invite me to the school dance in late November, and this year my invitation to him to attend our Guy Fawkes bonfire was a cunning plan to force a return invitation.

When I told you, dear First Dad, that I had invited Donald you were very understanding, you did not mock me, you were not jealous, oh no, you smiled your approval.

That day stayed for hours and hours in the same place, the middle of a science lesson where I tried to work out chemical formulae and at the same time gaze at the picture on the wall of *The Laughing Cavalier*. I knew the day would sometime start moving again, that it would be precipitated by some force, the nature of which I could not guess but which would not be the mere going down of the sun and the darkening of the world.

I went home from school. I had tea. The world had grown darker. I grew impatient for Donald's arrival. I walked

113

down to the gate and lurked there until I saw him and then I walked casually to meet him.

"Oh, Donald," I said coldly, with surprise, as if I had met him by chance and was not pleased to see him.

He blushed. I felt triumphant. Then I felt sorry for him with his strawlike hair sticking out at all angles and his face redder than usual, his excitement controlling his body in a way that left his body uncontrolled and his gait awkward. He reminded me of a portrait I had seen of Hans Andersen dancing before the Duchess in Copenhagen, clumsily, believing himself to be performing a ballet as his ambition was to be a dancer; while the duchess and her guests laughed at what they thought were his clowning antics. I remembered how his hair stuck out like Donald's hair, in gold spikes like a drawing of the sun. I remembered how he cried afterwards when he discovered they were laughing at him.

Donald took my hand. His hand felt like rabbit skin when the fur has just been removed: wet and cold. We walked up the path.

"I'm glad you could come to our bonfire," I said. His awkwardness made my face burn too.

"Dad is so pleased you could come, too. He's arranged a performance in the old summerhouse before we have the bonfire."

"Oh, you act?"

Donald looked respectfully at me.

"Only with properties Dad has collected. There's a mask he likes to wear, and a few weapons, a rifle, a bayonet, and so on, oh in fun only, and sometimes he likes to dress in soldier's uniform, you'll love my father, Donald, he's kindness itself."

"He sounds interesting," Donald said, as we came to the summerhouse where the preliminary drama was to be staged. "So many parents are out of touch with everything. Just plain dead."

"You wait till you see my father! Of course my mother died when I was ten years old and I've had the place to myself, being an only child."

"All my mother thinks of is the Women's Institute, and all my father thinks of is herd-testing and stud bulls."

"Oh Donald!"

My tone was sympathetic. Donald's father owned the town milk supply and a fine herd of Jersey cattle.

The summerhouse had always been ideal for a theatre. It was covered with banksia roses, tiny yellow roses with buds like dabs of butter, and inside it on this November night there was the smell of the roses, the manuka beams, the damp darkness and the kerosene from the lantern that stood on a small table on the improvised stage.

"Dad is such good fun," I said, as Donald and I sat on the manuka seats facing the stage.

"What, no audience?" Donald mocked, losing his shyness. "Am I the only guest?"

"This is a private performance," I said. "A family affair. And as the family consists of only my father and myself we are the audience. Later the kids of the neighborhood will be swarming everywhere for the crackers and the bonfire, not forgetting the fizz."

"Half of the delight of a play is in the audience," Donald said in that exasperating way that some of the school girls and boys adopted when they collected new ideas and feelings: a happy confidence of being ahead of the rest of the dumb world and away ahead of the dumb older generation.

Suddenly you, dear First Dad, walked onto the stage.

"That's Dad," I said, my voice full of pride.

You asked us to come nearer the stage, and of course we did. I saw that you had put on the gas mask as a Guy Fawkes mask, and it was all I could do to stop myself from bursting into laughter at the comic sight. I'm sure you smiled behind the mask.

"I thought we might act a scene of war this evening," you said, still smiling.

"Hurrah, hurrah," I cried, while Donald looked rather puzzled at my enthusiasm.

Then you gave me an old soldier's uniform which I put on, and the mock weapon, the rifle and bayonet, all in fun of course, and then disappearing backstage you appeared with the Guy, such a peculiar Guy with his red face and small eyes painted on and his hair sticking out like wayward straw and his ragged clothes.

"Bayonet practice," you said, in your military voice.

Naturally I tried to take advantage of my acting lessons although I confess that just a second before I advanced with the bayonet I had a dizzying feeling of strangeness and sickness that vanished almost at once, and then with you, dear First Dad, urging me, dancing up and down in your gas mask with muffled cries of Kill, Kill, Kill I lunged forward with the bayonet and thrust it at the heart of the funny old Guy with his red face, and hair sticking out like yellow straw, the silly old Guy that later we would put on top of the bonfire, in the hot seat, and set fire to in an explosion of fireworks and feasting.

Well, that was that. I doubted if I should ever be called on to play that kind of military role, but you were pleased with my performance although Donald was not, complaining that he had not been able to see the Guy clearly as the kerosene lantern kept flickering and making shadows.

"Don't worry," you said kindly. "When the Guy is on the bonfire you will see him clearly, the lighting will be the clearest in the world."

And you laughed in that kindly reassuring way you had, and our happiness brimming over we all smiled, smiled, smiled.

We made our way to the clearing where the bonfire had been set. You wheeled the barrow with the Guy in it and when

116

we arrived at the place you lifted the sagging form over your shoulders, and, climbing the lower logs of the fire, you set the Guy on top of the pile where it reclined, supported by a chair-shape of logs and old table legs while its straw-colored hair stood in silhouette against the sky. And then suddenly without one firework having been lit, the neighborhood children arrived and began drinking from the bottles of fizz—raspberry and orange—we had provided for them. As keeper of the Flame in the cement factory you had special skills with Flame and therefore you organized everything perfectly and just as everyone felt that the suspense was too much to bear you lit the first sky rocket, whosh-shsh the signal for the beginning of the festivities. It soared into the sky, surely hitting a few stars before it fell to the other side of the world while the children danced up and down in excitement, begging to have their small slabs of crackers lit, and there was the sour after-smell of gunpowder returning on the wind into our noses and eyes and mouths, and blue misty scribbles of smoke rising in the air, and Catherine wheels, lit, were spinning with blue flame, filled with hundreds of red, blue, green sparks, and with so much banging and crackling and exploding you might have thought a war had started and snipers had begun their fire.

When almost all the fireworks had been set alight, and the time came for the bonfire, there was a sudden hush as effective as if it had been an explosion of sound, and we sat on the grass waiting for the climax of the evening and you, dear First Dad, came up to Donald and asked him, very politely, as he was the guest of the evening, would he have the honor of lighting the bonfire.

"Oh yes please Mr. Livingstone," Donald said.

He and I walked hand in hand, while the children, seeing us together, began shouting rude rhymes in the way children have.

117

The boy stood on the burning deck,
his feet were full of blisters
he had the pants burned off his bum
so he put on his sister's.

And,

The boy stood on the burning deck
picking his nose like mad
he rolled it into little balls
and threw it at his Dad.

And,

The boy stood on the burning deck
playing a game of cricket
the ball flew up his trouser leg
and hit the middle wicket.

The children shouted and screamed with laughter; they were quite uncontrollable, and if I had not known the words of the sung rhymes from my early childhood I don't think I should have been able to understand them. Nobody seemed to mind the gaiety. We couldn't help being gay when the silly old Guy was about to be burned to death.

A new silence. Donald was the center of attention. You gave him the matches and you smiled, smiled, smiled while Donald, his face flushed, stooped, struck a match, and put it to the kindling where it flared, spluttered, and died, and instantly there was a sigh of disappointment from the children, and once again Donald stooped and struck a match, and this time it flared into flame that, seizing the fuel in a ragged scissoring clasp and glare, rose, leaping, crackling, hissing where the wood was damp, in the first few moments driving from the wood like the exhalation of breath all the insects who lived there and now scurried to and fro a second before they shriveled and disappeared; and suddenly in a huge catapaulting of flame the Guy was in sight, the poor crazy Guy, the silly old Guy, his straw-colored hair sticking out like the spokes of the sun, his red-painted cheeks flushed, and as I watched a fantasy came to me that this Guy in his ragged clothes and red face and straw-colored hair was Donald Parker transformed from flesh into rags. The fire roared now to its full height. The Guy was almost burned. Donald and I stood close, watching the body twisting and turning like a live thing in the flames, and it was only my imagination that Donald's face lost its rosy blush and became pale as the face of a dead man, and I did not cling to him, sobbing, digging my fingers fiercely into his wet shirt-covered flesh and there was no startled sigh as if the world had witnessed everything, as if a fire had begun and could not ever be stamped out, oh no, all was gaiety, the children leapt and flew about like birds, the skyrockets soared in showers of multicolored sparks above the scarred face of the silly old Guy, up and up to the stars, and the moon had risen, and the stars, catching the fever of fire seemed to explode in the moon's face leaving there scarred dark hollows, and the pine trees in the valley grew darker and darker as the last leap of the fire filled the sky, and the only light left in the day settled softly on the leaves of the great pear tree until darkness, heavier than light, plummeted through the air to lie on the earth.

And all was over. The children tasted the last of the gunpowder-raspberry fizz sitting on the rugs and groundsheets and looking up, up at the Guy whose face only remained a few moments before it was burned. I looked across at you, dear First Dad, and saw that you still wore the gas mask. Then you took it off. Your face was kind, so kind. Then you fired the last rocket. This was the highest rocket of all; no one ever found it.

Donald was far from being a pale trembling schoolboy as he put his arm around me as if I were feeling sad to see the last of Guy Fawkes Day.

"It had to end sometime," he said.

119

So the children went home to bed, called by their mothers who *coo-eed* into the night like birds calling from their nests. *Coo-ee, Coo-ee, Cooee,* all over the neighborhood the voices rising and falling.

Donald and I walked to the gate.

"It was a wonderful Guy Fawkes night," he said. "Everything was like a dream. The crackers, the kids, everything. And the silly old Guy burned beautifully."

Then he kissed me goodbye, seizing me fiercely in a way that robbed me of my breath, and later, when I snuggled into bed, I kept remembering it and how it felt. And that was the end of a very happy Guy Fawkes Night.

Yet I never went to the dance. I knew I had to be loyal to you, dear First Dad, and when Donald Parker hanged himself from a gas bracket in the chemistry laboratory I was shocked, yet I recovered quickly, it was so wonderful to be alive with a father who was kindness itself.

19

"I'm thinking of ending my single blessedness," Tom said to Greg Newell, the grocer, as he bought his weekly supplies.

Greg Newell was a good shopkeeper. He wanted genuinely to please his customers, he was quick in serving, accurate in giving change, and he earned enough money from the summer visitors to the botanical gardens and the high prices he charged them to keep his business in his family and not be taken over by one of the supermarket firms. Although he no longer bagged his own sugar, flour, oatmeal, and biscuits, he still weighed ham and bacon, and cut cheese with the wire, and used string for unwieldy parcels, and listened to his customers' tales of woe and happiness.

"Moving again into married bliss, eh?"

He already knew from local gossip and from seeing Peggy in Tom's car who the "lucky woman" was but he waited for Tom to say.

Tom had meant to tell but he found he could not. Giving the news, carefully confining it to cliché, was enough for the moment.

He repeated, "Yes, ending my single blessedness."

Greg waited.

The flow of news had stopped.

Tom picked up his groceries and with a cheerful good-bye he went out of the shop, feeling a sense of relief at having given his news and an unaccountable gratitude to Greg Newell for having accepted it.

"He's a good chap, that," Tom thought warmly. "One of the best. Not many like that around today."

One morning three weeks later when Tom and Peggy were still thinking about arrangements for the wedding, Tom collapsed in the street outside Greg Newell's store. Greg phoned the ambulance, Tom was taken to the public hospital where, barely conscious, he named Greg Newell as his next-of-kin. A day later he died suddenly of a hemhorrage from a stomach ulcer that no one knew existed, and Greg Newell, serving giant-size packs of ice cream to the last of the autumn visitors received a phone call from the hospital. Would he kindly call to make funeral arrangements and take delivery of the possessions of Tom Livingstone, his next-of-kin who had died that day at three o'clock? The hospital, the voice on the phone said, extended its deep sympathy to him in his loss. Greg hung up the phone and returned to his customer.

"Sorry about that," he said. "Now was it two giant-sized or one giant-sized? Raspberry, strawberry, vanilla? I haven't hokey-pokey in stock at the moment."

Later that evening his wife took over the shop while he drove to the hospital where, embarrassingly but unavoidably, as official next-of-kin of a man he scarcely knew, he was given details he did not want to hear and was not interested in. They were getting in touch with Livingstone's lawyer, they said. Greg Newell drove home with the pathetic loot of the official next-of-kin—a small bundle of crumpled clothes: trousers and coat, frayed braces, underpants, the contents of an old man's pockets—a wallet with a handful of coins, a cracked, faded photograph of a woman holding a parasol over a young man lying on a lawn, a driver's licence, pension card, a few stamps, R.S.A. discount book, and a wristwatch with a broken face. When Greg had tried to tell the clerk at the hospital that he was not really the next-of-kin, that Tom Livingstone had a brother living on his property, the clerk had said he was sorry but he could only obey instructions which said that Greg Newell was next-of-kin.

"Otherwise," the clerk said, "we'd have every Tom, Dick, and Harry ringing up for information. We have to protect the patients, you know."

"But Tom Livingstone's dead."

"It's even more important to protect them when they're dead and it's a question of inheritance and personal property. You'd be surprised what people would get away with if they could. Don't worry, Mr. Newell, the lawyers will see to everything else. In the meantime we've checked these things out with you and that gets rid of our responsibility in the matter."

So Greg Newell, grocer and small goods supplier to the Waipori tourists and campers, found himself recovering all that remained of Tom Livingstone. The lawyers came to the Livingstone home, shut the newly cleaned windows, drew the blinds down across the newly hung curtains, locked all doors, and returned to their office to study Tom's will and to set against his meager cash assets the payment of their fee, his coffin and burial (which on paper became casket and interment), and his many hire-purchase debts for household goods from Prop and Fancy. And while the lawyers were going about their business of translating common phrases into the legal syntax of death, the news reaching members of the family and the neighborhood acted as a key which opens many long-closed doors, trunks, boxes, some of which were found to contain tightly coiled springs which uncoiled suddenly and which, like those uncontrollable maps of cities of the world pored over by lost panic-stricken travelers who cannot refold or return them to their original shape, lay released, wantoning in disquieting anarchy.

The funeral was small, attended only by Leonard, the Secretary of the R.S.A., and a black-and-white fox terrier that happened to be passing. Pearl and Henry, Colin and May sent wreaths and cards. Tom was buried in the already overcrowded cemetery on the hill, where vandals had broken and scattered the pioneers' tombstones and the marble vases and the angels and their wings, and there were now more weeds —cocksfoot, wild sweet pea, dock, nettle—than flowers. Eleanor's grave had only lately sunk to its correct level and was covered with clay puddles from a recent heavy rainfall. There was barely room for Tom beside Eleanor and Tom's father and mother and seven of his brothers and the two sisters. The graves of the ten less-recent dead, responding to the diplomacy of time and weather, had disappeared with few traces. There would be room, finally, for Leonard; but if burial remained the human custom, daughters and grandchildren would need some other place to decay, some place that would match in its secrecy of attendants and their destructive duties the first privacy of their conception.

The Secretary of the Returned Services Association read the shortened version of the funeral service printed at the end of the soldier's pay book, opposite the will form. The coffin was lowered and covered with mounds of clay that resembled uncooked dough heaped in a pie dish; and even the few wreaths could not disguise the suggestion that this was not burial but the preparation of a monstrous meal that in its own time would be cooked and eaten.

The mourners went home. The fox terrier lifted its leg on a wreath and hurried on at a small sniffing trot. There was no funeral party. Leonard bought a dozen bottles of beer, went to his cottage, drank the lot and lay on his bed dead drunk until the following evening. One could not say that Tom's dismissal from life (it could scarcely be called farewell and mourning) was made more "human" by the appearance in the evening when the autumn chill was in the air and the dew was heavy on the grass and the shrubs and grassheads were shawled with glistening cobwebs, of a woman carrying flowers, a simple bunch of early chrysanthemums to lay tenderly upon the grave. No one came to visit Tom's grave. Peggy, shocked and frightened at the news, stayed in her room at the Bideawhile Home. That a man should die of an ulcer he never knew he had while he was receiving treatment for a broken leg that would not heal! Why didn't they know that his body was moonlighting in its disabilities? Why didn't Dr. Friar know?

As his wife, she thought later, more calm, I'd have had the house and land and everything. No one would have contested the will. And we'd have been good company, such good company. As it was, no one knew about their planned marriage, she was officially a nobody, with no claim. She couldn't even claim the new kitchen curtains or the furniture covers she'd sewn with her own hands, or her drawerful of nylon lace underwear lying ready in the duchesse in the newly decorated front bedroom.

Peggy wrote to Pearl.

Dear Pearl,
    Your father often spoke to me of you and your sister Naomi, and I'm writing to send my deepest sympathy to you in your sad loss. We were very good friends and had planned

to marry. He appeared so healthy and in such good spirits that it's hard to believe he has gone. I'm enclosing the cutting from the local paper. I shall miss your father very much. He was a good man—kindness itself to me.

In sympathy,
Peggy Warren

The cutting read:

Obituary. An Old Soldier Passes. Another veteran of the First World War passed away suddenly at Waipori today. He was Tom Livingstone, sixty-five, of Eagle Street. The son of Scottish immigrants, Mr. Livingstone was born and bred in Waipori and served overseas during the Great War as a sapper with the First New Zealand Expeditionary Force in Egypt, Belgium, and France where he was wounded in action and invalided home. During the Second World War, Mr. Livingstone was an efficient member of the National Reserve. He was also well known as a local Lodge and Union Member and for many years was an employee in the local cement works where he saw many changes take place in the manufacture of cement. He married Eleanor Madigan who predeceased him, and he is survived by two daughters, Mrs. Henry Torrance of Birkenhead, Auckland, and Mrs. Alfred Whyborn, and one brother, Leonard of Waipori.

When Peggy was putting the cutting in the envelope she reread her letter, tore it up, and rewrote it making no reference to her marriage plans. She posted the letter and returned through the cool night to her room at the Bideawhile. How small, stuffy, and stale it appeared. There was her pile of sewing on the table by the window—a gay print linen bag, bright bias-bordered kitchen aprons, a pegbag, and on the chair a tablecloth and six table napkins in a plastic envelope with the sales slip, Prop and Fancy showing through. Her room had never appeared so disagreeable. It was like a cage, there was simply nowhere to walk or stretch, and the bed with its hospital linen and its fawn bedspread was narrow and raw looking as a plank of unseasoned wood.

The prospect of setting up house with Tom Livingstone had meant more to Peggy than she had dreamed. She found herself thinking nostalgically of the pine plantation in the valley, of the lilac bush by the window (she had always "loved" lilac), of the big crippled-looking pear tree, the biggest pear tree she had ever seen, that still bloomed, Tom had said, year after year, dropping pears as numerous as hailstones in a storm. She imagined herself walking from room to room of the house looking at *her—their*—curtains, *their* furniture, knowing the joy of possessing kitchen utensils, stacked or hanging in rows on hooks or arranged on shelves, in compartments. She had not dreamed, however, of stoking, lighting, "boiling up" the copper on wash day or even of setting aside a day to be known as wash day. A washing machine with a built-in spinner and drier had been high on her list of conveniences for her new life as Mrs. Thomas Livingstone of Eagle Street, Waipori City.

She sat in the cane easy chair by her bed. Even after an event as shocking and unique as the sudden death of someone she had grown used to being near and, as a result, to loving, it was unlike her to feel both at a loss and unable quickly to compensate for the loss. She sprawled as if unmasked, exposed like an emptied sack. She fidgeted her fingers and toes like a hungry child trying to get to its milk. She wanted to cry because Tom was dead, and yet she was restrained by an anger springing from her realization that she was not an official mourner, she was nobody in the Livingstone story, she might as well have been annihilated by Tom's death. If only he had spoken to someone! If only he had said, "Peggy Warren and I are getting married," instead of secretively talking of the marriage and giving no names. It was names that mattered. He could have been planning to marry the Queen of Spain for all anyone knew. If he'd said her name she would now be existing as an important person in the Livingstone story instead of which Greg Newell, the grocer, a mere merchant acquaintance, had sprung to the center of Tom's life and death, simply because he had been *named.*

"Greg Newell," Tom had said, scarcely conscious of the power he was conferring. And instantly Greg Newell became entitled to receive news, sympathy, material remnants, to stake his claim in another person's life and death.

Peggy knew her reputation as a tart. During the Second World War she had shown visiting Americans the town and a good time. Her tricks of coquetry were learned from the *Confess*! magazine which had real photos of real people and told real stories of what men and women really did, how they dressed, what they said, the woman to get her man and the man to get his woman, and what they both did in bed, and Peggy, meeting these "real" people when she was eleven years old, had many years to imitate and practice their tricks. She had assumed that what others had done she could do, and she did; and when the first visiting American arrived she was waiting for him, and he never dreamed he was in bed with a shy virgin and not an accomplished whore. Later, over the years, Peggy had no need to act her part, for her performance lay over her lost shyness like icing on a plain cake and as only the icing was visible it promised (and gave) sweetness and satisfaction of appetite.

After the war Peggy moved from Waipori to Maheno where she took the live-in job in the old people's home. She was popular with the residents and staff and with the one or two local men friends who discreetly provided her with finely perfumed cosmetics, expensive underwear and—once the prime factor in the equation of prostitution, carefully solved by the alert citizens of Maheno who had named her Furcoat Peg—two fur coats; one black sealskin, the other Persian lamb. She had now, unknown to herself, the pathos that attends the aging coquette, where the blush in the cheeks is a combination of girlish self-consciousness, high blood pressure, and rouge; where the light in the eyes is eagerness, gaiety, desperation, vaseline, and tiredness (a final flicker before sleep, as an almost burned coal flares swiftly now and again with the ignition of its remaining chemicals); where the energy necessary to sustain a love affair is retrieved from a diminishing store with the knowledge that the requisitioning officer (who cannot be bribed or flirted with) has made his last issue of supplies.

Sitting in her cane chair by her planklike bed, Peggy at last cried with disappointment and rage to think that she was now nothing and no one in anyone's life. She could not face the prospect of a lonely future with no one to visit and cuddle with; of long punishing years that could not be appeased with offerings of finely stitched linen (from Prop and Fancy), furniture coverings, household notions and repairs; of an imprisonment within her body from which she would now find it harder to free herself with men other than Tom, her hands bound; never again to touch Livingstone flesh nor, equally as frustrating, to stroke Livingstone furniture, linen, cutlery, crockery; the eyes in their feasting, restricted more by their freedom to see everyone and no one than when they might have been enjoying a richly satisfying private meal as mistress eyes in the Livingstone household.

She cried. She did not deliberate upon her specialty of grief. She just cried with heartache and tears and when her supply of tears dried up she said aloud, "It's not fair, it's not fair to anyone. And poor Tom. After all that trouble with his leg. Nothing but his leg for weeks and weeks and he goes and dies of something he never knew he had."

It was like a ruthlessly planned trick, poor unsuspecting Tom, defending his leg while the enemy occupied his stomach.

Late that night Peggy phoned her barman friend.

"I'm free for the weekend," she said.

He was, too.

"Let's go up to Christ Church on the Friday night. We can stay at the French (the racing hotel). We can even go to the museum and look at the moa. Ha, ha."

"O.K. by me. But what about your boyfriend in Waipori? I thought it was serious between you two."

"It was. It's over. Haven't you heard? He's dead, caput, a goner."

Peggy's voice trembled saying the last few words. She hadn't said it aloud before, and instead of going over the telephone wires to her friend, the announcement of Tom's death seemed to return to her with its harsh reality undisguised by facetious evasive remarks.

"So, off with the old, on with the new."

"No. You know you're different."

"Let's go then, for a lark. It's dull as ditchwater here. By the way, I suppose you come into property now as the old man's intended. What did he die of anyway? I didn't know he was ill."

"An ulcer. No he wasn't except for his leg. There's nothing in it for me."

"What do you mean nothing in it?"

"We weren't married yet."

"No kidding! So you were going to marry him."

"Why not? Why shouldn't I settle down at my age?"

"Why shouldn't you!"

"Goodnight," Peggy said. "I'll tell you all about it in the weekend while we're looking at the moa."

"The moa, eh?"

"The moa," Peggy said softly. In her role. She was a full-page photograph in black and white, she and the man half-dressed in the hotel bedroom, he with a three days' growth of beard. And she?

The caption read: "Now that Tom was dead I was deter-

mined to make the most of my affair with Ted. I knew he had
been deceiving me but as we lay there in bed ..."

Full page. Black and white. A relief from the exacting
subtleties, the light and shade of the full range of the spec-
trum of loving. Turn the page.

20

The door opens
like an electronic eye;
streaked purple and white
irises grow
at the edge of the pool
tall flowers
of throats and ears
and one root-foot
sunk in water.

The dark frame of the doorway
encloses hell
that is, hole,
all things visible
removed. Fill
in burying the dark
the wreathed images
the word everlasting;
everlasting
is encompassing but brittle
dead leaves break
underfoot
but do not
I know
break under snow.

It is the company
of weather I crave

in this weatherless room
the thermometer
reads me only
is it safe to be
inhabited much longer
by this hot
inland sea?

I would shed leaves
not this waste stream
of mustard-yellow
stinking paste.
Were I a tree
the loitering wind
would lean against me
and I would have
company, company
in the wild wood.
Most of my fleshy being
has gone. I do not ask
to stay long, so alone.

Breathe in the gas mask, father,
or the poisonous air, like a scorpion,
stings your lung.

In the last dream that was not a dream day by day with a
        feeling of dread
I watched the snow disappearing
the torture takeover with the sky's spring coloring,
the waxed pine sharpen its needles for darning the holes in
        the sunlight with green shadows
stitching the light with tailor's chalk of moonlight; smooth
white rubbing off on the last hunchback huddles of snow and
the human faces; yours too; days of stillness; the ice cracked
like
glass into splinters flying
the footprints icy realities, vacant footprints filled in a mo-
        ment's freezing,

the clinical coffin-care of the sealing of surfaces with glass,
   the attentively timed returning kiss of the sun
embracing, winning to waken
the fatally frozen year and yearning; I watched all with wonderful horror;
the scabs of snow peeling, the skin of the earth healing; the
   old fever over.
Bring back the petrifying hand of snow!

2.

A Kind of Moss, a Sudden Cry

21

Not long after Tom's death Leonard had a note from Peggy Warren.

Dear Mr. Livingstone,
   As Tom's very good friend I'm writing to express my sympathy with you in your loss of a brother. I shall miss Tom very much. I wonder if I might call at the house one day and collect a few things?

   Leonard delayed answering; he had to have time to think. Then one night he wrote to Peggy inviting her to come to the house and hinting that many of the contents needed sorting, rubbish needed burning, dust had settled everywhere. On his way to post the note, he stopped outside Greg Newell's grocery to recover his breath, for his breath had a habit lately of deserting him. Greg Newell came to the shop door.
   "Mr. Livingstone, I've been looking out for you. I've a bundle of things belonging to your brother."
   He looked self-conscious.
   "I was next-of-kin, you know. I don't know why. Maybe because he collapsed outside my shop."
   He fetched the brown paper parcel of Tom's things and gave it to Leonard.
   "You'll see the receipt I signed. Everything's there. I must say," he hesitated, "it was really an honor to be named next-of-kin by someone who was almost a complete stranger, I mean I haven't been long in the neighborhood have I, and to be named like that, just named."
   Leonard took the parcel under his arm. It weighed so little, it was shapeless, yielding instantly to the pressure of his arm, like the remains of the kittens he'd found dead in the hemlock and put in a sugar sack to bury; and

in a sense this bundle was Tom's official meaningful remains which he would carry home and unwrap and identify and even value, put a price to.

Leonard posted his letter and returned to his bach, while Greg Newell in the shop preparing bread orders for the weekend said to his wife,

"I gave Tom Livingstone's things to his brother."

"The whole lot? They're yours really."

"Well he was standing looking in the window. His face is a mess. Has it always been that way? Has he always had that broken nose?"

"Ask me."

"The War did it?"

"No. Motorbike accident, I believe."

"No woman would look at him with that face."

"Did you give him everything, the watch too?"

"Yes. Why?"

"We could have had it mended. It had seventeen jewels. You could have kept it."

Greg Newell sighed. "I thought of keeping it. It was a good make. Swiss. Shockproof. Waterproof. Antimagnetic bloc . . ."

"Antimagnetic bloc?"

"Antimagnetic."

"What does that mean, exactly?"

"Something to do with the North and the South Pole, related to the swing of the compass, the tilt of the earth an adjustment of time."

"Really? Funny how you never think of the earth moving. I don't believe it myself, I just can't believe it, not because I don't trust those who say it moves, spinning and spinning like that, but because I can't take it in. And the experts have been so wrong about so many things, haven't they, they get everyone believing this and believing that, then they change their minds. You can only take in so much can't you? And there's enough to worry about in everyday life, not to mention the bakers' strike for next week. I don't suppose any woman has gone near Leonard Livingstone for years with his face like that. He smells too. He was in the shop the other day. You feel you want to stand well away from him, otherwise you get it in the face, full blast. Still, maybe it's just as well you got rid of Tom Livingstone's things. They were beginning to worry me. Next-of-kin is really only a term isn't it? It doesn't really mean it."

"It's a convenience. But there's power in it, you know. I was the only one they'd give information to. And I could have demanded they deliver the body to me. Tom Livingstone's body was officially mine."

"Deliver the body to you?"

"Yes, remember we went over all this at the time?"

Greg finished making the bread orders and turned to the display of new improved cornflakes with R.X.N.

"In the end Tom Livingstone belonged to me. The family might have fought to recover him but he was officially mine."

"Like the watch and the clothes and the wallet?"

"Like the watch and the clothes and the wallet."

"We should have kept the watch. It told the days of the month, too, through a little square window, and what year it was, and you hardly ever had to wind it."

"And it was antimagnetic bloc, don't forget."

"Antimagnetic bloc. North, south, east, west."

"True north, that's it. True north."

"Oh," Greg's wife said, stacking the last of the cornflakes. The packet was transparent and the new ingredient R.X.N. caused the flakes to glow as if they had tiny lights inside them.

She turned to stare out the door of the shop along the deserted dust-covered road.

"Oh. True north."

The following week Peggy came to Waipori City, her first visit since Tom's death, and as the bus steered into the terminal she was seized by a feeling of dread as if Tom might be there as usual to meet her, and as the bus slowed down she could not help looking towards the book stall where Tom always waited, where he could turn the pages of the magazines—*Man, Stag, Jokes Galore.* She was unhappily aware of the lightness of her shopping bag. She had no domestic knickknacks or purchases, not even her smock and apron. Her bag held only half-a-dozen Belgian biscuits that surrounded her with an odor of spices, and a rainhat so that her piled blonde coiffeur would not be spoiled if it rained. There was no bottle of gin in her handbag.

No one met her at the terminal. She had not expected anyone, yet she felt dispirited standing there alone, and no Tom to fill the moment between arriving and setting out, with his jokes cribbed from the radio or the magazines he'd been reading at the bookstall. Then, her spirits reviving at the thought of seeing the Livingstone home and of claiming some of her personal possessions, she stab stabbed in her high-heeled shoes, briskly swinging her shopping bag, to the taxi stand, found a taxi, and set out for Eagle Street, musing, as she noticed the street sign, why on earth was it called Eagle Street.

As she paid the taxi driver she noticed the milk and the newspaper were still at the gate.

She hesitated. Shall I?

Why should I? She thought. Leaving them she walked towards Leonard's cottage following the path she'd seen him take through the pine trees. The needles were deep and damp and their rust color seemed phony, like a dye that rubbed off on her black shoes. She bent her head passing the last deep-boughed pine trees and came upon Leonard's cottage in its clearing by the side of the valley creek with its water tank outside and the small concrete backyard littered with buckets, brooms, gardening tools, and a sagging clothesline hung with long brick-colored woolen underpants and a blue shirt with a tear in the sleeve. And there was Leonard in his familiar crouching pose leaning over a bucket of washing, wringing out a shirt, sweeping it this way and that to get rid of the wetness.

"Oh," Peggy said, slapped suddenly in the face with soapy spray.

Surprised, Leonard turned and saw her, and instantly with a shy movement he dropped the shirt into the bucket and stood in front of it as if to protect or hide it. He looked guiltily at the already displayed line of washing.

"I meant you to go straight up to the house," he said.

"Oh. I'm Peggy Warren," Peggy said, as if they'd never met.

"I know. We met. I thought you might like to go over the place. There are one or two things of yours."

"Tom and I were going to be married," Peggy said. "Tom and I had fun together," she said defiantly.

Leonard looked sourly at her.

"Tom was my elder brother you know. He had a rough time with all his women."

Peggy looked curiously at him. "All his women?"

Leonard grinned his ugly red-faced grin. His eyes were clear blue and there was a ginger light in his brown hair that was bushy with no sign of baldness.

"It only takes one woman to ruin a man's life, and when he had three . . ."

Peggy, so used to thinking of Tom as hers, felt herself on the shifting ground of jealousy.

"He and Eleanor were not right for each other," she said.

"They were, once. You should have seen them at first, before he went on active service. Two days married. I was sweet on her myself, I used to think. She could have had anybody but the War ruined everything."

"If you don't mind," Peggy said suddenly, "I'd like to go up to the house. And," she said boldly, "don't be afraid to hang up your washing in front of me. I've known bachelors before today. I know the way they hide their underpants rather than let anyone see them hanging on the clothesline."

There. She was bold. She spoke the truth.

Leonard did not smile as he spoke. His eyes had a cold blue light.

"We'll go up to the house then. You know the way. Here's the key. I'll be with you in two shakes."

He took the key from his pocket and gave it to her and their hands touched and Peggy knew a flash of unreality as if the whole story was being retold with the same procedure followed, words spoken, acts performed. For so long she had had a habit of seducing or being seduced that it never seemed stale to her until now. The touched hands, the meeting eyes, the wordless promise, anticipation, the same old routine, everything asked for given—and what then? She fancied she could detect the sudden greed in Leonard's eyes and she despised both him and herself; of course he was a dirty old man and she was well on the way to being a dirty old woman.

She shook off her sudden gloom and tiredness.

What did it matter, she told herself. After all, it was the best form of company, wasn't it; another person's sex and skin was the best company in the world, and that was all anyone needed, wasn't it?

There was no seduction that day. Peggy and Leonard worked quietly, coldly, examining Tom's possessions. Peggy packed in her shopping bag her few cosmetics, kitchen aprons, bedroom slippers, and the nylon lace underwear from the front bedroom. Leonard carried bundles of old rags and newspapers to the oil drum in the garden to be burned.

"I don't know why Tom kept all these joke magazines," he said. "And look at this."

He had opened the trunk containing three soldier uniforms including hats, puttees, overcoats, badges; two identity discs, an old first-aid kit, a rifle complete with bayonet.

"Look the bayonet's polished."

He picked up a tin of brass buttons, a German gas mask with ribbed gray tubing attached to the snout, and windowed eyes. He put it down hastily beside the crumpled uniform. He remembered the gas attacks. The sight of the mask made him feel sick. Even the feel of the uniform—what had Tom been thinking of to treasure these things? But of course all the chaps brought home souvenirs, Some from the dead, their own or the enemy's. They picked the dead clean, like crows. What else was there to do? He'd done it himself, a boy of eighteen. You had to have some kind of loot. He'd expected more than the War gave him. Like marriage.

Leonard Livingstone, eighteen:

Dear War, I'm just writing to tell you that I shall be coming to meet you in the near future. I hope that you and I will be able to build up a relationship satisfactory

141

to us both. I cannot tell you how much I have looked forward to meeting you and now I am writing to you after studying the *Letter-Writer's Handbook.* I have heard so much about you from older men, and dreamed of you, it's hardly likely that we will not come to an immediate understanding. I am young, eighteen, male, handsome, a good worker, and I'm sending this letter in advance of my arrival and hope you will be waiting to greet me with your traditional passion. Believe me to be, dear War, yours faithfully ever and always,

Leonard Livingstone.

"Oh look, a mask!"

Peggy picked up the gas mask and put it over her face and breathed in and out, sucking in and ballooning the gray cheeks.

"It's horrible," she said quickly. "Why bring that home from the War?"

"Souvenirs," Leonard said calmly. "Souvenirs. Want any?"

"No thanks."

Peggy was puzzled. Surely Tom was the last person to keep war souvenirs? He must have cleaned that rifle and polished the bayonet regularly. But didn't it sometimes happen that way, that you kept what you hated most?

"And here is the woman," Leonard said, staging the news, taking from a small ivory-inlaid box the faded photograph of a dark-haired woman in a long black dress with small pointed buttoned boots showing beneath the hem; and a young handsome man, not as tall as the woman, standing slightly bowlegged in his soldier puttees with his wide-brimmed digger hat set jauntily on one side and one arm tight around the woman's waist. Peggy stared at the woman with a feeling of recognition

142

—she'd seen those eyes before, though heavily made up; and those skinny feet, like the end of wooden spoons, wearing sharp pointed shoes; the hair too, braided like that; she'd seen them so often, they were as familiar to her as her own face and body in the mirror—

they
were
her
own
face and body
in the mirror.

Her face went pale.

"Recognize her?" Leonard asked.

Except for the hair, her own face and body.

"Now you come to mention it," Leonard said, though she had not mentioned it, "she looks a bit like you."

Peggy felt herself trembling. "Ridiculous," she said.

"Did he tell you? He was crazy about her."

"Yes, of course," Peggy said. "It's hard to face the idea of dying isn't it?"

Within two hours the house was neat, the rubbish was burned, and Peggy, with her shopping bag of treasures, was saying goodbye to Leonard at the gate.

"You forgot your milk and paper," she said. "Look after yourself in that lair of yours. And never be too shy to hang out your washing."

Leonard snorted.

"Women!"

They grinned at each other as they said goodbye. As she waited for the taxi she watched him walk along the path by the pine trees stopping now and again to get his breath. He did not look back.

22

The clock in the steeple strikes one, you sang.
Whom?

Dear First Dad, sleep is in our faces.
We wake to toys—a John Bull printing set,
a tiny Kewpie doll with painted eyes,
arms strung by sprigs of elastic, legs likewise,
all limbs working like catapults; and a gold ring
with a green-glass jewel glued in, sparkling.

Breathe in the gas mask, father
or the poisonous air, like a scorpion,
stings your lung.

Father Christmas redfaced with passion, white-bearded with
    age and rage,
redclothed with blood cottonwooled where
the deepest still-bleeding wounds are,
bayoneting the morning like a good soldier,
arriving by troopship instead of reindeer,
growing poppy-promises in a scarred field of summer—
Father Christmas, dear first Dad, like the clock striking one,
    everyone,
and mother dead in the sad song,
and Uncle Leonard at the pub willing to drown in the marble-
    colored sea.

Breathe in the gas mask, father,
or the poisonous air like a scorpion
stings your lung.

Roast lamb, mint sauce, roast potatoes, green peas, plum
    pudding full of silver money, a tiny silver bell,
a horseshoe, each a good-luck charm,
strawberries or raspberries and cream,
cake with icing and crystalized cherries and copperplate

icing writing, green angelica and pink cochineal,
hazel, brazil nuts; black-heart cherries with bloody stone;
fizz, all colors of the rainbow spinning with effervescent fury
    in the belly;
and clear golden jelly.
Such was the Christmas meal followed by the love-sleep
in the embrace of toys deformed and blind and dead
and under the pillow the blot-filled page that read
Naomi Livingstone, Pearl Livingstone,
New Zealand the World, the quick brown fox, how
now brown Kewpie doll extraordinary
hangar, airplane, aerodrome
Hollywood star, this is only //////7574333333
a printing set*******!!!!@@@¢¢¢¢¢¢
dndn#####%%%%%%"$+"#=2333=234##$'***!
    ¢;/.p
....??????..,,,,,1/21/2-***
@@@@@@@@@@@@@@@@
A John Bull printing set%%%%%%%%%
**********;;;;;;;;made in England
imported. This is a Christmas pre444444444 sent $$$$$$ No
    SMOKING.
KINDLY LEAVE THE BATH AS YOU WOULD LIKE OTH-
    ERS TO FIND IT.
Brightly shone
the moon that night through the frost was CRUEL. We bring
    good tidings.
Trespassers will be prosecuted.

Breathe in the gas mask, father,
or the poisonous air like a scorpion
stings your lung.

23

They found Leonard wandering around the streets of Waipori City in the middle of the night, plopping along in his check-felt slippers with the turnip-colored lining; with the waistcord loose from his pyjamas and his thing hanging out of the fly; and they thought he was drunk as usual until they realized he was delirious with pneumonia. He lay for six weeks in hospital with no one to visit him, and when they asked him to name his next-of-kin he refused to answer. The day before he was discharged from hospital the Secretary of the R.S.A. came to see him, bringing a bag of red Delicious apples, a packet of cigarettes, and a packet of Kleenex for Men.

"If there's anything else you need, Len, just tell me."

"I don't need anything, thank you. Nothing at all. Except to get my breath back."

"Who will look after you?" they asked him as he was leaving. The question made him angry. They knew he had no one. Then why did they ask? Then he grew afraid that perhaps they might put him in an old people's home, they might stop him from going to his cottage by the pine trees and the creek where he'd be happy to die. He knew what old people's homes were like—there was one out by the slaughterhouse, "Convenient if you ask me"—where they mooned around, slack and slobbery with watery eyes, and if that was old age no thank you.

They sent him home. He found the front windows smashed in the house on the hill by Eagle Street, for the house was empty now and though it had been up for sale for two years since Tom died, no one wanted to buy it, and the seasons had passed with the big pear tree blossoming and bearing its fruit which the boys of the neighborhood picked and ate as their undisputed boyhood right; and because the place looked uninhabited, though Leonard hung a torn tea towel like a flag of occupation on the upper clothesline, the boys with their boyhood right had taken over the grounds, made paths through them, short cuts and hideouts for gangs, and when challenged they replied with an arrogance that could not be questioned.

"We're cutting through. We're only cutting through."

After his bout of pneumonia Leonard seldom visited the R.S.A. for his drink and the company. He stayed at home working, very slowly as he now found it difficult to get his breath, a small vegetable patch: cabbage, and spinach that grew wild and needed little care. He kept four Leghorn pullets in a small run near the cottage, and though they kept escaping through the torn wire netting he discovered their favorite nesting place in the hedge and collected their eggs each morning. He bought oyster shells from the fish shop and ground them in the small machine by the fowl run; and generally he was kept busy with the hens clooking and clucking for their morning grit and water and their evening bran mash, the cat wanting its food, the garden waiting to be hoed clear of weeds. There was food to buy, prepare and eat, the newspaper to read, the lavatory to visit, fill and bury, and each week a new burying hole to be searched for; and there was beer to drink. Sometimes Leonard lay for two or three days, dead drunk; lay, slept, dreamed, and woke. And on pension day he dressed in his best brown suit and joined the queue at the Pensions, Driver's Licenses, Radio Licenses, Money Orders window at the post office.

He still received, each birthday and at Christmas, the handkerchiefs and socks from Pearl and Henry, Colin and May, though he'd met only Pearl. He had not kept in touch with Peggy Warren; he was not the kind of man who "keeps

147

in touch"; he had a fear of being trapped, of being asked to fulfill promises he could not remember having made. One day he thought he saw Peggy Warren sitting alone having a snack at the Dainty Doris. She had a disused, derelict appearance and wore a brown costume and a small round hat shaped like a ginger biscuit and her eyes stared restlessly out of the window looking this way and that like a whirring camera recording the scene. She had been a pretty smooth bird, Leonard thought, but she had changed, something had ruffled her, she seemed to be all side-to-side and up-and-down like a common sparrow riding a storm.

It was a bitter July morning nearly three years after Tom's death that Leonard, during his monthly check at the hospital, was asked to stay a few days for tests, and five days later, when he was still in bed, they told him they'd arranged for him to go to the Special Chest Unit at Maheno Hospital and the ambulance would take him, the new ambulance making its first journey, and wouldn't he be honored and proud to travel in such style! They gave him a hospital dressing gown and clean pyjamas and wheeled him out to the ambulance.

"What about my things? My things from home?" he asked as the attendant shut the door and the nurse in her neat uniform and red flannel cape took her place beside him.

"Oh you don't need things," she said, "We've got your bundle."

So they'd reduced him to a swag man with his brown-paper bundle of crumpled clothes and nothing in his pockets but a few fivers he'd stowed away and his pension book and R.S.A. discount card.

"At least I'm not traveling in the hearse," he joked. He remembered Tom, and Tom's small bundle of things and the way it had kept circulating, like a part of animal that stays alive when the animal is dead, and the way it sagged in his arm, collapsed like a bundle with nothing in it when it came home finally; even the watch had felt somehow limp and lifeless.

"This is the way to travel!"

How sick was he, really, that he had to be taken to Maheno for further tests? What was wrong? Had it a name? Would he be more afraid if they gave the suspected disease a name? There were several frightful names to choose from. But the nurse was pretty and it had been too long since he was alone with a pretty girl; dark hair and eyes and the soft curls at the nape of her neck.

"What are you reading, nurse?"

The nurse shut the manila folder and looked across at Leonard.

"Do you have friends in Maheno Mr. Livingstone?"

He was about to say No, when he remembered Peggy Warren.

He said, "No."

"I believe the hospital has official visitors for those from out of town. They have patients from all over the South Island. Maheno Hospital is the center, you see."

"They're the experts there, right?"

"Oh yes, the unit in Maheno is one of the finest in the country."

He didn't ask, center for what, unit for what? He knew.

He lay in the ambulance bunk, tucked up in the red flannel blanket, his head propped against four pillows so as to be able to breathe more easily, and realizing suddenly that he had been picking at the black stitching around the blanket edge and had unraveled a long black thread, he looked dismayed.

"Oh nurse!"

She smiled. She had brown eyes. Her lips smiled with her eyes.

"You nurses are always so neatly turned out," he said.

She smiled again.

"Do you know the Maheno Memorial Hospital?"

He did not know it. He had heard of it, he'd heard of people who, living in parts of the South Island, had attended the hospital for special treatment, the cobalt-bomb treatment, an unfortunate name, surely, for hospital treatment. He'd heard people say of others:

"He's under the cobalt bomb you know."

Spoken with same dread as if it were the atom or hydrogen bomb; imagined as a dark blue missile-shaped explosive set underground in a lead-lined room.

"They've the cobalt treatment there, haven't they?"

He spoke casually, leaving out the word bomb. Saying "the cobalt treatment" gave it and the disease it was reputed to conquer some of the apparent harmlessness of cures such as the "salt water treatment" the "milk treatment"—something slightly eccentric—with treatment not a matter of life and death but a whim, an indulgence.

The nurse smiled again with her lips but not with her eyes.

"Yes," she said briskly. "The Maheno Memorial Hospital is where they have the cobalt treatment. My sister's husband had it and has never looked back.

"Well Mr. Livingstone, it's not far away now. You'll like the hospital. It has a view over the hills and the harbor and the air is pure." He fancied she spoke mockingly. "How about a little sleep?"

She tucked him in. My god, he thought, what would an old man like me feel like crying for?

He slept. He dreamed he was a small boy in bed between his two big brothers who kept hitting and pinching him and digging their elbows into him and he called out for his mother to come and rescue him. She came to the door in a long black dress, brandishing a huge wooden spoon, and immediately his brothers stopped hitting him and he closed his eyes pretending to sleep, and when he woke the ambulance had stopped.

A white-coated attendant opened the ambulance door and wheeled a chair up the ramp and the nurse helped Leonard into the chair while he protested that he could walk, he could walk ten to fifteen to twenty miles a day if they wanted him to, he was so fit.

"And I'm only here for tests," he told them, half-laughing, half-struggling to get his breath. He turned his head from side to side, taking in everything, as they wheeled him into the main reception hall.

"It sure is a beautiful view over the hills and the sea."

At the admissions desk where they studied his file and asked him questions he kept telling them, "I'm only here for tests you know." His name and address? That was simple—they had it right in front of them on the file didn't they? Surely they didn't think he was an imposter? It was just too bad that he couldn't prove that he was Leonard Livingstone and not someone else; there was absolutely no way he could identify himself, so they would have to believe him, wouldn't they? His occupation? They had that too, didn't they, written down? A pensioner and proud of it. Religion?

"Never had any, knew nothing about it."

"I'll put you down as Presbyterian," the nurse said smoothly.

"Next-of-kin?"

Pause.

Then, "Peggy Warren, the staff of the Bideawhile Home and Hospital for the Aged."

"That's nice. You'll have someone to visit you, you won't be lonely," said the blue-uniformed ward sister who had appeared to "receive" him and who, with the air of a porter taking charge of goods in transit, now signaled a nurse to remove him to where they had planned he should go to occupy the carefully planned and rationed hospital space.

They wheeled him to a four-bed ward where three of the beds were occupied by men who appeared on the verge of death, they were lying so still with gray faces. Leonard tried to suppress his surge of horror by telling himself, I'm only here for tests, this is where they bring you for tests, it's the only place in the South Island where they have reliable tests.

He lay in bed looking through the huge windows at the hills and the sea and the cloudscape. He waited for the tests to begin.

"I'm in here for tests," he said aloud to the three men, separating himself at once from their sickness. The man in the opposite bed, still half-conscious from a lung operation, was suddenly besieged by five members of his family crowding around him, trying to get him to wake up and notice them and speak to them; huge with energy and health, they tried by their manner to punnel him into consciousness while the other two patients and Leonard watched.

A nurse came in.

"Please nurse," the man in the bed beside him whispered, "Get them away from him."

The nurse understood. She approached the visitors. "I'm sorry. Only two at a time for each patient."

This was a signal for the visitors to begin arguing about who should go and who should stay, who had claim to the most time, who was most dear and near, while the sick man whose eyes were open gazed dumbly at the ceiling.

"Leonard Livingstone," Leonard called suddenly, making a general introduction.

The nurse put her finger to her lips.

"Sh-sh. These patients are very sick."

"Why am I here with them then?" Leonard asked resentfully. "I'm only in for tests."

The nurse looked at him, frowning.

"What about your operation."

Leonard started up in bed.

152

"My what? They're not opening me up! You've got the wrong patient if you think I'm going under the knife." ·

"The doctor will come to see you shortly," the nurse said.

"For my tests?"

The nurse soothed. "Yes. To arrange for your tests."

Leonard lay for two days in the ward. One of the patients with lung cancer, a scheelite miner from Central Otago, was to have an operation the following week and the doctor was trying to persuade him to make the journey home to settle his affairs as it would be better for him to prepare for the worst, but he was refusing to go, he would rather not face it, he said. Another patient with hydatids, the manager of a High Country sheep station, lay trying to decide whether he had more hope with hydatids than with lung cancer, and reached no conclusion. Both had before them the example of the third patient who entering the hospital seemingly well had emerged from the operation with the appearance of a corpse, and whenever he was away from the ward being tested or receiving X-ray or other treatment, the others made bets on his chances for survival. Leonard's contribution to any discussion had so far been his denial of sickness, his assertion that he was "different" from the others in the ward, that he was in for "tests only" and when the question of an operation was put to him, this time by the doctor, his indignant protest that anyone should want to "open him up."

"I'd rather have the illness I've got than be opened up," he said. "You keep your knife to yourself, Mr. Sawbones."

He was allowed up. He wandered around in his pyjamas and dressing gown. He explored the wards, the sitting rooms, the recreation rooms. He listened to the racing commentary on the radio headphones attached to his bed. He took his wallet from under his pillow and counted his hoard of fivers.

"By jove," he said to himself one evening during visiting

153

hour when he was amusing himself by sorting the contents of his wallet. "One of Tom's birthday cards."

By chance or design he'd brought the last birthday card Tom had given him, and as he looked at it he felt ashamed of having brought it, as if he had been like a child taking a toy to hospital. After Eleanor's death, when Leonard went to stay in the cottage was the first time he and Tom had been alone with each other since their childhood, and he'd just begun to enjoy their mutually antagonizing brand of happiness when Peggy Warren came on the scene and claimed Tom, and Tom died. That Peggy Warren.

"Think of the devil," he exclaimed, sitting up in bed one evening rereading Tom's birthday card and seeing Peggy herself come into the ward.

"A visitor for you Mr. Livingstone," the nurse said.

Think of the devil. There she was, looking her age tonight, he thought. She smiled at him.

"I slipped on a coat and came over. The Bideawhile's not far from here. I could have come before only ...," she shrugged. "I've brought a few things. How are you?"

She rummaged in her shopping bag.

Just because I'm in bed she talks as if she knows me, Leonard thought resentfully, and could do nothing about it.

"I'm in for tests only," he said. "I don't need anything, thanks."

She stopped rummaging in her bag and looked at him with her violet eyes, widening them a little and smiling again.

That blonde hair's dyed, he thought, seeing the dark roots. It's a wonder Tom didn't cotton on.

"How like Tom you are! I've brought you a couple of handkerchiefs."

Leonard was angry.

"Don't you go buying things for me, spending money on me. I'm only in for a few days."

"Oh, at least you can take the handkerchiefs. They're a

ton weight to carry. And I didn't buy them, one of the men at the home gave them to me, his family keeps sending him handkerchiefs, handkerchiefs, handkerchiefs for birthdays and Christmas, and he's collected so many he doesn't know what to do with them."

Leonard grinned.

"Don't I know it! It's like a plague! If I thought I'd be here more than a few days I'd have brought my own private collection."

Peggy giggled.

"What do you know! Here, take these."

She gave him the two cellophane-wrapped handkerchiefs, white with the initial L embroidered in one corner.

"Well thanks anyway," Leonard said, "I could do with a couple, but I don't want anyone buying things for me. I've money of my own here."

He reached under his pillow and drew out a bundle of fivers, spreading them like a hand of playing cards. "See. They don't know I've got these. Enough to last while I'm here."

He looked at her then, and there was pleading and fear in his eyes and voice as he half-stated, half-questioned, "They're thinking of opening me up."

Peggy said nothing but her eyes were sympathetic. Poor old codger.

"It's my breathing. They want to fix me so I can breathe properly."

Peggy said nothing. She looked around the ward at the three other patients. One lay listening passively while his wife explained to him the gospel according to medicine and surgery. The other two, frail, exhausted, lay propped against their pillows.

Leonard pointed to the bed opposite him.

"Operation. Still not out of it."

He pointed to the bed next to him.

"Hydatid cyst."

And to the remaining bed. "Lung cancer. Scheelite miner from up Central. They want him to go home to fix up his affairs, to take the *train* mind you, in his condition, but he's refused."

Then he reached behind him for a tube.

"See, private oxygen supply. Everything's fancy here. Private oxygen, radio, T.V. in the sitting room, and look at the view. Hills and the sea. The gorse and broom'll be out soon. A chap could die in peace here. I'm beginning to like it. If there's any question of dying, this is where I'd like to be. Hotel with the panoramic view."

He showed Peggy Tom's birthday card.

"Bit of a lark isn't it? His last card to me. Goodness knows how it happened to be in my luggage."

"I miss him," Peggy said quickly. "Sour and sweet. How are things at the house?"

"The place on the hill is shut. Being put up for auction."

Suddenly breathless he leaned back against the pillows. "I can't understand this trouble with my breathing. I just don't seem to get enough air."

"They'll fix you up," Peggy said cheerfully.

"I've had today to think about it. It scared me at first, the idea they might open me up but I think I'm used to it now. What is there to lose? I might as well die here with this view —the hills, the sea, not to mention the pretty nurses—that one's nice but you should see her offsider. I like to kid the nurses. I kid the doctors, too. I know what they're talking about when they gather round. They're having me for a demonstration tomorrow. May we have your permission they said and I said, 'Yes, all in the cause of medicine.' So the head, the chief is coming to give them a lesson about me."

Visiting hour finished. The lights in the ward were switched off and the patients lay like children with the night-light burning in the center of the ward. They lay in comfort, their pain eased, their sleep coaxed by sedatives; tucked in, quiet, while the hills outside loomed black against the sky and the sea flashed with the reflection of the city's lights. Leonard felt at peace. For all their careful talk and smoothness he was beginning to suspect he had cancer—otherwise why was he in a cancer ward? Yet if he had to die, why not, he thought, die here with the view of the sea and the hills?

His few days' stay in hospital became more than a few days. He was given repeated tests, X-rays, examinations with and without students, and the operation was spoken of as a reality. He became bold with the nurses. He plugged his borrowed electric shaver into the wrong outlet and nearly fused the lights in the whole hospital. He joked with the doctors. He was a cheer germ indeed, everyone said. He asked if he could have a glass of beer and the next thing he knew—as he told Peggy on her visit—was they brought him and the other patients a glass of beer each. He could scarcely wait for Peggy to visit him, he began to feel he had so much to tell her. He found himself anxious to see what she had brought for him, though each time he protested loudly that she should not spend her money on him.

One night she brought him a bottle of lime cordial with a strong urine color and a sweet smell and taste.

"They told me you needed liquids," she said.

He was instantly suspicious.

"Who told you? What have they been saying about me?"

"Oh nothing. The nurse told me."

He reached for his bundle of fivers.

"Here, take one. I've money to throw away."

She took a fiver.

"Now we know where we are," he said, "we can enjoy ourselves. How's life at the Bideawhile?"

"Same as usual. Old Mrs. Walker's passed on. Bob Waterbury—what a name—has come to the home. Remember him?"

"No."

Leonard listened to Peggy, occupied in his mind by preparing what he had to say to her, scarcely able to wait to give her the simplest craziest information.

"Be happy to die here," he said again. "Up here on the hill with the gorse golden and the sea bright blue and the ward clean and airy and the nurses like angels, everything provided, tucked in at night and so on, the only snag's the illness, this breathing; still when they open me up I should be O.K."

He was no longer afraid, he said, at the thought of the operation. He was quite looking forward to having it, he'd be happy to die if necessary, for what had life to offer him now except this clean bright airy ward, and the pretty nurses feeling his pulse, and the hills and the sea?

Peggy did not try to say, as others did, "None of that nonsense, life has everything to offer." She said little. When she had given her news for the day she listened. Leonard talked of his childhood and boyhood. He told her of his discovery of reading, the burning of the candle at night, his work in the school garden while at the time he longed to read.

"I've read all the works of Dickens."

When Peggy said, "Would you like me to get hold of them for you to read now?" he looked dismayed, alarmed.

"Oh, that was *then*," he said, as if she were deliberately disturbing a dream. "Too late now. That was *then*. All I read now's the paper and the weekly scandal sheet and the writing on the food packets."

He told her how when he and Tom were small they made a boat and paddled out to sea with a dog, and the boat overturned and they had to swim for shore, the dog too, and the dog reached the shore first and waited for them, and they made a fire and took off all their clothes and danced round the fire and you couldn't do that kind of thing today, they'd put you in Borstal. And he told how a sailor down at one of

158

the pubs gave their father a monkey, so they had a pet monkey at home and you wouldn't find that today, it would have to be quarantined first. And he described how he acted as go-between in his sister's romance. Peggy listened.

Before her visits he would wander up and down in his dressing gown looking out of the window, waiting for her, hoping to see her walking along the flood-lit flower-bordered path towards the hospital entrance; and if he saw her he would feel happy, as happy as a child on its birthday, and when she came to the ward he'd be propped against the pillows waiting to see her.

"The hydatids chap has been transferred. The lung cancer chap's gone for treatment. Anyway, he's disappeared."

He did not discuss the rumor that he had died.

"So we've a couple of empty beds now and only me waiting for my op. How'd you like to move in?"

Peggy smiled. "Now you're talking. It's a lovely outlook."

"It sure is. I'd be happy to die here. I really mean that. They're going to tell me soon when my op's arranged for. I'm a bit jittery, the sooner it's over the better, but I'm used to the idea. I've never had so much peace and quiet in my life. Nothing to worry about here. I'm an old man now. This is the life for me."

On the days when Peggy did not visit he lay gloomily in bed while the other patient consumed his visitors, all of whom had news to tell, and when the supply of news was over they would glance furtively at Leonard and ask questions about him. "What's he in for? Is he having an operation? Where are the others who used to be here?"

And the barrier between the sick and the healthy became so clear that the healthy seemed to become caricatures of themselves, and the sick of their sickness while Leonard, still ruddy faced, fitted nowhere. He would look out each morning to see the sun rising onto the yellow mist of broom and gorse and as the days passed he watched the mist deepen to gold, and though he could not see the sun go down he watched its light gradually withdraw from the hills and sea, leaving a dark twilight purple. He tasted the silence, too, of his leisure. No sound but the reassuring hospital sounds, and in the evening across the valley the gentle humming of the transformer that fed the city its electric power. All was peace. He wanted peace. More and more he wanted his own death to be a part of that peace. He had no affairs to put in order; anyone who wanted his cottage could have it. He had no money, no goods, nothing for relatives to quarrel over, and except for the card-handkerchief communication, he might have been said to have no relatives. He'd named Peggy Warren as his next-of-kin and why shouldn't it stay?

At noon a week later, the doctor on his usual rounds stopped in front of Leonard's bed.

"Well Mr. Livingstone, how are you today?"

"A box of birds."

"Good. Good."

The doctor then told Leonard of the decision they had made, that he was not to have an operation after all, that he could get up, get dressed, and go home.

"Home? You mean now?"

"Whenever you like. Yes, now if you like. We've decided it would be best not to operate."

The doctor moved away, talking, explaining, questioning with his small group of registrars and students, while Leonard lay against his pillows. He was breathing heavily. His heart was beating fast with panic. When he had calmed a little he tried to remember what the doctor had said to him. His marching orders, they'd given him his marching orders.

Oh no. They were sending him home to die. Economy. Hospital economy. Or because he hadn't many relatives inquiring after him, keeping the doctors up to scratch. They'd done nothing to help his breathing. They were sending him home to die because they couldn't be bothered with him. They did that, he knew, with some patients, particularly the old and unwanted. In fifty or a hundred years' time maybe they'd get rid of them by killing them off. This was the way that sort of thing started. Not caring. People not caring for other people. Who wanted an ugly old broken-nosed alcoholic cluttering up precious hospital cubic feet in a slow convalescence from an operation for lung cancer?

His panic was followed suddenly by relief. No operation. No operation.

The panic returned. Loneliness. Why couldn't they let him die here in the silence with the hills outside and the view over the sea? Why couldn't they let him die his dream death?

He called to the nurse.

"Nurse," he said, his voice high-pitched and afraid. "How will I get home?"

"There's a train in the morning," the nurse said in a matter-of-fact tone. "The express."

"But I came in an ambulance, a brand new ambulance, a special trip, the first trip it's ever made!"

"The express will do you this time, Mr. Livingstone."

"Me? Like this? They said the ambulance would bring me back to Waipori City. They promised."

He sounded almost in tears.

The nurse was brisk.

"You have a good day today and a good night's sleep, and take the train tomorrow. We'll have everything ready for you. You'll be away early tomorrow."

"But the train doesn't go till twelve noon."

"Oh? Oh! Is there somewhere you can wait? We need the bed sharp in the morning."

Leonard had recovered some of his calm.

"You can have your bed," he said coldly. "I'll find somewhere to wait. Funny, one day they're treating you as if you're sick, don't do this, don't do that, the next day they're turfing you out, telling you to take the train home. They can't do anything for me, is that it?"

The nurse was smooth, diplomatic.

"They thought you might prefer to be home. That's natural isn't it?"

"When I die, you mean?"

"Who said anything about dying?" her lips said, but her eyes spoke differently. She stared at him uneasily and looked away. She was young and new and had not yet learned the varieties of hospital clichés in words and facial expression.

That evening Peggy made an unexpected visit.

"It must be telepathy," Leonard said. "If you'd come tomorrow at your usual time I'd be gone."

"Gone? Where to?"

"Home."

Leonard's voice and lips trembled. "Not having an op. They're not going to open me up."

Peggy looked at him shrewdly, observing his air of homelessness.

"It's good news isn't it? You're going home. No operation."

"They're sending me home to die," Leonard said abruptly.

Peggy was as quick. "Nonsense. Is there anything you need?"

"Is there anything I need?"

The echo was spoken both as question and as exclamation mark.

"Yes. Clothes, money," Peggy said, reducing the implied immensity of the reference. But Leonard stayed in it.

"No thanks," he said. "Here, take this cordial and these biscuits."

"Don't you want them?"

"You have them."

"What time do you leave tomorrow?"

"First thing."

"First thing? In the ambulance?"

"By train."

"By train? But you've been ill."

"They don't care about that."

"But the train doesn't go until twelve. Where will you wait?"

"The station, I suppose."

"But you've been in bed all this time. You'll be weak. You could"—she hesitated—"you could wait at the Bideawhile, if you liked."

"No thanks, I've plenty of places to wait. I know a few spots. I'm not alone in the world you know."

"You'll get in touch with me if you need anything?"

"Sure. Thanks for coming to see me. I'll be right as rain. Get home to the old cottage, smoke as many cigarettes as I like there, have a cup of tea any old time, ha, ha, no nurses bossing me around every hour of the day, none of this milk and water hospital food, wild horses wouldn't drag me back here, let me tell you."

"As long as you'll be all right."

"Who said I wouldn't be?" Leonard said sharply.

Abruptly, without any preliminary straining, the bond between them had been broken. He had saved up so many things to say to her, he had imagined his talking to her would not cease until one day, some time after the operation when he'd grown weaker and his face had lost its healthy color and Peggy was there listening to his tales of childhood and boyhood, for these were the tales he most wanted to tell, one day he would die, just like that, painlessly, cared for, nursed, with the hills and the sea and the dark silence around him and someone to prepare his body for burial, and no one, as would happen in the cottage were he to die there, finding him by accident, dead many days, decomposing, smelling, a dirty lonely old man whom no one ever visited and whose only signals to the world in his death were his uncollected newspapers and bottles of morning milk. Peggy guessed his pride. She had not known how to deal with it. She'd been able to deal with it only through initialed handkerchiefs from Woolworth's; other ways and means baffled her.

As she was leaving she said, "You know you can't wait, in your condition, at the railway."

"I'll be at the R.S.A.," he told her. "That's my second home in any town."

"Good. Goodbye then."

They shook hands, formally, and looked a moment into each other's eyes, both with expressions of bewilderment, yet also of furious power force that tried to exert denial over the world, that said to the sick, "You are well," to the lonely, "You have friends, lovers," to the dying, "You are immortal."

The next morning people who visited the R.S.A. club rooms in Maheno might have seen an elderly broken-nosed man wearing a crumpled suit and clutching a brown-paper parcel, sitting at a table in the cafeteria drinking a cup of tea. Sometimes he seemed to gasp for breath and moved his head from side to side as if the air were eluding him. He spoke to no one though he appeared to joke with the waitress who removed his tea cup. Then at half-past eleven the porter called,

"Taxi for Mr. Livingstone."

The man started to his feet, swaying a little, then steadying himself. He appeared to be drunk or ill. With his brown-paper parcel under his arm he went towards the waiting taxi.

"Where to?"

"Maheno railway station."

When the train arrived at Waipori City, Leonard took a taxi home, paid the driver, and was alone in the annihilating aloneness that rises from there being no one in view, no people in the street or in the driveway or among the pine trees. There might have been no one else alive in the world. No one at that moment was witness to his existence. It needs only a moment's inattention, separation of a man from his fellows, for his being to vanish from the face of the earth as if it had never been; and then in a flash the sun, the earth recover all. Some say that it is a God who recovers—"The earth is the Lord's and the fullness thereof, the world and they that dwell therein," which is as comprehensive a statement of ownership as can be found and names the earth as its own recovery unit.

Leonard walked through the pine trees to his cottage. He'd been in hospital five weeks. It was now September. The daffodils showed firm, strong shoots in the grass, the crocuses had pierced the earth. The pear tree was covered with the first snowy mist that is the aura of the arrival of its blossoms. Birds were nesting, crowds of small flies swam dizzily in the air: mayflies, dragonflies, bees. These were the few living creatures that witnessed Leonard's homecoming, each with its particular awareness of him whether in his shape, smell, dance, movement, density, lightness, darkness, even his geometric relation to the stars and the sun, the patterns he formed of light and shade, for he *was*, he blocked the light, he jostled the surrounding air and these creatures received messages about him—we see him, we affirm his existence. A bee might sting him, a fly brush his face, a swarm of flies block his path. A bird might twitter at his approach and if he put out food it might value his being there, might watch for him. A tame bird might even learn to say his name—Leonard, Leonard. And thus he might have existed. Yet there was no one to take his yesterdays and shake them free of dust, putting them out like patterned hearth rugs in the sun. And there was no one to say to him "Hello, how are you," and wait for him to answer, "I'm well"; unless there were a God or other self, the slender affirmation of Leonard threatened to break down even before he reached the door of his cottage, negation taking over as lover and destroyer. Sycamore trees, pine trees, the big Livingstone pear tree might remain through centuries uncircled by human language. Unvoweled, unconsonated, unexclaimed, a man must soon die. Even the alphabetical atom may be subdued by the hydrogen atom, unless those who work with language, unless people who speak, learn also to split and solve the alphabet.

Three weeks after Leonard came home from hospital he died. He died rejected, negated, extinguished, yet recovered, for his death reclaimed in some the affirmation of memory. People at the R.S.A. heard of it and said, Leonard Livingstone. Remember Leonard Livingstone? Peggy read the news, and Tom rushed into her life again, and Leonard too, and she remembered how he had wanted to die in the hospital overlooking the sea when the hills were gold with gorse and broom, but they had sent him home, alone with his brown-paper parcel, to a death that was witnessed only by . . .?

Old yellowing newspapers and photographs; a dust-filled hearth rug; rows of empty beer bottles—dead marines; a white-painted chair; small square dirty window; rag of lace curtain; unsprung blind; nobbled shoes his feet had lived in; unwashed dishes; a spring day; a pear tree, unconcerned, in blossom: these the witnesses. Unless a God looked in?

24

Dear First Dad, summer will not come any more. I have been prepared for it. I have lost count of the seasons and their distribution of color and their ways of deceiving. My memory is lost. I have known for years that the footprints are too small or too large, their pattern is alien. The season came down like splinters of ice in the Gerdastorm and little Kay has gone. There was a time when, looking at the snow falling, I saw white thread worms dropping out of the sick belly of

childhood. There was a time of searching in the snowfields.
The snow swallows, its big
white mouth turning over and munching the sugared people
limbs go down into cool columns of pressure,
the sky is spinning out the flakes like webs
they drift like lantern spiders across the sky
catching the air
hammering silver fang-nails into its nothingness.

O deep unaccountable earth
the cannibal snow like pear blossom smiles white with its
    white mouth
the plains lie bandaged; none know the outcome;
a spring morning will uncover the eyes
and the trees with leaves to their elbows will lean down over
    the earth.
Can you see? Can you follow, unwavering, the light of the
    sun?
The black jellied people
detached from the white night
bud waterlilies and the fungus of a green frog singing in
    marble.

Snowstorm, grains of snow red in the desert,
and the blind pool we drink from, the brackish water we
    hoped not to find
at the end of winter, lying stagnant in our eyes.

25

Clerk Tamas loved fair Annie
As well as Mary loved her son,
But now he hates fair Annie,
And hates the land she lives in.

I dreamed a dream concerning thee,
O read ill dreams to guid
Your bower was full of milkwhite swans,
Your bride's bed full o'bluid.

Colin, Pearl's son, unlike his grandfather Tom Living-stone, had no war to blame for his foundering upon a new passion. If one thinks of a man's life as contained only within its span and not bearing its own responsibilities towards yesterday and tomorrow, one might say that Colin was born and lived in a time of peace, yet like his father and mother, and their father and mother, and so on and on to the start of the stream in Scandinavia and Scotland, Colin had a dream. The people in his dream had density, lightness, and with a thrust of feeling could leave dents or red marks on his skin where their love or hate touched him; and those who died were shatteringly dead and could not be pieced together on his waking. His wife, May, was not in his dream, although they had been married eleven years now and the eldest of their three children was ten—a boy of ten!—secretive, sullen, absorbed. May still worked in a factory designing chocolate wrappers; Colin was still a junior partner in an accounting firm; he had not made the fortune he hoped for when he resolved to make money his profession. Eleven years mar-ried, a wife, children, member of the Cricket Club, the Rate-Payers' Association, the Parent-Teachers' Association; and now alone, dreaming of Lorna Kimberley. Oh, his dream was so real it could not be set beside dream or reality without contaminating both and itself, growing a mold of reality over his dream, of dream over the reality.

Lorna Kimberley worked in the office. She lived in a monotonously level northern town that had gardens, a Shakespeare festival each year, and boating in spring and summer on the willow-bordered river. She rented a room in Maheno where Colin had come to live. She was not beautiful, rich, talented. She was plump with coarse blonde—real blonde not wigged or dyed—hair, big lamppost legs, and violet eyes like liquid quicksands. At first Colin tried to avoid glancing at her and talking to her but gradually he felt himself being sucked into her presence as if he were a plant leaning over a treacherous pool. She began to haunt him, rather more than he haunted her, though he had not the power of judgment which gauges this balance correctly and which is usually suspended when those who wish to use it or need desperately to use it find themselves "in love." The image of Lorna Kimberley began to occupy the background of Colin's waking thoughts and sleeping dreams. Her face, her eyes, her hair, the back of her head, her neck; her body in as many positions as his imagination could conjure; with each image giving his heart the familiar sick overturning sensation of desire and love. He tried to emphasize to himself that his feelings were madness, to remind himself of his list of responsibilities—father, husband, rate-payer, member of committees raising money for charity, sports facilities, community centers, a citizen, perhaps an aspiring mayor, member of Parliament—the list sounded to him like the suburban equivalent of the witches' evil chant where before it had been his rosary of respectability.

One evening he invited Lorna Kimberley to a local dance. His conscience, in a fantasy of optimism, hoped she would refuse and this refusal could give him firm ground to stand on, because it seemed that otherwise the only firm ground he would ever know again would be that graciously provided by Lorna Kimberley. He brought all his power of conscience to bear to try to persuade her to leave him the necessary anchorage, just a small square of reality, but she did not receive his unspoken message or perhaps he deceived himself in interpreting the nature of his signals. She accepted the invitation. And other invitations followed and were accepted. They danced, they spent summer evenings on the beach, they went to the pictures and sat like young lovers cuddling in the back row among the knife-split broken-down seats, and soon her invasion of him was so complete that she no longer haunted the background only of his waking and sleeping, she stood sharp, clear, hauntingly clear, wherever he gazed, in reality or dream, until he suspected that he might be going mad. He'd heard of men driven crazy over a woman. He knew the story of his grandfather Tom Livingstone and the impossible wartime romance. And soon his wife, as his Grandma Livingstone had done, sensed his relationship with another woman and he found himself telling her about Lorna Kimberley, though not naming her, and even inviting her sympathy, and to her remark that it was infatuation and would pass he countered, "Why keep calling it names? It's not a name, it's a feeling."

Then while May recited to him the magic list of his responsibilities he said with the universal presumption that flatters and makes secure, "She and I are made for each other."

He left home. He took lodgings in town, and because open adultery was not countenanced in Maheno he and Lorna were dismissed from the office and the day after the dismissal both made the decision; they would go to Australia and live as man and wife.

They sailed for Australia as Mr. and Mrs. Colin Torrance and arriving at Melbourne they found a job together as housemaid and kitchenhand in a tourist hotel and they had been there only two weeks when their dream life was invaded by Lorna's parents who had traced her and wrote to her condemning her "conduct" (a word used only by parents of a nineteen-year-old girl), reminding her of all they had ever taught or tried to teach her, insisting that she would break their hearts if she lived in sin with the dreadful Colin Torrance who had shown no sense of responsibility to his wife and three children and who, when the time came, as it would, they warned her, would show no responsibility to her; finally demanding that she return home at once. When Lorna received the letter she was immediately affected by it and took it to Colin who was on late-afternoon duty in the kitchen preparing the vegetables at the peeling machine. He read the letter, shrugged, and turned his attention to the more urgent demands of the peeling machine. When he heard and understood what Lorna was saying to him, however, he switched off the machine and someone observing him might have supposed he had had news of a sudden death by the way he sat down suddenly on a stool and put his hand to his head, rubbing his forehead and closing and opening his eyes in a mime of shock and loss.

He reached out to Lorna and caught her plump wrist and ran his fingers along her bracelets of flesh. He drew the hand close to his face, studying it. Then he touched it lightly as if afraid it might break in pieces.

"What do you mean?" he said. "You can't go home just like this. You're with me. We're together."

Lorna looked at him innocently, almost happily. She had not withdrawn her hand.

"Oh I have to go home," she said, in a scatterbrained way that only endeared her more deeply to him. "Mum and Dad are awfully angry. Besides . . ."

"Besides what?"

She looked at him coolly, slowly widening and closing and widening her violet eyes, like a cat caught by a ray of strong sunlight.

"Well it's all been a bit of fun hasn't it, but we're really not all that keen on each other, are we?"

Here was the judgment that Colin had been unable to make and that Lorna in her perverted innocence had not thought to make. In the early days of their escapade there had been a shrewd measuring, from time to time, of their love, each of the other's, but the balance had a trick of disappearing, almost of denying its own existence. Colin felt the familiar overturning of his heart, his heart grown huge like a hippopotamus in a sea of love. He felt a wild despair, a dread of separation such as he had not known before, and an overwhelming disbelief, an unreality within the unreality. He

171

looked around him at the kitchen with its sordid peeling and chopping machines working nineteen to the dozen for the big evening spread and he shook the scene from him as Lorna Kimberley the housemaid might have shaken a duchesse cover in a bedroom, but desolation stayed like ice inside him. He laughed.

"Don't be silly, Lorna. Don't be a kid."

Her intentions were clear.

"I mean it, Colin. It's true what Mum and Dad say, I *am* only a kid. You know yourself we've been a bit wild."

There was nothing he could say to that, it was so removed from his own sense of actuality. My god, she had been—she *was* like a giant advertisement put across him so insistently by his feelings that he bought her up, like an irresistible product, he added her up, like the only sum left in his accountancy. He was dreaming within the dream when he heard her say:

"And of course we're tired of each other now. I'd better go straight home as Mum and Dad want."

As if home were a mere ten minutes away by bus instead of hundreds of miles across the Tasman Sea but that was Lorna Kimberley all over again, it was the same trait that made her so ready to accept his proposals in the first place when he and his conscience tried to will her not to. She had no sense of enormity. In this she was like his mother who had dispersed herself among the household furniture so much that by the time she came to her family she had only triviality left and when she came to investigate the Battered Children she had no enormity to embrace their suffering.

"Yes. I'm going home straight away."

The awareness of Lorna's lack and his own plenitude did nothing to diminish Colin's feeling of anguish and dread. It was like a physical gnawing in his chest, like a rat eating its way through a wall to get to food. He looked at Lorna again, trying to find in himself some reasonable foothold supplied by her (as he now lived wholly within her country) but he found none. Her going away would remove any he had, and at the thought of this he felt, sinking it in his mind's heaviness almost before he had time to identify it precisely, a surge of rebellion against her power over him. He was the victim, the settler robbed of his land by lovelight, he was the drowning sailor without a sea to drown in, the underprivileged beyond the castle gates. She was the captain, the commander, the rich, the privileged, the earth, the sea; she was "they."

"Don't go, Lorna," he pleaded, aware of a rising hate against himself.

Lorna looked shocked.

"I'm not doing right you know. I can't disobey Mum and Dad. And you can go back to May and the children and everything will be almost as it used to be."

"You can't really believe that, Lorna. What's come over you? We're like man and wife now. We can't go back to the old days."

Lorna tossed her head.

"Why not? If you go back won't it be?"

"Listen," Colin pleaded. "We'll get out of this hotel and find a job somewhere else, I'll do accounting work, not this peeling potatoes and emptying slops, we're clever, we can go places, you can't just go and leave me."

"Why not? It's over isn't it?"

She was being cruel, endearingly cruel because she did not realize it, and he looked at her with longing and if it had been as far away and as recent as that morning when they woke in bed together she would have responded to his glance with a sudden budding of warmth that reversed the roles of power: he was the sun then, and she was the droopy rosebud revived in the midst of its languor; and he was the rain and there she was thirstily drinking every drop. In his anguish he laughed to himself at the wild comparisons. He'd been reading love poetry. Love poetry! He guessed that perhaps he could make a fitting poem out of his accounts to sum up Lorna Kimberley and himself if he had been ready to account what they had only begun to record.

That evening he found she had taken a room by herself. Her parents were cabling her the fare home, she told him. He had the impulse to carry her away and lock her up.He remembered again how his grandfather had been involved with some woman in the First World War and how the rest of the family had made a joke of it. Granddad must have been out of his mind, they said. And they were right, though not in the sense they meant. He too was out of his mind in the sense that he now inhabited the territory of Lorna Kimberley body and soul, and what was marriage and love but just that?

He made a last plea.

"Stay here with me, Lorna. I'll come back with you, then. I'll get a divorce. We'll be married, and have children."

Lorna's voice was sharp. "Can't you see, Colin, it's over, it's just gone, it was fun, it was marvelous while it lasted, and of course we'll be friends."

Fun. Fun. As if it had been a picnic excursion.

He felt suddenly diminished as if they had both taken a potion to reduce his life, with Lorna acting as the catalyst to perform the operation upon him. How strange it was! He had been such a milk-and-water child and boy and man, and had made no protest at the people or the world and he'd studied so hard, cost accounting, and knew about debit and credit, in the red, in the black, and he had been an only child and his parents had big soldier faces full of care for him, how strange it was, and it was under a spell that he met May and fell in love with her and his mother managed everything, from the engagement party to the wedding and the births of the children, all part of the spell, until Lorna Kimberley came by—how was it?—*O what can ail thee Knight at Arms alone and palely loitering.* He felt now if he did not take some action he might shrink and disappear, Lorna had such power to annihilate him. Unless her love continued to bear witness to him, what existence had he?

He felt confusion and panic and terror and could understand nothing of his turmoil. He lay on his bed that evening and conducted a dialogue with his reason, an argument which he won after his reason, offering solutions of sleep it off, time heals all, talk to someone about it, surrendered. He realized there was no one but Lorna to whom he needed to talk. He longed to explain, explain, explain to her, and as if in explaining himself he would restore his imperiled identity.

The next morning, when he went to give notice at the hotel he found that Lorna had already left. He collected his previous week's wages and set out to wander the streets of Melbourne. He came to a flower market and walked in and was surrounded by tropical blooms, perfumes, and colors that made him feel sick. He walked up and down peering into the hearts of the flowers as if he were some kind of insect on the trail of stolen honey. Then shaking the accumulated sweetness from him, he went out into the streets once more. It was raining, a subtropical shower pelting down on him, soaking him to the skin. He licked the drops as they splashed by his face. He felt that unlike him the rain (that he had imagined himself once to be, he remembered) had a destination and his thrusting out of his tongue was a way of arresting it, as a bewildered traveler may stop another to ask the way; he drew the raindrops to his mouth like a lizard receiving food, devouring his chance of help. The raindrops tasted like soot.

Evening came. He returned to the hotel and decided to sail the next day by the TransTasman ferry to New Zealand. He gave up his job that evening, paid a night's board and lodging, and the next morning still unable to believe that Lorna would not be with him he walked to his cabin aboard the ferry wholly expecting to find her waiting for him in the cabin, for if she had gone from his life at all it was only to inhabit his mind, there to take up more room than she had ever done; in fact from moment to moment even the curve between her neck and shoulders, like a bend in a white road in a mysterious country where the sand and dust are made of silk, occupied more space than the ship he had walked aboard and the sea it would sail upon and the sky it would sail under.

The Tasman ship was old, battered by many storms, and on its second day it reared to face yet another storm from the treacherous seas that surrounded the Australasian countries. Most of the passengers stayed in their cabins. Furniture was anchored to the floor—one of the passengers described it dramatically as "lashed" to the floor. Colin had an inner cabin on the lowest deck with no porthole and only a cream-colored air blower like the elbow of a drainpipe for ventilation. He lay on the bilious-yellow coverlet of his bunk and stared up at the cream-painted ceiling and expected to see Lorna Kimberley as a visitor to the Sistine Chapel expects to see the work of Michaelangelo on the ceiling, as a man spending the night in the open would expect to see the stars in the sky. He closed his eyes. The image of Lorna remained, a love-haunting deep with pleasure and pain, swimming around him within a warm element of promise, starring the circumference of his feeling with white sparks from the center that burned like a white-hot stone he'd plunged his hand in the farthest part of the earth or the sea or the sky to retrieve.

He tried to reason. He cared for reason. He was a calculating man, he could add and subtract, divide and multiply columns of figures and get the correct solution and know it was correct. He had a wife and family. He had been a respected member-citizen blah, blah, blah, the evil list sounded like an incantation in his ears. He was an ordinary man in an ordinary town in an ordinary country of an ordinary world, yet even as he tried to persuade himself that this was so he knew it not to be: love (and hate) transformed all, including the lover, to the realm of the extraordinary. Now he might just as well have been any of the men in history who suffered from the obsessions of loving. He had no voice to speak of it but they spoke for him, their speaking searched his most private thought and desire.

Colin was trapped within the limitations of a self unable to continue either sophisticated dialogue with reason or an exchange of anguished exclamations. He tried to use arguments as a bait, as it were, to bring reason up out of the darkness but it was no use, there was not even a ripple of sense in what was happening inside him. Lorna Kimberley, Lorna Kimberley. Her name echoed in his mind like the name at the top of some magnificent gold-scrolled register delivered to him by an angel. Lorna Kimberley, Lorna Kimberley. The storm at sea roared it and when the storm was over the calm seas and wind lapped it gently in his ears. And as landfall approached in the blue and white gull-crowded seas surrounding New Zealand and the albatrosses turned back to sea, abandoning the ship, leaving it strangely motherless until it should be adopted by the harbor-pilot launch, Colin walked on the deck, round and round, and every passenger he saw had some resemblance—in glance, gait, strand of hair, smile—to Lorna. Once he fancied he saw her turning the corner by the bow of the ship towards starboard.

"Excuse me."

Hurriedly he thrust past an elderly man and woman who, on deck for the first time since the ship left Melbourne, were attempting in one morning to complete the "turns" of the deck they had planned for the entire voyage. They walked with sticks, tapping them sharply on the boards, now and again reminding each other of how many "turns" they had made and how many were still to be done.

"Seventeenth," he would say, looking at her for confirmation or denial.

"Yes. Next is eighteenth, then nineteenth."

Hearing them, Colin had a strange idea that words were "over," "done with," just as a day or century is over, that numbers were the language. He felt proud then to have chosen numbers to work with: the cool calm calculators that never spilled blood or accumulated pieces of flesh and skin.

He rushed past the tramping couple, veered round the corner sending a quoit flying from someone's hand, and spinning bowls askew from the game of deck bowls.

"Hey! Watch it!"

And wasn't that just what he was doing—*watching it? Watching his love.*

The sunless side of the deck was deserted except at the far end where members of the crew prepared the cargo hatches, and on the deck railings a few feet from Colin where a black-backed gull with a beak like two crooked sharpened bones set together, and amber glittering eyes, balanced, swaying slightly to the motion of the ship. Seeing Colin, the gull flapped its wings heavily and swooped and rose on the back of the wind uttering its raucous mocking cry, Lorna Kimberley Lorna Kimberley, while Colin stared at it with a concentration of hostility. It flew farther away and then sank down a funnel of the wind to skim and splash over the surface of the water and ride there, full-breasted, dipping and rising in the little hollows of the waves as if within the wilder ocean it had discovered its own personal tide and thus was able to secure itself against seas and men. A rush of fury made Colin want to strike it from its fortunate nest, to scatter it into the wilder buffeting seas. That would teach it, he thought. That would teach it there's no immunity.

He stood a while on the sunless side. The decks were damp from their early morning scrubbing. Night spray lay along the railings. He could see beyond the shadow of the ship the spot in the water where the sunlight struck sending up a dazzling shower of sparks of light. He peered over the railing. The water sucked against the side of the ship, in huge kisses, clinging and sucking with rhythmic motion. He could see where its harsh persistent salt touch had scoured the paint from the side replacing it with specks of rust. In fewer than twenty-four hours the ship would be in dry dock with the crew tramping their board and rope ladders, hurriedly trying to conceal her devoured appearance. Below the waterline she would look like any old wreck that had lain on its side a hundred years, exposed to the attentively leaning sucking spitting scouring seas.

She.

The ship.

She.

Another bird alighted on the railing. A white gull. It balanced, tipping backward and forward, its wings folded making it appear plump and white and smoothly feathered. It put its head on one side, stretched its neck and crying out suddenly, Lorna Lorna, it took off into the sky flying until it was out of sight. Colin watched it disappear. Lorna Lorna. A cry of extravagant scorn or promise, he could not decide, as, lonely, he tried to conspire with his surroundings to force them to share some of his longing and pain.

He drew his dagger that was sae sharp
That was sae sharp and meet,
And drave it into the nutbrown bride
That fell ded at his feet.

Now stay for me dear Ennet he said
Now stay my dear he cryd
Then strake the dagger into his heart,
And fell deid by her side.

Perhaps the white gull would fly to Lorna to deliver his message of love. Perhaps receiving the message she would go at once to her parents.

Colin Torrance has sent for me. I'm leaving home to live with him. He's like a magnetic sea surrounding me. I'm never any longer where I am but where I will be. Where is he.

And when in a few hours the ship berthed at Wellington, miraculously Lorna would be there waiting for him and together they would find a place to live and love.

He clenched his fists as he tried with the force of his thinking to compel Lorna at her home, by now, in Waihuna to recognize and surrender to his demands and desires. It did not seem impossible that so much overwhelming feeling should not arrive like a pistol shot or bomb or guided missile exactly where it had been aimed causing upheaval, explosion, revolt, surrender. He simply could not imagine its not doing so. In his excess of feeling his imagination reacted in concertina fashion, now stretched to limits where it had never been before in his waking or dreaming, now shrunk to admit only the narrowest of possibilities and impossibilities. He could not imagine, as the ship sailed into harbor under the guide of the pilot launch, while the thought of Lorna occupied his mind, she was not occupied simultaneously with thinking of him. Yet where was the logic in that? Was it not as logical to suppose that the thought of Lorna Kimberley also occupied the mind of Lorna Kimberley? Colin did not even try to search out the faults in his reasoning. He walked from the sunless deserted portside towards the sunny crowded starboard with a feeling as if he were emerging from the other side of the moon to look down on the peopled earth, and he may have been, for there was the earth, the harbor with the red and white houses, the dark bush-necklaced hills rising steeply from the turquoise waters. His heart, set to be pulled anywhere, it was so much a spring of longing, and desire, surged towards the familiar land and hills, the gray splintered wharf buildings, the drab downtown streets with their towering biscuit-colored wooden buildings and the black entangled scorings of telephone and electric wires—progress darning the gulf left by someone's failure to plan a city.

It was the sight of the wires that moved Colin, imprison-ing rather than freeing his view, allowing him to keep his visions momentarily close to him like an overcoat against the coming storm, to prevent perhaps the invasion of the fabled white bird that would strip him of his overcoat and fly with it into the sky leaving him unprotected. He folded his arms across his chest as in the pictures he'd seen of Napoleon, and then he closed his eyes, surveying his own battlefield, in-credulous that so much should have happened to him with his consent, that he should be separated from May and the chil-dren, that separating himself from them he had cut his, not their, moorings, so to speak, and it was he who was adrift and defeated. He had known a man who left his wife after a week of marriage because he felt he was going mad with the con-stant thought of her, the way she stalked in his heart like a creature of prey. He remembered his advice to this acquaint-ance—Bill Hench—that everything would settle down, that he'd soon be back to normal. Play it cool, he had said. And he'd tried to tell this to himself after Lorna's calm statement in the hotel that they had "lost interest" in each other. He felt as if he had lost the sight of one eye—as he had, for his love was blind, and the eye that had looked and still looked on Lorna Kimberley saw nothing but his own dream images.

He knew that he would not recover. Yet Bill Hench had recovered and others and others, but there were those unfor-tunate wrecks who never did—for instance his grandfather when Grandma died, rushing off to London after all those years to try to find his lost love, and then not finding her but breaking his leg and coming home like a wounded hero and taking up with an old whore. Colin had wondered about Peggy Warren, that his grandfather should have been so fascinated by her that he risked his label "dirty old man." He understood now; he knew the craze; the recklessness, the overturning of all so-called respectability in the storm of love, just as the tables and crockery had risked overturning in the Tasman storm, while the conventional meal, the dull daily nibble could not be taken in the midst of such a storm. Lovers do feed on air; on sea and sky; on nothing; the peril is that if their love died they, like the woman in the nursery rhyme, "Whatever Miss T. eats turns into Miss T.," may become, man and woman, nothing. The peril is in the poverty, in the annihilation that follows the poverty.

And so Colin refused still to believe that Lorna's love for him had died. He decided that as soon as the ship berthed he could take the ferry and the train to Waihuna and call on Lorna at her home. He reminded himself that he had panicked stupidly. It was not as if their love, his love—the morning wind was cold with reality between his eyes and his heart—were anything unusual, it was merely a need that demanded satisfaction, a habit that could not be put aside, a habit of seeing, of being warmed, of touching, of discovering the topsyturvy life cycle of happiness that allowed blossoms to be picked before the seeds were noticed or fruit eaten where there had been no revealed blossom; of uncovering and recovering in no fixed pattern layers of darkness and mystery.

He disembarked from the ship and at half-past three that afternoon he found or lost himself in the long long Waihuna street where Lorna lived. The street was like a nightmare with its seemingly hundreds of houses, all alike, all with holly, olearia, or privet hedges, flower gardens blooming in spectacular display, each garden with its particular flower of late summer and its first flush of autumn berries—cotoneaster, rowan, rata, and the passion fruit vines with their plump yellow fruit encircling the trellis gates or sprawling across the latticework of the verandas. No home in the street had a "view." There was nothing to look up to or over or at except the clouds in the sky, the high white-and-blue sky of the land of the plains; and the other houses in the street. Arrived in the street, one had the dreadful sensation of final arrival as if there were nowhere to go from here, here was finality where future events could happen as there was no "beyond." The houses, the gardens, the few people and the vehicles in the street acquired suddenly the defenselessness of being assigned the containment of history.

Colin stopped outside Number 361, Kimberley's house. Although the house was barely halfway along the street the number gave added finality, an end-of-year reckoning where the events of the past year could be added and blotted out or carried forward, all in *now*, as yesterday and tomorrow seemed to merge in the shelter of *now*, like drops of water or digits running irresistably together.

Number 361 was a small house with two front bay windows, with the lace curtains tied back with bows to display the ornaments on the windowsill of one room and a vase of flowers and two plaster cats gazing out at the gladioli in the garden (evidently gladiola was the Kimberley flower) two rows of tall furled blooms in delicate shades of pink, rose, pale and deep gold bordering the path to the front door which had a brass knocker in the shape of a lion, as well as a modern electric doorbell. The front door was glass, with upper panels of frosted starred glass and side panels of the rich deep-blue glass, the color of the old-fashioned bottles of castor oil and milk of magnesia that mothers spooned to their children in sickness.

Colin stood as if entranced gazing at the house, absorbing the detail, the carved steeple on the deeply pitched red corrugated iron roof, the cream-painted wooden walls with some of the weatherboards beneath the two bay windows weather-warped, the paint curling away, and between board and overlapping board the homes of various insects in a kind of Insect Street—milk-white woven cocoons, spiderwebs, fly bodies stuck to the paint, web entrances leading to lairs between the boards—Colin knew it all so well, for as an only

183

child he had played for hours at home beside the wall of the house with the weatherboards close and familiar like the streets of a known city, where the beetles promenaded, the spiders crept or darted out like muggers to seize and kidnap their prey, war was declared, there were processions and disasters that could be caused by the insects themselves or by Colin, when with one movement of his powerful human hand he demolished the buildings and inhabitants of Insect Street.

He looked up at the roof of the house. He saw again the spouting and the downpipe. Spouting. Downpipe. Magical words came to him. Pitch, cornice. The roof needs pointing. He absorbed the details of roof, walls, the dressing table of the other bay-windowed room which he supposed to be a bedroom, that of Lorna's parents, perhaps, and though he could not see it immediately he imagined the adjacent room at the back to be Lorna's; he could see the tiny opaque window of the lavatory and bathroom between the two. Then summoning his courage he opened the gate of Number 361, walked up the path noting without effort his exact number of steps, and rang the doorbell. It echoed shrilly inside, stirring and stinging rather than striking the silence. He pressed the bell again. Silence. No door opening or shutting. No footsteps. They're not at home, he told himself, finding this impossible to believe. He was finding unbelievable even the simplest normally credible circumstances as if his belief, like an artery, had suddenly narrowed and clogged with the old age of love. He waited. Still no response from within. He felt that if no one was at home then all must be dead, murdered in their beds without having had time to defend themselves. He rang the front doorbell again. The front door of the neighboring house opened and a woman came out.

"They're away for the day," she said, and went inside again and shut the door. Colin scarcely had time to observe her. She had not even asked if it were the Kimberleys he was visiting. He might have been calling on—oh, Smiths, Andersons, Wallaces—anybody, and mistaken the house. Why did the woman not ask him, to make sure, why had she taken it for granted that he was visiting the Kimberleys? Away for the day. The desertion was impossible to believe or bear. He would phone them, he decided. He would collect his gear from the railway station, find a place to stay, read the *Star* to look for a job, and phone the Kimberleys.

He collected his gear, found a place for the night, read the *Star*, chose a likely job, a clerk in an accountant's office —Solomon, Garstang and Treat—then having in this way reinforced his capacity for action he phoned the Kimberleys.

"Hello."

"Is that the Kimberleys?"

"Who's speaking?"

He was suddenly shy, seized with terror.

"Oh, a friend of Lorna's. Is Lorna at home?"

"No, she's out."

"Do you know when she'll be back?"

"I'm sorry, no."

He heard an exchange of conversation in the background. Lorna's parents trying to decide when she would be home. If she were at the pictures, Colin thought, they would have known. Or somewhere definite—a concert perhaps. She liked dancing. If she were at a dance they would not be likely to know when she would be home. That was it. She was out dancing the night away with some bloke and not a thought in her head for Colin Torrance.

"Is there a message for her?"

Colin spoke carefully to prevent his desolation from escaping into his voice. "No. No. I'll phone again."

He hung up, left the telephone booth that was downstairs in the hall of the hostel where he'd found a bed, and climbed to his second-floor room, a large room divided into four cubicles, each with headboard panels reaching to within

185

three feet of the high ceiling. Each cubicle was slightly larger than a cemetery plot, containing in place of a coffin, a single bed, chest of drawers, a bed table and a curtained wardrobe. The surrounding earth-colored walls were painted yellow near the ceiling as if to imitate the penetration of sunlight into the earth-room. Colin lay on his bed and looked up at the ceiling. First thing tomorrow, he said to himself, I'll see about a job. And then Lorna. He closed his eyes, and closing them was like opening all the doors and gates and lids and pocket flaps into loneliness and longing. The released loneliness came to him for company and stayed and stayed, and he did not try, that evening or any other day and evening, to drive it home or capture it and lock it away, for the doors into loneliness were unhinged, the gates broken, the lids mislaid, the pocket flaps torn with no woman to sew them.

He fell asleep, weighed down by his loneliness and he woke still heavy with the pressure of his desolating perma-nent attendants.

He did not get the job with Solomon, Garstang and Treat. They were suspicious of him, of his separation from his wife and family, of the circumstances of his leaving the accountant's office. Instead, he was hired as a kitchenman in a hotel with his bedroom in the attic. He found it attracted him because it was work he had done when he and Lorna were together. Even the commonplace tasks like peeling potatoes, slicing carrots, slopping around in a big apron and gumboots to put out the garbage were charged with a prom-ise of mystery and sadness of memory and dream, as if these were to be the tasks performed on the last day by the last man left alive on earth. Even the waitresses with their squabbling over tips and "stations" would belong among the inhabitants of the heaven and the hell.

Colin telephoned Lorna again. She was at home. Her voice, he noticed, had acquired overtones of an Australian twang, a comfortable lazy intonation like the swing of a hammock in the sun. There was tension between her words as she identified Colin.

"I told you, Colin, it's all over. It just happened that way. I promised Mum and Dad never to see you again. It's better that way."

He wanted to cry out, What was better, why was it better, who or what was "it" that its welfare should take precedence over their love.

"But it's up to you to make up your mind, Lorna."

"I've made up my mind. It's just one of those things, Colin. We had happy times, it was marvelous in Australia, the whole thing was really wonderful but it went away more or less suddenly, like a headache or something . . ."

"A headache!"

"You know."

"I don't know. It was your parents sent it away with that letter."

"I'm hanging up now. Goodbye."

"Wait."

She waited.

"Have you got another boyfriend? Is that it?"

She laughed nervously. "I'm not exactly swearing off. No, there's no one else at the moment. It's just that you and I . . . it's over, Colin."

"You can't just go off and leave me . . ."

"You went off and left your wife and family didn't you? Just like that. Mum said . . ."

"To hell with what your mother said. I'm talking about us. I need you."

"Goodbye. I'm hanging up."

"Wait."

She did not wait. He heard the sound described as the line "gone dead" when she put down the receiver. He half decided to phone her again to make sure he had heard and interpreted her correctly. There may have been something she said that he did not hear. Perhaps in his excitement he had misheard what she did say. And what had she said? As he tried urgently to remember, his mind played tricks by suggesting possible alternatives to what he thought she had said, so confusing him that, to make sure, he dialed the Kimberley home once again and once again Lorna answered.

"Who's there?"

Her voice was sharply impatient. As if he were at her home knocking at the door and she was alone and feared he might force an entry. He tried to be casual. He laughed as he spoke.

"Me again, Lorna."

He spoke her name caressingly with the special tone that he knew she liked, that had often been a summons and an invitation to make love; and the now familiar fog of incredulousness shrouded his mind as he heard her reply, devoid of all tender feeling.

"You!"

She hung up. The deadness of the line communicated itself to him, numbing him. She couldn't mean it, of course. She did mean it. She couldn't just leave him. She had left him. He would wait for her to calm down and think things over and in a few days he would phone her again, just to make sure. Perhaps he might even call on her, surprise her, and when she answered the door and he was standing there all the old feelings would surge in her and they'd be in each other's arms again. That was how it would happen. He couldn't quite remember where it had happened, but books had it and films had it and if so-called real life didn't have it what hope was there in living at all?

And dreams had it.

That evening he resisted the temptation to phone or visit Lorna. To calm himself he decided to take a walk along the riverbank. The evening was cold with autumn mists rising from the water. The willows showed their first glimmer of gold. He sat on one of the seats under the willows overlooking the river. There were few people about. The circulation in the heart of the city had slowed down following the rush of concerts and theatres. Colin, tired and depressed, still felt the steamy air of the hotel kitchen while the sound of the vegetable machines ground in his ears, alternating with Lorna's voice saying, "I told you, Colin, it's all over, it's just one of those things, we had happy times, it was wonderful." He half-closed his eyes and peered at the water and the trees and the reflections of the city lights. It was a slow-moving stream. In summer you could hire a boat and row upstream to the source or downstream to the estuary by the harbor beach. In spring the banks were lined with daffodils which people came to admire and to photograph as a yearly spectacle, with the photographs appearing in magazines and tourists brochures labeled a scene from one of the English cities of New Zealand. The flatness of the city depressed Colin. Walking in it was like walking in a dream with the sense of getting nowhere, seeing beyond nothing, although beyond the city and the plains, against the too distant sky were the snow-covered Alps and in winter the wind blowing from the Alps first filled its mouth with snow and arriving in the long desolate streets of the city, spat out the snow not caring who was hurt or chilled. It was a city encircled on three sides by sheep who kept their dreams, if they had any, to themselves, and on the fourth side by the sea's intruding clamor.

A man passed Colin, walking his dog. A young couple passed. Colin began to doubt if they were real. He would have liked to put out his hand to touch them. He could feel from time to time the clinging of his children around his neck, the small child's foot placed firmly, perfectly upon the palm of his hand; with astonishment and disbelief he remembered May, her skin like the feel of nylon, the clinging drops of water when she bathed, the dew-sweat in the night of their loving. Detached, he felt and watched these sensations come and go.

But when he thought of Lorna Kimberley he was seized and held by a force like a hurricane that condemned him to play the part of its eye, while it moved along the path of its destruction. He half-dozed, wanting to escape. He woke abruptly. He noticed a young woman sitting on the next seat about twenty yards away. She had not been there when he arrived. He turned to observe her though even before he did so he knew without being told that the young woman was Lorna Kimberley. She wore a blue coat, and a small blue hat over her long blonde wavy hair. She has a new hairdo, Colin thought jealously. She had worn her hair braided and curled about her head and pinned with a dark-grained wooden comb. Now it fell free, making her appear even younger than nineteen. Her hair was that of a wraith or mermaid, not of a clerk in an accountancy office. I wonder why she's here, Colin thought, his heart setting up a staccato beating until he began to feel as if he were suffocating. He got up and walked towards her and she turned and, seeing him, she smiled, Lorna's warm inviting smile, and when she spoke her voice was gentle.

"Colin. I was hoping I'd find you here."

Colin looked wonderingly at her. Her hair had a gold mist about it like the mist of the willow trees.

"How did you know I'd be here, in this exact spot?" he asked.

She smiled again. Her violet-colored eyes widened and stared at him and her lips caught the smile of her eyes. Her face was paler than he had ever seen it.

He sat beside her and together they stared at the water.

"I like to look at water moving," she said. "Don't you?"

He put his arm around her and took her hand.

"Yes, I like to see water flowing."

She was so quiet, so still. She turned to look at him.

"Have you heard from your wife and children, Colin?"

He spoke in a grave voice.

"They died," he said. "It was some months ago. I never knew. They are all dead now."

She touched his cheek and began to stroke it.

"Oh Colin. You loved them didn't you?"

"Yes."

They stared again into the water. A scatter of early willow leaves, narrow as exclamation marks, golden, floated by, twirling on the surface.

"You didn't mean what you said on the telephone, did you?" Colin asked.

She spoke quickly.

"Of course not. I've never stopped loving you, Colin. I'm sorry about your wife and family, but it's us now isn't it, we'll be together. Now. Now."

He took her gently by the shoulders and turned her face to him. They stared at each other, their feelings and their gaze flowing in and out, swimming eye into eye and back and forth, longings and thoughts propelled by desire in an element of love as easily as little fish swimming in water or the agile willow leaves navigating the current. He bent to kiss her, looking deep into her still-open eyes and a cloud of confusion came over him and he felt the blood draining from his face. He became aware that he was leaning over the water, staring at the floating willow leaves. His flesh felt as if it were coated with ice. He shook his head, and was awake, yet still in a dream he got up from his seat and walked slowly back to the hotel, climbed to his attic room and lay on his bed and slept without dreaming or with dreams too deep to remember.

The next day he moved slowly, dazedly. He peeled the potatoes and sliced carrots and cleaned the kitchen and pantry floors and emptied the slops and stood by to help with the dishing up of the meal orders, with an air of studied patience that caused the staff to agree when he had gone off duty that the new chap was a "good sort." A bit moody but a good sort.

191

Quiet, would probably keep himself to himself but would pitch in to help others, maybe exchange time with the cleaner or the third cook if they wanted to go to the races. Quiet, moody, a bit sickly looking around the eyes but hadn't someone said his wife and children had been killed in a car crash two years ago? Or last Christmas. Or last Easter. And that would make anyone look sickly. Someone said.

That evening Colin walked up and down the street where Lorna lived. He stopped outside her home, on the other side of the road, feasting on the house and its details, imagining what was happening behind the lighted rooms with the drawn blinds. He saw a light on on in one of the back rooms. That's her bedroom, he told himself. Then a light shone through the small window of the lavatory. He imagined her there.

Each night now he came to the house to watch, and once he strode up to the house, opened the gate, walked up the path and rang the bell. When he heard footsteps he had the impulse, like a small boy doing mischief, to run away and hide but it was too late.

The door was opened by a woman—he supposed it was Lorna's mother.

"Is Lorna at home?"

She stared at him a moment. Then she said,

"No. She's out."

There was a pause.

"Are you that chap Torrance? Because if you are I'll ask you to keep away from our daughter. If you bother her again we'll call the police." She shut the door in his face.

The injustice of it infuriated Colin. He wanted to rush into the house and strangle the woman at once. Then a terrible sensation of loneliness came over him and he saw his dream of the other night, that had kept him warm, receding, as he realized that even his imaginings had cheated him. For a while following the dream he had been bathed in sweet warmth as a child is for the first few moments after it wets the bed, or a parent may be when he is holding his infant and feels the surprise and intimate warmth of sudden wetness. Now he shivered though the night was not cold. There was cold enough within him to freeze his flesh and his skin and clothes and the breath coming out of his mouth and all thoughts and all feelings coming out of his mind and heart.

He walked back to the hotel. He found a letter from May's lawyer. He lay on his back and closed his eyes and his constant attendants cared for him, administering once again the subtly served varieties of despair.

On the day he collected his second pay check Colin went to the gunsmith's in Talbot street and bought a rifle and a supply of ammunition, telling the gunsmith that he was preparing for the duck-shooting season.

"Pigs or deer?" one of the hotel staff asked, seeing the rifle.

"Pigs," Colin said.

"You're right," said the third cook with the presumption of one who habitually completed other people's sentences in conversation.

"You're right, there's no comparison. Not if you have a good sticking dog."

Colin cleaned and oiled the rifle and put it in its case under his bed. Then he lay on the bed and thought about what he would do. And every night for the next week after he had first walked up and down the street where Lorna lived, or taken the bus past there, for he no longer dared to watch the house openly, he returned to the hotel and lay on his bed and imagined that he took his rifle, walked to the house, knocked on the door, and when Lorna came to the door he shot her. Or her mother came to the door and he shot her and went to Lorna's room and he and Lorna lay on the bed and made love and then he shot Lorna and shot himself. Or her father tried to prevent him and he shot him too. All in the small wooden house with the red roof; and the carved steeple like a weatherbeaten chair leg stuck up there; and the latticed veranda with the passion-fruit vine clinging to the lattice and the big bruised yellow black-seeded fruit hanging from the trellis; and the front door with its rich blue glass like the old-fashioned bottles of castor oil and milk of magnesia that mothers spooned to their children in sickness; and the warped weatherboards in front where the insects lived their separate vulnerable lives down Insect Street; and the bay-windowed front room with the two plaster cats on the window sill; and the front doorsteps and the front path and the furled gladioli with the blossoms opened at the top of the stalk and the younger blooms at the foot of the stem with their petals reticent against the heart of the flower, the color therefore deeper, like the sunset sky close to the sun.

The house, the garden, and what he observed of them were dear to him now. He saw the imagined rooms, the paths, the flowers, the back garden with the Kimberley washing on the line and the rows of vegetables—spinach, cabbage, silver beet, and the worked-out earth where the vegetables had been dug and eaten. He saw these now in his mind as frequently as he saw the image of Lorna. Her parents, too. They rose vividly before him. And the neighbor who years and years ago had said, "They're away for the day. They're away for the day." Where had they been that day? He still wondered. He thought, If only they had been at home that day, that first day, none of his sufferings would have been so intense. But they had been away, and the doorbell sounded unanswered through the lonely house with the blue-glassed panes in the side of the front door, the dark blue like blue velvet, a sacred untouchable blue.

And now his former life was remote from him. What had he to do with a wife and family, the local cricket team, the Rate-Payers' Association, Accountancy? All the past properties of his life were as remote to him as moon furniture, his wife and children as moon people who even existed in another atmosphere where the thoughts they might have thought, the feelings they might have felt, the food eaten, the dreams dreamed were so far removed from him as to be extraplanetary.

Each day he performed his duties in the hotel kitchen, being carried here and there, like a piece of flotsam on the rising and ebbing tides that were controlled not by the moon but by the number of race meetings and conferences in the district. He washed and peeled the potatoes, sliced the carrots, washed the cabbage and the silver beets and the silken artichokes with the spiked hearts, unbedded the frozen peas, thumbed out the broad beans from their long narrow fur-lined retreat, scrubbed the parsnips, cut up the rhubarb; with his mind on his work and on his desire, on the intensity of his desire to possess Lorna. The light of what reason remained in him was beginning to illuminate the idea that nothing is truly possessed that has life or the promise of life.

It was one warm early March evening of Indian summer that he took his rifle and went to Number 361 and rang the doorbell and when Mrs. Kimberley answered the door he shot her dead and when Mr. Kimberley, hearing the shot and seeing what had happened, ran to the telephone he shot him too, dead, and then he went to Lorna's bedroom and she was in bed there and suddenly his life became incredible no longer because what he had dreamed had happened, Lorna was there, lying in bed asleep, but she was awake now and preparing to scream. He did not try to make love to her. He aimed the rifle at her and shot her and she fell back on the pillow dead, and he lay down beside her, still holding the rifle, and he kissed her, and there was blood all over her face. He aimed the rifle, then, at his own head and pulled the trigger.

And there were no witnesses. And when the bodies were discovered the newspapers carried a photograph of the house, of the "scene," an ordinary wooden house with weatherboards that needed painting, a veranda with a passion-fruit vine, a wooden steeple, front bay windows with lace curtains, a garden path and gladioli; but it was not the house Colin had seen, and no one, looking at the photograph could have known about the Insect Street, the young and old gladioli and their sunset colors or that two panes of glass on each side of the front door were blue glass, the dark rich blue of old-fashioned bottles of castor oil and milk of magnesia that mothers spooned to their children in sickness.

26

Dear First Dad, it is Christmas, family-time. Pain
and Santa, white and red are In,
getting down to it, distributing upon branches of green pine
the gifts guaranteed to break, stain, fit, keep warm,
beautify, startle, harm, amuse. The favor, your favor is
we never grew out of Christmas: hard bright gold blue
sea and sky Christmas; a swim and sunburn
snowcarols out of tune where the gold-brown cicadas
flake the sky, green crickets swarm
in the grass
caroling with their arse as men and women are doing
on the lupined beach. Our Christmas was
enjoy, swim, eat, sleep, wake to grief of destruction.
What was it? We had it. It is gone. Tears then,
tears, and a handkerchief for us and Uncle Leonard to fold
    the grief in
The annual lesson
of trying to throw a saltstorm of tears to catch time
or spreading a sticky mess like cake icing, pretend it is bird
    lime.

Growing up we grew in
like unhealthy finger and toenails;
you cut us to the quick

which was wrong, confusing the necessary
circle with the necessary straight line.

Hands touch. Hands and their fingers cling.
Feet stand to give the head
headroom an unacceptably lonely
distance from the sky. Clouds, head in.

Let the soldiers die, father, and the pears blossom and fruit
green and russet; decay is brown
like the earth and the singing cicadas and an old man's or
woman's
sparse pubic hair and skin
decay-spotted like the fallen pears.

Breathe in the gas mask, father,
or the poisonous air like a scorpion
stings your lung.

27

In Pearl's garden that summer the gladioli were a picture, everyone said so. Sunset-flushed, swanlike smoothness
of petal, though they did not last here, in the north, as summer flowers lasted down south, they bloomed feverishly and
died suddenly but there were always more flowers to take
over the display. That summer Pearl redecorated the house,
rearranged the furniture to include one or two pieces sent to
her by the lawyer from the family home; she stored the others
in the cellar with two old suitcases belonging to Henry who
insisted on keeping them "on hand" for the overseas trip
they would make—he said "they" but he might have meant
"he"—some day. He meant when Pearl died. He did not
desire her death so much as to want to hasten it; he needed
her tyranny and hugeness and her ability to repair what was
broken. Her passion for doing and making, for controlling

things and people, had been struck a blow in the early days of Colin's marriage when after knitting layettes for the children, advising May on their birth and upbringing, preparing her own plan for the redecoration of their kitchen from its present "ugly shade" to one with more harmony and illusion of space, she was told that her help was not wanted, that May preferred her children and their clothes and manners and her kitchen to stay or be changed according to her own plan and not that of Grandmother Torrance.

"All the toys returned!" Pearl exclaimed the Christmas before Colin went to Australia. "All that trouble and money I took to make or buy those toys and I find them on my doorstep. What haven't I done for Colin and May and the children? And this is all the thanks I get!"

Henry, accounting, said nothing.

The following Christmas when Pearl heard (by the Christmas-card holly vine) that Colin had left May and the children, she was divided in her feeling between incredulity that Colin who had been given "everything an only son could have" should be so irresponsible, and her pleasant anticipation of the sympathy and help she could offer the deserted family.

"I feel for them," she said. "They'll not return the presents this Christmas. They'll have to eat humble pie. And if I offer to redecorate the house she can't possible refuse."

May returned the presents. She refused to accept Pearl's plans for redecoration. She wrote (in her Christmas card):

"Dear mother, Thank you very much for the offer. But it's our home and we want to redecorate in our own way. And the children do not want or need all those presents. Please don't send them again, mother, and don't mind my saying this. You are far too generous. Yes, it is true about Colin. It is, as you say, unlike him as he has been a good husband and father. I'm managing, thank you. You really are too generous, you try to do too much for other people. Thank you for

198

the things from the Livingstone home. Your daughter-in-law
May."

Pearl read the letter.

"Too generous. Of course I'm too generous, I'm generous to a fault and everyone says so but it's my nature to do
things for people. I'm a busy woman, I like to be busy."

She wondered why her busyness did nothing to reduce
her bulk as the books on metabolism and diet had promised.
My dancing days are over, she would say to herself, with a
kind of settled sadness in knowing that her dancing days had
never been, that what had never been could yet end and leave
her in a state of nostalgia. There was nothing she would not
have done for Colin and his family or for Henry. She would
have liked to see her grandchildren dance ballet, with her
paying for and supervising their dancing. Why did they
refuse her gifts, her offers of help? She was comforted by the
thought that at least the Society for the Protection of Battered Children were pleased to have her help with their correspondence and casework, although they had relieved her of
the duties of visiting the homes and interviewing the parents
and children. She had wanted to love and care for the Battered Children; she wondered why the society no longer
needed her for the interviews when they were so short of
helpers.

Besides, she had knitted her fingers to the bone for
Colin's children—jerseys, suits, caps, mittens, bootees, sing-
lets. She had always done her utmost for those in her care.

Yet, a gradually acquired, slow monotone in her voice
told of hopeless loss. When birthdays and Christmas came
round again she would have to resist the temptation to go to
the toy shop, she would have to accept only the ritual communication by card and handkerchief.

The news came in autumn. When Pearl heard it from
Henry who had been given it by the local police constable she

fainted. Her faint was momentary. Henry helped her to the newly covered sofa where she lay with her eyes closed making small groaning and whimpering sounds; big, on her back, as if she were giving birth or making love.

Henry swallowed a brandy.

"My god, a swipe in the face, that's it," he said. "A swipe in the face. The whole family, the whole family, Pearl. He was sweet on the daughter."

Pearl opened her eyes.

"I don't know what you're trying to tell me," she said, "but if it's murder he had provocation, that Kimberley woman lured him away from his family, led him on, led him a dance ... dance ... dance"—her voice became shrill—"a dance to Australia and back."

She closed her eyes again. Henry put his arm around her shoulders; it was like trying to encircle a mountain, a soft mountain. Pearl was even bigger than the dream.

"I have to identify his body. Tomorrow morning."

Pearl opened her eyes and was awake.

"I'm coming too."

"It's not for a woman."

"He's my son, I'm coming to see him and bring him back home to give him a decent burial."

"Yes, we'll do that," Henry said. "But they have to keep the body in the meantime."

"They? Who's they?"

"The law."

"But he's my son."

Henry swallowed another sip of brandy.

"Apparently if someone does what Colin did, he belongs to the state ... or something. They take possession of the body."

"But we want him home."

"I suppose we'll get him eventually. I don't know."

Pearl gave a roar of laughter.

"Ha, ha, ha, they'll divide his body, I suppose, distribute it to anyone who wants a share, for the sake of justice."

Then her voice quiet, her eyes wondering and the tears falling she asked, "Is it Colin, our Colin? Isn't there some mistake?"

"May's Colin," Henry said harshly. "May's had a shock, but she will claim the body, she's his wife. He belongs officially to her."

Pearl got up suddenly from the sofa.

"I'm going with you tomorrow."

Then with large deliberate movements, almost as if nothing had happened, she began to unpack her day's shopping—giant packets of detergent, cornflakes, dishwashing fluid, insecticide, new shoes for Henry (chosen by Pearl), a bolt of curtain material, new towel rails for the bathroom.

"They'll be against him," she said, gripping a large packet of Moonwash. Her sudden energy contrasted with Henry's sudden exhaustion, as if the two had exchanged roles.

"There are no witnesses," Henry said quietly.

"All the same, they'll tell lies about him and because there are no witnesses no one can contradict them, they'll besmirch his name.

"The sink's leaking," she said in a monotone as she opened the cupboard under the sink and stowed away the detergent. "I know the plumber didn't fix it properly."

"There's nothing we can do to help him now."

"I'll ring him or the Waterboard."

"We might have been able to help him if he'd come to us."

"It's her fault. He was crazy about her and she lured him on. Dad was the same. Lured on. And tomorrow it will be in the papers, splashed up and down the country. We won't be able to show our faces in the street. And they'll be against him, everyone, you see. What went wrong? He was a clever good boy, respectable, never a show of anger. He should never have married. Think of the kids, their father a murderer. They should never have sent back the toys I bought and the clothes I knitted specially for them. I should think that Kimberley girl deserved everything she got. Her parents too. They probably connived. Colin would never hurt a fly.

"Splashed up and down the country," she repeated, putting away the cornflakes.

"Have you got a clean shirt for tomorrow? Clean socks? And wear your best suit, your dark one, and a black tie, and shave off those sideburns you look like an undertaker."

She started to cry. She shut the kitchen cupboard on the last of the groceries and came to where Henry was sitting, still with his glass of brandy, in the kitchenette.

"He grew away from us didn't he? We grew away, Naomi and I, from our parents. I'm glad Mum and Dad are dead. Did you know I had a Christmas card from Naomi posted months ago by seamail. She hasn't much longer to live. She's in a recovery unit."

"Sounds hopeful."

"No, it's only a name. She's a mere shell."

Henry shuddered. From his seat on the bench he could not see out of the kitchen window. Pearl blocked his view.

"Yes I'm glad Mum and Dad are dead, and Uncle Leonard, and there's nothing left for Naomi except to die, but they might have stayed alive to share this, it comes full on us, doesn't it?"

She sat on the sofa again and began to cry remembering as she did so with a feeling of unreality the last two occasions when she had cried—the film of the dog and the thought of her father's remarriage; pity and anger; but this was loss, stronger than loss, theft, as if a child of hers had been born dead and then been stolen. They wanted Colin's body. They thought they had a right to his body. The law thought so. His wife thought so. They were the law and he was the murderer.

They were justice and he was the criminal. And they wouldn't
let his dead body go, oh no, they would keep it until the last
possible moment as if it might up and speak and they wanted
to have it in secret, to silence it in case it began to tell the
truth, for the truth was always with those who told it and
against those to whom it was told; the truth was rightness,
Colin's rightness; but only the police would hear it from the
dead, and hush it up.

The next morning even before Pearl and Henry left for
Waihuna by the early plane they saw the morning paper, the
headlines on the front page, the photograph of the house
along a row of houses in a long, long street, with arrows
pointing to the front door.

"Let's not read it," Henry said.

They left for the airport and were attacked on the way
and at the newsstand by the headlines "Murder," "Quiet Man
Murders for Love," "Murder and Suicide," "Accountant,
Cricketer, Rate-payer Murders."

"I didn't know Colin was so many people," Pearl
thought, as she saw the divisions the reporters made from
their privileged view of the circumference of Colin's person-
ality, as they focused upon the dead, the dead center that was
her dead son.

They identified Colin. May identified him. Warm in triple
identification he lay dead but alive, named in memory. May,
sleepwalking, was inaccessible.

"I don't want him. You can keep him."

"You can have him when we've finished with him," the
police said. "After the inquest."

"I'll say it was self-defense all the way," Pearl said.

"Father, husband, rate-payer, cricketer, accountant," the
evening newspapers repeated.

"Quiet Accountant, Cheerful," the weekly newspaper,
the scandal sheet, *Tell* said, with subheading "Torrance on
the Path of Murder and Suicide."

Cheerful.

Wife and three children.

Fatal infatuation.

Buys Rifle.

Number 361.

There was a photograph collected from the newspaper's cricket records of a slim fair-haired young man in cream cricket flannels and a knitted cable-stitched pullover with a contrasting border around the V-neck. Another photograph of Number 361 with arrows of the bedroom where he and Lorna had been discovered; but the photograph revealed only its dutiful negative and illuminated positive and a blurred hint of confusion where the light intruded.

Relatives who traveled up from the paper-milling town down south to identify the Kimberley bodies were also given headlines and histories, quoted with paragraph headings of "Fatal Infatuation." Torrance seduced Lorna Kimberley while she worked in his office, they said. She left the office and fled to Australia. He followed her. She returned home after her parents pleaded with her. He followed her home to Waihuna where he "hung around" making a nuisance of himself, the relatives said. He rang the doorbell at all hours of the day and night and annoyed them by phoning at all hours. One of the neighbors described how he used to "watch the house" standing opposite it a short way along the street, no doubt so as not to arouse suspicion, sometimes watching all night, and you don't keep watch like that unless you plan to do harm, do you? Obviously he had already made up his mind to murder. I watched over Colin all night when he had scarlet fever, Pearl remembered. And I wrung out a flannel in cold water and wiped his face and forehead with it to get down the fever.

Pearl and Henry were asked, "What was the story. What was behind it all. What kind of child was he? Had he shown any signs? Was there a family history? Could they explain his fatal infatuation, his final 'brainstorm?' "

But there was no story to be told, and because there was none there were many created, bringing glances, words, feelings in the watching eyes, with Pearl sensing that she, more than Henry, was receiving a larger share of the blame if only because her bulk was larger. And it was the kind of disaster that, happening, put its hand at once over the mouth of the murdered and the murderer; and it was a human disaster striking like lightning or tornado with the victims a cluster of people instead of trees growing together in family or neighboring soil, and the event remembered afterwards, as storms are remembered, as part of a season of the year, a winter, with death, violent death a variation of the weather that composed the normal climate.

28

And they wouldn't let his dead body go
the windows are shut against me
I looked into them
the blind was drawn at once
it was a brown blind
the house had a pale face
the house said
and the windows with their drawn blinds confirmed the say-
    ing
there is an invitation no longer
Go away, go away
I am not at home to you.

Change said let nothing stay or be
but become; and now you ask me, *me*
what do I know of distance
when every time I look at the windows
I am turned away
to walk if I cherish what was

more than what is and will be
a thousand miles through time to yesterday.

Cold face cold as on a tomb.
No lights within. Why, I remember them
shining at all hours, my welcome.
Blinds down, door shut. Frown. Goodbye
stranger, strange son, never try
again to come in
though coming out of me you
cried, once, the morning away.

29

The Recovery Unit, late winter. A dark morning of one
of the earliest spring rains when the dead leaves clinging to
the trees are at last washed to the earth and the last ripe pine
needles drift from the two pine trees at the gate, and the
spears of the crocuses thrust through the two round flower
beds on the front lawn, and the violet leaves down by the
goldfish pond, grown almost overnight, flop glossily green
like Greta Garbo hats. Match-heads—the grape hyacinths—
have struck their clusters of blue flame; and when the rain
falls around the trees it forms a lingering cloud of pale-green
light shed, on a sunless morning, by multitudes of wet green
leaf buds.

"The Recovery Unit," the patients say, choosing their
season, "is best in spring."

The winter-thrashed grass uncurls from its low crouching under the foot and whip of many storms. The steadily
falling rain begins slowly to open the stone-hard frost-bound
earth. A walk on the lawn, for those able to walk, is a treading
of springing turf as if it were air. The patients look out of the
window of Culin Hall and taste the newly remembered plea-
sures of sunlight and full daylight and color. The walls of

their buildings are painted autumnal brown. The winter dream outside always corresponds so closely to the world of sickness within that both have been taken—mistaken—for eternal truth; people fastened like dead leaves to a blossomless tree, the incomplete bodies, the lost limbs, the icy paralysis, the slow reptilean or swift lush cancer growths nourished and sheltered by the old house as a forest accomodates its fungi; the amputation of limbs seeming as natural as the loss of limbs from the trees, the institutional withering of mind and body accepted as is the withering from time to time of healthy trees in a forest or orchard. With the first signs of spring, of branches believed dead, suddenly necklaced with green growth, the accepted truth is denied, the miracle dream—"stones have been known to move and trees to speak"—begins again to bud in the hearts of the patients of the Recovery Unit.

And now Miriam, outgrowing the pylon and the kneeless tiral leg has her new permanent leg which she can bend, stride, walk, dance with should she choose to dance. Were it an old fashioned wooden leg it might break out in leaf to assert its life.

Miriam plays the violin again. Soon she will leave the Recovery Unit to join the city orchestra and to give violin lessons. She is happy. What more does she need?

In the dream, in the dream.

Peter also is well enough to leave the Recovery Unit. His one lung functions so well that thoracic surgeons are beginning to question the need for two lungs. Peter has been offered work as a private tutor. He is happy. What more does he need?

In the dream, in the dream.

Wombless Bertha has reconciled herself to her loss. Who needs a womb, anyway? It's only a status symbol, no part of the body is indispensable.

In the dream, in the dream.

And Mrs. Dockett smiles, smiles, smiles her example of sweetness and courage.

One day the doctor arrives later than usual at the Recovery Unit. He has an air of efficiency and purpose. All morning he has been picking over lymph glands trying to decide which are edible and which are so diseased they must be thrown in the slop bucket; and which will make fertile gardens for growing the new crop of spring viruses. He smiles at the patients grouped in their wheelchairs outside the dining room, waiting to be wheeled wherever they wish to go, and having no one, as usual, willing to wheel them.

"Be of good cheer," he says, sounding strangely archaic. For whatever the dream offers the reality is one of misery; the one-limbed, no-limbed, one-lunged, wombless, no-eyed, not to speak of those with inner deformities, are refusing to smile, smile, smile, accept, adapt, at least not under the persuasion of the reasoning that the seeing and the blind, the lunged and the lungless, the wombed and the wombless will be as they have been, that all will be well, that the crooked places will be made plain instead of being made acceptably, recognizably crooked; and the valleys exalted—rather is it not debased—from their valleyness; that being blind is simply not seeing, that courage is simply not cowardice.

Kindness itself.

Happiness itself.

Today the doctor works harder than usual. By suppertime when the visitors again queue in the hall waiting for the patients to finish their meal, the doctor has left by the back door while within the surgery a blind woman sees through Miriam's eyes, Bertha, the wombless, has acquired Miriam's womb, Peter has one of her lungs, while Miriam herself, dead of course, still has the best chance of surviving by the record she has made of Beethoven's violin concerto which all the renewed whole shining impure recovered people will agree is "pure Miriam."

Yet their assertion will be made only because they have been witness to Miriam's existence. The concertgoers and music lovers who have never known her will say, when they listen to the record of the playing, that the music is "pure Beethoven." Who will speak of the transplantation of the spirit? Which crooked place has been made plain, which valley has been exalted? Who has recovered the city by night-

30

Dear First Dad, I shan't write much more.
I am sick.
The house is empty.
All is a dream at Christmas time.
Blood, woods, the War,
the snow falling or fallen,
grandma will spin a white woolen shawl to cover me
grandma is the sky in a dark dress
with lace collar
cuffs of cloud
the shawl is my shroud.

The dream of dying is not dying itself.
The barrier is broken with death
pain walks the tightrope up and down, up and down,
the shawl is gray steel wool
splintering the skin where it is worn.
Look, there's a honeybee
with a basket of poisonous fruit under its arm.
No, it's grandma with apples and pears red and green
picked from the once-white wild orchard.

Death is the spell of minuteness
the microscopic last look
at the words between the lines between the words between
    the pages

of the going going gone book.
Hammer hammer down
at auction
the discriminating prejudiced earth that will always save
what it makes a move to save
because it is there, on fire deep within,
and may move a stone shoulder to shake off
childlike piggy-backing you and me and yesterday and to-
    morrow
clinging to ice and rock
human flesh arms tight around glacial neck
and it is we and they who strangle, who die
of volcano and earthquake shock.

Breathe in the gas mask, father,
or the poisonous air like a scorpion
stings your lung.

The crossword pain.
I have not solved it.
What are the clues?
Six feet down and three across?
A kind of moss? A sudden cry?
Dance dance dance
on the small square corner of your life
while over the full page glitters
the death-dealing news; you and I and we and they and they.
are recovered, father,
six feet down and three across.
A kind of moss, a sudden cry.

3.
Pear Blossom to
Feed the Nightmare

My name is Colin Monk. Because I believe that any group of human beings may demand to elect within itself the characters of folklore—the Idiot, the Wise Man, the Kind Man, the Cruel Man, Father Wizard, Mother Witch, all of whom have risen in the beginning from Everyman—I have decided to write my story without claim to be writing as the Wise Man or the Cruel Man, and I leave the Village Idiot to Milly Galbraith, but write to seize a place for myself and my memory in the folklore that will take root and grow from this terrible time. I'm not telling the story of my life. I'm only describing the part I have played in the enforcement of the Human Delineation Act, beginning from that day in January of this year when I received an urgent telegram from Government House Wellington commanding that I fly there immediately to take part in a conference to discuss the passing of a new law.

I remember the day, one of the warmest of a long warm summer that started as early as October though we'll not remember it that way, we will say we have never known a summer of such caprice, storms, and sudden rains, profusion of unseasonable flowers. We will say—those of us who live and are able to remember—whatever we need to say to share the burden of our memory. My wife Gloria had a friend who offered their house to us in January and part of February and we were about to go to enjoy ourselves at Queenstown when the telegram came. Gloria suggested going on ahead with the children, Robert and Sally, but I refused to let them go for I'd received this kind of telegram only during the recent war, after the devastation of the North Island, when my job was to make a statistical study of the wounded, the dead, and the survivors for a report that was never made public.

Even a loyal mathematician may confess that the quickened senses of the survivors could perform calculations with a computer's accuracy, writing into the solutions a complex tally that no computer had been programmed to make; and equations that would make a mathematician weep, unable to solve them: thousands of faceless wounded, equal rivers of tears plus deserts of tearless anguish. Fanciful? There were wars and wars and wars, and old men reliving them, and searching for them as they would search for long-lost loves.

I might have known that the Government was planning to rid itself and the nation of the burden of results got best by human calculation; to wipe out the sum and the need for it; to dissolve the problem as so many have been dis-solved —in a breath of white dust blown away by the southwest wind.

When I arrived in Wellington I was told of the Human Delineation Act, the date it would be announced and the date it would come into operation. I was sworn to secrecy, and with others chosen (we were the scientists) I took part in Sleep Periods where, I suspect, we were encouraged to think more kindly or tolerantly of the "plan," since at the first conference we all spoke against it, overcome with horror. Some went mad. The Director of Education killed himself, his wife, and his three children the day after the first Committee meeting. In Phase One which was personal and dealt with ways of breaking the news to our families to get their full cooperation, I was tempted to kill myself and my family before the news reached them.

I remember there was some comfort in the division of the process into Phases—the preparations for Classification; the actual Classification; and the Utopian vision of the effects, the blossoming of an economy based on primary products, where primary meant human animal. In those first days it seemed unbelievable that anyone could survive the revolution and remain sane and, therefore, human; the animals would outnumber the classified human beings; some might even disown their humanity; few would convert to it; while the factories, the mass graves out on the Taeri plains, the cages which varied from pits like ancient bear or snake pits to gilded bird-size cages in which would be folded, contoured to fit, the animal children—these made us believe we were dreaming, and we walked as in dreams where every movement is an effort; pursued, we could not escape; our clothes, lead-lined, wound like shrouds about our bodies, tightening their web and weight. It was a deliverance like a release from a death sentence when we began the first Sleep Period that was deep, dreamless, and lasted, we were told, for three days.

I remember waking refreshed, secure, happy. I sang a jingle, "Happy and Free with H.D.," as I showered. I flipped myself playfully with the towel. I thought, after our breakfast of scrambled eggs, coffee with cream (Wellington's new tourist hotel had been taken over for the conference) that I would go at once to my room and write to Gloria to tell her the news.

The preliminary work for the Human Delineation Act had been carried out by the Investigating Committee (whom we never met; some said they had been flown from America for the purpose) and only those whose families would be classified as human had been chosen for the Conference. I was now convinced that even without the preparatory Sleep Period, Gloria would share my enthusiasm, that she would agree to my arrangement for her and the children to spend six months with her sister and family in the neo-city, Palmerston North. We'd have a few weeks together, I hoped, before the news became public. There might be violence if it were known that Gloria and the children were the family of one of the men who would program the computer for Classification Day, though the tranquilizers in the water supply were expected to ward off this kind of violent protest. When I heard of the adulteration of the nation's water supply I was struck with horror that I could not express—the language that dealt daily with Giant Detergents and Packets and Free Offers and Monster Bargains simply collapsed under our weight of feeling. Yet, after waking from my Sleep Period, I had only a mild sense of indignation when I thought of the threat to the water supply; as if, say, my suit had not been returned from the cleaners, followed by a self-reassuring: the suit will keep; tomorrow, the day after, it wouldn't disappear, it would be there—how easily, you see, I took my vanished horror into cleaner country!

I wrote to Gloria. "The news is quite puzzling and disturbing," she replied. "No doubt you'll explain further when you get home. I'm dying to go up to Marian's to see the colors at Queenstown; you always said it was a disgrace that I've never seen them. Perhaps next year? Eagle Street is much the same. No one has yet bought that old property that belonged to the Livingstones, last century. There's still just a pear tree there, in a wilderness, hung with pears as a chandelier is hung with light . . . your absence makes me dream. And Milly Galbraith, that poor girl at the end of the street, comes by to talk to the children who find her great fun. But I really can't grasp the idea of this new legislation. Why be so secretive? You're awfully distinguished to be chosen to take part in it, aren't you? Do explain when you come home which you must do soon, soon."

The next few weeks were spent in detailed work on the program. I was surprised to learn that the Government had been planning this legislation for more than three years. The zoning, an extensive task even in a country as small as New Zealand, had been completed and the Classification Centers arranged for districts and boroughs, while the population had been numbered without any suspicion having been aroused. I found my assigned work absorbing: the coding of human and animal characteristics, borderline percentages, physical data, I.Q. results (thank heavens we have progressed from the old cumbersome I.Q. tests to the new one-question multiple-answer instant I.Q. gauge)—it was wonderful the way the numbers snapped these up as if they were usual diet, which they are. My senses expanded with pleasure. Working with numbers, I have a feeling of cleanness, and when my children recite the moon story, the distances, angles, temperatures, I despair that words will ever catch up again. How I admire the immunity of numbers, their untouchability, their inaccessibility; every moment they shine, newly bathed, concealing, never acknowledging the dark work they do.

And so I and my colleagues slaved all that summer while the population of Wellington and the rest of the country lazed on the beaches in the sun with the affairs of the nation and the world forgotten, buried in the sand by castles of summer that could not resist a spade's or wave's smack, yet, demolished, did not uncover the conference world and the new vision we labored for. I returned to Waipori. The news of the Act was made public. Gloria and Robert and Sally went north, flying secretly at night for we were thought to be in danger.

"But where shall we go?" Gloria cried. "We can't get out of the country. We're trapped. And you don't care."

"I do," I said. "I did."

I had not told her of the proposed heavier doses of tranquilizers and the Sleep Days and all the paraphernalia of H.D. which I'd accepted by then and took pride in; but even after the doses of tranquilizers there were parts of Gloria that couldn't be reached: women have so many secret pockets and undiscovered ravines, the government never dreamed. If protests arise, I thought, they will come from the women. The men wear their lives and thoughts like outhouses, big barns on their estates that can be burned down without trace of the harvest; but these pleated females with their folds and tucks and creases—some part of their lives will never be cleaned away; it is they who will keep the race-memory; flower seed in a crack of the world.

And so I was alone in the house then, working during the

day, sleeping or not sleeping at night, and from time to time being amazed that the city and the country should have accepted so faithfully the promises of the future. I began to live the life of a bachelor who has only his work to distract him. I was surprised that I did not miss Gloria and the children, although we exchanged weekly letters in which she gave details of her life in Palmerston North. She rarely mentioned the preparations for Classification. She and her sister and brother-in-law (who is town clerk) were living in a district already zoned and protected by the new police who had begun to arrive in planeloads from the United States of America. In my letters to Gloria I did not say that I missed her. Instead, I found myself praising the efficiency of the household machines and describing my satisfaction in working with them. When I came home from work I went at once to the kitchen. I would stand listening to the quiet reassuring murmur, like an inland sea, of the Feasterama Refrigerator and the insect-humming summer-sound of the electric clock, and I was glad that Gloria had not been the type, common among university wives, who suddenly abandoned machines and reverted to old-fashioned ways of housekeeping; sitting on the patio in the evening with their spinning wheel conjuring "raw" wool from greasy hunks of fleece, to make the family clothing.

The aristocrat of the machines was the Central Computer that already held most of the information required about each citizen. The newborn were to be classified at birth for a primary judgment and at five years for a secondary judgment which would be final, though in the early stages of the Act there would be annual reclassification and, later, regularly, reclassification or "pruning" where the animal content was thought to have increased. In spite of the doses of tranquilizers, I found myself often overcome by horror that seemed to originate beyond myself. One of my colleagues who was deathed, claimed that his feelings of horror were a gift from God. At these times I remembered that I was tallying people as commodities. If it had not been for my appreciation of the purity and beauty of numbers and forms of calculation I don't think I should have been able to go on living, especially during that early winter when the frosts were severe, as if each night as Classification Day came nearer frost formed also inside each heart in a cold threat of death, and morning and waking was a time of struggling free from the iron constriction.

During the summer there had been talk of postponing Classification Day until the following summer (someone suggested Christmas Day) when the sun, the green grass, the flowers in bloom might counterbalance the human winter season. Then came the argument for early Spring Classification—naive but more convincing. The struggle would be against the seasons; the prolonged darkness of awaiting the verdict would parallel the darkness of winter; the exhaustion of early spring would encourage passive acceptance of the verdict, as if those who waited were blades of grass without the energy to stand upright after their winter beating. Visitors from overseas pointed out that such a Wordsworthian approach was possible only in a country where trees and grass still grew and flowers bloomed and the sun was visible for several hours a day.

When the time came for the rest of the world to convert to H.D. after the New Zealand experiment had been studied and the methods improved and refined, it might be wise, the psychologists said, to try to retain human communion with the natural world of weather, landscape, seascape. To this end, in the Northern hemisphere (especially in Scandinavia where the experiment of biological control was being studied) the devastated cities and countrysides were being planted with forests of plastic trees and grass, while weather control units had been instructed to include the former seasons of the year to provide a variety of weather experience.

219

There had to be something, "they" said—and man himself said, in defiance of or in agreement with "them"—to ease the agony of the loneliness of beings separated from animals and vegetation and earth and the forces and guardians they had named Gods; existing soon in a terrifying Middle Kingdom; nothing yet to fall down in worship of; nothing to strike in revenge against; a human forest of beheaded uprooted trees still kept mysteriously in green balance by the winds blowing from eternity to eternity and nowhere to nowhere.

I told myself that other nations could find their own solutions and seasons when their time came. I tried to revive in myself the pioneering spirit of long ago. Instead of attacking and felling the bush to make shelters and clear the sky for the sun to shine through the dark-green world and make the crops grow, I was in charge of a weapon, a delicate axe that would choose and fell people, moral and ethical codes, habits and conventions. I recalled how the poets of that pioneering time were eloquent in their denunciation of the murder of the forests. In my childhood there had still been the old custom of Arbor Day where we planted trees, in atonement. It was a religious day. In the park where hundreds of tiny trees waited to be planted we took our place, one pupil beside each tree, stood it up to its neck in earth, then waited, crouched, squinting into the spattering sunlight while the teachers brought the spade and shovel to pat the soil around each tree. We stamped, stamped on the earth, making the tree bed hard. I sometimes wondered about the trees we planted each year, and it distressed me to think there was nothing to distinguish my trees from other trees, no special direction of leaning, or sliding of sunlight down the polished leaves. My only relation to the trees that later grew taller in the park was my memory that each year I'd had my share in firming the soil around the new tree's roots.

But I've digressed. It is because Arbor Day was held in early spring that when I thought of Classification Day I knew a similar feeling—almost of holiness—as if I were helping to stamp the earth about the roots of a new humanity. I had atoned, as it were, for the mass destruction. I was freed from guilt. And yet—how would I know, unless the new species bore a nameplate like a tree, what I had planted?

There's not much to tell about this past winter. When it became known that I would be among those responsible for the Classification of Waipori City the incitements to bribery began. I was visited by worried parents or other relatives with their little leather moneybag or wordbag of offerings—if I would only classify their Tom, Dick, Harry, their Marjorie, Jane, as Human. I'm not a trained psychologist. I don't know the techniques of interviewing. When people came to plead with me I relied on cups of tea and my unwavering belief in the New World; and for the children whom their parents brought, mistakenly and sadly, in the hope of influencing me, I became provider of things to eat—the human mouth is as convenient as ever for shortcut comfort; I became a mixture of politician and psychotherapist. Although all knew that bribery was a criminal offence, still they came with their mongol children (I name the obvious first), the mentally defective, the diseased, deformed. I never dreamed Waipori City held such tragedies. They came, people I had never seen, like hibernating creatures blinking into the sun, or holidaymakers from hell, noticed for the first time in the world. Except for those who had escaped into the mountains few could be hidden, yet I was surprised that there were not more attempts to hide the future Animals, especially those whose classification was not at first obvious. It seemed, indeed, as if some parents were proud of their exhibits, that they came not only to bribe me but to display to me, as artists do, what they had created. They asked, they received my refusal, questioned, perhaps threatened, then went home; and some, I knew, who had suffered much from their sad family, were happy to have their secret desires given official approval.

221

I found it hard to remember why I had had such violent objections to the Human Delineation Act. The moral arguments against it had been so overgrown by the arguments for its expediency, its convenience, and in a civilization and age of convenience these held much weight. Our nation was becoming, so to speak, the Comfort Station of Civilization. If the United States of America had not such a vast unwieldy population and area it might have been the first country to achieve this honor. The smallness of our population and the ease of carrying out social experiments favored our becoming the first nation of Convenience, where Convenience was not our God but our brother, our parent, our lover; we made it human and as an aluminum cuckoo in the nest it chose to thrust out all inconvenient human offspring.

And still the people came to me, pleading, with their numerous freaks of humanity. I remember one—Milly Galbraith.

Milly was the kind of person whom at first one does not "see," as one usually sees and places the members of a family; nor does one see such a person "second"—that is, in the shadow of the placing, when one has met the family and is shown the photograph albums. There are always intrusive "rogue" photographs in an album, people who are friends of friends, or completely unknown, who happen to turn up in the pages because no one knows who they are and each assumes it is a distant relative on mother's or father's side and no one likes to offend by casting out the unknown. As far as I know Milly Galbraith did not even appear in such "rogue" presentations, though I never knew the family well enough to be shown the albums. I simply *knew*.

I first saw Milly one evening about six years ago when I was walking along Eagle Street. It was spring, about the same time as now. I was going to the top of the hill for a breath of fresh air as I sometimes do when I'm working on a problem or wanting to escape from the family muddle—I use the word in a complimentary sense, though sometimes it is alarming; a mixture of flesh, tears, frying pans, food, nappies, kisses, addition and subtraction sums, spiderwebs, and magnets.

When I go out walking I do not make a point of noticing my surroundings. I take in things at the periphery of vision: shapes, colors, through a mist as if I were half-blind.

I was walking past Galbraiths' back section (it is next door to the old Livingstone ruin and what is known as the "Livingstone pear tree"—something of a monument in the town to a family who lived in the "old" way among moldy wars and moldier passions). The Galbraiths' house has two frontages, one with the house and the front path and garden, the other where Ted Galbraith and Winton, his son, in business as landscape gardeners, have made the vegetable garden and where the pear tree stood. I remember that as I glanced down into the back section I noticed someone I had never seen before in the neighborhood or anywhere, sitting under the pear tree nursing a black-and-white cat. I can't explain, but at first I didn't believe what I saw. I'm not superstitious or fanciful, yet I had a wild notion that here was a creature emerged like a rabbit or hedgehog or elf to exist in a moment of twilight, perhaps, with plants and animals, as if that were the only time allowed it. I suppose this thought came to me because I had lived several years in Eagle Street and I had never seen Milly Galbraith. In the aftermath of war, one had time to observe or not to observe; often it was easier for one's peace of mind to turn away from people one met, certainly not to seek them out in twilight gardens.

I looked again at the girl or woman. Now she had the cat on the lawn beside her and though she surely could not have seen clearly enough in the fading light, she had begun to knit a scarlet drape that was already the size of a small bedspread. Suddenly she glanced up from her knitting and saw me. She stood up. She was a woman, a little over five-feet tall, rather stout and well-developed. She walked up the path towards me, delaying my retreat with a conversationally called, "Hello!"

"Hello there."

"You must be Mister Colin Monk."

"Yes. I am."

I was annoyed. While I knew nothing of her she evidently knew of me. I could not see her more clearly. Her face was not gentle, unlined, untouched as one might imagine the face to be of a creature kept in hiding from the world. Her face startled me. It showed the wrinkles and lines of an old woman, not the birthlines, which daylight irons out, of a newborn child; these were lines of exposure, sun, weather, and people—exposure, with the deepest marks those of self-exposure.

"I'm Milly Galbraith. I'm dull-normal."

She pronounced it *doll-normill.*

She repeated it.

"*Doll-normill.* I'm mature but just past doll-size and my brain is doll-size."

She was mocking me! She was speaking for all her kind whom we had condemned. I looked at her clear violet-colored eyes. If one ever perceived intelligence in the eyes one perceived it here. She seemed to be playing a role expected of her.

She pouted and smiled.

"Pleased to meet you, Mister Monk. How is your wife?"

She pronounced it —*whife*—blowing on the first two letters like someone blowing on soup to cool it.

The little spy! I realized then that my reaction to her was as to an elf who might know more secrets that one would prefer, inhabit more places than was wise for the comfort of others.

"And your children, Robert and Sally?"

Robbitt. Chilldrin. Chill Drinn.

A kind of dizziness came over me.

"They're fine."

"And Sandy, home from the War?"

I was pleased at last to find a point of strangeness. There was no Sandy, there has never been a Sandy, I have never heard of a Sandy, and no matter what Milly Galbraith in her fantasies was dreaming up I had to make it clear to her that there was no Sandy.

My voice was protesting, almost whining.

"There is no Sandy."

It sounded stupidly like a cross between There is no God, There is no history, and There is no justice!

She smiled slowly. I'd been skeptical of novelists who wrote of "slow smiles," but this smile had a beginning, a middle, and an end, and the time in between seemed measureless, almost like a new kind of geological time.

"Many people," she said—again contradicting the verdict of herself as "doll-normill"—"many people never know their own twin."

"My twin? Don't be ridiculous."

"Your twin. Sandy. Home from the War."

Poor girl, I thought. Worse than dull-normal.

I said goodbye abruptly and I didn't continue my walk to the top of the hill. I went home, pausing just a while again, as I always do, before the white glazing archaic fire of the Livingstones' pear tree. I was haunted by this strangely invisible child-woman. I did not see her again until recently. She came once or twice to help with the children while I was away in Wellington. My wife did not speak of her except to call her a "treasure"; she became like something borrowed from the earth. Whose earth?

My second meeting with Milly Galbraith came in the early days after preparation for Classification Day when her father brought her to plead for her life.

That morning I had walked as usual through the botanical gardens and I stopped and sat on one of the seats overlooking the creek and the avenue of flowering cherry trees. In Waipori we were rather proud of still having trees, and birds, and gardens.

Since the announcement of the Human Delineation Act I'd refused to take the armored car lent to me by the university, as I found it hard to imagine myself a target for violence. Yet as Classification Day drew near I realized I would soon have to give up my morning walk through the gardens: I'm not a nature lover but I do like to sit in peace, and green shade and trees and lawns still provide that peace; the discipline and shape of formal gardens always had for me the delight and pride similar to those found in a solved equation. There had been a time, before the War, when I had believed —plants, yes. People, never. Never people clipped and cut and caged and subdued but still growing towards the sun.

The creek flowed not more than fifteen yards away. I stared at the water. I saw a white bird that I thought at first was a swan with its head bowed towards the water and its body huddled behind the long grass. Then it stood tall with its beak and head slightly to the left in a different pose. I remembered there'd been news of a white heron in the botanical gardens. It had been a timely distraction with a kind of hysteria in the reporting of the news: white herons, all birds, were the only creatures remaining blessedly immune and free. The comings and goings of birds in unboundaried spaces of sky were now events to set the human heart thudding with excitement and, perhaps, hope; birds had removed themselves from our element as if they had never inhabited it, and the film of air had closed about them, transparent yet unbreakable and inaccessible.

"It should have flown to Siberia," I said aloud, resentfully watching the heron. Who sees a white heron twice is blessed; three times he may enter heaven.

It stood motionless, its beak sunk in its breast. It did not have the air of preparing for migration. Where was its mate?

I whispered to myself, thankful that fellow members of the Delineation Committee could not hear my thoughts—I've seen the white heron!

Then I became angry. The bird was breaking the law, its own law and that of the sun and the wind and the stars. It had fallen from the orbit of grace and brought harm to the world of man. The stars and sun and moon had fallen out of the sky. The white heron should have flown in season; then the stars might be replaced in the sky and the seasons strike again as accurately as stated and solved equations, and all remain certain, unaltered and unalterable.

I was in no mood for work that day. I felt irritable and tired and depressed. We had been warned to expect this: my hysteria over the white heron, my unvoiced but no less passionate longing for fixed stars and seasons and times, were merely symptoms that I dared not reveal to my colleagues. All the data of all the citizens in and around Waipori City had been processed and I felt I could not bear to study another assessment or medical record or quotient. I had been appalled by the secrets, the revealed disasters and deformities in the minds and bodies of people I had known all my life and recognized with that "recognition of the spirit" as whole human beings and whom I was now forced to classify as animals. Also, the office dealt with the letters, mostly from elderly people, requesting an early merciful death before Classification Day. These requests, most of which were addressed to the Mathematics Department of the University as if the Computer must be consulted when the decision was made, were passed to the Public Hospital where the Humane Department dealt with them. Most requests were readily granted. This necessary devision of man and animal had not annihilated the compassion of man for man.

The Humane Department and its Early Disposal Unit had almost a festive air with the bright-blue station wagons drawn up at the entrance, and the old men and women in their best clothes, the women with flowers in their gray hair, waving and singing. My window at the University overlooked the street where they passed and I found myself waving cheerfully as the passengers traveled to their lethal picnic. One might have thought that with such cooperation from the public the Early Disaposal Units would be a success. They were not. The old men and women who said they wanted to die and who believed they were speaking the truth, discovered, when the time came for their proud willing surrender that the death they craved was life itself, disguised in its most convenient mask. Their horror at the double deceit practiced by their selves and their own lives roused them, in the end, to a furious energy of resistance. I heard from colleagues at the hospital that the Early Disposal Unit might have been filled with birds, the way these people clawed and struggled to retrieve life. It is easier now, as I write of them, to think of them as the "old people"; anonymity drapes a kind of emotional velvet, whereas grandad's torn suit and grandma's worn dress may let their bones show through, and bones are the direct form of human poverty.

That day I took the University taxi home. I planned to spend the afternoon reading and sleeping and trying to ward off a cold in the head. I took two aspirins after lunch and I was lying half asleep on the couch in the sitting room when the doorbell rang. I felt afraid. It was not good to be even slightly sick, and worse to let others see it.

I knew Ted Galbraith by sight and I recognized Milly as the creature I'd spoken to in the garden. She was dressed in conventional Sunday best, including pearls and white hat and white gloves—how we retained the historic wear!—all the Waipori female trimmings of formality, expectation, underlined innocence.

"If I could speak to you a few moments?" Galbraith began.

Perhaps he thought I did not recognize him. He introduced himself as Ted Galbraith my neighbor, and Milly as his afflicted daughter and stressed that he knew how busy I was and he would not take up my time, and so forth.

I was tired and annoyed and I showed it. I knew why he had called and I didn't want to admit I knew, either to him or to Milly or to myself. I resented the formal way he had introduced himself when the few times we had met our words had been.

"Hi Ted."

"Hi Colin."

He'd pruned our roses too. He and his family were certainly sitting pretty and wealthy now that Waipori City had deepened its passion for the earth and its plants.

And I remembered how he'd brought us all those daffodil bulbs from out the Taeri plains when Gloria wanted to plant daffodils in the grass under the trees at the back of the house.

"Hi Ted."

"Hi Colin."

A democracy.

Except that judgment, death, are formal, autocratic. The victim makes a formal acknowledgment of his murderer. The condemned man wears a bow tie, polishes his shoes, wipes his mouth on a starched table napkin.

I was tired, tired, tired. A common cold, uncommon now, could lead to common death.

Milly had not spoken. She sat correctly, her feet side by side, her back straight, her eyes downcast. Like a maiden being introduced to a prospective husband.

Her father turned to her.

"Milly would you like to go outside a moment?"

"Perhaps," I said, "she would like to go onto the sun-porch."

When she had gone Ted did not sit down again. We stood facing each other.

"I want to save Milly."

I did not answer.

"She's our only daughter."

"Many people," I said calmly, "have only daughters."

"Mind you, I'm not saying anything against H.D."

"I should think not."

"I just thought . . ."

"What did you just think?"

It was as swift as that. My manner was grim. I suppose I was playing the role of the overdog whose pity for the underdog is submerged in despising; in pity all drown, in despising, the strong are rescued. It is that kind of sea, and the wrecks are deep, irrecoverable.

Ted Galbraith's face was flushed. He looked like a pig. He looked as if he had just had a heavy meal. I remembered that he had something of the reputation of a know-all. The neighbors liked him, though. The nature of his job kept him at home often during the day and he was looked on with envy; his own boss and doing work that never seemed much like work. Sometimes he rang up my wife and (I discovered) other women when the wild winds came raging down North East Valley.

"Your washing's in trouble."

"My washing? So kind of you to tell me."

"You know what it will mean to us if Milly is saved."

I told him that I did know. I also knew what it would mean to thousands of others, I reminded him, if members of their family were saved. I reminded him it was a sacrifice we had to make for the general good, yet even as I spoke, the lines from the sonnet came to my mind:

Tir'd with all these for restful death I cry.
. . . .
Right perfection wrongfully disgraced,
And strength by limping sway disabled,
And art made tongue-tied by authority,

230

And folly doctorlike controlling skill,
And simple truth miscalled simplicity,
And captive good attending captain ill.

No, it was not far from Captive Good to General Good. Of what significance was his military rank when his bones were exposed in the end to the poverty of weather polish?

My head was not clear. The cold made me feverish. I felt that Ted Galbraith was trying to confuse me by dropping me into the eddying force of human relations and stirring with a big gold stick that smelt like money.

He and his son, he said, had built a flourishing business since the War. The people of Waipori City were garden mad, sometimes you had the feeling they wanted to dig their own graves, but most wanted their share of earth dug and decorated by a professional gardener, and by God they wanted their gardens clean and neat with not a weed in place or a flower out of place; trees amputated by special surgery; lawns sheared. He and his son Winton were skilled workers with a growing nestegg in the bank. Enough money for a trip overseas. Formalities could be arranged. Connections. . . . Everyone had connections!

We began to argue then. Mothers, fathers, brothers, sisters, lovers, daughters, sons whirled about me.

"We could band together," Galbraith said.

As if we were not already banded! That, I told myself, reviving, was the glory of H.D. Happy and Free with H.D. I believed in happiness as an expansion of being, not in the prolonged painful contraction that had been man's condition of heart as he suffered and was suffered by the exiles, the outcasts, the pitifully deformed, diseased, inefficient; the idiot pools that gave back no reflection to the searching sky.

"We *shall* band together," I said, proudly.

Then I told him to get out.

He called Milly, and, her presence seeming to give him

extra courage, he began to rage. I heard reference to roses, daffodils, and a startled exclamation by Milly as if she were seeing a vision.

"The dwarves' heads, the dwarves' heads! Their machines wore out!"

Then both were calm and I walked them to the door as if I were saying goodbye to old friends. I remember thinking that when they had arrived both were smart in Sunday best clothes, and yet seeing them walk along the path to the gate I was struck by their disheveled appearance, as if in the fifteen minutes they had been with me they had worked hard: Ted Galbraith perhaps at his gardening, was that a crease of mud on his coat sleeve? Milly at washing, not in a white machine but at wooden tubs, dark and splintered with use. Washing, and the wild wind raging down the valley and the phone ringing and ringing . . .

"Your washing's in trouble."

Shall I rescue clothes that dance with nothing inside?

My head throbbed. I, the mathematician, could not cope with probable subtraction. I slept, and when I woke it was dark. I looked out at the Galbraiths' house and their light, still burning. I could see the smoky white burst of the Livingstone pear tree, a vegetable lifeline that still spoke of people; their story flashed through my mind. I knew that I was afraid.

32

My name is Milly Galbraith. I'm writing my story in an exercise book with a ballpoint pen that you throw away or stamp on or break into pieces when the ink finished. When my brother Winton saw me sitting under the Livingstones' pear tree and said, "What are you doing Milly," and I said "I am writing my story about the Deciding," he said, "Never mind, Milly," and I said, "Mind what?" but he did not say what, only that one day someone might take my story to show everyone it is not right to decide about people, that dreadful mistakes are made that cannot be undone. Winton was gardening near the fence.

"The first frosts are here," he said. "Rhubarb is a gross feeder."

The roots are called crowns.

My father and my brother work as gardeners cutting hedges and growing plants and putting in fancy ornaments and statues, dwarves and fat boys; and pruning the prize roses of Waipori, our Friendly City of the South.

"It is heads and not roots that wear crowns," my brother said. And then he said you would have thought the King would save some of the people because the King had been to school in Australia our neighboring continent, and when he passed through Auckland airport years ago on his way home from school he smiled at all the people and shook hands for two hours with crippled children and soldiers and patted babies' heads, everyone said like a true politician or like the President of America. Fancy that.

The roots of the rhubarb are called crowns. Kings no longer wear crowns.

And then Winton looked at me without joking and said solemnly.

"The Deciding Day will be your birthday, Milly, and the Livingstone pear tree will be in blossom."

My birthday!

Now when I was born and the nurse took me to my mother in the ward of the maternity hospital that is now a student hostel, I kicked so hard that the nurse said, "She is as strong as an ox," and throughout my life when my mother has been talking about me she has not forgotten to repeat, "At birth she was as strong as an ox and even before birth I think she had hooves instead of feet, how she could kick."

233

And when I was small and searched for an ox and could not find one except several inside a hymn:

Not in that poor lonely stable
with the oxen standing by

I thought they had big white faces like the moon, only the color of milk, and their black eyes were like stones and I remember this only because The Act was passed in Parliament which said there was to be Deciding, and some were to be People and some were to be Animals, and I heard my mother talking over the telephone to Mr. Colin Monk of the University whose computer will decide, and my mother was saying,

"From birth she has been as strong as an ox, surely it will be in her favor." And I felt lonely again to see them with their big white faces glistening and their black eyes like stones.

I am twenty-five. There has been a war but now there is peace. I wonder which of us will be allowed to go on living in houses with mothers and fathers and food and television sets and electric heaters and gardens outside where Samuel cat plays and the Livingstone pear tree grows bigger and bigger into the sky, and I wonder which will be called Animals to be put in cages, stared at, killed, eaten, or sent to factories to be made into shoes and shoelaces and lampshades and soap and even teacups and saucers. Everything is secret now but soon it will not be. When I tell my mother that I do not want Samuel cat to be killed, she says that is not the point, it is people who are the point to be decided about and that means us, and anyway Samuel cat was the Livingstone cat, a descendant running wild among the ruins, and the Livingstones loved too much, like bombing, and I know I am truly Human because I have a mother and father and brother and I live in a house with a television and electric heater and I sleep at night in a bed, and in the daytime I sit with Samuel cat near the pear tree and the sun shines warm on his fur and on my skin and the pear tree is the biggest tree in the world and cool to sit under on the hot dry days when the grass is shriveled with burning.

I have lived all my life in this house on this street in this Friendly City of the South, Waipori, and I know my way in and out of doors and in and out of rooms and up and down the front path to the gate and up and down the back path to the garden and through the side gate to the Livingstones' and I know the chairs and beds and tables and windowsills and cupboards and where to find things, cups and saucers and spoons and knives, and how to cook things and how to sew —they taught me this in the Occupation Center where I used to go to school, though not always, for at first I went to school on the hill and the teacher was annoyed because I would not stay in my seat. "Milly Galbraith, there's plenty of time for moving around, we have to learn to sit still, stop jigging your foot, dear," and she said to my mother, "Milly jigs her foot and won't keep still and her reading readiness is never going to be ready. She's afraid of words but it's inborn, there's nothing to be done, her speaking is mixed up too, you mustn't talk baby talk to her though she's retarded, doll-normill, maybe worse, but her routine number work is average and some things are above normill, it may be something chemical but it's beyond our comprehension."

So I built a city of red and yellow blocks and knocked over its towers with one swipe of my hand that has been as strong as an ox from the day I was born, and the teacher said, "The frustrations of the retarded."

So I stopped going to school on the hill. At the Occupation Center we sang rhymes:

Two little apples hanging on a tree,
Two little apples smiling at me.

And when I said I wouldn't smile if I knew I was going to be eaten the teacher was annoyed.

We sang:

I have ten little fingers they all belong to me.
I can make them do things would you like to see.

and the teacher got annoyed again because we did things with our fingers she didn't like.

And then I became interested in counting, and I began to count things into my birthdays like my fingers and toes and the people in our family including Samuel cat with his white apron and white nose and whiskers and now I'm up to myself twenty-five and on my twenty-sixth birthday I'll count in the biggest pear tree in the world, a pear tree out of history and the days when people went up and down in their lives day after day without a murderous thought, with love in their hearts, and the pear tree has not learned to sleep at night or in the daytime and the birds sing in it and the branches sigh and rock and seesaw and creak and drop their shadows down on the earth, and I put my face against the tree and love it because I am old enough to love something. I am mature now. I saw loving on television with them kissing as I kiss the tree and I kiss Samuel cat and my life in Waipori this Friendly City of the South is happy enough.

Now also at the Occupation Center I wore an apron with a bib front, and at first I played with blocks and tried to get silver rings in and out of other silver rings with only one small gap for them to slide through; they were silver links in a chain that I couldn't break and neither could the other pupils and sometimes from early morning until the sun set in the west we used to play How Does Willy get Home, starting him from the Center and trying to find the way down long straight narrow streets with nowhere to sit or stop for morning or afternoon tea and no bed to sleep in if he got tired, but the teacher said "Boys and girls there is no time limit, you have all the time in the world because of your special intellygents," but Willy never got home not on my page. With my pencil prodding him on he stayed in the maze and slept standing up like a horse at midday in the corner paddock, with no shelter from the sun at the time when people look at one another and say Oh, for the cool of the evening.

In this way we were taught to be useful citizens and we were taught to play, they said, in a manner fitting for the retarded but they did not call us We they called us They. They do this and They do that, They think this and They think that, why they knew everything about us only they did not call us Us they called us Them. Truly the teachers had a wonderful way of knowing our secret hopes and fears and thoughts.

And so I, Milly Galbraith, was a child, and after many years I came to a-doll-essence.

A-doll-essence is upon her, I heard my mother say.

I glued my legs together and crayoned my eyebrows and eyelashes and the big white clouds in the sky scattered and broke in pieces like curds and whey sprinkled with blue and gold sugar, and my future was decided. They talked about me and said it was natural I should be baffled, so they sent me to a private hospital to stop me from being baffled while they decided, but it didn't take them long to decide and they said I could stay home sitting under the Livingstones' pear tree with Samuel cat and that sometimes I was oughtistick, very, but I would be mother's help knitting jerseys to keep everyone warm, though first they tried a laundry for me to work in, but the hot sheets made blisters on the tips of my fingers and the throbbing machine came nearer and nearer so I went into domestic work for a time, cleaning and polishing with Brasso the nameplates of the doctors and dentists along the Main Street of Waipori City, but in the end I found that home was best and writing my spelling way in my notebook but especially knitting jerseys to keep everyone warm with the icebergs waiting in the corner of the world with their white teeth jagged and polished like white nameplates. Oh I know about the world, but they said simple people are always happiest because simple people have not much furniture to worry about, how dare they, because I have always wanted a little house with furniture, a television, a chair, a bed, a table, and I want the house to be built near the pear tree but when I told them my dream they said there's no harm in wanting is there, and only Samuel cat understood.

Still, my heart is not broken. I am happy except that the pear tree does not sleep or keep still. I learned gradually to sleep and stand still and not walk up and down, day in day out, but I do not know how to teach the tree, and everyone is angry with it for moving and tossing and nodding and waving and never getting tired and all this overtime and it is bigger than everybody and can see more, and I know this makes people jealous and one day someone is going to try to kill it. When I am twenty-six I shall take the tree under my protective arm and care for it as a loving mother cares for her child through all adversity. Some of these phrases I use are out of books, as you will see.

My reading readiness was never quite what people wanted it to be, I wanted my own language, for if you have your own language nobody can take it away from you, it's not like taking chewing gum out of your mouth and throwing it in the wastepaper basket when it's worked its chew and stretch to death. Still I don't care for reading much and hymns are my favorite, *Who is he that cometh from Edom with all his garments stained with blood*? Also knitting patterns rep25th $k_3 s_3$ isp al psso psso psso; and the Bible that the minister told me will help me when I need help and I am not to run out into the street and call Help Help Help, that is only for Stop Thief, and the ground is giving way beneath me and all are murdered in their beds; but my kind of help is different, it is not stealing and earthquakes and murder it is how I was made, chemical or not, therefore the minister said I am to read the Bible or if I don't want to read it, to touch it, to turn the pages and dwell on them like a plot of land "Shemehiah, and Joia-rib, Jedaiah, moreover the Levites."

33

Here today gone tomorrow is money, so my father says when he breaks a note, is life on this earth my mother says when she reads the death column, the shock was great, the loss severe, was it only last year. My father put his arm around my mother.

"Don't worry Decima. At least we live in a democracy."

"A democracy!"

My mother screamed, not making the ordinary sound Samuel cat makes when you tread on his paw but a fierce scream like *peril, peril.*

"Milly," my mother said looking at me with great kind-ness, "why don't you go outside?"

Now if like me you have found it hard to be what people want you to be and have quarrels with their sort of learning and speaking the right words and phrases, and in your mind you are confused with your meaning and their meaning and why not, and if you are then labeled doll-normill or worse, you will find it hard to convince people that you know more than they think you know, that you understand more words and phrases than they would give you credit for, credit means owing you money but they are owing you respect for your in-telly-gents. When my mother said, "Go outside to play," she thought I did not understand what was happening, but I learn in my secret ways and I knew they were talking about the Act of Parliament. Why worry, I thought, unconcerned.

Now let me tell you more about this Act of Parliament

called the Human Delineation Act. On my birthday, the Deciding Day, everyone will be counted and tested and with all the information gathered the computer with all our history inside it will look at each one and say sharply like a soldier, Human, Animal, Human, Animal, depending on what you are, and if you are human everyone will smile at you and say "Fine weather we're having, congratulations," and you will go free and be able to live in the world as a human being; on the other hand if the computer decides you are animal, how different it will be for you in your future life, for at once they will kidnap you, capture you, and put you in a cage and take you to a factory if you are suitable and they will experiment on you or keep you locked up and stare at you day and night, study you until the situation is more than you can bear. Your legs will wither from not walking and you will be forced to screw up your eyes to see in the dark, blindness will come eventually and death, and if you think I paint a grim picture of what will happen, then I can only say that you who are reading this are lucky not to be living in the time I write of. Do not be deceived—you may be living in it and not know, because two times can live together and the one doesn't know that the other time is living because if you're in one time whatever would make you want to think there is another there going on through the light of day and the dark of night? Is your world my world? Do you still have seasons in the year, Christmas followed by autumn when the leaves turn gold and float from the trees until the trees are bare and winter has come with frosts and cold mornings, and then before you know it spring has come round again with the flowering currant. If you have seasons like this then you are living in our part of the world and you will know about our Act of Parliament which sets an example to all other people who love freedom and democracy. Are you preparing for the Deciding? Are you afraid? I think that most people in Waipori are afraid to talk of the matter and the mayor has gone insane and has boarded up his house and all the windows with his wife and family inside without any food, and nobody can get into them to break the news whether they will be Animal or Human but it is said that if you behave in a peculiar manner, antisocially or strangely, you are automatykilly Animal. I know that my parents think that I will be Animal, disposed of on my birthday, because I have my own way of learning and secrets and I couldn't get out of the maze when they tried it on me with paper and pencil and my earning power is low— I've heard them say these things about me, and even if your memory is bad you don't forget what people say about you and you don't even have to learn it like dates in hisstree. Perhaps they have forgotten that I am as strong as an ox and that i can count: they may need me to help them with their calculations.

And still the minister tells me to sing: *When gathering clouds around I view and days are dark and friends are few on him I lean who not in vain experienced every human pain.* And he tries to make me read the Bible and turn the pages though my opinion is the print is too small for comfort and I really only listen to them singing on the radio and television. Also many of the words don't have enough meaning because I am doll-normill and I will never be able to include the whole range of knowledge in my brain because my brain won't take it, still I have enough for comfort when you consider all there is to know.

If I am made an animal they may keep me in a cage in the garden under the Livingstone pear tree or they might take me to a factory out on the Taeri Plains where they are building new factories nineteen to the dozen, so my mother says when she thinks I am not listening, to cope with all the people who will be brutally murdered because they are de-formed or were not born strong as an ox or because they say the wrong things in company and are not polite and agreeing but have different ideas to express, the frail and the weak, the idiots and the insane, those who are slow in the race, who are a burden on the community, and those in hospitals costing thousands of dollars a year for board and keep, the old and neglected and the young with ill health, I think I have covered most of the world of Animals. Perhaps when it is all over there will not be many people left and those who are left will have more—that is what the radio announcer said. He said there will be more for everyone in a new world, more goods and services, a higher standard of living with every home boasting a television set, a washing machine, central heating, a dishwashing machine, electric blankets with double heat control on each side for husband and wife, a motor mower with rotary blades and instant switch, a stove, with eye-level grill, a double-sided pop-up toaster, carpets wall to wall, cocktail cabinets, stereophone record players, not to mention a deep freeze and the thousand-and-one inventions of this latter day. The announcer kept telling us over and over how we would have more, that the Deciding would be a time of pain for all, certainly, but afterwards when the ugly sights were gone from the community we would settle down to a life we have never been able to live before and we would even have bigger homes and bigger sections and swimming pools and barbecues and plenty of leisure time, it would be like heaven on earth, but my father right from the beginning was worried about it.

"Something is going to happen," he said, "the way they are buttering us up."

And it has happened.

Also people get excited about having more, and I thought of all the things they would give me, for though I do not want a cocktail cabinet or a double electric blanket I want more than other people, I've always been a great wanter right down to my own language and I want chiefly a house to live in with Samuel cat under the Livingstone pear tree and the husband I want to live with is called Sandy and you may laugh and laugh to your heart's content when I tell you about Sandy but that does not hurt me, nothing hurts me because Sandy belongs to me as much as my brain, and when I write in this notebook to tell my experience no one in the world is going to know my experience unless I tell it and I wanted to use my special spelling to make the words show up for what they really are the cruel deceivers.

I will tell you about Sandy. He is Sandy Monk, twin brother of Colin Monk of the Computer Center. He was wounded in the war and is the First Reconstructed Man with new gold skin and new eyes of a dead person, and after he had been mended he came to live with Colin Monk and his wife and family and sometimes he still comes here to talk to me and he treats me like an equal though his knowledge is more than mine. Admittedly he is not handsome for he was burned with the bomb that writes its name on you with graphite and with the other bomb that leaves a glare in the sky and blinds you, but not if you hide in concrete under the earth with air excluded and supplies for many days until the bomb loses its deadly power and you come out on the earth and you have all the fresh air you have saved in containers, but the earth is razed into an unfamiliar desert and you have to start all over again the task of building the western world safe for democracy.

When I saw Sandy's face and knew no normill girl would take a second look at him now that he had been thrown on the scrapheap of humanity, I felt pity for him, and when he came into the garden to talk to me I loved him with all my heart. He did not look at me as if to say, "She is doll-normill, her brain is too small and occupied to hold learning, she will never manage the complications of the world. No. He looked at me and I smiled and I smiled at him. How considerate he was!

On my twenty-sixth birthday he will propose to me. He will address me in gentle tones.

"Milly there's something I've wanted to ask you for a long time."

"What is it Sandy?"

"First do my deformities and knowing that I am a Reconstructed Man make any difference to you?"

"I accept you as you are, Sandy."

"I'm grateful, my dear."

"You were going to ask me a question?"

And so it will be, with me pursuing my point, and we will go hand in hand to the kitchen where Sandy says to my mother as she cooks the meal.

"Mrs. Galbraith meet your new son."

Then Humans all, we will celebrate.

Now our street is Eagle Street I do not know why because we have no eagles here, but perhaps that is why it is called Eagle Street because people are pining for eagles to be swooping down from the sky and are sad that when they look up there is space and clouds and no eagles. We have a view over the two chief hills of Waipori City, called Swampy and Flagstaff, where the morning mists begin coming out of their lair and swirling into the quiet streets swallowing up the view. For our street is a quiet street and you would not know that some of the people and places here were wiped out in the war, that is you would not know unless I told you, and it is good for houses and people to be wiped out sometimes for then it cleans up the world and the world has to be clean for democracy. Mr. Warburton Maurice the old crippled man lives in our street. He used to work at the Meddykill School among the rabbits and rats, testing them and experimenting on them for different diseases to see if they could stand the strain of being sick, putting cancers inside them, and consumption and pneumonia in a cruel way but only to make the human race more healthy and improve conditions and make the world safe for democracy. Now that Mr. Maurice is retired and crippled his daughter has everything fixed for him, with a stool in the kitchen for his crippled legs and kitchen drawers to pull out and swiveling things to make it easy for him to get his own meals, for his daughter is a busy woman with welfare work and has not much time to visit him. However she does provide for his comfort in these ways. Every day a lady from the Meals on Wheels comes to give him a piping hot meal in an aluminum dish, meat and two vegetables for vitamins and proteins and minyrills, and to make him want to go on living in his lonely state his daughter has brought him a television to look at in the evenings when no one comes to visit him and you can see him sitting in the front room watching the programs right through from the children's to the murders to the documentaries of people in other lands who wear no clothes or a piece of stuff in front of them hanging so everyone can't look, which is different from our society where no one sees anything because it is all covered except when you undress at night, but in the society on television they wear just this little patch of stuff and sometimes if you look fast enough when they are walking you can see something, or when they are lying down but you have to be quick because they move again and your view is gone and then you don't really know whether you saw it or not and you begin to wonder until they move and you see it again. Television is fun and I'm sure Mr. Warburton Maurice enjoys watching people of other lands. Sometimes also he works in his garden, kneeling on a rubber mat, and I hear my mother and everyone say it's amazing how he does it when he is crippled but then he has to have some interests or he will go to pieces alone in that big house with his wife dead so many years and his daughter keeping clear of him with excuses. He has sometimes spoken kindly to me when I pass on my way to get the bread at the store near the bus stop where you can buy groceries, fruit, food from the deep freeze, lollies, and small items for the kitchen like potscrubs, dishcloths, also perfumed hair-set called lacker that we have been told is inflammable.

"Goodmorning Milly," Mr. Warburton Maurice says cheerfully.

His face is big like a murderer's face on television.

"Doing your shopping?"

"Yes Mr. Maurice."

Then with a cheery wave I am gone up the road to the store where people are already waiting to be served and I am in the kew. They always smile when they see me and tell me how nice I look and ask me if I am being a good girl, much to my annoyance as I am a groan woman as they know from looking at me with my breasts size thirty-six and my hips thirty-nine and my waist twenty-nine going on for thirty, anybody could tell how well-developed I am. In fact I am old enough to conceive and bare a child, so mature is my development. I do not speak when they ask me such insulting questions about being a good girl, and they smile again, talking and very free with my Christian name and I get annoyed and frown and wish there was somewhere for me to go away from everybody and not feel so awkward, but I repeat it is only because they treat me like a child because I have not been able to learn as fast as they have and I am oughtistick but when you are mature you don't really need to know about books written or about volcanoes and mountains and populations, when you are mature you don't have to know anything, for you can pretend everything all the time and no one knows any different so skillfool is your pretending. However the trouble is that you might forget what you are pretending to know and what you really know, with the result that you are muddled and don't know any more and can't pretend that you do, so you have to think fast of some other plan but you can't find a plan so good and you feel you will never be able to bear the disgrace of not having a plan to pretend you know more than you really know, and even if you rack your brain the

246

answer is hidden from you, especially if you are known as doll-normill or imbecile which is what someone called me the other day causing me to flush with anger at their impertinence.

34

I am Sandy Monk. I am a hero, the Reconstructed Man with the mechanical memory, the golden skin, the implanted glossily dead eyes, the Brand-X penis. I hold the first Human Reconstruction Certificate presented to me by the Governor General at a special ceremony in Wellington. I hold the Charles Cross, the freedom of the city of Waipori, I am the first reconstructed man . . . open-windowed stillness in a hot climate, moveless air, the public touch. I am marigolds, sunflowers, brass urns, goldfinches, coins, the Midas man. I do not bleed.

I am Sandy Monk, fraternal twin to Colin Monk, mathematician, guardian of the University Computer Center, husband, father, householder. Fraternal twin or shadow. He survived the Greatest War and the lifework of his survival is housed now in the Central University Building where in the clock tower, originally the haunt of seagulls, the sentries now guard and shoot on sight. I will not try to compare our degrees of mutilation. Accepting conscription or death and attached to life as a chrysalis to a leaf, I learned to kill by remote near control until I woke, candlelit, a birthday for surgeons who snuffed me out, sliced me, swallowed me, then relit my shadow to make my years burn full and bright and tall in golden flame.

I am a hero, the first experimental man. To Sir Horace Mutimer I owe my mechanical memory. His theory that memory and forgetfulness are one, the newly minted or worn coin and its protective glaze that preserves the mint condition of time's currency, while allowing its constant circulation, and his testing and proving his theory at the surgeon's birthday party earned him many awards. To Sir Mackenzie Dobie who was able with the grafting of my golden skin and dead eyes to prove the worth of his Red-Herring Virus, I owe the gold and the gloss that were not rejected but were given immediate shelter, rest, and function. To Sir James Watson I owe my Brand-X penis and its streamlined faultless mechanism.

I am Sandy Monk: in debt for money, skin, and sight; and yet I have no rage; no rage to be free or to pay or to die. I am content to sit under the Livingstone pear tree and wait for Milly's birthday. I say to her, "What do birthdays mean, Milly?" Her reply, paraphrased, is: Birthdays are noticing the morning is the earliest of the year, are getting ready for smiles and presents and hating knots and are waiting for too long after it happens for it to happen. And then it is over and all the wishes come home to hide in the pillow and people are angry with you because you lost your temper and cried.

And I say to her, "What does this birthday mean, Milly?"

And her reply is, "I will build my house forever under the Livingstone pear tree, it is everybody's pear tree now, it gets bigger and bigger and every year it is blossoming and there is fruit on it."

I am Sandy Monk. I have a clear memory for what I have and what I have lost. I have a full-blown ease of tranquillity. Sandy Monk, the golden rose. On the birthday party to celebrate my rebirth there was no surgeon in attendance to replenish my supply of love. I said to Milly "There is a word I want you to spell as the rest of the world spells it because if you do not, or forget how to spell it, it might mean that you lose the word altogether, that it falls down the cracks in the world and can never be found again, so you mustn't lose it because no one will even have time to find it or realize it is lost. You're a watching, waiting person, Milly, in the country

248

of the simpleminded whose shores are washed and littered with the flotsam and jetsam of the Seas of Complexity; and you're a natural beachcomber in your own land. Things are changing, Miss Doll-Normill and you are changing and I have a golden skin. I could say the winter should be past and the rain over and gone ..."

"Oh Sandy you mean the time of the singing of birds, like in the Bible, but we have no turtles only sheep, but it will be the bleating of sheep because it is spring come round again and my birthday soon."

"I am changing Miss Doll-Normill. I have decisions to make. I am proud of my metal memory. My experience is golden. If only you could tell the tomorrow you write for, in your own words ... "

"I have no words, Sandy. They are not my property though no one has stopped me from using them, and I help myself to them when I want to speak and I share them with people except Samuel cat and the pear tree who have their own words or perhaps it is the same for them, for other cats speak Samuel's words and other trees have the same kind of sound, other trees can't bear the wind at them not leaving them alone to move in a dainty way instead of their heads shaking with fright and crying words that trees have for 'Let me alone, please,' and despair words for, 'What has come over the world up here near the sky, what will I do, what will I do alone up here with my head in the cold clouds and my feet stuck in the earth weighed down with mountains of clods and grass and heavy people stamping on me and my roots are red where the earth wears away over me and my bones stick out and I can't reach down to cover them. What will I do, what will I do?' That is the trees' own words and it is a smelling tree that breathes out smell instead of air, and crying, and some trees are light green and make words like paper and dresses and fire crackling and some are dark, dark and the wind won't go away from them to let them sleep; they are irritable trees, complaining trees with their brain wrapped in clouds. My tree is light green and meant to be light of heart but it is bigger and taller than any pear tree anyone ever remembers and it was here when the Livingstones had it at their back door. What is it, Sandy?"

"You and I, Miss Doll-Normill, are going to be exterminated. The Prime Minister has said, 'Think not of the human race in the abstract, think of people you know who have struggled for years under the handicap of being human and who would be eased of their distressing life by this new legislation. Moreover you may think of their fate, if fate it can be called, without guilt as the decision has been taken out of your hands. And those close to you who may be suffering in other ways—mental defects, gross physical handicap—and whom you love, love, love and wish to remain near to and fear to lose, think of it only as an advance of death, think of their loss patriotically as a gesture to your country on their and your behalf. For are we not at War, a declared war against human customs and accepted morals? For how many years have we tried to mend, to recover and care for broken bits of humanity without realizing that disposal, with other waste, is the solution? And is not this legislation a form of conscription that must be adhered to in order to give us future freedom to enrich, purify our country and its people, bring a new phase of humanity? Let it never be said that we do not lead the world in social legislation. In a year's time our country will have settled to its new way of life and will be thriving with its new industries and customs in a reality of economic prosperity. We shall have observers from other countries to study our Human Delineation Act and return to set it up in their own countries.'

"End of quote from Prime Minister.

"I heard him speak these words, Miss Doll-Normill, while the Speaker of the House prayed for the 'peace and tranquillity of New Zealand almighty God.' "

"Is that truly what he said, Sandy? He has borrowed plenty of words."

"No one will be able to blame the tussock, the paddocks, the sheep and their price, the fences, the cabbage trees wearing their innocent swords like stars.

"Loyalty to H.D.

"Freedom for you and me.

"That is the slogan, Miss Doll-Normill. Now to continue the Prime Minister's Announcement:

" 'The new schools of Preventive Medicine will keep the new population shining with health and in-telly-gents and normality. There will be no more prolonged dying, nor prolonged recovery, no need to turn away at the sights made unbearable by one's compassion for others. A vast diseased unproductive area of each human mind will be removed by the enforcement of this law. The process may be compared to amputation. And, remember, packs of maimed in their hallucinatory guise as jungle animals did not roam the streets fifty years ago as they do today, haunting and terrifying with their unintelligible cries. Some of you may remember your city as it was last century with people living out their ordinary human lives, even after having known two World Wars. All that is changed. There is no longer room anywhere in building or heart for those members of our population who are more clearly animal than human, while the sacrifice of those who are deformed, diseased, handicapped in any way, whose strangeness has been accepted over so many years, is a necessary price to pay for the continued survival of whole, normal, in-telly-gent beings. I will use the phrase *a Clean Sweep*. It will be an objective process. No concessions will be made. Even in our Cabinet there is the example of the Minister of Public Works whose untimely illness has made him a possible sacrifice for the principles of H.D. For those who suffer mild illness—flu or the common cold and suchlike—a time limit has been set for quick recovery; each man's desire

to survive will ensure that no illness goes undetected for long
—there is always hope of a quick cure. And the best watch-
dogs (pardon the expression) and police in any country are
one's neighbors in competition for survival. In the end a man
is loyal to his own survival, not to his neighbor, not even to
his wife, family, parents, friends.' "

"Did the Prime Minister say that, Sandy? It scares me. I
am afraid of important words not borrowed from the Bible
or the knitting patterns or the cookery books but from pages
and mouths I know nothing about."

"Miss Doll-Normill, Swampy and Flagstaff loom bleak
with storm clouds big and purple as bruises blotting the
late-afternoon light. I hear the shouts of children playing; a
referee whistles from the park; a bellbird chiming from Mr.
Warburton Maurice's rowan tree; birds in the Livingstone
pear tree; a dample-dample sound of a tennis ball bounced
on the footpath.

> *"Dustfree, germfree, and human*
> *stone wings angels of stone*
> *flying without motion above a clay grave*
> *the snowgrass is tufted silk beautiful*
> *the lily of the valley*
> *its little white pearl-drop and its green spears."*

"Why do you say that, Sandy? Did they put it in you when
they fixed you? Am I human, Sandy?"

"You know yourself what you are, but the final decision
will come from above."

"From God?"

"Not as high as that."

"From the King?"

"Not as high."

"From the Prime Minister?"

"Still not as high above."

"If you get lower you will come to me, to us."

"Why do I have to remind you, Miss Doll-Normill, that the decision is from Colin's computer because you and I and everybody else have been fed into it, meals and meals of people, and even before we knew about the Act the computer was digesting everybody in a magnificent feast of *bits*.

"Milk honey
flesh fire
sweet salt
sweet sour
sour bitter
salt sour
flesh fire
sweet bitter
earth sky

"sour milk
salt honey
bitter flesh
sweet fire

"sweet water
salt flesh
sour sky
bitter wood
sweet earth
bitter fire
salt sky
sour flesh

"sweet wood
sweet honey
sweet milk
sweet fire
sour earth bitter sky.

"You see it is all there and we are there too but the strangest thing is that it is not the parts I have written about that are in the computer, not flesh, honey, fire, earth, sky, milk which is people but 'When did Columbus discover America? Who is the Prime Minister? How many yards in a mile? Which is the intruder—goose, swan, tiger, sparrow, godwit, albatross?' Remember, Milly, they came asking those questions many months ago now, and they said it was for research and it was, it was research for the act, re-search but it was not soursalt sweetbitter it was different food the computer wanted—Columbus, gotwits, albatross; foreign countries—America, Siberia—and the birds and the earth. The computer's appetite is capricious, it swallows bits and pieces —of us and of history and of the seasons of the years."

"Have you seen the computer, Sandy?"

"Yes. It is guarded by guns and dogs and if you want to see it you must have a special pass because it is busy deciding and when Deciding Day comes it will be buzzing inside, Milly, from morning to night, working with all the names and classifications of everybody in the Southern Zone while Colin and his special helpers stand by, pressing buttons and watching lights flash. But think of other things, Milly. We live on a strange planet. The landscape supports no life because the heat is too hot and the cold is too cold and there is no shelter of forgetfulness and the days and the nights, real and in memory, are longer than men could ever bear."

"Which planet, Sandy?"

"You and me and they."

35

Waipori, Friendly City of the South, is my city and here are its inhabitants. First, most of the people who used to live on Eagle Street in what they call the old days are gone because in the War there were upheavals and some of the places including the Livingstone's place were left in ruins. Dora

Nightshade is new here and my father is helping her with her sexshun by clearing the weeds and preparing the garden so she can grow her own vegetables and have flowers in vases. Sometimes I go with my father to Miss Nightshade's where I help her hang out her washing and save her from getting varicose veins from standing and hanging out her washing, because she is older, about sixty or more and soon will be retired on a pension. At the post office she weighs parcels and sells stamps and has her name "Miss Nightshade" written on her dress and across her heart, and when it is lunch time with everyone coming and going and saying, "Stamps please," she has two red spots on her cheeks from being flustered with people asking and her not having enough time to get the stamps and weigh the parcels, and the other positions saying Closed Apply Next Teller. Miss Nightshade wears a straw hat in summer and straw shoes, and because it is always blowing up here she has to hold onto her hat and her elbows are skinny like chicken's. However she is kindness itself to me and asks me in for a cup of tea and a scone and she speaks heartily and cheerfoolly and has china cups and saucers around the room on stands painted black in the latest fashion. Sometimes she lets me use her steam iron which is one of my favorite occupations, and after the washing is brought in I go inside to iron all the clothes. How exciting it is to fill the iron with the tiny cup of water just up to near the top and turn the switch, though Miss Nightshade likes to do the turning herself but she lets me watch and she flicks it and everything is ready and the clothes are stacked in order and after each one is ironed I fold it cairfoolly ready for it to go in the hot-water cupboard to keep warm, and I put my face down to smell it, a lovely ironed smell, and suddenly I want to be cosy, so cosy but you can't be cosy when you're walking around in the world with the wind coming at you from all directions and you can't hide in the hot-water cupboard on the shelf because Miss Nightshade wouldn't let you, besides

255

you wouldn't fit in, not if you are mature like me, there's no room. When I have finished ironing, Miss Nightshade gives me coins to buy hair-set or something and a lolly to eat, though she does not approve of lollies because of the tooth decay and she has said that she would die if she had to have false teeth, that her teeth are her most precious possession and it is rare for someone her age to have her own teeth. In her bathroom she has rows and rows of tooth-stuff, she is so determined, and she has a different brush for every day and in her broom cupboard she has different brooms for every day, for the floor, and different dusters for the furniture and the windows, and several times she has confessed to me that she wants her house to stay in its original condition. She does exercises too, but not when I am there, only when I see her against the blind at night and my father is unkind and laughs at her. There goes Miss Dora Nightshade keeping in trim for the great day. She dances too and one day she asked me to join a class for creative dancing where you do what you please to music, but I don't like classikill music it's too slow, dum-de-dum, boom, boom, and gloomy and when it comes on the radio my father says, "Get a move on can't you," to the musicians and if they don't get a move on he turns it off and when I listen to the transistor I don't bother to listen if it is dum-dum-dum boom, it is too confusing.

Miss Nightshade goes to the class for older people. How busy she is, not a spare moment, up with the lark, burning the candle at both ends, and you can see her being busy whenever you look up to her place and she is almost never away Closed Apply Next Teller, she is always there ready to send parcels if anybody wants her to send parcels. One thing, she does not knit, she has no spare time and I have knitted several garments for her, even in the few months she has been here, as my own way of life is very leisurely. One day she told me that I was a treasure and that the people in the neighborhood were lucky to have someone like me to do little jobs and that more use should be made of the hand-icapped, we are such treasures. I felt so pleased, she has never said anything else is a treasure, only her teeth. I am conscious of the distinction of being doll-normill. It is rare, rare as having your own teeth, so I suppose that is why I am a treasure, like Miss Nightshade's teeth in their original con-dition. Pearls are treasures too, and diamonds, but some are real and some are artifishool. I had a double string of pearls given to me on my twenty-fifth birthday. I wear them for visitors and I wore them for an interview when they wanted to see how much I knew and how much my brain worked and I am wearing them the day they decide whether I am Animal or Human. On that day, my birthday as you know, I shall wear my best dress and shoes and pearls and I shall have my hair set and I'll have a bath before I dress so as to smell nice to be near.

Oh, oh, I sometimes gasp with terror to think of the Day. It's coming nearer. Last week for instance my father did not go to work. He told my mother he was taking me to the botanical gardens to see the pond and the hothouse and the fernhouse and the Peter Pan statue and he told me to wear my best clothes, but when we got to the gardens my father said, "This is a secret Milly, we're going to see a man who may be able to help you." And do you know it was incredible, he took me another way round to where Mr. Colin Monk lives and Sandy lives there too, but no one will admit it, and Co-lin's wife and children are gone away to be safe.

My father knocked at the door.

"Mr. Monk may we see you about a certain matter?"

"Come in," Mr. Monk said sternly with a severe frown lining his manly brow.

He ushered us into a room graciously furnished.

"What can I do for you?"

First my father said, "This is Milly, Milly say hello to Mr. Monk."

I said, "Hello." Then I made the mistake of saying, "I know your twin brother Sandy Monk, he is my special friend." (As I spoke I lowered my eyes modestly and bit my lower lip as they do on television. I looked maidenly.) Mr. Colin Monk looked aghast and I was promptly ushered out of the room and I heard voices getting angry and then my father came out and Mr. Monk was saying the Act's law, you know there can be no bribery, it's in the hands of the government. My father sounded as if he was going to cry, and I felt like crying too to see him, because he is my first and only Dad.

"If I'd known," he said, "I'd have kept it secret from the time she was born."

Mr. Monk looked solemn.

"The suffering is not confined to one family. All must bear great grief."

My father looked sly. "Milly's no fool. What about this Sandy, the First Reconstructed Man. How do we know you're not hiding him?"

Although Mr. Monk looked guilty he said, "It's a figment. Let's not talk about it any more."

"It would surprise you," my father said, "what Milly knows."

Yes it would, I thought, it would surprise you all. I was glad to get back to the botanical gardens where we looked at a few flowers and sat on the seat by the band rotunda but there was no band playing, it does only on Sundays, The Ladies Pipe Band and the Waipori Brass Band, because the Government said that music will help us. While we were sitting there we saw a white heron standing by the creek.

"That's a white heron," my father said. "It should have flown, Milly. It's a migrating bird. This is not the season for it to be here." He told me he read in the papers the best place for white herons was Siberia in the northern hemmysfear near the land of the midnight sun.

258

"Does it mean a moon?"

"No a sun, a shining sun. Don't you remember we saw it on television?"

I said I didn't remember. I see so much on television that the geography is confused with the love and the lions and tigers and the insex are confused with the people, and though I remember them I don't remember which is which.

My father sighed.

"Let's go home, Milly."

He made me promise not to tell about going to Mr. Monk's to plead our cause.

How glad I was to get home and into the garden and to see that Samuel cat was still alive. I went and sat with Samuel under the Livingstone pear tree and I didn't feel like talking to anybody and I heard my father say to my mother, "It's beginning to tell on her, she knows it without knowing. There's nothing to be done."

How gloomy that sounded! Meanwhile I was safe under my tree and I tickled Samuel's tummy, but he did not like that and he growled and scratched, in fun only of course, but it made me feel dismal and gloomy, I don't know why. I hit him to teach him a lesson and then I felt better and we were friends again and I sat there dreaming of my future.

36

This is in which I go for a walk in Waipori City. My parents had forbidden me to go anywhere outside even to the neighbors but one day when they were at an official meeting, filling in fawms and giving information about their family and its hisstree, I decided to take a walk.

The city as I used to know it when I went to the Occupation Center was an ordinary place with streets and shops and plenty of cars and people. On Thursdays or Fridays my mother used to take me into town while she shopped and then it would be extra busy with more people and cars and no room to sit for a cup of tea and cakes unless you sat with other people. "Excuse me may we sit here?" my mother would say, and they would say, "Of course, delighted," whether they meant it or not. One of my favorite experiences was having tea in town from the moment we went in and walked along by the railing where the sandwiches and cakes were waiting on plates (you had to use a special fork because of the germs) to the moment we sat at the table and started eating. The people made a buzzing noise all the time and the dishes clattered and the knives and forks tinkled and the money being paid into the till rang bells every time it dropped and I wished I could be a seller in a restaurant pressing the button to make the cash register jingle and then opening the drawer smartly, and quickly slamming it shut and then with the notes pinned down inside the drawer so a wind could not blow them away, and saying, "That will be so much," giving the exact price and change. I used to dream of being there selling coconut cakes and milk shakes and so many things including egg and lettuce sandwiches and tomato and ham, and when I dreamed and it did not come true though I waited for it to come true I got very annoyed and going into restaurants began to annoy me and sometimes I dropped a plate accidentally on purpose but no one knew and everyone was kindness itself to me. And then when I dropped a plate I felt better and I thought perhaps my future was not in restaurants at all but somewhere else, for instance in a dress shop or grocer's or selling jools at the corner.

When I used to go to town there were so many things to see that I became dizzy with looking everywhere: shopwindows with pink ladies staring over their shoulder and sometimes wearing clothes and sometimes not wearing clothes; and hats on heads that had no body, just wire heads like cages stuck in the window with wire and arms and legs lying everywhere like in a war but dressed in fancy clothes with prices on them; and the hare dressers with heads in the window; and the shoe shops with spare feet left and right wearing shoes of every fashion and the butcher's with bluddy bodies hanging on hooks and swinging and their cream-colored fat and blew kidnees and the mints in a pattern like chain stitch on the plate and when the butcher opened the door to the deep freeze a wind blew from the South Poll and icicles came on everyone's nose.

In the middle of the butcher's window there was an artifishool sheep with a necklace of artifishool mint leaves to remind you to make mint sauce. His eyes were like brown and green marbools and his legs were stiff from standing and there was dust on his artifishool wool and in front of his eyes was a plate with an artifishool dinner on it—mutton and mint sauce and potatoes and a green vegetable like cabbage or collyflower; but the artifishool sheep was standing on a cold marbel flaw and didn't move, not like in some shops where the animals and the artifishool people nod their heads all the time, they are so pleased just to be there in the window with everyone looking at them and thinking how clever they are to smile and laugh all the time; but it is electricity and batteries and switches and if you go inside the shop near the window you can hear them humming and clicking, though from outside all you can see is smiling and laughing and you don't hear their masheens working. In one shop there used to be dwarves digging for treasure and their song came out into the street, a song about digging for treasure, it was a jewelled mountain that they owned and they all went there together so no one could cheet and take maw jewels and when they went to the mountain they sang their mountain song to make it orderly. One year they sang in Bradley's shop for months before Krissmiss and after Krissmiss, singing and singing and never getting tired but it was electricity and batteries and all artifishool and one day when we went into town the singing was ova and the dwarves who owned the jewelled mountain were gone and they never came back and my father said that when he drove out to the plains to the rubbish dump to throw away the daffodil bulbs that people didn't want because the daffodil population was increasing too fast, there were dwarves' heads, not their arms and legs or bodies, just their heads lying everywhere because they wore out and could not be replaced with overseize funds, but soon you couldn't see their heads, they were buried in daffodil bulbs because the daffodils decided to grow there, nobody's going to throw us away they said, let's grow, come on, and they did, making a pretty yellow sight in the rubbish dump. I was sorry the dwarves were gone because I used to like watching them and though I never saw them digging for jools I used to hope I would be first to see their jools coming out of the mountain and then everybody would have said, Milly Galbraith was first to see the jewels, and I would have gone for a tour of the world in a Bowing seven-oh-seven with a black nose and silver wings, but now my secret hope is gone and the dwarves are berried in daffodil bulbs, their punishment for wearing out and being manufactured overseize.

After the butcher's and the shop with the dwarves there were the bakers with rows and rows of cakes arranged like on a grandstand at a football match, one above the other and all facing onto the street, all on plates with prices, some cheaper because they were stale. And then there were shops with domestick goods such as pots and pans and bean slicers and cake mixers and all the labor-saving devices and masheens in gleaming white and crome taps and specially colored lavatrees and then the material shops and the fruit and stationery, it was all without end, and all the people buying and buying and the money jingling and knocking in their pockets it was the most exciting city I knew and everyone was always bizzy with motor-moas and painting and planting and going to the beech and to the mountains; that was Waipori Friendly

262

City of the South and if you don't believe me you might be able to find postcards with pictures of it to see how gay it used to be.

Then the War came, the last war, and at first it was all right because nobody bothered and everybody went on just the same and then a few men went to phite and then they started putting people in jail because they didn't want to phite and they demonstrated and the pleece came with truncheons and put them in black vans and shut the daws and they looked out wite faced, demonstrating, and then maw men went to the War because they were balloted in the Art Union, First Prize the War, and maw men and maw men and then they started coming around the houses knocking in broad daylight and the dead of night. "Have you any able-boddied yewths or mail sex any age, come at once." Like a tellygram. People hid, but it was no use they were smoked out like rabbits. Everyone went to the War, some of the women too, mostly the normill, until the War started coming here and the North Island was raised, with everyone seeing the smoke and the wite clouds in the sky and the firy light. And then the men started coming home from the war and some had no faces and no hands and no feet and no skins and no nothing and there were men with blew faces like kidknees only it was the graffite writing on their faces and their bodies. The hospittles were short of peepill to help the wounded and they asked my mother if I could cleen the operating rooms where the wounded were treated and though they said I was doll-nor-mill and they talked in my presence and laughed, there wasn't reely much time for laughter only they started the laughing where you cry at the end and some cried and some laughed and the ones who began laughing ended crying and the ones who began crying ended laughing and then crying and then they all started ova again until you lost count of which was which and it was all mixt with the screams of the wounded having their skins torn off and mendead with anny's thettix. It was a noisy world.

Then everyone gave up hope and the doctors got tired and only the doll-normills continued working, but soon there was nothing to clean up because no one bothered, it was too much to bear, instead they prayed and prayed but God was not in the mood for listening to so much prayer ovatime. He said, why didn't you ask me before when I was not rushed off my feet with work. And when maw of the wounded men came home in the Bowing seven-oh-seven with the black nose and silva wings an ambewlants met them at the airport and they were taken to the hospittle and put in rows on the flaw like seed potatoes, and most went rotten and died and there were whole rooms full of such people with special sprays being showered on them to stop them from spreading diseases, the sort of spray used on insex. And everyone was dazed all the time and didn't bother about shampoos and home perms and though I'm a natural counter I couldn't tell you how many years that war lasted because I was growing up past my a-doll-essence and it was a dream with monsters and carboard faces and queer things and you forgot that people were people there were so many who didn't look like people and then gradually while the Prime Minister kept reminding us of our duty to dim-mock-crissy and the need for curridge and building a new world out of the ashes of the old the city of Waipori began to look normill again only the people were worn out and defawmed and produckshun fell and exports that are so necessary to the ekk-onnimy, and there was unemployment and hunger and no clothes in the shops and no food except what you grew on your sexshun and they said it was the sexshuns that saved everyone and growing your own food which is why Miss Dora Nightshade is so anxious to have a garden in case it all happens again, because it is only a few years ago as the crow flies. My father and brother took ova the old Livingstone sexshun then and when I said I thought the house had fallen apart in a war and the Livingstone's had been razed in a war, my father said: no they did it themselves, it was their own country, their own family histree pulling its weight, which I did not understand, but you can imagine that my father and brother became wealthy, they had so much work to do helping to grow vegetables and fruit and they maid so much money that they achieved what they said had been their ambishun for a long time, that's just it, to be rich, to enjoy the lucksuries. And that was when they bought the Livingstone sexshun with the pear tree and the pears to eat, but before I had time to enjoy them, as part of their ambishun they sent me to a private hospittle to tide me ova they said and to see if I could be fixed not to be ought-istick and diffrint in my brane. They thought the hospitle would make me neat so there would be no threads showing, like when you sew a dress or tuck in the wool when you are knitting but when I got there I found I didn't like it so they took me home and I was not tided ova and I was glad to be home because there was a man asking questions about Waipori and the Prime Minister and our house and my perrints in a most inquisitive way and naturally I had been taught not to answer every Tom, Dick, and Harry who asks questions, for you never know. So that I kept mum in the hospittle, laughing to myself when they tried to test me but it was chiefly this man with wite hare and thin face, middle-aged. There were lots of flowers in bleum there and lawns being watered with hoses and motor moas mowing and everyone was in such a hurry to get us up in the mawning and then to get us to bed at night, they were never satisfied and what was the reason was there something going on what we had to get to and it would be terrible to miss? I was glad, as I told you, when my mother and father came to take me home, not like some who had relations who kept them in the land of the lost. The man who was cheef doctor said I could work at simpool jobs and even micks, be socially active, go out and about, and it was important for me to feel usefool in spite of my so-called mentill defeck.

So when I came out of hospittle the city had been cleaned up after the war (except for the sick and deformed and old) and then the announcement came not many months ago about the Ack and the people being divided into Human and Annymill to help the eek-onnommy. My father wished then that he hadn't put me in hospittle, as it told against me in the wreckawds, because the officials would inspect such wreckawds when the day came to decide.

So now have I brought you up to date about my life? And now to continue my walk in Waipori City.

My mother and father had gone out and I was there in the garden getting annoyed with Samuel cat because he was mooving around and didn't want to be patted though I wanted to pat him, I was in the mood for it. I tweeked his ear I was so annoyed with him and he jumped down from my knee and climbed up the pear tree, up and up, higher and higher until his black fur was colored green like the tree and I could see only the wite of his paws and his apron that makes him look like a baker but the clouds in the sky were wite too like a baker's apron. I knew that if I called out, Samuel, come down this instant, he wouldn't come because he was annoyed with me, he was not in the mood to be patted. How I hated him! I wanted something alive to pat and be friends with, but not something that would climb up the Livingstone pear tree if I started to pat it, something that would be pleased and ask for maw and say would I like to be patted in return, fare's fair; that's what I wanted and fat hope I had to getting it in this cruel world.

So I thought I would go for a walk in Waipori City. I went to my bedroom and found my best clothes, my dark-blue costume with the wite blouse that has buttons the color of milk and the neck frilled nylon easy wash easy care. I made up my face and put on my broach instead of my pearls and my hug-the-head hat for there was a cold wind blowing from the southwest and wite clouds turning gray with rain, and taking my handbag, imitation leather, I set out walking in my comfortable shoes. First I wanted to walk through the gardens, then I decided not to, as it reminded me of the day my father and I went to see the birds and flowers but really to ask for charrity in the future from Mr. Colin Monk.

I walked down the road. Nowadays there are not many people in the street at all, you'd be surprised, and my mother says the only ones you see are the ones who are sure they will be Human and so are not afraid, but I say how can you be sure? Certainly everyone looked the picktewer of health, pleased to be alive and not worrying. When I came to the town it looked as if the wind had blown away something that used to be there and I don't know what it was, it was something like the pegs that keep up the tent when you are camping; it would be terrible to wake early in the morning and find the pegs gone but it would be worse if the tent had been blown away too and you were exposed to the weather. I began to feel gleumier and gleumier because I thought everything in Waipori City was dead with ghosts walking in the fires of hell with their smiling and smiling that said, "We're not walking in the fires of hell," when it was plane they were, only the world and the city had changed and the smiles told it instead of screams, so I felt like crying but I started to smile and smile because I learned it you see and my brane worked from tears to laughter.

Then when I had walked up George Street for some time I began to notice that the town was fool of euniformed officers dressed like the new kind of policemen come to enforce the law. There were hordes of them suddenly outside the City Hotel and I knew they must be staying there in readiness for the grate day. I walked boldly by one and smiled and he smiled back.

"Hello there, you're all dressed up aren't you?"

I admitted that I was and why not.

It dawned on me then that he spoke Amerrykin.

"Are you Amerrykin," I asked politely.

"Shaw," he said, and as soon as he said "Shaw" like that I knew that he was. I smiled a special smile and for a moment he looked at me as they look when they know I'm doll-normill but that look went wherever looks go when they are finished with, off your face and into the air most likely.

"I'm off duty in half an hour," he said. "Would you like to show me the town? Can you wait?"

By the time I've walked up the rest of George Street and Princes Street, I thought, it will be half an hour, so I said, "Yes, I can wait I'll be back, hunny."

I felt very bold, but as he was Amerrykin I thought it might be different.

"What are you here for?" I asked.

"To keep order," he said. "Your government decided to get help from another scenter because then you people won't be hostile against your neighbors for what they'll do to you."

I said, "Oh I see the point." Then giving him a friendly word of goodbye and promising to see him in half an hour I went walking up George Street and down Princes Street stopping at the Ladies Rest Rheum to go to the Lavatree and make up my face again, but the fat woman was cleaning the lavatrees with special disinfectant that smelt like rhubarb and the flaw was wet.

"I didn't expect anyone much today," she said, smiling and healthy and looking curiously at my fine clothes and hug-the-head hat and proberly my broach which would be twinkling in her eyes enough to blind her. In fack I almost said, "Stare, stare like a bare sitting on a monkey's chair when the chair begins to crack all the fleas run down your back," for she did stare at me and made me quite embarrassed. So I did not go to the lavatree though I wanted to but I held on and set out for the City Hotel and my appointment with the Amerrykin which had come round faster than I dreamed in my excitement. My conscience said, "What about Sandy Monk the First Rekinstruckdead Man," and I went wite. I have seen it on tellyvision how terrible it is to be a double-crossing two-timer. Still, I thought, no harm will come from a friendly walk in the Queens Gardens where I will show him the statue and the view of the Early Settlers Museum with all the photographs of the battle-axes who colonized the province and their scared husbands, little men with kind faces and kind but troubled eyes. Yes, I thought I will show this Amerrykin our city and its innerscent sights. My heart began to beat quickly as I had certain thoughts. After all, I told myself, Sandy is far away at this moment.

I came to the City Hotel and suddenly I felt gleumy because I didn't know the Amerrykin's name, so I waited and waited and nothing happened, and then I saw him coming out of the hotel and my heart soared and I knew we would go to the Queens Gardens and be private together with his strong arms around my little waste so tight I wouldn't be able to breathe and I would be so excited and he might be intimitt with me.

I looked at him coming nearer and nearer and then I saw he had a smart piece with him, a blonde without a hug-the-hat, and smiling all ova her face at her capture and though he walked past me he didn't even see me, not one blink of his sea-blew eyes. So much for Amerrykins I said fiercely to myself, and continued on my way with my head high but my heart was disapointed I confess.

I decided to go home along George Street. I had wanted so much to go with the Amerrykin to the Queens Gardens which is a bewty spot with First Church standing tall against the ever-blew sky. I did not want to go down by the railway station as I know that is one of the places where they keep the cages ready for Deciding Day and police and dogs surround that area. I saw the hawding that the City Fathers had put up to remind us to be good:

Happy and Free with H.D.

And it showed a wonnderfool picture of a family being happy, with them eating breakfast and between smiling and eating they were waving at everybody to remind them of the good time coming when the Deciding Day was ova. When I looked at them I felt so pleased that they were happy because it is good to be happy and smiling and eating breakfast all healthy and normill with brains working so fast they wear out and have to start ova again, but some people's brains don't mind, they are used to it. How pleased I was to see the family Happy and Free with H.D. When I talked later with Sandy he said, "It's not a special kind of cornflakes, you know." He said the advertisement makes it look as if it is something to eat, but H.D. is being put in cages and sent to fracktrees and smiling and eating breakfast because you are pleased to be put in cages and sent to fracktrees. I do not want that to happen to me, going to a facktree and being tipped in a masheen with my hair everywhere and untidy in my eyes so I can't see, which is done on purpose so you can't see the terrible masheen.

My thoughts were gleumy as I walked along the street and saw the people laughing and gleumy and the maw I saw of them the gleumier they looked though they were happy and free. And at every corner there were T.V. entertainers employed by the government to make people laugh and forget their troubles but they all looked as if they found it hard to forget and the entertainers looked strange away from the tellyvision screen because their faces were gray instead of black and wite. They sang, "Happy people we embracing our H.D."

He was kissing her and she had H.D. printed on her blouse making her nice to be near. And while they sang there were rebels beside them singing a *Ballad of the Times* which Sandy has written down for me. It goes:

Sandy he belongs to the mill
Sandy he belongs there still,
Sandy he belongs to the mill
and the mill belongs to Sandy.

which is an old rhyme from the nursery.
The ballad begins really with:

Spin doctor spin
a soldier's new skin
use your studied skill
to turn the human wheel
the wheel the weal the well
black water and black oil
a white bird's blood and meat
a black skin's winding sheet.

Scour doctor sour
the national sheep that bore
the dirty fleece of war
scour doctor scour
to find the soldier's cleanest hour
to wrap him safe and warm within
his private shawl of skin.

Scan doctor scan
to read a whole man
quell the animal rage
sign the form that keeps him warm
within the human span
in bach and barn
in house and hut
in room and flat and not
and not in cage.

He washed with human soap and was unclean
His new eyes that would have flowered
were nipped in the bud
by the blight of the dead
and here I should cry for human sake

and here I should sleep
cold in a country of shorn sheep
while the southwest wind doth blow
and we shall have snow.

    That is what Sandy said the rebels were singing and who am I to question him?

    So I continued my walk through the city. I had to pass a crowd of young people who created a disturbance at the sight of me and they were not nice at all, they bullied me. However I did get past them and their stony faces and rude jokes, though you can't blame anyone for enjoying everything while it lasts, having a whole world party with dancing and singing and drinking and eating and making love in their spare beds and in the summerhouses in the gardens and in the streets, really making love with them taking their clothes off and him putting it right inside her and them jigging up and down which is what they do in a whole world party.

    Further along the street there were people with placards which said, "Where are the Sheep?" and some policemen were putting these people in black vans for disturbing the peace. By now I was tired and didn't bother to look into the shop windows but in one shop there was a funny little man standing at the door calling, "Everything free!" and everyone was looking at him and nudging each other and tapping their heads but not stopping to speak to him.

    "Everything free, take yaw pick, this shop won't be open long and we all know why, we all know why."

    I saw a passing euniformed Amerrykin say to his companion.

    "Get him!"

    But the other man said,

    "No, it keeps the crowd happy. Leave him."

    They walked on, leaving him. I thought, however, everything free. Why don't they believe him? For you see people were not believing him at all. I stopped and said conversationally.

"Hello."

He looked at me.

"Help yourself," he said.

I questioned.

"Really?"

"Shaw."

He was speaking Amerrykin, shaw thing baby. It is catching.

"Can I come in then?"

"Shaw. Help yourself."

I followed him into the shop which was selling camping and sports gear, footballs, golf clubs, bicycle lights, and clothes for wearing in the mountains and skis and bright jersies and blankets.

"You'd think they'd want these," the man said. "I've heard of some who've escaped to the mountains, but they must have bought their kits elsewhere. Help yourself."

Now if only it had been a hare dressers or clothes shop or china and other gifts, or even food. The man had not stopped screaming his message.

"Why is it?" he asked, "that you believe when the others don't or won't?"

"I dunno," I said. "Just because you said, 'Help yaself,' I thought you meant it and why shouldn't you mean it?"

"Why shouldn't I? I can see you have an uncomplicated brain."

So that was why, I thought, and I felt pleased that someone was saying nice things about my brain after all these years.

"I do indeed," I said. "My brain is special."

"So is mine," the man confessed. "And that is why this shop won't be open much longer and as I've no relatives I may as well give everything away. Don't you think that's a good idea?"

"I certainly do. I wish it was a hare dressers for me to get a hare-set."

"Help yawself then. What would you like?"

I didn't know what to choose. "Can I have anything at all?"

"Certainly madam."

Slowly I walked through the shop. I'd have to choose something I could carry away with me, therefore I could not take the skis or the inflatable dinghy but I took the crash helmet. There was a rubber bed too that I wanted to blow up and lie on and it would carry me away on the waves as far out to sea as I wished to go and I would lie in bed looking up at the ever-blew sky and feel the Passifick rolling around me and washing me gently to a forrin shore.

I took the crash helmet and a dynermow lamp for a bicycle, because there wasn't much else I wanted. Perhaps Sandy would like the dynermow, I thought, because when it is switched on it makes a pleasant humming sound like a bird. And while I stood there musing on what I would like and what Sandy would like I thought there might be other shops such as hare dressers where they were giving away things so I decided to take my crash helmet and dynermow lamp but first I thanked the shopkeeper who had been kindness itself and who had approved of my special brane.

As I hurried from the shop I saw that people were still not accepting the invitation to help themselves because they were not believing it and I thought it very strange. Perhaps they suspected a trick and they couldn't bear to be tricked but if it was a trick the shopkeeper would be put in jail. What they are missing, I said to myself as I hurried along in search of a hare dressers but there were none in view so I stopped walking quickly and went ordinary and because the crash helmet was heavy and because I wanted to see how it felt I put it on and I climbed the hill and turned up the road toward our house. One of the neighbors looked over the fence at me.

"Hello Milly."

I did not know him but he knew me.

"Hello Milly."

Being familiar.

Then he called to the woman in the garden, talking as if I was invisible.

"She thinks, paw soll, that wearing a crash helmet will save her on the Day."

Then he said to me,

"Nice crash helmet you've got, Milly."

I did not answer as I like courtesy and when you are there people talking to you as if you are there and not talking to other people about you as if you were not there. I walked along the road, my head at a proud angool, feeling pleased at my black shiny crash helmet.

When I arrived home my mother and father had come home from their meeting. They seemed worried about my absence.

"You must never go out by yourself again, Milly," my mother said. "Not now the Ack is in force."

They were worried, too, about my crash helmet.

"Where did you get this?" my father asked, going wite.

"A man in a shop gave it to me," I said calmly.

They looked at me as if they didn't believe me.

"Now Milly," my father said, "you're old enough to know better. We've trained you carefooly. No one gives away crash hellmits."

"Your brane is different from mine," I said angrilly. I would have gone on to explain that my brane was a believing brane and most people's was not but I saw they were troubled and I knew we were living in troubled times, therefore I did not boast any maw about my brane.

I heard them deciding to put a special lock on the

gate and door. Then my mother was crying.

"Though what good it will do when the time comes, I don't know. Perhaps we should let her enjoy herself while she can."

Enjoy myself! They did not know how much I was enjoying myself already with walking in the street and having a crash hellmit and a believing brane and sitting under the Livingstone pear tree with Samuel cat though I think Samuel knows about Sandy and is jealous and that will teach you, Samuel, I said aloud, that will teach you not to scratch when I pat you.

It was time for him to learn that I could go elsewhere to eckspress my affeckshuns.

37

Poor Sandy. He sleeps in a back room at Colin's place and they stand at the door and call out, "Come in for tea, Sandy," and he comes and does not mind, he has no dignity. I care about dignity and if people are rude to me or call out angrily or speak nastily, I get angry too and don't speak to them because I am so angry but Sandy does not care, he said they took his care out and forgot to put it back and when no one was looking it was stolen or lost and they were so busy with his golden skin and special memory, they forgot to look for his care.

"Come in for tea Sandy, tea's ready," they call as people do to a child who does not know the time by the stars or the sun or the clock. They come with their voices like the tidill waves and drown Sandy and that is why Colin does not even see that he is alive or admit that he is his twin brother. Colin lives in a double-brick house with a patio and two ferns in pots in front, a carport at the side and walls that face the northwest, made of glass so that every morning when all the

family used to be home you would see them sitting at breakfast and after Colin Monk went to work you saw his whife
standing in the middle of the room wondering where to hide
or walking around the room touching the furniture, dusting
it with a shammy leather duster, vacuuming, washing, plenty
to do, and all the appliances to do it because the Euniversity
pays Colin plenty of munny, enough to keep Sandy too free
board and lodgings tellyvision installed, own room, weekend
outings, extras, plenty of spare time, and the more salary
they get the more appliances they get but that is not always
so, because Sandy said that with some of them the more
salary they got the more they become pioneers making their
own clothes and gathering firewood and pine cones for their
wood stove and planting native bush on their sexshun to
make it look as if they had never arrived in Waipori or in the
country, but Colin was not like that and the Monks sat in
chairs, not on the floor, and they have a masheen underneath
the sink that chews and swallows the waist food except
knuckle bones and it eats quietly because it is called a Velvet
Eunit, a Plush Mistress, and their refrigerator is a Feasterama holding food for forty days and forty nights it is so
big, rows and rows of eggs, pounds of butter with the extinct
bird on the wrapper, Canterbury lam with red stripes only the
best is good enough, and other meats, bottles and cartons
and jellies and vegetables and ice cream and extra joints for
emergency, certainly enough to feed a city and once when
Sandy said, "Can I clean out the fridge, Gloria?" She said,
"No, it's automatick defrost daws adjustible shelves foamwall." And when Sandy told me this I felt jelliss because ours
is not foamwall but one can't complain, Sandy said and I
admitted I like outside best under the Livingstone pear tree
and my head in the shadow of the tree is colder than my hand
inside the silly old refrigerator. Sandy explained that in Colin's house people and masheens live on eekwill terms. Colin
is chiefly interested in masheens that remember and calcu-

late and decide and like people they get hungry and irritable and have to be fed bits and pieces that are numbers left ova after people have eaten them but Sandy said, "No they are just special numbers and special counting one, two, ten, eleven, twelve, twenty, and so on."

Little Robert and Sally Monk were such pretty chilldren. Robert used to be at school before they closed the schools until it is all decided because chilldren will be decided about too and there were some rheumas that chilldren were being taken beforehand to make it kwick and eezy for everyone because people usually smile when they see chilldren and what will happen if the time comes to put them in cages and take them to factrees or just to kill them if they have to be smiled at all the time? They will smile back and the people taking them will smile and everyone will smile and nothing will happen and the law will be forgotten and the Prime Minister will be angry and the world will go on as it used to be with nobody Animal and nobody Human but all a mickstewer and the standead of living will be lower and exports lower too and goods and services poor even nil, that is what they said it would be like and you'll have to wait ours for a bus and a letter posted in one place will get to another place twenty miles away two weeks later which is gross innyfishency and there will be rebellion and poverty and hunger with people eating each other and being kept in cages for experiments and then no one will have a better chance than anyone else at being able to eat people, and you have to be fair when it comes to eating people and experimenting on them and manufacturing paper and clothes out of them, otherwise there would be a racket in people and that is why the new law is best, it's fairer. Now to return to Robert and Sally Monk whom I used to know before they went North. Robert was an ordinary boy ten years old, a bit cheeky and too brite, but Sally was best, she was in a pram and had to be tucked up. They had to be looked after all the time, such a lot of looking after with their mother peeping at Sally to see if all was well and Mr. And Mrs. Monk talking to them as if they were groan people saying, "What do you think Robert, have you an opinion," and Robert, who is brite but not as brite as they wanted him to be, would look around for an opinion and when he couldn't find one his perrints were disappointed in what they had brought into the world, but they hadn't time to be disappointed in Sally because crying and smiling were all her opinion and they could really say she was thinking whatever they chose her to think and what her crying and smiling meant, oh, a very in-telly-gent opinion she had and they were pleased and they looked at her and said she will learn bally when she grows up. The Monks were special perrints the way they talked to their children but I think I would find it hard and would feel like going away under the Livingstone pear tree where you don't have any opinions because I admit that when I myself am looking for an opinion I can't always find one but then I have no training to look for them, they must be everywhere, they are talked about so much. Somehow it comfits me when I look at Samuel cat for shawlly he has not menny opinions either? And nobody cares or is angry with him for that or calls him doll-normill. But what are opinions anyway, not of much importants after all. Even if I found one I would not use it because I hate opinions and never ask other people for them and I think it is crooly when they ask me for one on my behalf because they can see them lying everywhere the way housekeepers see dust and specks in places where others can't see them, so they take one and say to other people that it is mine and I am kwite pleased at this, really, and I smile and feel golden in my skin when they announce so firmly, "That is Milly's opinion isn't it Milly deer."

Then the other people turn to me and smile because they are pleased with my opinion.

I used to feel like warning Robert and Sally about the world and the people and all the things that get lost or you never had them yet you are expected to find them in a hurry, but you mustn't tell anyone you never had them so how can you find them if you don't know what to look for?

Robert as I said was quite an ordinary but brite little boy and still is as far as I know. Children in fack are like kittens without their eyes open and it is only when their eyes open that you can see they are all different, some scratching and some purring and happy to be patted and some sleeping and some going away to hunt berds and myce, well it is a long time before children have their eyes open and you know what color they are. There was once a cat next door, a lady-cat, you could tell when you turned her upside down to look she had a little pleat just there so you knew she was a lady-cat. She had kittens, five, one after the other, they were wet where she licked them and their faces were screwed up and their mouths thin like rubber bands stretch stretch to get at the milk and they used to snuggool together so wawm, one curled over the other and all breathing together up and down tick tick their hearts and their skinny legs with big feet and I wished it was me there breathing but I mean to be telling you maw of the neighborhood.

Most of the houses are very old or new. The only real ruin is where the Livingstones had their home and they all perished, they were a tippykill family of the old days everyone says but something went wrong with their pattern, the world came in and washed them all away. Miss Dora Nightshade's house is old and Colin Monk's is new, it was photographed on a calendar the grocer Mr. Newell gave us, it said a tippykill house in Waipori City; and our house is old with the Livingstone pear tree older than all the houses. One by one the houses are being pooled down and new ones built, and at the corner there is a motel owned by a dentist, fancy little houses with letterboxes like birdhouses with pointed roofs and windows and front doors with a number on them and every nite you hear the tellyvision coming roll roll roll the horses in the new Westerns galloping farster and farster. And then there is the house further along Eagle street built by a speckulator with no one living there at first and then it was advertized Kintemperry double brick, open-plan living, ceiling to flaw windows, and as it was being built all day the carpenters hammered and the painters painted and they played nice musick on their transistors and sometimes a car came and people inspected the house because they had seen it advertized For Sale, and the man would look at the house and then at his whife and say tendaly, "What do you think my darling?" and she would say, "Oh deer, the windows are not to my taste, the clothesline does not swing in the write direction, the kitshun sink is in the wrong place," and he would say tendaly, "Very well, my darling," then it is decided and they would get into the car and drive away as happy as the day is long. Every day someone came to look at the house and sometimes the man would say, "My dear it is not suitable, lets go hunny," and they would go, but everyone liked the view, the view was mentioned as something speshill, as it is for us, ova the seven hils of Waipori City. Dream house, sun all day, eezy care sexshun. I thought that perhaps people did not want a dream home, when one day I saw the furniture van arriving and the next day there was a china dog on the front dawstep; he was black and wite and so reel but he stayed still and no real dog would do that, for dogs have to walk about and wag their tails and sniff after everyone to see if they are enny relation. And now there are people living in the house and you can see them in the morning having their breakfast, you can even see what is on the table. My father and brother have been helping them to plant their garden, for before the house was built, naturally, the builders dug out the old garden and chopped down the trees and shrubs and maid it all clean for the new people who would have been angry if they had come and seen old flowers and trees growing around a new house doublebrick contemperry. It would not have set off the new house at all and they would have said, "Why that tree's been there fifty years if it's been there a day, a disgrace, whatever are the builders thinking to leave it there." Now however there is a new neat garden growing up, although it's taking time, because when the plants were put in, the earth said, "What do you think you are doing here taking the place of those gone before my lost deerly beloveds with such indecent haste there has to be a decent interval you know, like after your husband dies. Oh, no you don't, you can't come here," so the plants didn't grow much at first because they were scared and every night when the new owners looked at them they frowned because they did not know about there being a decent interval after something is lost and gone and dead. Gradually, however, the earth forgot its scentermentill nonsense and was glad to start keeping compinny with plants which could look around and see what's going on when the earth can't, and another thing the plants can sneak down pots and pots of sunlight for the earth, a happy arrangement if you ask me. So now there are plants and no more bare clay and the garden is trouble-free and the earth is healed because everything heals even when the beloved is wrenched away to make the sexshun neat and clean and new.

38

Much time has passed since I wrote in this exercise book. It is now the end of July and it is snowing and at the end of next month is my birthday and the Deciding when one by one we will be separated and classified. The city has become fool of people in euniforms, maw than were here when I wrote about my walk and nearly all are Amerrykins for the special reason I told you earlier, and a number of officers have been given to the streets and families to get to know them and play games with the chilldrin and give them special toys and smile at everybody as if it were a happy world fool of happy people and no doubt it is, for one officer, called liason, has come regularly to our place and has brought with him a sewing masheen such as I never saw before in my life although I have heard of them, a big masheen glittering with knobs and switches and let me tell you about it because as you know I am interested in sewing and can do chain stitch and lazy daisy and different seams which all come naturally to me since I learned them at the Occupation Center. When Miss Dora Nightshade said she wanted all her bed linen to be handmaid, someone told her of my talents in that direction and so she came to me, "Milly wood you sew my sheets and pillow cases please for a small sum?"

"Certainly," I said, pleased to be usefool.

Carefoolly she instructed me about the color and stitch and all, and I sewed them on our masheen at home which is modern but not with as many attachments and bright lights like a city as the sewing masheen brought here by the Amer-rykin officer. You can imagine my excitement when he brought it. I thought I would die of loving it and touching it, only there was a catch I'll tell you about it, there is always a catch.

"Wait Milly dear. Wait," he drawled when I leaned forward.

He smiled and nodded at my mother who didn't really know why he was smiling and nodding, although my mother is a sensible person. And then when everyone was looking and ready and I didn't know whether to laugh or cry, wanting so much to touch the masheen the officer said,

"Go ahead Milly it's all yaws."

I could not help smiling and smiling, and wiping my hands on my apron in case there was a speck of dirt on them and wiping and wiping them they had to be cleaner than clean and with everyone getting impatient and all pleased at my wonderfool present, I plucked up courage, and at last I touched the masheen gently at first and then when I saw they were waiting for me to try it out, to take off the pretty blew cover and spread out some stuff and sew it in front of them with the nobs turning and the lights flashing and the needle like an icicle darnsing along hop skip, hop skip, or fancy stitching if I wanted it, whatever I asked it to do because I was boss of it, well then I took a chair and sat down and getting a reel of cotton from the table draw I began to thread it into the masheen and it surprised me at first until I saw it was a special masheen that the needle would not go in the ordinary way. Oh this must be a modern masheen indeed I thought, but the maw I looked for where to thread the masheen the maw I couldn't find it anywhere and it was then I discovered that all the nobs and lights were pretend nobs and lights; the nobs were stuck on ornamentilly and the lights were bolbs of colored plastick, in fack nothing in the beautifool masheen would work. I felt sad and sick, as if it was the end, and angry with their tricks, and my shoulders were shaking and I thought my arms would turn and hit and slice everybody in the furious wind blowing. My mother and father looked sad too because they had been tricked. The Amerrykin smiled in a puzzled way because his heart was really good.

"Don't you like your new toy, Milly? If you don't like it yew can choose whatever you like from a hole range, yew can have a toy refrigerator, a toy washing masheen, life-size, a motor moa that really mows a little plastick lawn two feet square, the lawn is provided in a complete outfit to fold up and put away in a glove-size kimpartmint." Yawr telling me, hunny, I thought. I knew it was only a fairy story where the dress was folded inside a thimble all in a million creases and when the lady who was a princess took it out of the thimble all the creases dropped out of it and she waw it to the ball where the prince danced with her and said, "Yewv a natty laundry maid, hunny, to steam-iron that model."

"Oh yes," the Amerrykin said, "yew can have any toy you choose Milly."

Certainly his generosity was ovawhelming and as he stood there smiling and smiling with his liaison smile I couldn't feel angry with him any more and when he persisted, "What's the matter, Milly, don't you like your masheen."

I said, "It's a very nice masheen Mr. Liaison but I'm groan, I can really sew, my sewing is treasured in the neighborhood."

I went on, thinking it might sound like skiting but it is true, "I sew. I gnit. I have several pattern books and I have learned to gnit skillfoolly."

Looking puzzled again the Amerrykin opened his briefcase and consulted the papers they always carry with them so they know which houses to go into and which people to smile at specially and which to bring toys to. I saw him frowning as he read down a column of numbers.

"According to my notes," he began, and then stopped, and the paw man looked embarrassed.

"Yew never know," he said. Then he turned to my mother and father who were looking puzzled and annoyed.

"The notes are of necessity brief and many details must be excluded."

My father and mother did not speak.

I think the Amerrykin was pleading when he said in a kind way,

"Now Mr. and Mrs. Galbraith this is just a task our nation has been called on to perform. I hope you have no ill feeling towards us as we have none towards you. I'm only doing my duty. It is best for our notes to be brief for in our posishun we must remain detached."

My mother was going to say something but she changed her mind.

The Amerrykin looked stern and then said in an official voice, "No decisions are made until the day. It's only our duty to spread goodwill in the waiting perryid, and naturally we choose the most likely people, to give them sum final pleasure before they are taken from us in the interests of the new society. We like to make their last thoughts of us not unkindly."

My father exclaimed impatiently and his face grew red. "It's bryberry," he said.

Cool and killecktead the Amerrykin smiled at my father and when he spoke he sounded menacing.

"I repeat that no decisions are maid until the day. Yew yourself may be in for a surprise, my man. Who knows which members of the community are cheerfoolly thinking their future is assured and what a blow it will be to them to learn of their classification."

If my father had been on tellyvision he would have advanced a pace or two and shaking his fist in the man's face, he would have muttered, "Is that a threat? Because if it is . . ."

And the Amerrykin, surprised, would have stepped back and slunk shamefaced threw the daw. But my father was not on tellyvision where everything is safe and where you can hit if yew want to and not have police coming, and say what yew want to say whatever you think of with no one to stop yew. Oh no, my father was in the house in Waipori City and just as scared as all the other people of the country with the day coming nearer and nearer. He had to pretend he wasn't angry.

He smiled at the Amerrykin.

"Yaw meaning is clear," he said. "We just have to wait and hoap don't we?"

Mind you there are people who would have spoken angrilly without caring what happened, but my father is not that kind of man, he obeys rools and keeps the law and is a respected citysin and therefore after a little while there was this Amerrykin and my father and mother having mawning tea and cakes and I could hear the pleasant laughter as if the world were a happy place and you'd be surprised when I say it is, it's a happy world with the sun shining wawm on yaw skin.

Ecksept today. As I write this it is snowing and I'm inside at the porch window looking out at the snow falling. We don't often have snow falling like this. It came secretly in the night; sometimes in the night it is cars coming and motor bikes, sometimes it is wind and rain, or it is the engine shunting at Pawt Chalmers or ferther round the coast towards Mihiwaka; and sometimes it is cats wailing and dogs barking, watch dogs mostly when they hear the burglar sneaking in the gate and trying to open the window to steal the jools, diamonds, pearls, bracelets, gold watches, munny, enny kind of treasure which they can get if they know the combination of the safe and the watchcogs don't nip them with their strong teeth doing their duty against the criminal types that abound. Also, sometimes in the night, it is people laughing and talking or thunder and lightning, or explosions of dynermite; and from here it is the sea at St. Clair and St. Kilda with the hewge waves dashing on the rox and the serf rolling in as high as the post office, and green and brown with bits of wood and then wite on top like soapsuds when you wash the dishes or clothes; how the sea roars at night; and with all the other noises not to mention the allnite radio—oh, the night is never quiet.

Except last night. It snowed secretly and the snow was so quiet that the quietness drowned all the noises in the world. How could that be? But it was. It was snow and it snowed and it blocked all the noises like filling yaw mouth with cotton-wool and stopping you from laughing or talking or eating and this morning everywhere was filled with snow the white gobstopper of quiet, but as soon as people woke it nearly stopped, it was half-hearted as if what's the use, with space between the flakes, and ouside on the street it turned brown though on the Livingstone pear tree it stayed white like best

287

flour and it's still white in grate lumps along the branches like wite of egg when you beat it and it grows stiff, and sometimes thud the snow shifts and drops to the ground and the branches spring up in the air as if to say good riddance because snow is heavy on your arm.

It is lunchtime now and the snow has almost stopped which it does here. Here it doesn't snow and snow until you forget everything but the snow, here it snows a little while and then it remembers that it's not supposed to snow and that's when it gets half-hearted and stops and the clouds blow away and the sky is blew again and the sun comes out though sometimes it doesn't get to yew because there's a long way to shine and too much cold in between to sneak the warmth that's coming to you by write. I think that while it was snowing my perrints and some of the people might have forgotten about waiting for the day because the snow blocked their thinking and maid them think snow snow snow and not Deciding Day Deciding Day Deciding Day.

Since I last wrote in this book there has been violence in Waipori City with riots and people being knocked down and some killed or ushered away to prison where they will never be heard of again. And for some funny reason everyone started to storm the bakers' shops asking for maw bread until the baker had to ration the bread, and Sandy told me the psychologists were saying that the tenshun was making people eat maw. One day when there had been a raid on a baker's shop, George Street had a mountain of loaves in the middle with people fighting ova them. My father said that some people know how to profit from the world's troubles, look at Frank Peterson the baker whizzing round in his new convertibool and look at the farmers hoarding their wheat so they can ask for higher prices.

In some of the gardens now they have asked my father to plant weet instead of lawn and the tellyvision doctor speaks every night trying to ask us why we should eat maw bread than usual when the human constitution has not changed, don't panick he says, eat other things. One day recently the churches had a Pavlova Sunday to get everyone's mind away from bread and everyone brought pavlova cakes to church, praying over them and eating them afterwards just like a bunphite to get them in, my father said. And there was a tellyvision program showing the Minister blessing the pavlova and frowning on the loaf of bread.

You know when it was snowing I thought the world was the same as it used to be, because when yawr looking out of the window and don't see people in the gardens or the streets you forget that anything has happened like War, but you can't get back into remembering what it was like before the War, it's like when you dream a dream and wake up and try to go to sleep again to get back into the dream only you can't because your awake and you keep trying to rescue the dream and it floats away, well when the snow was here it was like being in the dream but now it's waking and as far as I can see the only thing to do is to start knitting knitting knitting and finish the jersey I started in double nylon and in the middle of knitting think about Sandy and my birthday and what I would like for a present and hoap the sky won't fall down on me which often frightens me, for it seems there's nothing to hold it up because the trees don't reach that far and the mountains might only hold it in a few places and when it fell down of course as any fool knows it would bring the sun and the stars and the moon with it, thud thud heavier than snow and the sun might just hit you when you were in the garden sitting under the Livingstone pear tree it might fall through the branches and burn you so much you had to be bandaged with a wite bandage round and round your body like a horror person. But it's funny whenever I said, "What about the sky falling?" people have said, "Don't you worry, Milly, that would never happen," and they've said it so often I don't like to mention it any maw, as they might laugh which is what they do, but a funny thing is they've never explained why it stays up, if it's poles and invisible lines or glew and nails. They just smile and try to tell me it's not really there, that sky isn't something, it's all nothing going on and on into nowhere and it happens to be colored blew on fine days. Sandy is best for talking to about these things because he believes the sky is real he says it's sucked up there and that we're sucked down here on earth like the rubber thing you put the teatowels on, sucked to the wall so you can find them to dry the dishes, and that the world wouldn't be the world if it was the other way round and we were sucked up in the sky and the sky was sucked down on earth, that it's best for it to be up there because it's a pretty blew and it changes color and we can look at it and it helps us to see where we're going and to look around and know if we're being followed and it tells us when to take our coats if we go out for the day, also that night is coming when we mightn't know the sun is getting ready to disappear, indeed the sky is usefool, maw usefool than some people might admit.

Wait.

I'm writing this in peace.

Something is happening.

Not the sky falling down.

A branch from the giant pear tree, its cracking and groaning going down into the garden, crash.

What's the row, my mother says.

"The pear tree, a branch with snow on it, Mum."

"Time and again I've told your father, time and time again."

It's not a very big branch only middle-sized, and by a stroke of good luck it hasn't fallen where Samuel and Sandy and I like to sit but in the empty part of the garden where the earth is cracked like sore hands; the bits of snow are lying all mouldy-looking along the cracks, but my father says it is good for the soil to be broken and cold with frost, it knocks some sense into it and freezes nasty things out the way yew freeze corns out of your feet and bunyins, so the tellyvision advertisement tells us, and all winter the earth is numb and can't feel like when you sleep on your hand all night or tuck yaw foot under you on the seat by the Livingstone pear tree and everything is dead and when yew wake yew have to slap your hand and yawr foot, hit them hard and that is the way the sun comes shining out of the sky after winter, slap bang slap like being born and the garden tingling and starting to breathe first pins and needles and then the curled up plants uncurling like your dead hand.

My father has gone outside to inspect the damage.

"That's what I mean, Milly," he says to me as he comes inside again. "The pear tree's out of control. I've never known another pear tree like it. They're usually well-behaved trees. It's only for your sake we've done nothing about it, because ever since you were kneehigh to a grasshopper it's the place you've liked to go. But any extra weight on it now, like snow, and hey presto it's a wonder we're not dead in our beds. Sometimes trees are more nuisance than they're worth, if they're not interfering with the sewer or the view, they're blocking the sun. The trouble I've had with trees in my work, Milly. The day's not far away when we'll have artifischool trees that stay where they're put and don't go wandering and sneaking around under the earth and reaching so far into the sky where nobody can see what's going on."

Now yew can lose things when you drop them or can't find them or when the time comes that you're not supposed to have them and that is the kind of losing I know most, for ever since I was a little girl people said to me, "Oh Milly shawlly you don't want to play with such toys at your age, yew have to learn to grow up, it's time you moved on to something else," and so they would move me on to something else, and all the way there was losing with people pushing me on and on to go somewhere everyone is expected to go and

I still haven't arrived and nobody cares now. That, as I say, has been my chief losing. The other losing is burglars that never happen when like me you have no treasure or bank-noats hidden in the safe or jools insured for a fortune. But when my father began to talk about the Livingstone pear tree, my that will be officially *mine* on my birthday then I know that burglars had come at last and there was a new kind of losing for me—barefaced robbery. My father said he was going to cut the tree down, that there were plenty of other places to sit and what was a tree anyway when the human race was threatened?

"Come my dear," he said or language to that effeck. "Do not mawn. It has to happen. There's no use moping. It's a danger."

This is the kind of burglary where you don't call the police and how can you put up in the sherriff's office, Wanted, Fifty-thousand Dollars Reward, when you know it is your own father?

I am writing this in my bedroom now. I can hear my mother and father talking. It was a shock for them when the branch fell, it was like the tree speaking and it scared them I suppose, because they do not know it as well as I do. My brother has gone away to collect tools for chopping down. I cannot trust anybody any more. I wish Sandy would come to talk to me. Where has he gone? And Samuel cat has been away since early morning, whatever can he find to do in the snow, just sneaking around the neighborhood pretending he's a stray cat and coming to people's daws and gazing at them as if to say I'm hungry I'm a stray cat, I used to belong to the Galbraiths and my ancestors belonged to the Living-stones and nobody feeds me and that is why I am all skin and bone whereupon the people look at Samuel and say, "Paw pussy it's a crying shame left out in the snow with nobody to feed you and own you, paw pussy, those Galbraiths have no conshints to let you go roaming for food like a commin alley

292

cat." They give Samuel a piece of fish or meet and a saucer of milk and doesn't he lick his chops, however, it is his superior intelly-gents that makes him so cunning, his brain being equill to many a human brain and that makes me ask if on Deciding Day there will be any animals that will be declared human, but I don't suppose they have all the computers and calculations to deal with animals and birds.

I am robbed and betrayed. Under the Livingstone pear tree is like being under some kinsiderate creature where its ribs have leaves growing on them and stretching out and waving to josstle the rain and snow off your head, keeping you dry, and it's a place for me to be when there are not many places in the world just to be. Oh, I know there's my bedroom and the chair or the bed and there's the corner of the sitting room which I always go to watch telly-vision and if I'm going to town, and it's a long time since I went to town, there was always the Ladies Waiting Room where I used to sit and look at the magazines, and in the shops there was sometimes a place to sit away up in the fernishing department where you sat comfittiboolly and looked at the carpets and the tent set up to show you how to go camping at Krissmiss; but none of these places are reel places like the Livingstone pear tree because you can't leave any part of yourself in those other places, for if you did and went away and came back it would be gone because the dusting woman or the cleaning woman had pinched it, but under the Livingstone pear tree I always find myself waiting. I can't think where I will go when they chop it down and what about the birds living up there like living in molty-story flats and having them collapse with an earthquake and out you go homeless.

Where has Sandy gone? Where is Samuel? The snow has long ago stopped, the sky is innerscent blew and the little green birds, the ring-eyes, that are only pieces of leather patched together as big as a wristwatch, have floan.

39

My birthday seems so far away and I feel as in I'm in a desert with everything dry and thirsty and nowhere to hide from the sun. I've waited years and years to put the Livingstone pear tree into my scheme, all that counting and counting without a computer, making friends of my fingers and toes and my family and myself and Samuel and Sandy and the Livingstone pear tree a place to sit under out of the sun and look up at the world partly green and partly blew with the fat oily leaves and sometimes the blossim and sometimes the pears, all these years waiting and waiting with everything worked out to my twenty-sixth birthday on the dot and no one but myself suspecting my skeem. My perrints know I was fond of the tree but they do not know the real story of my life, the story that happens between times of ordinary being and sitting and working with embroidery, for as it turns out I am not really the same age as all the people who are supposed to be my age because most of the day for me is not living but sliding along in great peace or sitting while the day slides along like sitting in the water down on the beach with the waves coming ova yew whoosh whoosh tick tock the clock and sometimes I shake myself like a little dog and the waves fall off me and my brain starts thinking about being alive and catching up on being alive because I haven't the alive time that other people have as I'm supposed to be doll-normill which means being short of everything in your brain and in your daytime too, so I sit and sit and quickly a wave comes and I'm alive and then it goes and I sit some maw until the next wave and my perrints know nothing about all this because naturally it's secret, for they seem to be living all the time except when they're asleep and they look at everything and notice things and are quick and have a memory all the time without being tired and it means they get sick in a different way of looking and noticing because it's all the time like birthdays every hour of the day and year, but my noticing times are like visitors come specially but not often even coming just standing at a distance and saying, "Look where we are, get an eyefull before we're gone," and it's peeping through the fence at the flours in the other people's gardens and perhaps picking a small bunch of their flours when no one's looking. It's all a terrible bother as visitors are, and its good to be back sitting without having to notice because one thing people expect of you whether you're normill or dullnormill is noticing. My father said, "If you're not quicker than this, Milly you'll be had," but I don't know whether he means had like had up where the pleece get you or had like food, weather, sore throat, and holidays.

As Deciding Day draws near, every day is still every day. I was sweeping the front path lately when someone passing said, "Hello, fancy sweeping your front path at a time like this." And even my perrints have begun to apologize to everyone and to themselves because they do ordinary things like washing, and there was my mother hanging out the washing and me helping her when Miss Nightshade who was also hanging out her washing called out, "Isn't it awfool the way we just keep washing and hanging it out?"

And my mother replied shamefaced,

"It's terribool the way we wash and hang out washing."

"And do you know," said Miss Nightshade, "I'm making plans to redeckorate." Miss Nightshade looked guilty.

"Well," my mother said in a stern manner, "I don't blame you." But it was almost as if she was talking to a pickpocket—keep picking pockets just as you're used to though it's an offence and you know it.

And even my father sowing the seeds in the glasshouse looked at me in an annoyed way when I came to watch him as if I shouldn't have been there but because I thought I should have been, I stayed, and for a while he didn't speak, then suddenly he turned to me and said in an excusing voice,

"It has to be done, Milly. We can't just not plant our gardens. I'm shaw you understand, Milly."

His face was all gilty.

And one day when my mother said, "I think I'll alter this dress, my middle-age spread is spreading and I do want to be able to wear this florrill in summer." She looked at me apologetikilly.

"You don't mind do you?" she asked.

"Why should I, Mum? You don't want to look awll fat in summer do yew?"

"It's all this bread we keep eating," my mother said.

"I'm getting fat too," I said, thinking she mite be happier to have cumpinny in fatness as cumpinny is nice to have.

My mother gave me two looks, a first one that said, "You're a little child, are you feeling tired, it's time for bed Milly deer," and a second look that said, "Be your Age Milly Galbraith, we all have to be our age and take what's coming to us." She was just going to give me another look like the first when she decided to go out of the room. But there's no denying that she seemed to have a gilty conscience about something. And these days when people in our house do anything they either do it quickly so that no one will notice it or very slowly as if they are dreaming and not doing it at all—I mean things like cutting their hair or reading advertizements for summer holidays or talking about Krissmiss which comes but once a year bringing good cheer; and if I happen to be listening with my big ears they stop talking about Krissmiss or summer and they talk about something else like the weather which is a grate standby, especially since we have snow.

The snow.

The snow and the Livingstone pear tree.

Shall I tell you now?

Shall I tell you now about the Livingstone pear tree.

One morning before I was up, the rest of the family was up and moving about and my father and brother were outside and something started whining and whining with the sound going round and round the seven hills of the city like a big sirkill spinning and spinning maid of metill, and yew could not tell where the whining came from unless you knew it came from our place from the garden and it was the Livingstone pear tree coming down. I knew it was the tree and I couldn't pretend not to cry. Also I stamped my foot and screamed when I looked out of the window and saw them working away at a branch that lay like a huge cut-off leg with the knee all wet and wood-colored, just imagine a slice of knee, and big green arms cut off, not holding anything any more and gradually it all filled the garden, knee and feet and arms and hands and fingers and last was the thick body standing with its roots going down down until a yellow trackter came and said, "Move ova, come out of there taking up standing room, you grate big pear tree," and heave heave the yellow vehikill with yellow pointed teeth bit into the body and pulled it out by the roots and there it was lying on its side and everywhere bits of tree and sticky blud and berds nests filled the garden. My father and brother had to climb ova the tree to move around the garden and once my brother said, "A nice bed this would make," and my mother looked out and said, "When are you going to clean up that awfool mess, I never knew there was so much tree, it's about time it came down."

I was crying and could not stop at first but gradewlly I stopped and began to knit the sleeves of the swetter I'm making for Sandy, knitting both sleeves at once, moss stitch on number five needles double knitting. I felt as if there were big stoans put inside me like the bottom of a basket and yew couldn't pick up the basket and walk away, you couldn't even lift it and the stoans were round and flat colored gray and I felt like what my father says sometimes when he has a big meal and my mother asks him, "How's the digestion Ted," and he says, "It's lying heavy on my stummick Decima, give me a dose of chalk." For my father is gnawed in his stomach.

Suddenly I looked out and there was no Livingstone pear tree and the sky was fast filling up the space and sweeping away with its clouds any leftover shadows of the pear tree.

"We'll get the wind from the sea now," my father said gloomilly. "That bitter east coastill wind."

"You should have thought of that," my mother said.

"But it's better down," my father said. "I've never known a pear tree like it. It's been more trouble than it's worth."

As I listened to him I tried to think what trouble, because as far as I knew there had been no trouble with the tree, it had not interrupted anyone's conversation and it had not complained about the weather or the view or the dark night when it had to stand outside in the cold or even about the snow, and it had not been bossy and hadn't come visiting without being arsked and it hadn't started classifying people into Human and Animal; in fack it had been a neutral tree like a country standing apart in the war; and it was full of things to give to us to make us say, "Oh," and "Ah," and "Isn't that pretty, that pear blossom," and then "These pears are tasty." Just dropping them in our lap when they were ripe; though I do not guarantee I know what it was up to there with its head so high in the sky, and what conversation it might have had that no one could understand.

My father called out.

"Milly! Come out of your bedroom. It's no use crying ova spilt milk."

Which was trew.

"We'll get the mess cleaned up. Just look Dessy how it's covering the whole garden. Soon you can go outside Milly and sit on the seat with Samuel and everything will be as it used to be."

"No I want to stay in my bedroom," I said coldly and distantly.

It has always seemed strange to me that they keep trying to move me around. If I'm sitting on the seat they don't like me sitting on the seat. If I'm sitting in my bedroom they don't like that. They're never satisfied and never will be. It's just as if all my life they've been trying to take a photograph of me and want to get me in the best light with the sun shining in my face and so on, though it's different now with photos and you can be taken in the dark now with a small explosion; so they've been moving me from room to room and placing me to see where I look best and the paw fools it never dawned on them that I don't look best anywhere, that as long as I'm alive they'll keep moving me and studying me like a vase of flowers.

"They look best in that light deer, they catch the rays of the setting sun."

"No they're best slightly in the shade."

"Oh no, to get them at their best they need the first light of the mawning sun shining on them."

"You're better outside on the seat, Milly. You can't stay in your bedroom forever."

Well I had no intention of staying in my bedroom forever.

"I'm busy knitting," I said coldly. "I have to finish these sleeves."

My perrints spoke in chorus.

"As long as you're doing something, Milly. It's better than being idle. Yew know yew can't bring back the tree."

They spoke as if it had been someone else, not they, who had felled the pear tree, as if they had watched helplessly unable to prevent the death. Thinking how sinister it was that they should pretend it had nothing to do with them, I thought perhaps it is like that when people die and when their best friends shake their heads and wipe the tears from their eyes

299

and say, "Nothing we can do will bring them back." When it really means, don't you believe it, we took our circular saw and our acks and our yellow earth masheen and chopped them off the earth and dug down to find and kill their roots. It seems to me that people are not always what they pretend to be and I shall have to be carefool what I say and what I do, and I will warn Sandy in case he too is trapped and cut down because he is too much trouble, but one thing is a laugh, now my pear tree is down it is being a nuisance it never was when it was up, for it is taking nearly all the sexshun room and perhaps that is what people do when they die, to get their own back, they start taking up room in other people, they spread everywhere and are bolky and although they're dead and still, all the living people have to get out of their way and curl up in corners in a very cramped position with their growth strangled by what should not be there like weeds that my father says are "usurpers," though they are mostly people who are unknown until one day they seize the king's crown and put it on and stand in front of the mirror and like the look of the crown on, so they keep it there and become king faster than it takes to say "Jack Robinson" or "my sainted unkill"; but understand I'm talking now of ordinary dying and not the new dying where it's a decision, and it's the new dying we've had most of in my time, thank you very much, also with bombs and car accidents and smashups at night and in the early morning along the Peninsula Road and Ten Mile Gully and Flax Hill and Muttonbird Swamp, but those days are hisstree since the cars stopped coming into the country and being maid here, for every manufacturer is preparing for the maw profitable trade in hewmans which will commence soon on my birthday, and, oh, the Deciding Day draws nearer and nearer like a seeryill with the masheen in your path or the tyger and lion crouched ready.

Sandy is speaking. He says:

A sudden flood melted butter pouring down
an afterthought of the sun to touch
the day-burned street with wind and twilight shining
the tearoses filled with cream
the japonica also and the olearia
crackles with yellow flame.

Is the heart eased? Too soon to say.
The sun has gone revealing
yellow is a kind of bruise.

Yes, it was Sandy came to see me and dicktate to me writing about the sun and the butter and the day-burned street, and when I looked puzzilled he said don't try to understand, Milly, I'm just polishing my metal memory, it has to be polished every day or it will tarnish. Still puzzilled, I said thinking of the mirrers and clean flaws,

"Do you have to see your face in it?"

"That's right," he said, impressed with my in-tellygents. "I have to polish it until I can see my face in it and sometimes I see other faces looking over my shoulder."

"Whose faces? Relations?"

"Sometimes. And sometimes people I knew before I turned to gold."

We both laughed at that for it's a queer thing to imagine, Sandy being turned to gold and being made new and precious. Sandy guessed my thoughts.

"Yes, it's queer," he said. "Particularly as Mutimer, Dobie, and Watson who were responsible have been struck down with streaks and arthritis and corrinnerries and whatnot and their knighthoods can't save them on the Day."

"Will you be saved on the Day?" I asked politely.

"If you want to know, Milly, I think I may be. But only because of my gold. I was turned to gold and my value went up."

We laughed again then and Sandy said, "I've been watching the Livingstone Pear tree coming down. It's a signal for destruction, Milly. What will yew do?

"Do? What? When?"

"Yew know. Now the pear tree has gone."

I felt shy then, and annoyed that Sandy was thinking about me and the tree and I couldn't hide my grief for I cried anew and said, "It's not fair." And as I cried I thought and hoaped that Sandy would put his arm around me and I would cry on his sholder as yew are meant to do if yew are betrothed, but Sandy maid no movement towards me, though I kept crying and hoaping. Still, he looked tenderly at me. And one consolation was that he did not suggest impossible things like, "You'll forget it, something else will turn up to occupy your time and affection." No he knew that something that has lived as long as the Livingstone pear tree, knowing so many people, and giving them pears right and left without asking for any munny, doesn't just "turn up." No, Sandy looked out of the porch where we were standing and said, "It's fallen all ova the garden hasn't it, like dirt or porridge, how will they carry it away and where will it go?"

Samuel was in my arms. I could feel his purr moving like a worm in his throat, wriggool wriggool, while his throat shook and throbbed like a little boat with its engine ready to put out to sea. Samuel was in a good mood after his two days holiday abroad, somewhere so confidential that I couldn't guess where it was. Sandy watched jellissly as I paid maw attention to Samuel. He repeated his question in a sharp toan.

"What will they do with the tree?"

Whereupon I told him they were going to cut it up gradewlly for fyrewood and cart it away in blox and perhaps make something out of it.

"A little house for you as you said you wanted on your birthday?"

I was touched by his special memory. I had been trying

302

to forget my dream, but when he mentioned it it all came back to me, the little house, the front daw, the passage, the bedroom with our big double bed, innerspring mattress, two-hundred-and-fifty longlasting springs facktree-tested guaranteed seventy years, blonde sweet crackle finish, turned legs, his and hers, everything, wall to wall carpet, sewing masheen, space heater, tellyvision, deepfreez, modern woman's dream kitchen, nursery, everything imaginable to make the heart gay and glad, all for nothing down and a lifetime to pay interest free if yew get it before the end of the month, not to speak of the curtains and the knitting room with colored wools around the wall on special stands, and the laundry with me there washing and spindrying clothes and linen to my heart's content three or four washes a day I so desire, just to keep busy. Oh, what a busy houswife I would be in my little house under the Livingstone pear tree and that was not mentioning the shopping I would have to do on my special budget.

"Don't remind me, Sandy," I said tearfoolly. "I just want a modest place. The pear tree is covered with sticky bubbles of stuff from the tree's inside," I said, changing the subject.

"That might be brown blud, an agglutinous substance," Sandy said wisely.

Then he persisted in asking.

"What will you do without the Livingstone pear tree, Milly? It will let in the sky and the wind and the sun and the birds that used to fly around and ova will fly strait through. And there's your birthday coming soon."

I admitted that my birthday was barely ten days away. Then to change the subjeck again, I asked him why he hadn't been to see me when it was snowing and the first branch was broken.

"I've been completing my diary of a Reconstructed Man while there's still time, Milly."

"Yew must write fast," I said. "I'm slow, for I have to

look in the recipe books: meat fritters, cut half-a-pound of meat into strips about a quarter of an inch, season with salt and pepper, dip in batter and fry a nice brown; in the knitting books: continue thus until the work measures fifteen inches; in the newspapers: Grate Battle ova, thousands Dead the Day of Deciding Draws Near; and the Bible: the Lord hath rejected and forsaken the generation, son of his wrath, then will I cause to seize the city of Judah and from the streets of Jerusalem the voice of mirth and the voice of gladness and the voice of the bride, for the land shall be desolate. . . .

The glory of Lebanon shall come unto thee, the fire tree, the pine tree, and the box together, to beautify the place of my sanctuary; and I will make the place of my feet glorious. . . . How is the gold become dim; how is the fine gold changed; the stones of the sanctuary are poured out in the top of every street. . . . And behold six men came from the way of the higher gate which lieth toward the north, and every man a slaughter weapon in his hand; and one man among them was clothed with linen, with a writer's inkhorn at his side. . . . And he spoke unto the man clothed with linen and said, . . . Go fill thine hand with coals of fire and scatter them over the city.

Now Sandy looking over my shoulder as I pointed to the story in the Bible went wite with terror.

"Is it all written at random?" he asked curiously.

"Of course it's at random," I said, not quite knowing what he meant.

"Although the print is too small and dark for me to read, but it is terrible things in the Bible, Sandy, it is all blud and fyre, desserlitt cities, wildernesses, and all the trees of the field shall know that I the Lord have brought down the high tree have exalted the low tree have dried up the green tree have maid the dry tree to flourish."

"Is it really at random, Milly? Isn't something guiding your hand when you pick out the verses and chapters."

"What do you mean, Sandy? The minister told me just

to sit and turn the pages and look now and again to see what was there. I see the words. In the books I look at I see the words. I see *fire*, place ova a sharp fire, let the fire not be too hot or the wheel-cake will burn, that's an old recipe, light the fire and warm the oven before you put in the little biscuits in their frilly paper cases, colored pink and blue and yellow, so I see fire and I know fire and I know blud it is written blud blud mud thud and shudder; and I know trees branches and garments from knitting and sewing and I know gold from treasure and from your skin and from the wasps and dande-lions; and that's most of the Bible, Sandy, fire blud, gold garments, and desserlitt cities. What have you written in your diary Sandy?

How small is the smallest world
it is less than a seed
fire blood and garments
I will. That is a God's intention
a city of desolation
the sun to crack open all life and draw forth
the shimmering garments of growth.

That is filling my inkhorn, Milly.
Now this:

Mutimer, Dobie, and Watson
strode in the sun one day.
Shall we reconstruct a dying man
Dobie was heard to say.
Shall we give him golden skin
said Watson.
Shall we steal his best finest fear
Said Mutimer.
How blood-stained will the snow be
said Dobie.

Mutimer, Dobie, and Watson

polished a memory
to dazzling mint condition
and paid it as salary
legal tender in all consciousness
for life, to Sandy.

Dobie, Watson, and Mutimer
peeled the skin from the dead
picked two eyes from a glass bowl
to fit in Sandy's head
with a virus Herring-Red.
Watson, Mutimer, Dobie
men of love and lust
fashioned a Brand-X penis
(if you have you must)
for Sandy out of gold-dust.

Mutimer, Dobie, and Watson
lay breath beneath the rib
worked for several months
on their reconstruction job
slicing, measuring, gilding, fitting
with no intent to rob.

But the receiving dark
blinder than blind love took
wholly the mature care
of hand heart compassionate look.
How can I read you Roger, if they have destroyed the book?

40

Sandy and I could no longer sit under the pear tree. The
weather was bitter following the snow storm and we found it
warmer to sit inside and watch the all-day tellyvision program
where men and women in evening dress with wite shirts and
glittering diamonds danced and danced to tunefool musick

and sang for variety about luv. There were no programs about our country because our country had all been sensored in case people panicked without thoughts of times to come, so my parents explained to me, so it was ovaseize where it doesn't matter if there's dying and violence in the streets and the police have masheen guns and gas and truncheons for truncheoning. At first there was a debait in Parliament about whether it might be good to show maw violence to get us used to it or to sensir it and pretend it didn't happen and the sensirs won the debait and that is why lately we see loving and dancing and roses on tellyvision, especially roses in our country. Theres a man from the Bottinny Department of the Euniversity who appears on T.V. every day to show us roses growing, being bred and bawn and sprayed to keep them pewer, and the insex that attack them are shown with big jaws like stainless-steel jugs ready to pour in the rose blud and jewce. These programs are called *Rose Coltewer.* We have a laugh at them because Winton who went to Agricoltewerill College said the man is not really from the Bottinny Department because the bottinny man Professir Boyd has gone mad and gone away, and the staff have taken all the secret sprays and poisons including arsinick, no I don't mean by drinking them, but they have maid off with them to a crib in Brighton and have built a huge manuka stockaid, and if anyone comes near they threaten to spray them with the deadly poisins they have been working on in secret to kill the nasty insex that keep sucking the blud of roses and other fare flouwers also the blossoms of Scentrill Otago where the farmers rely on the fruit for their livelyhood and are surrounded by enemies including diseases, insex with big mouths, and frost that comes so secretly they have to have warnings like air-raid warnings and stay up to lite the little pots of fyre in the orchards to beware the frost away by melting. They say that if the police try to get the members of the Bottiny Department they will be sprayed with deadly insecktyside, but if they pull down the stockaid and sneak into the crib the professor and his staff will commit sewyside with the poisinus sprays, first shooting them at the police at a last resort, and then all will be dead a sad sight with boddies strewn around the little seaside resort where the lupins grow tall with shiny leaves and blew and yellow flours scattered among the sandhills and the sea rolls in, unaware of what dreadfool misery has been suffered but ready and willing to bury anything that happens to be in its path and to say nothing with its tongue in its head, not still yet still not giving the game away, room is scarce on earth for burying but not in the sea.

You can imagine then that by now we have all groan tired of roses. Winton said the coltewer is all wrong anyway and the names which they say are of new roses are only invented for the sake of properganander with emphasis on the fewture. When my mother heard him say this she said, "Oh Winton!" And my father said,

"It's best not to voice such thoughts, Winton. More especially now when the Amerrykin Everitt Morse is coming any day to make, I believe, final assessment and judgment before the Day. You know they're being very fair."

"Fair!" My mother screamed.

"As fair as they may be," my father said. "They come so often to see if they've missed something in people's favor."

My mother was worked up.

"If you ask me," she said, "Everitt Morse comes here just for a good meal and to sponge on us. Look at all the food we've given him and the hospitalitty he's received is noboddy's business. And those toys are of no use to Milly. She's grown up."

I nodded agreement that I was groan up. It didn't seem to matter that sometime my own mother and father forget the fack.

"Yes, it's nothing but corruption," my mother said.

My father, who as I told you is law abiding, tried to soothe her.

308

"In every legislation, Decima, there are people who take advantage and try to cheat."

"That's all very well, Dad, but with this legislation we can't afford to let anyone start cheating. Human life is at steak. One man gets cunning—then where are you? Unable to trust your oan friends and family. People will sell their loved ones, the clothes off their backs, to be declared human."

My father put a restraining hand on Winton's sholder.

"Yew just watch what you say. I'm told some unscrewpulus fokes are already dealing in human remains to get a start on the others, and once markets are open in someone's favor it's hard to get the buyers to switch, first in, first served. Harry Heron and his wife of St. Clair have disappeared. Been gone since last week and they're not the only ones."

"They might be in hiding?"

"Not from what I've heard. I tell you, they're victims of black marketeers."

Then looking very solemn my father said, "I don't want to hear any maw talk of this matter. Just all keep quiet from now on. Keep your thoughts to yourselves. We'll have enough to talk about in dew time."

But even as he spoke my thoughts were going round and round. What had Winton said about people selling the skin off their backs to be declared human? They might think of selling other people's skin too?

Later, when my father and brother were out clearing away maw of the Livingstone pear tree and my mother was visiting Miss Nightshade for an exchange of gossip and vegetabools and Sandy and I were in the sitting room watching tellyvision, *The Perfeck World of Tomorrow*, I questioned Sandy.

"Yaw skin is gold but is it real gold, the gold sort of gold?"

"Why of course. When they were experimenting they

309

found that gold dust was best for manufackturing human skin and as I am the First Reconstructed Man they decided to try it on me. I believe they've found a synthetick substance now, but of course with the Ack they've given up reconstructing."

"Does everybody know you're maid of gold?"

"Most people do."

"That means treasure doesn't it?"

Sandy smiled.

"A few years ago it mightn't have meant that, when gold was lower in value, but now I believe it's scarcer than diamonds or wite roobies."

"Are there wite robbies?"

"There's one somewhere, all milk wite on top of a mountain in the moon, not far from the Sea of Tranquillity."

"I've never seen a red rooby, Sandy. I haven't any jewels except imitation pearls. I wonder what it would be like to have jewels and have to keep closing yaw eyes, they dazzle so much and having other people close their eyes with so much dazzle."

Sandy smiled at me again. I thought, "He is fond of me. He will not let me be declared animal. He will save me."

"Oh Sandy, it is terrible with the Livingstone pear tree gone, there's nothing to hide under and my mother won't let us go to my bedroom and we're here watching roses grow on tellyvision in a new world of tomorrow. And what if someone steals your skin? Couldn't you put it in a bank or something?"

Sandy smiled.

"You've given me an idea. My skin is safe with me as long as I need it and want it, and I'm snug and safe inside it. I'm not a snake you know or a catterpiller or a silk worm to be putting my skin off and on like an ovacoat. It's my special container."

I put out my hand to touch it.

"It's warm, with moving like Samuel's purr going through it."

"That's my blud flowing."

"Have you got a way of showing like Samuel cat that you're pleased. Does something like a purr travel threw yaw skin?"

Sandy smiled again and said nothing. I was troubled.

"Sandy my birthday is Deciding Day and you know what will happen to me because of my doll-normill brain and not earning a living and being a burden on the community. I'll be going away with other people who are like me."

"Perhaps I'll be going away too, Milly."

I became annoyed and said sharply, "Why are yew talking about it all the time, yew and my mother and father and brother all talking about it and chopping down the Livingstone pear tree, there's only Samuel who has the scents to keep quiet, he just lies there with his paws curled ova his ears and his eyes harf-shut and his legs stuck out like handles of pots and he just lies there and breathes and breathes. If that's what it's like being animal then I don't mind."

Sandy did not smile. I felt irritable, and anyway the roses on tellyvision were fool of blight, yew could see them with spots all ova them and bits eaten out of their velvet petals, so yew could see they weren't safe even on tellyvision, for something came with its big mouth and chewed them and stained them and it was all very well for the man from the Bottinny Department to smile and smile and say everything was perfick.

Sandy went home early and I went to bed early and as I lay in bed I listened and listened and at first I did not know what I was listening to. I felt lonely. I listened but there was a big gap in the listening where something used to come into the room and into my eyes and ears to send me to sleep. I tried to think what it could be and then I knew—it was the Livingstone pear tree that used to say shiver-shiver hush-

hush rustle and it was gone and yet it was still there, but its branches were lying on the ground and it didn't move or breathe or take any notice of the wind and they were no longer on talking terms, their conversation had been made into a quarrill that was settled by killing. Thinking about it I became frightened and hid my face under the bedclothes and was soon fast asleep as innerscent as a babe.

41

This morning I lay in bed wondering what it would be like to be twenty-six and remembering how I used to wonder this before all my other birthdays and then when my birthday came I wasn't quick enough to find the secret of it, and this was why I became maw and maw determined to surprise my birthday, to capture it and find what it meant and make it give me all the good things it had in staw for me, as I am sometimes the sort of person who misses the good things because I don't know where to find them or they are too quick for me like the train going out of the station just because you haven't a ticket and they could have waited while you bought one and got yawself arranged, but they don't wait because they are going somewhere else and don't really care whether you miss it or not and that is why they are called Limited Trains, meaning there's not enough room for everyone so yew have to be quick and buy yaw ticket perhaps years and years in advance even the day before you are bawn. I want all the good things I can get and birthdays are for getting them, because on that day people acktewlly ask you what you want and sometimes they give it to yew though they can be cruel like the time I, being twenty-one, said to my perrint I want a house to myself and husband and children and a broom to sweep the flaw and a vacuum for the wall-to-wall carpeting and my father said, "You're asking for the moon, Milly." Which means that he did not understand my language and I remember that night how I crept under the pear tree that used to be there a long time ago blocking the sun and the view and keeping out the cold southeast wind and I took Samuel cat on my knee, though I was surprised he wasn't roaming for he roams at night, and I looked up at the moon. I was so angry with my father for not understanding and with my mother too for she agreed with him, "You're asking for the moon, Milly." Well, I looked up at the moon and there were shadows in it moving around like people against a yellow window and I knew that my perrints had spoken the truth because do you know what those shadows were, they were a lady vacuuming her best wall-to-wall carpet, you could see the vacuum cleaner and you could see the lady's husband sitting in his armchair saying, "I'll move deer," and his whife saying, "No, don't move, I'll vaccuum around you," and all up there in the moon in the sky with no neighbors except the stars, but the view would be exceptional there was no doubt, and if they were selling it they would say Cannot be Overlooked or Built Out, Superb View. I felt maw kindly then towards my perrints for I guessed they must have thought I wanted that place because they themselves must have looked up many a time and thought, "How secluded, yew could do as you liked up there and no electrick bills." Therefore, when I went inside I said as I passed the kitchen on my way to my bedroom, "It's all right Mum and Dad, I don't want what you think I want for my birthday." My mother said, "It's best to accept the way we're maid, Milly. And your knitting is most beautifool. Your moss stitch, Milly!"

My moss stitch! The rain sometimes makes moss on our back doorstep and in our spouting and drainpipe. People do get excited ova my moss stitch and that always makes me feel pleased and I feel that I could pick up my knitting and knit moss stitch for ever and ever, only that would put me off wanting what I really want, not the moon because I think I would be loanly up there, even with the house and the husband and the vacuuming and the wite rooby, but a place of my oan and my oan familly; and, privately, I get tired to death of moss stitch.

This morning I was disappointed that no one remembered there were only five days to my birthday. There was no talk of birthdays or presents. My father and brother have not been out lately to work at other people's places and it seems as if nobody in the world is going to work any more or maybe there will be no presents. The weather has been like spring and my father and brother are picking up the last of the Livingstone pear tree, what an ugly tree it is, lying far too big and blocking the view and the sunshine and being too old and seeing too much in its lifetime and doing nothing to help, and its roots too deep for comfort and too near the people's sewers, and the sewers might have burst and flooded the gardens and germs might have come with diseases and everyone might have been dead in their beds because of the big overgroan Livingstone pear tree. How peacefool it is without it and soon it will be gone and the garden will be pewer again. So many trees are a newsints, not to mention the hazidds like lightning which strikes from trees and yew must never stand under a tree in a thunder storm, I can't think how I have risked my life for so many years with a pear tree in the garden.

No talk of presents today not even suspicious questions that make yaw heart thud ready for the grate day, you know, like, "What exactly is your size shoe Milly," which makes you think that on the morning there will be a pair of blew satin shoes in tissue paper in a white box.

"These are for you, Milly, your exact size."

Or they might say, laughing, "What are yaw measurements again Milly," and even though you're not a modills measurements yew might find on the grate morning a new dress with spangills for dancing and even shoes to match. Or

they might choose something that doesn't need measurements like a waltz-length nightie or a dressing gown where
it's enough to know yawr women's size. Or there could be
cosmetticks—skin perfume, hare spray in lilly of the valley.
Oh any number of things. And Sandy might even bring an
engagement ring.

But all day there's been no word from Sandy. In the
morning Everitt Morse came to visit us and when I saw him
coming I thought he knows it's only five days to my birthday
and the Deciding Day and he has come to ask me what size
shoes I wear or what size dress or because he has such an
interesting supply of things he might ask what size house I
would like for myself and my husband and children bawn one
by one at regular intervills so that I can give them proper
attention and not hit them all the time when they eat coal and
keep dropping the tellyphone off the tellyphone table. But
once again I was disappointed. Everitt Morse did not even
talk to me this morning. I saw him looking out of the window
to where I was sitting with Samuel on the green seat that
we've moved near to the back daw, and he seemed to be
jestewering to my perrints, probably about the Livingstone
pear tree and the newsints it was while it was alive and the way
it blocked the view and people's sunlight and the way its roots
went down too near the scenter of the earth which is on fyre.
I thought perhaps Everitt Morse might have been arranging
a birthday party for me because people have been known to
do that. It has to be arranged severill days ahead and yew
know nothing about it until on the day someone comes to
yew and says, still not telling you, "How would you like to go
for the day to the beech or see the seals around the Peninsula." And yew say, "How nice," or they might say, "How
would you like to go to the picktewers," and then when you
come home from the beech or the picktewers where they
were living cozily and opening daws with musick playing
every time the daw opened and going down in lifts to the

315

street where it was dry without thunder or lightning and there were no trees blocking the view, only little ones under control in tubs so that if they started to grow and hurt the sewers and steal the sunlight you would not need axes and circular saws to get rid of them and put them out of harms way, for with just one flick of the wrist yew would yank them out by the roots and put them in their place which would be the rubbish bin collected on a Tuesday and thrown among the daffodils and the dwarves heads at the rubbish dump. Well as I was saying when yew came hoam from your treat yew would be led into the dining room and there it would be, your party.

Although it did occur to me that Everitt Morse was arranging a party, I dismissed the thought with some contempt when I remembered his cheating ova the little sewing masheen that would not sew. He's come ova business matters, I thought. Perhaps our house is going to be sold unless a morgage is arranged and he will arrange it or we will be turned out of house and hoam, throan into the streets to die. And then thinking about that I remembered the pear tree as it used to be a long time ago when I sat under it and listened to it, looked up at its leaves growing and its blossoms getting fat and sweet, and it was so old and big it maid me feel safe from the sky which is too much space really and has to be filled in heer and there or people would be frightened of it, as rabbits are, who live in burrows out of sight of the sky, also muttonbirds who have enough of sky when they fly around in it and so choose to sleep in burrows also. I remembered about the pear tree and yet I didn't really remember because it seemed too long ago and it was gone, it was gone the moment they chopped it down, for then it was still and I'd never seen it still like that before, taking no notice when the wind was blowing, it was just a sulky dead tree not wanting to play anymore but then it shouldn't have taken up so much room in the world and blocked the view, it had to be taught a lesson, and sewers should not be interfeared with either for they are an important part of our civilization and without them we would be meddy-evil again with plague and the cries in the street, "Bring out your dead."

So all day I have pottered about not knowing what to do and waiting and waiting for Sandy and getting maw annoyed at the leftova bits of the Livingstone pear tree. Thank the Lord, I said, that today the last of it will have disappeared. I didn't even feel sorry that all the insex who thought they had found a place to live forever had their roof lifted off and the weather coming into their house though the insex don't mind, they are waterproof in little black mackintosh coats and they don't need much of a house to live in, not one with beds and tellyvisions and carpets wall-to-wall.

No one, therefore, said to me, "Milly it is only five days to your birthday." Just mother and father and Winton and Everitt Morse hanging around with an unemployed look that everyone has these days, I mean an unemployed outside look but a busy inside look as if everyone's thoughts are going round and round like on the race track at Wingatui or the Forbury Trots with the big lights ova the track and everyone hoaping to win the double. Once Everitt Morse waved to me out of the window as I sat musing. The Reverend Polly has told me to read the Bible but I do not belong to his church and my perrints said the Bible is there for us if we want to read it and we don't need a minister to preach at us on Sunday when our thoughts are on the Sunday roast and a day of rest after a week of slogging. Yet lately the family have let the minister come in and chat but after he is gone my father says, "Good Riddance," for my father doesn't mind talking boldly about ministers as they can't arrest you or not now, so make hay while the sun shines for you never know.

"Such is life," the minister said to me when the tree was cut down and silly old yaws truly was grieving. "The reed cut down in the wind. The blossom perished. Such is man."

"It's a tree not a reed," I said.

"Metterfaw, Milly."

And then he told me to prepare my heart and soul and not to think evil of those who do evil or something like that and being of a generous nature I said I would do as he advised. But I became suspicious when he talked of Sandy.

"Yew have this friend you call Sandy?"

"Yes."

"Yew have this idea that his skin is maid of gold?"

"It's not an idea it's the truth."

"Of course, of course."

He smiled and I said conversationally, "He's the first Reconstructed Man," whereupon he smiled slyly.

"There are no reconstructed people, Milly."

My anger flaired.

"What about your Christ?"

"Oh that's different," he said, "Yew say that Sandy has gold skin?"

"Of course he has gold skin. He's reconstructed."

The minister adopted a neutrill stand.

"Gold skin is rare," he said.

And then he told me to seek comfit from the Bible which would help me, although they were always a trifle gloomy in the Bible with death and destruction and the lord is my cumfit and all ye that labor and are heavyladen, which I have heard sung on tellyvision by a woman in a glittering dress with pearls around her throat and her hands clasped ova her bosom to help her get her breath, otherwise she would be short of breath she would have to gasp when she should be singing and she would look maw like a fish than a holy singer cumfitting, and the program would not be a sickcess.

"And now Milly would you say a simple prayer with me."

I said, No I did not want to say a simple prayer because I did not think prayers were simple in fack they were complicated. I prefer to leave them to be said by people with intellygents. And, although the Reverend Polly said no maw about Sandy, I heard him say to himself, "A golden skin what an opportunity for a parable."

Where is Sandy now? Sandy said to me one day, "Why did they reconstruct me, Milly, if it has all come to this in the end? Why must I give it all up when I have tried so hard to keep it?"

I said I didn't know.

And he said it is the law and the profits, it is the greatest house cleaning the human race has ever had. He said you can talk of eppydemmic, natural disasters, geological phenomena like the Ice Age, but the most efficient way of sorting things out is the law, the plain law maid by humanity. Yew might say (he said) it's all very well but what if the law is against you then you won't be so keen on it surely. Well you have to take it, he said, for in the Ice Age the ice is against you and in the epidemick the germs are against you and these enemies are indiscriminate, whereas the law as an enemy can bring the power of reason to its judgment and even if you are doomed you know it is fair doom. Oh, I thought not again, not again about things being fair. Sandy must have been listening to the Reverent Polly or Colin or perhaps he has been to the instruction classes in H.D. held every night in the Sports Pavilion and the Scouts Hall and the play centers and such buildings constructed from grants from the Golden Kiwi which is an art union, a golden bird as symbol, but it cannot fly and is getting extinct, and it has given grants for Colin's computer as well as for the special community halls where the lessons are now held to teach us to love, love, love the new law.

"It's very cunning," Sandy said, "the way they are teaching, and during the lecture they have roses in big bowls around the hall and people come in as if they are dreaming and sit down and a prayer is said and the lowkill man from the Euniversity who will be taking part in the deciding stands up on the platform (surrounded by his body guards) and instead of saying, 'Ladies and Gentlemen of Waipori City,' he says, 'Sisters and Brothers of the Roses'; and then he goes on to tell of the new world and the prosperity and maw goods and services."

When Sandy has talked to me I remember it all. He is very close to me.

"It seems like doom," he said once.

He said all the people who lecture are nice quiet people who would not harm a fly and that is why they are chosen because no one will think ill of them when it is all ova, and people alive will think only of the liaison officers who will have returned to their foreign countries with their toy sewing masheens with their lights flashing like a city.

"Who would ever have thought," he said to me one day, "that wheat would be planted in the back garden and the bread-baking day be the holy day and that roses would assume the importance they once had centuries ago, which is remembered by us away in our corner of the world because they keep putting it in the history books. The Wars of the Roses, red and white and the battlefields strewn with the dead people and the dead roses but not mechanical people like dwarves whose masheens no longer worked."

And then he talks of the dissolution of everything that the human race once held dear, and then he sounds like a prime minister, for prime ministers and presidents often talk of freedom and demockracy and such things because they love them so much, and I said, "Sandy isn't dissolution where everything is solved like arithmetick and the answer comes out, and isn't that what the computer will do with the humans and animals."

"Oh, no," he said, "a dissolution is when the meal plate is broken and the worst dissolution is where there has been a famine and there are no crumbs of food to hold in yaw hands; and sometimes the plate has a pattern on it and that

320

is broken too and can never be fitted together not even with the new special glue from the new special human industries. But we shall see," he said. "We shall see."

"Yew already see maw than most," I said. "Do your eyes hurt with seeing?"

He didn't answer that. His eyes were kind when he looked at me.

"I wonder is it a dream," he said, "and you and I are aloan, the golden man and the doll-normill woman, Adam and Eve in the botannykill gardens."

But this mention of the botannykill gardens brought everything back to me about myself and my father and the wite heron and Colin Monk's angry face as he spoke of bryberry, a kind of fruit that would poison him and feed us.

It is night now. All the pear tree has been cleared away. There is only dust left and bird dirt where the birds were afraid as people are when their houses are pulled down; and the birds skittered down their legs onto the leaves and the beginning pear blossom without being able to hold the skitter in.

42

It cannot be Krissmiss and it isn't War because the war is ova and it can't be a volcano and everyone in the ruins with the ashes in their hair and on their faces and their clothes but it is most like a volcano and my father who as you know is a law-abiding man has been almost the only person in our house to speak much today, and all he has said is, "Why are we taking it this way? Why haven't we banded together?" He keeps saying that. Why haven't we banded together.

For today is the day before my birthday and Deciding Day.

And it is strange that though the Livingstone pear tree

has vanished in the cleanest sweep in the world it has returned to hush everybody, or what is it then saying hush hush hush hush to everyone, like a fierce wind blowing the tree, only there is no tree, but there must be leaves and blossoms in our heads or hidden in the walls of the house for the hush hush to be sounding for everyone in our house and in Waipori Friendly City of the South. And though it's cold today there's no smoke from any chimneys and no sounds of cars and the dogs have stopped barking and all you can hear is the sea and the wind blowing in the leaves and the secret pear blossoms.

"Why haven't we banded together?"

There's my father again talking of banding, bandits and so on.

When the volcano erupted they found people loving each other and their loving had turned to stone and they were wite-faced with the ashes.

My father has begun to smile. He is preparing lunch. We are having a boiled egg and brown bread because it is the healthtiest lunch you can have and it will do us good, he says, with protein and vitamins and we are having winter greens from the garden though it is spring the day before my birthday and I'm not going to start saying that the flowers and leaves are scared and are not blooming because they might be caught in the Deciding, no feer, they are coming out all right as cool as cool and all our moaning and groaning is like water off a duck's back to the forsythia and the flowering currant who like rich ladies in the films when they pass the cringing beggars draw their satin cloaks around their shoulders and put their heds in the air and flower on regardless.

As I said, my father is smiling. I suppose he has thought of something funny unless his smiling and crying have got twisted. He is cooking all the meals today because my mother has a headache and is lying in bed with a cloth soaked in vinegar wrapped around her head to ease the headache and to stop her from seeing the light because her headache is a tellyvision headache where a drum beats in the middle of the masheen and the brain is shown with all its complicated workings, wheels and screws and little hammers knocking like the inside of a kitchen clock, and no wonder then that my mother has a headache. My brother is moping because the coming of the grate day has let in the light and he thinks it is too late, you see he has been working all these years and years in the garden with my father and he has such a pink face and doesn't shave much, and yesterday someone said to him, "Why don't yew shave." And do you know it seems as if he has never thought about it before, all the roses to prune and other people haven't bothered, but with the Ack they wonder and wonder about normill. Anything could affect the Deciding once the computer starts to work.

What is my father smiling at?

He looks up from the cooking and he sees me writing in my exercise book with Sandy telling me how.

"Milly, I've never known a day to take so long."

"I know why. Because we got up too early this morning like Krissmiss or Birthdays."

I feel his kind gaze upon me.

"Birthdays?"

"Yes we got up too early and there were no presents."

"And tomorrow we'll be up even earlier for the grate day."

"Yew mean my birthday?"

"Why of course, your birthday. What would yew like for a present?"

When my father said, "What would you like for a present?" although I had dreamed it for so long and planned the answer everything happened trew to form like in the Bible when the angel comes down too suddenly and asks the riddle that cannot be answered at once or ever because it's too late.

I had nothing to say to my father.

323

I was going to say I wanted the pear tree in blossom, but what use was that when it was gone and I did not care for it anyway. And I could not say about the house and the husband and the children at regular intervals so I wouldn't get angry when they ate coal and dropped the tellyphone. My father was standing there with my mother's apron on and the ladle in his hand and the saucepan where the boiled eggs had been and inside the saucepan there was a blew stain that comes when yew boil eggs and unless yew scrub and scrub you never get rid of it and it's hard to understand what has stained it because the eggs are not broken and the water is just boiling, but it's kemmykill I suppose like my brain and my mother's clockwork headache, though I'm told that vinegar removes stains and a cloth soaked in vinegar can freshen the dollest wall to wall carpet until it looks like new. Cold tea is usefool too; and both vinegar and cold tea are golden when yew put them in a glass and hold them up to the light, they are amber and gold, but gold is from the earth or the water, mined or dredged, and amber is, quote, "a yellowish translucent resin resembling opal, found in fossil in alluvial soils with beds of lignite and on seashores. It makes a fine polish. By friction it becomes strongly electrick." End of quote. Which proves the dictionary is as good as the Bible and the knitting patterns, but it does not change the color of the gold and the amber when they are held up to the light or the cold tea and the vinegar put to kill stains and headaches but not the carpet that has the stain or the people who have the headache, it is a selective killing like the weedkiller that says, "Oh here's a flower, stay flower, here's a weed, out weed." Like the games we played when I was a child at the Occupation Center and yew lined up and people were going to chop your head off but they wouldn't chop it off if your dream was the same as theirs, so if you thought of a little gold jool or a pearl and they thought of it too they said you could live, but if you thought of something foreign, something they had never thought

324

about, then they were intitled, it was in the game, to chop your head off; it's like with the weedkiller and the insecticide too that chooses the insex that are not allowed to live and it chiefly lets the good ones live, those that are good because they eat the bad ones, while it kills those that are too strong to be killed by the good ones and so become a nuisance to people who are on top and boss of them all, deciding which animal and bird and inseck and flower is allowed to live. Then God looks down seeing that everything works for its living and cumfitting those people who get hurt by mistake either because the kemmykill was not the right one or because the one they thought was bad turns out to be good, you can't always tell, and the insecticides and weedkillers haven't the clockwork kind of brain that we have and my mother has, giving her headaches to be cured by a cloth soaked in vinegar, an old-fashioned remedy if you ask me when we are all so modern.

"I'm asking you what you want for your birthday, Milly."

I thought then that what I would most like would be everybody talking and noisy again and the radios going and the dogs barking and the ashes wiped off people's faces and the stone lovers being cracked open and a small red heart put inside them and enough blud to flow round and round and warm them from top to toe.

"I don't want volcanoes for my birthday, that's one thing I don't want," I told my father in a voice full of decision. He looked at me then as he and my mother used to look at me until they stopped bothering; a puzzilled look that said I was too bafilled and a hopeless look that said the baffillment would never end.

"This is the first time since you could talk that you've not had definite ideas on your birthday. We all know it means a lot to you, and you're clever at counting—we remember that too Milly. Can't you think of what you want besides refusing a volcano when you haven't even be offered one?"

I think he was angry.

"If your mother didn't have a headache we might have had a party for you. We might manage a small family tea."

A party. Being sent to the picktewers and coming hoam thinking of him and her in their room with the colored telephones, "Is that yew darling." Then seeing the table and the raspberry jellies with their sides shaking and everyone round the table, all the faces that have stayed only a few yards from you all your life and how strange it would be with even one face removed, it is easier to remove faces than trees because faces travel anyway but trees are locked for life until you kill them but if you kill people the police arrest you and the jury condemns yew to give natural pleasure to His Majesty for the rest of your life.

"But your mother has a headache."

From my father's expression I could tell that he was trying to work something out. Though I wanted to ask for all the things I have longed for, I discovered that I felt very shy about asking as I realized that perhaps they would say I was asking for the moon. I could have asked not only for the moon but for the stars and the sun and a private planet as a country or beach residence and I would sit at the daw and the waves of light like tides would flow in and out making a noise like an ocean otherwise it wouldn't be a beach house and everyone would go swimming in the light and then stretch out on the edge of the planet, light bathing and we would all turn Sandy's color and be Midas people.

"We might manage a small family tea today, Milly. Would you like to invite anyone special?"

"Yes."

"Who?"

I felt shy.

"How many can I have?"

"We haven't such a wide choice have we Milly? Do you want to ask Miss Dora Nightshade? She's a lonely soul."

326

"I don't see why we should ask lonely souls," I said.

"It's just that we're all together as a family. Close-knit. Why not ask Mr. Warburton Maurice?"

"Oh, no, he's a lonely soul too."

'Who then, Milly?"

"Mr. Colin Monk?"

I could see that my father was alarmed and afraid, and I supposed that he was remembering our walk threw the bottanyykill gardens when the wite heron should have floan to Siberia to escape the winter and when Mr. Colin Monk accused him of bryberry. Then I saw the thinking lines on my father's forehead; he had an idea but he didn't do as the people on tellyvision do and throw out his arms and grab the idea as if it were a wasp and cry, "Got it!"

Oh, no. He just smiled hopefoolly.

"If you wish it. It's possible he won't be able to come. There's no harm in asking. Anyone else, Milly?"

"Sandy," I said.

My father looked puzzled.

"Sandy?"

"Yes. I know he'll accept."

"Your Sandy is very accommodating."

I saw an expression on my father's face that I had seen only once before when he had the special job planting the peach trees in the town orchard and something—a frost or disease—wiped all the blossoms out the very first time they were meant to fruit. My father came home and sat with his head in his hands and my mother said, "What's up, Ted?"

And as if a town had been destroyed he said, "The peach orchard is wiped out."

As if it had been his fault. And his face seemed that way now, only where were the dead peach trees and what was the blame coming to him fast like knives being thrown or deadly bombs that spray other bombs that spray other bombs until there is not a square inch of people left? Some situations are beyond my brain and intellygents. If an orchard is destroyed by frost yew don't blame yourself for the frost do you, especially if you have been up night after night for years making sure the small fire pots between the trees are always burning to keep away the disaster.

"I'll ask Sandy then," I said.

"Yes, ask Sandy. It will be a pleasure to have him."

My father sat down then and sagged like an empty sack of potatoes in the cellar. If it is decided against me he will never be able to say that I have not been a dutifool daughter.

Sandy was walking casually in the garden trying to remember, I suppose, where the Livingstone pear tree had been, when I asked him to tea. I explained that my father had gone to visit Colin and that he and Colin would be my special guests and that the tea was to celebrate my birthday the next day and it could not be a party because my mother had a headache and was lying down in a darkened room with a cloth soaked in vinegar wrapped around her head.

Sandy smiled his golden smile.

"I don't think I shall be able to come. Tonight I must stay up late to prepare for tomorrow. Perhaps Colin may not be able to come either. We know that tomorrow is an important time for him. He will want to be fresh for tomorrow's work."

"Fresh to control the Deciding?"

"Yes."

"It's just tea. Some raspberry jelly and cream and a cup of tea and then you can go hoam. Yew must drink a toast to my birthday."

We sat quietly while he considered the invitation. Samuel came running and sprang on my knee and purred and I put my hand under his chin to feel his purr. He slobbered and his eyes glistened. I looked hoapfoolly at Sandy, waiting for him to accept my invitation.

He smiled.

"A happy birthday Milly, whatever that means. I shan't be able to come to tea. You understand?"

"Of course, I understand," I said.

And then he smiled his golden smile and gave me a solemn promise he would take care of me forever.

I said goodbye to him. I went inside and waited for my father who had gone to see Colin Monk, and by the way he came quickly hoam I knew that his mission had not been rewarded.

"Have you maid the raspberry jelly, Milly?"

"Yes," I said with housewhifely pride.

"Good. It's your favorite jelly."

I smiled kindly but I felt that my smiling kindly at people was wearing out and murder was coming after it.

"I'm going to bed early," I said coldly. "I don't want to see anyone. And the raspberry jelly won't set anyway."

I sounded like a film star or royalty, and I was glad because my father looked at me with respect amounting to awe.

"We thought all along that this would be best, Milly. Early to bed, Milly. You're entitled to that. You must have time to yourself, to meditate." He sounded like the minister. Angrilly I turned on my heel, said there and then a sharp bitter goodnight and went from the room and I know that my banging of the door caused the famous unset raspberry jelly to shake and shiver with fright.

And then in the night a dream came. In the dream there was another land and I was by myself which maid me afraid. The trees were standing up to their wastes and their heads had been cut off; they were all the same size but smaller than me and I was able to stand on tiptoe and look into their bodies and see the rings that are their birthdays like veins and bludvessills in their bodies. They seemed so strong without branches that would snap or leaves that could be torn apart, and some of them that had blossoms were so strong the blossoms were everlasting, and I waited for a gale to test their strength but the air was still, and I could not really prove their strength I had to believe it without proof inside my believing brain. I decided to pretend I was a pear tree, to play the game we had played at the Occupation Center where the teacher said, "Now be a flower, now be a tree," and we stood fighting a storm or looking beautiful with our velvet hats and blossoms on.

I looked down at my feet. They were deep in the earth. I longed to move but I could not. And then Sandy appeared. He was misty but I could see his gold skin like sunlight.

"Why have you come here," he asked, "to live in this deprived forest where the trees have their heads cut off and their nerve endings, and are no better than living posts that will not fruit or experience any seasons or learn to reach beyond themselves to shelter birds and other creatures? Why have you chosen to live in this forest?"

"I wanted to receive news," I said. "Fresh news."

"And now you are trapped in it; and tomorrow on your birthday you will be sacrificed."

My little house. The pear tree. Samuel, Sandy. The private planet view, unsurpassed, cannot be built out, sought after area. Happy and free with H.D.

"I could sell my golden skin for your life Milly. And then there would be no Deciding to dread on your birthday, for yew do dread it, don't you Milly and going out to the plains to the factrees. And while the Deciding is being carried out and surrounds you with this one and that one and him and him and her being chosen to be taken away whatever happens you need not be afraid, yew will be safe."

"Where will you be, Sandy?"

"Me? The Reconstructed Man. The metal memory. The golden skin. Who shall say where I will be?"

I pleaded.

"But where?

He did not answer. He had disappeared. And though I began the dream by laughing I ended by crying, though no tears came. My forest lips were wet; they were dabbed with bits of raspberry jelly, as if I had gobbled the jelly. And then the sun came out fuming with light and someone tried to put it out, Get In, Sun, and threw sand across its face and the sand struck like grains of sand boiling in asphalt, except the asphalt was golden. I can't remember any maw. I woke up. I heard the sea scraping its scraper on the foreshore. I looked at the luminous alarm clock on my dressing table and I'm looking at it now. Almost twelve o'clock, the magic hour. Almost tomorrow. Tick the seconds cruelly in the clocks face and it is Deciding Day.

43

I performed my duties, I may say, satisfactorily. Did you see the fires burning over Waipori City?

I welcomed my guests, poured them a drink, and before I joined them in the sitting room I tried once more, unsuccessfully, to shut out the haze and the sweet smell by closing the kitchen and bathoom window, but the bathroom window remained open an inch or two and still would not budge. I returned to the sitting room. I apologized to my guests. Hugh Craig, of the Psychology Department, smiled.

"It doesn't bother me, Colin."

Everitt Morse, an American, now on the staff of the University, assured me (a little too fervently?) that he was not bothered by the smoke or the smell. He did not smile as he spoke. He asked after Gloria and Robert and Sally.

"They're still up north. She feels safer there. I'll say, give them six months or a year. It's interesting how we've all misjudged the time taken to perform or suffer the human experience."

Sensing a reflection on his capacities as Psychological Adviser, Hugh spoke sharply.

"Even after the research we carried out! I agreed that many things have been misjudged. No one's perfect."

(Ah but you must be, you must be, Hugh Craig, to stay alive as a human being!)

"I never dreamed so many people would claim the bodies of their dead and decide to burn them in the back garden. These fires have been burning for days.We might have foreseen that. And some have even kept them burning as if they were on a desert island or in some such situation, waiting to be rescued. Ridiculous!"

"Most have chosen burning?"

"Yes. It had to be that, or the bodies had to be surrendered to be taken out to the Taeri Plains. What was left of the bodies, I should say. Another thing we misjudged or ignored —the human instinct to scavenge."

I felt that it might be wiser to steer the conversation to neutral topics. In spite of our training and position we were at that time rather apprehensive of our own safety; not sure, to speak ironically, which way the wind was blowing. Everitt Morse and Hugh Craig had grown to be close friends in the days preceding Classification Day. It was unwise, however, to have close friends. It was wise to smile, smile, smile, to appear joyful in our share of survival. If we were cunning we might live many years of clear fulfillment in the new world where we were invited guests. Our only obligation was to keep our invitation card clean by retaining our mental and physical health, our conforming behavior, our productive, useful, cooperative life. A dreadful strain might spread . . .

"One might have known," Hugh said, "I agree with you, one might have known that human processes like geological processes would take much time. The formation and melting of ice, the shifting of a mountain, the youth and senility of a volcano; and now the separation of Man from Animal."

I tried to speak uncritically in my practiced "neutral" tone.

"I never heard of an Act which decreed that ice should melt and mountains move."

Everitt Morse was watching me closely. I smiled at him. He returned the smile.

"It's built in, built in. Stands to reason the human laws are there as much as the physical and natural laws; we're discovering them as we evolve. God, just think where we can go now!"

"God?" Hugh seemed surprised. "God" was a strong exclamation, surely; and an unwise one. A word only, of course, a vowel linked with guttural force. A useful exclamation.

"I see," Hugh said.

"Another drink?"

Both declined.

I tried not to speak of it but I found myself saying, "All the same it's surprising how quickly the practical details have been taken care of. It's a marvel when you think of it, how everyone's adapted."

"But the fires are still burning."

Hugh spoke, I thought with sadness. I was tempted to share it. It was pure, wasn't it, a lament for the lost human condition, a nostalgia for the weak, the sick, the eccentric who had time to stare and judge and give their unusual diamond-shaped views, the challenging distortions of our assumed completeness.

"And they're still burning."

All right, then. Silence. Whiskey. Evening. The fires only to release the acceptable memories of autumn, a stereotyped sadness. Everitt Morse lifted his hand from the plastic cover of the armchair. His hand was moist with sweat marks. The plastic looked damp. Was Hugh Craig's evident sadness a trap? I could read the confusion in Everitt's face. Should he join the autumn lament? What was there non-human in the sadness of the autumn fires burning even though the time was spring and the fires were not of leaves but of people?

Hugh Craig changed the subject.

"Now this Milly Galbraith . . ."

He was cunning. I should not have invited him. Impulsively Everitt began to speak. I put my finger to my lips, silencing both Everitt and Hugh. I had a strange sense of overturning, *renversé*; I think I looked gratefully at my fellow murderers whom I had silenced simply by touching my nicotine-stained, crack-nailed worn index finger to my lips. Then the invading smell of the smoke sickened me finally, and I went to the bathroom and retched whiskey and a sweet taste and smell of death.

I returned again to the sitting room. I hoped that my guests would not notice my sickness. I had told them about Milly Galbraith from the point of view of her story. They were here to read her manuscript. I left them then and went out to the back porch and lay as the mythical Sandy used to do, on the sofa, looking out over the lights of Waipori City and its burning fires.

Two hours later Hugh Craig and Everitt Morse finished reading the story. They had both read quietly, and if at any time they may have wanted to exclaim or question they had not done so; but when the reading was finished they called to me, and when I returned to the sitting room I could feel the spring of being and feeling and moving as it was released, and I questioned my wisdom in showing them the manuscript.

Hugh and Everitt waited for me to speak. My voice was slow, evenly pitched, without feeling.

"The girl's father gave me the exercise books before they took him away. He thought I should have them, as I explained to you. He wanted to protect me."

"Protect?"

Everitt's question was sharp. He had much influence on the Deciding Committee. I should have given them more than snacks with their drinks, I thought, as I studied his bright moist eyes.

"Well he was just about crazy—as everyone else was. Oh no, I don't mean that; I felt remarkably composed, remarkably composed myself; but poor Ted Galbraith."

I laughed and snapped off the laugh halfway through it. I cleared my throat. It hurt from the vomiting and my clearing reminded me of the smoke and the smell and I felt the churning in my belly as another bout of retching began. Oh God, no. I smiled again and was in command.

"The whole family was so sure they would be saved, and their daughter condemned. The computer has been very careful about this business of extra genes—well, I should say, accurate; and of course the mother lost all reason. The daughter was the first to go, naturally. She didn't go as docilely as we thought she would. Seemed to be expecting a miracle."

"It's common. Common in times of stress."

Hugh Craig cunningly included in his voice the message that he, never subject to stress and therefore never liable to be declared animal, would never expect miracles. "Quite common."

"Obviously Milly Galbraith couldn't have written this."

It was Everitt Morse who spoke. Both were looking at me with suspicion. In the confusion following my sickness I couldn't remember what explanation I had given for showing them the manuscript.

"How do you account for the intellectual grasp, the power of recall? This isn't the Milly Galbraith as described in the records. As you know I visited the family often as liaison officer. The Galbraith woman doesn't write very kindly of me, I'm sure. No matter, of course, no matter."

Everitt Morse looked embarrassed. I thought to myself,

his too-ready display of feeling will get him into trouble.

"It seemed," I said pompously, "an historic document to preserve, for posterity."

Hugh Craig whistled.

"I'd forgotten about posterity."

Everitt glancing slyly at him confessed, "I'd forgotten too."

A majority. Confessions. I had to decide which, in the new world, would increase my eligibility to continue living—forgetting or remembering posterity. Every thought had to be accompanied now by such caution. I had said the document might be interesting to posterity. I could easily change my way of describing my interest in it, make it a detached, not a personal, reference and remark, omitting myself.

"There's a question of posterity, whether such a state exists or not."

The others, I felt, were waiting to hear my contributed confession. I wished that I hadn't shown the manuscript. I needn't have. Why had I, really? Why had I staged this evening, risking everything? I knew that since the Act had been enforced there had been inevitable rumors of bribery. These were inescapable as rumors: I wanted to declare my own innocence; I wanted to stay alive; I thought that a declaration and acceptance by my friends of my humanity would abolish many of the fears that haunted me and, I knew, haunted others. Since the meetings in Wellington at the beginning of the year I felt that I had grown used to the new ways of thinking and feeling, and I had observed, with detachment, my pity for those who would be condemned change to despising and loathing, and the deeper this well of negative feelings became, the clearer was my belief, drawn from it, to sustain myself in my appointed role of nursemaid to life and death. The well-nourished computer had drawn the boundaries that man by himself could not quite define; it had traced as confidently as the encephalographic or cardiographic let-

336

ter writes: Dear brain, dear heart you have a tumor, a fatal lesion, you have a normal pattern of electrical discharge, of blood circulation—the hate letters and love letters which communicated the decision.

"Posterity? As an observer I realized . . ."

I was safe. I had won.

I had lost. I began losing the first day, when the news of the Act came to me and I signed the oath of agreement. Why of course, I said, I'll do anything you ask, naturally, it's the only way, the only solution, as I see it, to an impossible situation, as if situations needed solving, I mean, looked at objectively, as it must be seen to be . . .

The skimming words and phrases that need leave no footprints; one might never have been there, but one had spoken; and the black water lay undisturbed beneath the ice; and not a blade of grass quivered or a dead leaf whispered; a race of words had lived and died and left no relic of their civilization.

As it must be seen to be, looked at objectively . . .

All was well.

Hugh Craig spoke.

"Why should Milly Galbraith have written her story? How could it have been possible? I never knew her of course. Are there more notes made by people as they awaited the decision?"

Everitt Morse smiled.

"The prisoners in death row have a privileged view, only if they have eyes to see the view and a brain to interpret it."

"And yet," I said carefully, "any human being with feeling, with a little intelligence, can make a pattern of the apprehension of death: not always in words, sometimes in dreams; or with the invisible writing of behavior where an understanding and special knowledge such as you have, Craig, can restore or create legibility."

Craig smiled his smug know-all smile. I'd heard he'd

337

been called to Wellington and was flying there the next day. Why?

"The Human Delineation Act," I said loyally, "is the greatest convenience of modern times, in an age of convenience; a labor-saving device more to be praised, more wonderful than all the housekeeping inventions of peace and war: the vacuum cleaners and the bombs."

The others echoed me.

"The Human Delineation Act is a marvel."

With our role thus affirmed we drank coffee and a small glass each of the new brew which we were privileged to get, in advance supply, from the new Taeri factories: blood-and-rose syrup, a recommended nightcap. I said good night then, to my guests, and as I opened the front door I tried not to be overcome by the sweet smell of the still-burning fires of the dead. Craig and Morse would be home before the curfew. By the time the town clock struck eleven there would be no one seen or heard on the streets of Waipori City, and the curtains and the blinds in the houses would all be drawn as in the blackouts of wartime.

I went to my sofa bed on the back porch. I'd not been able to sleep in any of the bedrooms. Even so I was troubled by dreams and sudden wakings, and tonight was no exception. I had not explained Milly Galbraith or anyone, just as I had not explained myself. I thought of her, of my golden twin brother, the Reconstructed Man. I dreamed of the three Knights: Mutimer, Dobie, and Watson.

"But there are only two knights," I murmured drowsily. "The black knight and the white knight. And now the man of the future, the Golden Knight. How Milly must have longed to die, I thought. That was the answer. She had longed to die. Some backwardness, trick of speech and thought, had branded her from an early age and she had become what she was believed to be. She dreamed that the Human Delineation Act would rescue her by condemning her to death, and the more she talked and planned her rescue the deeper her dream of survival became, so deep that she made first a reconstruction of herself, and then of a, of x, of y, of Sandy, the reconstructed human being; yet in her last-known dream she sacrificed both her death and her life. Nothing remained; nothing was allowed to remain. What a turmoil my mind was in that night. I came to the point of supposing it had all been a dream, that I had got myself into a fictional city at a fictional time, so strange that the present had split, like the earth beneath me, and the past and its people and seasons surged forth like a fountain, and then it was Now again, a season with pear blossom, and the fires of the dead were burning over Waipori City.

44

I am making these few last notes. It is nearly four months since Classification Day; it is almost the time that used to be called Christmas. I'm able to make these notes because I did not take part in the National Sleep Days, supervised by the Sleep Patrol, that followed Classification Day; but what I'm remembering may be distorted in that I do not seem to be able to find a place to be while I remember. After Classification Day, the Prime Minister spoke on television and read a congratulatory telegram from old King Charles. I remember I slept each night with a copy of Horrohda under my pillow in the porch and my dreams were haunted by the new code words—DOSP: Department of Sleep Patrols, MOB: Memory Order Board, AID: Animal Industries Division, SS: Skin Salvage, CUD: Corpse Utilization Department, DED: Dream Erasure Department, HADES:Human Animal Decision Enquiry Services, SPCV: Society for the Prevention of Cruelty to Vegetation. This society was unexpected, but even in the first weeks following Classification Day its membership began to grow. The official opinion had been that the National Sleep Days would eliminate most of the unrest and human concern which breeds such societies.

I cannot explain why the Act was enforced with so little violence and disturbance. The people lining up for classification seemed to be placid enough, both before and after the decision. In some cases where the classification was unexpectedly *human* there was unconcealed delight and tears that were hastily suppressed for fear the decision would be reversed; and there were some screams and struggles—I remember vividly the whole Galbraith family, apart from Milly, who of course was among the first to be taken, and their struggles and the screams not so much of terror but of rage at the imagined injustice. It was the sense of justice, the respect for the agreed law, strong after so many years of democracy, that ensured the successful enforcement of H.D.

And now as there's nothing left for me to risk I'll ask how many were there, besides myself, who managed to avoid the Sleep Days? The sleep drug acted as a strip of darkness lying across the country's memory, erasing its identity, as the eyes of criminals and the insane used to be covered to protect them when they were exposed to the curious public; and because the memory, like the eyes, contains the secret identity, when the Sleep Days were over and the daily routine began in the new improved democracy, most people experienced a feeling of well-being with their minds and hearts tuned to the perfect society. Life was fun again. Mass murder lay dreaming forever in Sleepy Hollow. The beings declared human awoke calm, vigorous, idealistic, their stains of memory and conscience removed by the country's expert housewifely operations. I notice that the question of personal and national identity has begun to emerge in underground writings and films.

I remember Hugh Craig's words—I think they were his —or were they mine? "I had forgotten about posterity." Did he and Everitt Morse take part in the Sleep Days?

Time is glacier-long fire-deep sun-high. Do a few weeks of lost memory matter? Surely in an age of dishwashers, clothes washers, floor cleaners, people cleaners, one may expect to be provided with an occasional memory cleaner? One might whimsically name it: Whirl, Splash, Clever Alice, or Shining Mary; or the Greek or Maori Gods might provide a name. What about Papa, the sky? A memory abrasive that does not damage the surface much, but will remove the stain of the spilled crime of the overturning of so many, many people.

If I look from my window I can see the Galbraiths' garden that is being used now as a vegetation laboratory. One can go there on certain hours of certain days to take part in flower conversation, and almost every home in the street keeps a flower, like a pet, for company and diversion, and of course the children love them and some have learned to speak their language. The Guardians of Vegetation have planted a pear orchard in the old Livingstone section, rows of tiny trees that will not blossom and fruit for two or three years, but already they are standing firm against the prevailing southwest wind.

There are mostly new people in Eagle Street: new, beautiful families. Dora Nightshade, declared human, is now co-manager of one of the Taeri factories with a smart house on the Peninsula and the beginnings of a lushly fertilized garden. There were many surprises in classification and behavior. We might have realized the error of human predictability. We employed experts—where could we have found people more expert than the experts? We would have needed to go beyond the realms of people into the world of gods, and perhaps we should have gone there, if we'd known the way—but then, only the Gods could have shown us.

But, did I say the *beautiful new people*? I have forgotten to mention the surge of nostalgia for things and experiences animal, how even in spite of the Classification and the Sleep Days the animal in man could not be subdued, and had the Government kept to its original plan the so-called human race might have been exterminated. Such has been the desperate need for survival at any cost that the conditions of the Act have become less restrictive. Hugh Craig and Everitt Morse in their hasty trip to Wellington formed part of the Committee which amended the Human Delineation Act. And now so deep is the nostalgia for that called—miscalled— animal, that the deformed, the insane, the defective, the outcasts, the unhappy have become the new elite. I have known a man, these past few days, break both arms, deliberately, so that he, intelligent, healthy, declared human, may escape sentence of early death; while I, of course, am crushed in the confusion, and find that my only hope is to proclaim myself to be the twin brother of Sandy, the myth, the Reconstructed Man.

These are notes at random. I do not know what will happen to me. My wife and children are dead.

I am not a literary man. I just wanted to describe the time of the fires in Waipori City.